ADVANCE PRAISE FOR *DIM STARS*

In his debut novel, *Dim Stars*, Brian Rubin blends the wonder of Douglas Adams, the imagination of Terry Pratchett, and the humor of John Scalzi to create a story that is extremely engaging. Rubin is able to take the silliest creatures and make them feel alive. With robust characters and a captivating story, I think *Dim Stars* is a must read.

—David Gallaher, author of *The Only Living Girl*

Witty and whimsical, but at the same time sharp and thoughtful, Brian Rubin's debut novel, *Dim Stars*, is a non-stop, uproarious romp through deep space that will have you holding your breath one minute and gasping between giggles the next. Though the book is ideal for both adults and young adults, young women especially will find inspiration in the teenage hero, Kenzie, who is pure STEM through and through. If the storm-trooper bonking his helmet on the blast shield door is one of your favorite parts of Star Wars, then you need this book. In the words of our hero: trust me.

—Sarah Hanley, author of *Matka*,
2019 Minnesota Author Project Winner

Dim Stars contains everything you could want in a space adventure: an octopus first mate, cannibal space pirates, and alien siblings. Rubin's wild imagination ignites the story with witty banter and nimble plot twists. But beneath the entertaining madcap adventure, *Dim Stars* asks important questions about the costs of perfectionism and what it means to be a hero—to others and to ourselves. There is no one I'd rather go gallivanting across the universe with than Dash and Kenzie; this book is pure and utter delight.

—Kaethe Schwehn, author of *The Rending and the Nest*

With *Dim Stars*, Rubin has choreographed a glorious, interstellar dance of lively vernacular and pulpy technobabble that is guaranteed to gratify any fan of farcical adventure on far-off worlds. I enjoyed every ludicrous moment.

—Chris Lockey, Writer/Producer for Critical Role

Dim Stars is a fun and energizing sci-fi story, filled with uniquely quirky characters and a well-paced adventure throughout an elaborate series of extraterrestrial civilizations. At the heart of this story is a young woman who is confident and capable and gets the chance to not only meet and set out on a journey with her swashbuckling space hero, but to show him up in every imaginable way and remind him who he is—or claimed to be. Brian Rubin's writing is crisp and witty, and his complex characters will stick with you in your own journeys right here on Earth.

—Amanda June Bell, News Editor, TV Guide

Dim Stars is a hilarious, action-filled space adventure with a motley cast of characters, who tackle obstacles as they hurtle through the galaxy in a worn-out spaceship. Kenzie Washington idolizes Captain Dash Drake, but she proves to be an agile leader herself, full of determination and heart. The story is a reminder that sometimes when things look bleak, we realize we've had the strength to persevere all along. And Brian Rubin's comic timing is impeccable.

—Kate Allen, author of *The Line Tender*,
2020 Minnesota Book Award Winner

Dim Stars mixes the colorful charm of *Guardians of the Galaxy* with the earnest redemption of *Galaxy Quest*. It's for everyone that looks at the night sky with wonder—especially those that have forgotten to do so in a while.

—Lawrence Sonntag, producer

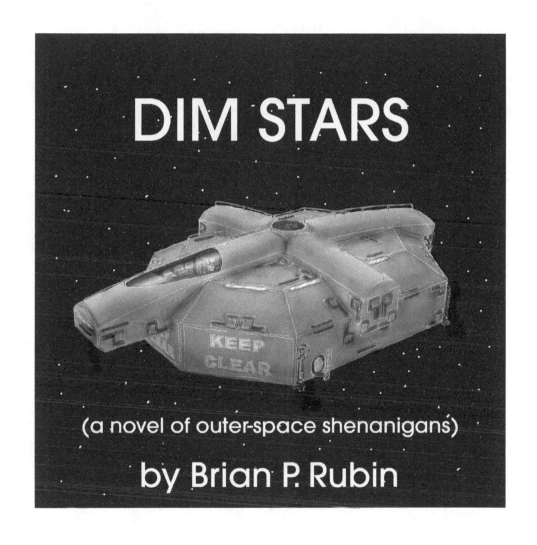

DIM STARS

(a novel of outer-space shenanigans)

by Brian P. Rubin

Critical Eye Publishing

Plymouth, Minnesota

Gremlin ship design, title page, and cutaway illustrations by William Lakey
Cover Illustrated by Collin David, www.resonantfish.com
Cover Designed by Beckie Hermans, www.foreverbeckie.com
Edited by D.J. Schuette at Critical Eye Editing, www.criticaleyeediting.com

ISBN: 978-0-9984293-5-9

Critical Eye Publishing
Plymouth, MN 55447

www.brianprubin.com

For Henry

Captain Dashiell Drake

Dash scrubbed furiously, but the dark stain refused to budge from the airlock floor. This is what happened when you had an Octopus for a first mate.

From the other end of the airlock came the hum of antigrav motors and the squeaks of tentacles on tile. Dash glared at Squix, who walked through the corridor on two arms, pushing a hovering cargo pallet in front while pulling another two behind. He was nearly finished loading their cargo onto the lift and marked the new additions on his handset with two free arms.

"I can't believe you."

Squix faced the captain, waving his eighth arm like a white flag.

"I said I was sorry!" Squix meant it, too, his mottled red skin flashing yellow with embarrassment as his exosuit translated his speech. "You know we've needed to repair this airlock forever. If the pressure fluctuates, even a little—"

"I know, yes, I know," said Dash, failing to mask the edge in his voice. He exhaled hard and stopped scrubbing.

"Look," he said, calmer. "It's just…the cadets arrive soon, and I'd rather they don't think the Gremlin is a dump."

There was a brief pause.

"But," Squix said, "it *is* a dump."

Dash started scrubbing again. "Well, sure, but I'd still prefer they don't know that until after we start our trip."

"Or at least until after their credits transfer into our account," added Squix.

"Right," Dash said, spraying more cleaner on the floor. "Remember Jonah?"

Squix thought.

"Nope."

"He got a rash from the sheets in his bunk after boarding two weeks ago."

"Oh yeah, the itchy kid!" said Squix. "He was disgusting."

"He was," said Dash. "Called his parents to get him before we even left port. They threatened to leave bad reviews and tell the other parents to stay away from our cadet immersion program—unless we refunded them. And that's why *you're* loading the cargo instead of him."

"Oh," said Squix. His head squeaked as he rubbed it with a tentacle. "I was wondering about that."

Dash shook his head and sighed. "Let's just not give anyone a reason to call home until we're a few star systems away, okay?"

Dash folded his rag in half, hoping to use the clean side to loosen more ink. Even as the rag darkened, the stain seemed like it might be a permanent fixture. The airlock corridor wasn't long—only a few meters— because it extended from the ship's port side whenever it docked with a station or another vessel. And that was the problem. Without much floorspace, and with the ink splattered right in the middle of the corridor, it was unavoidable. The moment anyone boarded the ship, it'd be the first thing they saw.

"How many more crates are there?" Dash said as he punished the floor.

Squix looked at his handset and scrolled through the display. "Only a few more pallets. Should be all loaded in twenty."

Dash dropped the rag, his shoulders slumped.

"You win this round, stain," he sighed, standing with a grunt. "Let's just get the boxes stowed so this place isn't a complete disaster. I still have—"

Dash paused mid-complaint. He sniffed the air.

"What's that smell?"

Squix flashed green, his tentacles coiling. "I don't know." Then, defensively, "You know I've always wanted a nose."

Dash sniffed again. "Goddammit."

He sprinted down the corridor. Squix yelled after him, "So, I'll just finish up here, then?"

He knew it wasn't the cargo bay trash compactor—he'd emptied it when he landed, like always. Dash ran to the galley at the center of the *Gremlin*'s top deck. Usually that was the first place to check for an unidentifiable stench.

He slapped the door control and ran to the sink, finding...nothing. He couldn't tie the smell to any spot in the galley. But the stink—a stomach-churning blend of rotten flowers, fermented synthetic cheese, and superglue—was definitely getting stronger.

This was bad. That smell could only mean one thing. And he knew it would only get worse if he didn't find the source...fast.

Dash clambered onto the counter and tore the magnetic air vent off the wall. The captain looked inside, saw nothing, and was hit with a fresh wave of funk. Gagging, he slammed the vent cover back into place. He bolted back into the corridor and pulled his jacket lapel over his face as the smell matured into adulthood. He breathed through his mouth, but somehow, he could still taste it.

Dash checked each room surrounding the galley looking for the stink-beast. First his room, strewn with dirty clothes and candy wrappers. Then Squix's room, which mostly was taken up by an aquarium in the wall and a rack for his exosuit—the mechanism keeping him hydrated and supporting his limbs out of the water. Then the empty crew and passenger bunks. Even the six-seat escape pod on the ship's starboard side, though he couldn't guess how something might've gotten into there. Nothing. The cockpit at the ship's bow, the dusty, disused weapons control room near the stern—all clean.

Dash ran into the medical bay. Its usual antiseptic scent was overpowered by the bastard smell. Bill, the flat, tablet-shaped medical robot attached to the ceiling, started chattering at him immediately.

"Captain, the ship's oxygen contains alarmingly high levels of—"

"I know!" Dash yelled, cutting him off. The screen displaying Bill's digital face buzzed with a burst of static.

"Well, I hope you find it soon," Doctor Bill said, crossing his medical probes in irritation. "This is the second time in as many months!"

Dash opened a storage locker and grabbed an emergency oxygen mask and a biomedical waste bag. He climbed onto an exam table while fitting the mask over his face and looked into the vent. Nothing.

"Come on!" Dash slammed the vent cover back onto the wall.

The handset on his hip chirped as he ran back into the corridor. He tapped it and shouted, losing his breath with each step.

"What now?"

"So," said Squix, "the crates are loaded, and I sent them all down to the cargo bay."

"Great job, Squix, really awesome," said the captain, squeezing every ounce of sarcasm festering in his body into his words. As usual, Squix didn't notice.

"Thank you!" he said.

"Anything else?" said Dash, racing toward the ship's rear.

"Yes, two things. First, the cadets board in ten minutes."

"Ugh." Dash entered the engine room. The chamber housing the *Gremlin*'s huge reactor core spanned both decks and was the largest room on the ship, featuring a ladder to the bottom and lots of air vents to check along the way.

"Second, I got a solution for the ink in the airlock! I think that—"

"Sounds good, thank you, bye." Dash tapped his handset to cut the connection. He removed another vent cover as he climbed down the ladder. The creature shouldn't have made it this far through the ship without being detected earlier…but the *Gremlin* was old, and Dash was losing track of its growing list of hiding spots for vermin.

Finally, after six vents and climbing halfway to the bottom of the engine room, he found it: a whole stinking nest of crungers.

Dash nearly threw up in his oxygen mask. Holding back breakfast, he looked closer. The small green creatures stabbed spiny beaks into a hunk of brownish-yellow meat. They flapped featherless wings as they ate, feasting on the rotting remains of their mother, which had birthed its brood and died for their nourishment.

She must've been living in the ship's vents for weeks—probably came aboard and mated with the other one Dash found in the crew quarters' vents on Antares Beta. The heat of the engine room was the perfect incubator for her eggs.

In some ways, the crunger momma's self-sacrifice was a beautiful expression of motherhood, an example of how love can take many forms throughout the galaxy. Creatures across the universe lived, fought, and died for the betterment of their species. The crunger turning herself into lunch proved that even from death could come life.

To Dash, however, it just smelled like his ship had athlete's foot.

Dash swallowed another wave of nausea and tucked the vent cover under his left arm, his left hand gripping the ladder. With his right, he slowly reached for his laser pistol. No sudden moves, or else the dozen baby crungers would bolt into the ventilation system. The new cadets arrived any minute, and he couldn't afford to cut the trip short because of the inescapable stink.

He leveled the pistol at the nest and fired, frying the crungers in a righteous fury of pest control. Dash let the vent cover drop to the engine room floor with a clang, wrapped his legs around the ladder rungs, and unfurled the biomedical waste bag. He carefully swept in the crunger family's remains, then climbed the rest of the way down. After cinching the bag, he opened the hatch to the reactor core and tossed the whole thing inside.

Dash tapped some commands into the nearby engineering console, and once he heard the air rushing through the ship's ventilation system, he removed his oxygen mask. He still caught the tail end of crunger stench, just before the overwhelming scent of lemon flooded his nostrils.

After changing clothes (but keeping his jacket despite the sleeves' fresh crunger stains), Dash sauntered into the airlock corridor, where Squix waited.

"We really need to upgrade our internal sensors," said Dash, tapping at his handset. "The Fleet's flagship would've found those crungers the instant they stowed away."

He looked up and saw Squix's tentacles slowly curling and uncurling with satisfaction. Dash looked for the inkstain on the floor, but it wasn't there. Instead, there was a towel, held in place with gray duct tape over each corner. The word "Welcome!" was scrawled in big black letters, the result of an Octopus wielding a magic marker.

Dash slumped against the wall, defeated. "Perfect."

"I know," said Squix. "Isn't it great?"

Mackenzie Washington

Kenzie's eyes flicked from the thief to her handset. Her fingers danced across the touchscreen's surface as she took notes on the perp's activities, his physical description, and even some theories about the root of his criminal impulses. Already she was divising a plan for how she'd stop the creep from making off with his loot, while also being sure she was prepared to disarm him if necessary. Kenzie thought it best to always be prepared for any contingency.

She did all this while standing behind a keychain display in the space station's gift shop.

Kenzie was fourteen years old and ready to dispense justice.

Minutes earlier, Kenzie was browsing the various space-themed knick-knacks and bric-a-brac available for purchase from Milky Wow, the souvenir shop near the elevators on Arcadia Station. She was due to report to her new posting on the *Gremlin* in about a half hour, and she was killing time.

She was one of a handful of customers walking through the aisles and the only Human. Across the store were two Crags, male and female, examining dermal polishing kits. Near the beverages stood a Marvinian—but because it wore the species' ceremonial tiny hat, Kenzie couldn't determine its gender, as she was unable to see the color of its cranial spike.

Milky Wow was brightly lit and crammed tight with narrow aisles filled with overpriced items that any well-prepared traveler would never need. Miniaturized toiletries, extra cables, data-storage cards, snacks with sodium content levels that had already been outlawed on most Alliance planets long before Kenzie was born. It was hard not to see Milky Wow for what it truly was. Kenzie saw past its brightly colored packages and admittedly clever name (she gave the store's owner credit on that one) and knew the shop was a galactic barnacle, clinging to the station as it floated through space and pulling in stray customers who couldn't ignore the siren song of Blazin' Hot Tortilla Blocks.

Still, when she saw the keychains, she was compelled to look for one featuring her name. She'd given up on the "Ks," and was about to switch to the "Ms" to see if she could find "Mackenzie" when she spotted a mirror off to the side, presumably for customers trying on pairs of cheaply made sunglasses.

She took a moment to study herself, checking to see if she looked presentable enough to report for duty later that afternoon. Her jumpsuit looked clean. Her dark brown skin was mercifully zit-free—for once—and her frizzy hair was relatively well-tamed, pulled into two tight, black poms at the back of her head. She'd thought about doing braids, but reasoned that maintaining them every day during her tour aboard the *Gremlin* might distract her from focusing on being the best cadet she knew she would be—and impressing Captain Dashiell Drake.

While fretting over her boring brown eyes, Kenzie spotted someone else in the mirror's reflection: an Aphid male, almost two meters tall, with purple spots dotted on his otherwise dull green carapace. Most Earthers compared Aphids to big, Human-sized mantises. Kenzie thought they had more of a giant cricket vibe. This one, she observed, was still a youth, probably only a few years older than her. He must've been crouching in his aisle, since she hadn't spotted him at first. But when she finally saw him, what he did made her gasp.

He tucked an inductive battery pack into his jacket pocket. He was going to *steal* it.

Kenzie's mind kicked into overdrive. She ducked behind the display, watching his every move, tapping at her handset, and looking for signs of weakness or vulnerability. Aphids were notoriously tough, physically. However, their tendency towards a group mentality—their need to protect the interests of the hive—was a trait that had been exploited in the past. In fact, Kenzie recalled, it was Admiral Robert Jawoski during the original Precursor Wars who found a way to turn a phalanx of swarming Aphid ships against one another by tapping into their comms and—

Kenzie shook her head to clear away the digression. The Aphid's predisposition toward group tactics wouldn't be useful now since there was only one here, and he was stealing a battery, not attacking an Earther outpost. She was a single Human girl in the Milky Wow gift shop, and she needed to protect it. She couldn't take the Aphid in a hand-to-hand match-up—he had the height, the strength, and the build, and despite her rigorous daily training schedule, she was still among the worst fighters in her jiu jitsu class.

Then she figured it out. As ever, her favorite book held the answer.

"Don't out-fight your enemy," she whispered as she stroked her chin dramatically. "Out-think him. Drake, page 59."

Kenzie realized she was focusing on the wrong weakness. This Aphid's desire to take property that didn't belong to him—his need to steal—that's what she would exploit. She felt her heart leap as she imagined Captain Drake's image from the book's cover, nodding with approval.

She finished typing her notes in her special shorthand (one she'd created during a day off from school, devised for maximum efficiency for situations just like these), and put her handset's echolocation protocols to work.

Kenzie had developed this program as a science class project a few years ago, when she was eleven. Most mapping programs worked by visually scanning an area beforehand. Hers, however, created real-time maps of physical spaces using sound, like how bats or dolphins navigated their environments. She'd thought it could be useful for ground conflicts, when soldiers needed to know the physical lay of the land but didn't have time to send out a scouting party. Her sixth-grade science teacher gave her an A, and for some reason set up an appointment for her with the school therapist.

The device sent out several short pulses of incredibly high-frequency sound—so high that neither she nor the Aphid would be able to hear them. But out of the corner of her eye, she spotted the two Crags suddenly wince and look in her direction. She hadn't accounted for the Crags' finely attuned hearing to give her away, but it was too late to worry about that now.

With a map of Milky Wow in front of her, she tapped in a few more commands. She set her handset to ping any available power sources in the area, revealing a long list of serial numbers on its display. Those were all the inductive battery packs in the store. Then she bridged those into her echo-locater program. Blammo: she saw exactly which battery pack the Aphid had stuffed into his jacket.

Kenzie tapped a few more commands into her handset and accessed the battery's power flow inhibitors and safety commands. She turned them all off. Then she tapped "connect."

The Aphid stood bolt upright and started flailing wildly, the power flowing from the battery in his jacket into the muscles throughout his body. He wasn't being electrocuted *per se*, though he was definitely uncomfortable and not in control of any of his body parts. His vocal cords constricted too, producing a high-pitched, buzzing whine. The battery pack was designed to wirelessly juice up power-hungry technology. And these were reliably safe, too…no one ever got their muscles electro-stimulated, not even when a few of the highly regulated products malfunctioned after being sold. Then again, most people didn't intentionally disable a battery's safety commands either. You'd have to be a truly determined troublemaker to do that—or a really smart fourteen-year-old with an overdeveloped sense of civic duty.

By this point, everyone in Milky Wow watched the Aphid, whose involuntary muscle spasms knocked antacids and snack cakes off their shelves. The store's owner, a faintly-glowing Drook, rushed out from the storeroom to see what the fuss was all about.

"Sir, are you okay?" the Drook said, panic in her voice. She hurried over to the dancing Aphid, and as she approached, Kenzie cut the connection, ending the battery's power surge. The thief collapsed into a heap. Before the owner could make it to the Aphid's crumpled form, Kenzie stepped in between the two.

"Hello," she said. "Mackenzie Washington, future cadet at the Alliance Academy. I'm afraid this Aphid doesn't need your help…unless it's help getting over to the station's security office."

Kenzie kicked open the Aphid's jacket and pulled out the battery pack. The price label reading "Milky Wow" was still on it. She handed the warm pack to the owner and smiled.

"You're welcome," she said.

* * *

The transport ferrying Kenzie to the *Gremlin* hovered down the station's corridors, its anti-grav motor humming, reducing the shops, restaurants, and service kiosks within Arcadia Station to a colorful blur. A hundred alien languages burbled over the transport's motor, while the acrid yet sweet smells of cuisines from around the galaxy hung in the recycled air as the vehicle rushed past.

Kenzie tapped at her handset—taking more notes—as the transport carried her and the two Crags to docking clamp 18. Apparently, the pair she'd seen in the Milky Wow were headed for the *Gremlin* as well, though she hadn't spared a moment to consider her new traveling companions. She was still trying to make sense of what had happened after she incapacitated the Aphid thief.

The Drook store owner certainly seemed appreciative of everything Kenzie had done. She'd thanked her and offered her some free bags of Protein Puffs, but the owner stopped smiling and offering her snacks as soon as Kenzie told her she'd alerted station security about the incident. That was weird. She figured the owner would've been happy the criminal was being apprehended and that he hadn't made off with her merchandise. Why did—

"She wanted to keep station security out of it," said the Crag sitting to her left—the female. Kenzie took a quick breath and tucked her handset into her pocket. How did she know what she was writing? Had the Crag cracked her shorthand after only five minutes of their ride so far? And wasn't it universally rude to read someone else's handset?

"Um, excuse me," said Kenzie, "but isn't it universally rude to read someone else's handset?"

"It is," she said, "but you were talking out loud while you were typing."

Oh.

"Oh," said Kenzie.

She stared at Kenzie blankly, and Kenzie stared back, unsure about quite what to do next.

She'd never been this close to a Crag, though she knew that a fair number of them—not as many as Humans—tended to enlist in the Academy. The alien girl looked to be about Kenzie's own age and had a smooth, lavender-gray face, broken up by hard edges where Humans had wrinkles and fine lines in their flesh. Crags didn't grow hair—at the top of her head were glittering spikes, like the inside of a broken geode. She looked not unlike a statue, sculpted from living stone. Her outfit was a one-piece jumpsuit, functionally identical to the ones traditionally worn by all space travelers, which were laced with fabric-thin life-support systems that could kick on in emergencies. But instead of looking drab and utilitarian, like Kenzie's, the Crag's suit flowed with slow, ever-shifting colors, like a rainbow inside a volcano. Kenzie had thought about dressing up her pale blue suit with an Academy jacket she'd gotten from the gift shop during a school trip to Earth's Moon the year before, but decided against it.

But there was more. Geometric patterns—faint indentations someone must have made with a fine chisel—crisscrossed the girl's face. Kenzie had read that getting your face "etched" was all the rage right now on Rhyolar, the Crag homeworld. The planet's youths decorated their bodies with these designs in rebellion against their parents and grandparents—the conservative generation that had first signed the agreement to form the Interstellar Alliance with Humans and Aphids in the first place.

"You're pretty weird," the Crag finally said, breaking the brief silence. Her voice was flat like a desert mesa. "Interesting, though," she added as she pulled out her handset. "Kind of."

"Thanks?" said Kenzie.

"Yeah," said the Crag, staring at the device to check her social feeds. Then, "I'm Jo."

"I'm Mackenzie. Most people just call me Kenzie, though."

"Whatever," said Jo. The Crag was done with her. And the other Crag, the male sitting in the row in front of them, didn't turn or say anything at all. Kenzie wasn't really sure what had just happened.

"So, why?" Kenzie asked.

"Why what?" said Jo, not looking up from her handset.

"Why didn't the store owner want station security to come?"

Jo turned to her. As the automated transport rounded a corner to approach the station's docking ring, Kenzie overheard an argument over the cost of a ship repair. The transport zoomed away and the arguers' voices faded.

Kenzie continued: "I mean, I stopped a thief."

"You totally did," Jo said, "but you also gave security an excuse to go to the store and poke around. And that Drook was definitely doing something shady with that shop."

"What?" Kenzie blinked. "Really?"

"Think about it," Jo said. "Arcadia Station is a major hub in this sector. Tons of people coming in and out of here every day. But there's that little store, off to the side, with hardly any customers. And did you see how old those ration packages were? They were all expired."

Kenzie cocked her head to the side. "Still not following you."

Jo rolled her eyes. "If no one's shopping there, how's the owner making money to pay the store's rent?"

It finally dawned on her.

"It's a front," said Kenzie. "Milky Wow is a front for..." she trailed off.

"For something she didn't want security to know about," said Jo, a hint of satisfaction creeping into her voice.

"'See with your mind, not just your eyes'—Drake, page 75," Kenzie said. Jo raised an eyebrow but said nothing. "I can't believe I didn't think of that. I mean, how could I miss that?"

The Crag girl shrugged. "Now you know. Don't worry, she probably paid security off anyway. But, like, good thing you didn't take any of those snacks she offered you. Probably loaded with parasites. Right Vor?"

The Crag sitting in the seat in front of them—the male who'd been with Jo in the Milky Wow—turned to face them. His complexion was a bit darker than Jo's, more purple than lavender. But, like Jo's, his face was covered with etchings, though much deeper and more defined. That is, except for the bottom half of his face, which held a jagged ruin where his mouth should've been. But he nodded his assent and smiled with his eyes.

"That's Vor, my brother," Jo said, turning back to her handset. "He doesn't have a mouth."

"I, uh, I can see that," Kenzie said.

Jo laughed. "He etched one time too many. So his face caved in."

Vor shrugged, as if to say, "Sure did," and turned back around. He didn't seem the least bit upset at his missing maw.

After a few more minutes, the automated transport glided up to docking clamp eighteen. Even though the trip had been strange up to this point, Kenzie knew things were about to improve significantly. She was going to meet Captain Dashiell Drake, hero of Gantoid IV and intergalactic adventurer. Better yet—she would serve on his crew for two whole weeks. Kenzie had been a Captain Drake fan since she was six, when her dad took her to see *The Glory of Gantos*, that old movie they made about him a few years after the Forger War ended—the war that took her mom. She didn't have any actual memories of her mother, but her dad and grandparents made sure to remind Kenzie of her absence on a regular basis.

Anyway, after that movie, she'd been hooked. His autobiography, *Drake: A Study in Courage*, was a frequent source of inspiration. Captain Drake was one of the main reasons she wanted to enlist in the Academy after she finished high school. Serving under him on his actual ship was a dream come true—and it'd look great on her Academy application too.

It didn't matter how weird Jo and her mouthless brother thought she was. This was going to be great.

Kenzie, Jo, and Vor grabbed their bags and approached the docking tube's door. It slid open with a whoosh as they approached.

At the other end of the corridor, a familiar-looking Human leaned against the corridor wall, looking strangely tired. Sandy brown hair, five o'clock shadow, and features that belied his Euro-Asian heritage. He wore a rumpled jumpsuit under a Fleet jacket—the same kind of Fleet jacket she'd seen so many times in *The Glory of Gantos*. There he was. Not an actor. Not a book. The real Captain Dashiell Drake.

Kenzie marched down the corridor to shake his hand.

"Captain Drake," she said, taking her first steps aboard her hero's ship, "Mackenzie Washington, future cadet at the Alliance Academy reporting for duty—"

That's when her foot got caught on the towel that was taped to the floor. She tripped and crashed to the ground in a heap.

From her left, she heard a computerized voice yell, "Holy crap!" She looked up: it was an Octopus in an exosuit that she hadn't noticed a second ago, his tentacles wiggling.

Jo spoke next. "Why does it smell like lemons in here?"

The Speech

Dash leaned against the wall, trying to keep the annoyance off his face. He was pretty sure it wasn't working.

"That's a Grade B dermal regenerator, isn't it?" the cadet named Kenzie asked Doctor Bill.

"Very good, young lady," the Doctor replied, waving the blue-glowing device over her hands and elbows.

She closed her eyes and shook her head. "That's so awesome," she said. "We only had Grade D regenerators at school. They took forever."

"And I imagine that patients itched like mad too."

"I know!" Kenzie threw her hands up, forcing Bill's robotic arm to readjust. "It itched like crazy!"

Doctor Bill and Kenzie had been babbling at each other since the moment Dash carried her into the medbay. After tripping, a nasty purple bruise formed on her already-dark cheeks, and she started bleeding all over the docking tube floor. Luckily, a towel was handy.

Dash was impressed that her questions hadn't slowed even when Doctor Bill applied the anti-inflammatory gel to her face. The gel didn't hurt, but it felt mighty strange. Every time Bill treated Dash's bruises with it, the captain made no effort to hide his discomfort. But Kenzie didn't miss a beat—she just asked Doctor Bill about the gel's various non-medical applications.

"One time at my school, a kid snuck out of gym class and put it in another student's uniform as a prank," she said. "It was nuts!"

"Now, that's hardly safe—or very kind," said a smiling Doctor Bill as he painted her face in the stuff, causing the swelling to go down almost instantaneously. "What happened to the victim?"

"Well…I was out of school for a week," she said, looking away. "But it was still pretty funny."

"Ah," he said, moving right past the anecdote. "Though somehow I don't think that's what the gel's manufacturer had in mind when—"

"Um, excuse me," said Dash.

Kenzie and the Doctor looked at Dash, who had left his spot on the wall and walked toward the center of the room, hands behind his back. By his side was Squix, whose skin had taken on a distinct shade of embarrassed yellow since Kenzie took her tumble. Meanwhile, Jo and Vor occupied two examination tables. Jo was on her handset checking her social feeds (for the fifth time in ten minutes), while Vor—the Crag kid with no mouth, Dash was alarmed to discover—busied himself by taking an extreme interest in the table's side control panel. With each button push, a new medical diagnostic application appeared on the display or the table itself revealed a new mechanical function. He took particular delight in seeing the fluctuations in his biometric readings as he raised the table from the floor before lowering it again.

"So, if you guys are almost done," he said, "I usually make a speech when new cadets come aboard, and I'd love to get back to our schedule…"

"Oh, so I get to hear the speech finally?" said Doctor Bill, putting his robotic hands on the bottom corners of his screen. The gesture would've been more effective if he had hips. "I've been on this ship for centuries, and I've never been invited to hear it once."

"Centuries? This ship is that old?" said Jo. She didn't look up from her handset. "No wonder you have to cover up the smell."

"Ha, uh—it's not nearly that old," said Dash, frowning.

"Yeah, actually it's closer to eighty," said Squix.

Dash looked up at the ceiling. "Thank you, Squix."

"You're welcome!"

A loud buzz accompanied by metal grinding on metal came from Dash's right. The examination table Vor sat on was at least two meters off the ground—higher than Dash had ever seen it go. Apparently the medbay itself was just as surprised and let everybody know with its alarm. It stopped when Vor began lowering the table again. His eyebrows were knit together as he considered the experience deeply.

"But, uh, anyway, I usually give the speech in the cockpit, so if you're almost done, Doc…" Dash said as he took a tentative step backwards to the door.

"I still have a few more minutes of work to do to patch up young Ms. Washington," said Bill, waving the dermal regenerator over Kenzie's elbow. Dash noticed the device had gone dark.

"It's not even turned on," he said.

"It's in low-power mode," said Doctor Bill.

"Dermal regenerators have a low-power mode?" asked Kenzie.

Doctor Bill looked at her for a moment. "Yes." He cocked a digital eyebrow. "Grade B dermal regenerators do," he sniffed. He looked back at Dash. "Do please continue, Captain."

Dash glared at Bill, saw Kenzie watching him intently, then cleared his throat.

"First I'd like to thank you all for coming aboard. Squix and I have been running this immersion experience for a while now, and we've worked with a lot of great young cadets looking to have, uh, real-world experience on a—a real-world ship."

Dash paused.

"I mean, um, a real ship," he said. "Not a real-world ship. I mean, we're a real-world ship, I guess. If that's a thing. But anyway. I'd like to think our reputation speaks for itself."

He looked at Squix. The Octopus stuck two tentacles together into a ball, then poked the tip of one up through it. His version of a thumbs up.

Dash took a deep breath—this next bit was usually pretty good.

"So. We who gather on this ship will embark on a grand adventure together," he said. "An adventure…of learning." Dash gently tapped a fist into his other hand.

"And an adventure of working—working hard to achieve our fullest potential. Working to keep the *Gremlin* flying. Working to prepare ourselves for the vast wonders of the galaxy. And working to make that galaxy—" Dash looked at the three cadets, two of whom were busy looking elsewhere. "—a better place."

Kenzie yelped. Everyone in the room turned to see Doctor Bill's robotic arms shaking, his face replaced with the chaos of static.

"What's wrong with him?" asked Jo, finally looking from her handset. "Is he broken?"

"No," said Squix. "I think he's laughing."

Dash folded his arms. After another second, Doctor Bill's face returned.

"Terribly sorry, Ms. Washington," he said, squirting a pain-relieving cream from his left arm onto the other elbow he'd just whacked. "I really should be more careful. Here, good as new."

Kenzie inspected her hand, her right elbow, and other, her newly cream-smeared left elbow, and smiled. "Thanks."

"My pleasure," said Bill. He pivoted to face Dash. "Now, Captain Drake, if I may ask a question? How, exactly, will you and the cadets here…" He smiled smugly. "…'make the galaxy a better place'?"

Dash folded his arms again. "Actually, Doctor, I don't typically take ques—"

"Yeah," Jo said, glancing from her handset to side-eye Dash. "How are we gonna make the galaxy a better place if we never leave Arcadia Station? We've been here for, like, days."

"It's been fifteen minutes," said Dash. "And actually, we're going to—"

"Because I really think we oughta get this trip going, so I can get back to, like, my actual life," said Jo, scrolling through her feed again. "I can already feel my social skills draining into my feet. Where are we even going first, anyway?"

"I think—"

"We have a delivery to make in the Motomondo system tomorrow," said Squix. "And then we're stopping at Pumbar, Grtbrl, and New Kentucky before heading to Rax to load more cargo for our trip back."

"Thanks, Squix, but I—"

"Ew," Jo said, sticking out her tongue. "Rax? Guh, don't tell me we're actually landing on the planet. I heard it's all just moss and hair everywhere."

"Now that doesn't even sound plausi—"

"From what I've read, there is a lot of hair," said Doctor Bill, his display nodding on the hinge connecting him to the medbay's ceiling. "The Raxians are a very…hirsute people, and the planet's chief export is wigs."

"Wait, wigs? That can't be—"

The medbay's warning buzz came back, this time double in volume. Sparks shot from the control panel on Vor's examination table. More than a few wires had been exposed since the last time Dash looked in that direction.

"Now fix that this instant, young man!" scolded Bill. Vor patted the air, possibly looking to put Bill at ease.

"He does this all the time," said Jo, unfazed by her brother's brush with electrocution.

"Okay, so, uh, I'd like him to stop," said Dash, his voice starting to crack. "Seriously, I don't even—"

"Well, he only does it when he's bored, so maybe this one's on you," Jo said.

Dash's face was getting hot.

"Captain, I have a question," said Kenzie.

Dash wheeled on her, snapping, "What?"

The room went silent, and Dash's hot white flash of anger was quickly replaced by a green gut-plop of humiliation. He felt everyone's eyes on him—finally quiet and listening, but not quite in the way he'd hoped.

But Kenzie kept his gaze, a blank expression on her face. She didn't even flinch at his outburst. After the briefest of pauses, she spoke.

"Shortly before boarding the *Gremlin*, I discovered the owner of the gift shop near the elevators on Arcadia Station was likely involved in some, uh, shady business," she said, jumping down from the examination table. "We should go back and investigate. 'Always leave the galaxy a better place than you found it,' right?"

Dash stood up straight, realizing as he did that he'd been hunched over. He had a tendency to hunch when he got frustrated. And he'd just been very, very hunchy.

"What?" he said.

"'Always leave the galaxy a better place than you found it,'" she repeated. "Page 113?" There was a pause as Dash just stared at her.

"From your book?" she said, her eyebrows scrunching together.

He coughed. "I don't really, uh," he scratched his armpit, looking at the floor. "I'm pretty sure station security can handle whatever's going on at the—" He looked at Kenzie. "—gift shop?"

Dash looked around the rest of the room, then turned to leave. He rushed out the door.

"Thanks, Cap'n! Great speech," said Squix as he left. "Now, how about I show you cadets to your bunks?"

* * *

When Squix walked into the dimly lit cockpit, Dash was practically laying across the main helm console, his head and face buried in his arms. At the sound of Squix's entrance, Dash sat up in his chair, trying to pretend he hadn't been wallowing in a heap for the past several minutes. The only illumination came from a few scattered screens and some of the more important buttons on his console. Otherwise, Dash liked to keep the cockpit pretty dark—well, when he was in one of his moods, at least.

Dash's display monitor, hanging above his seat, showed a live broadcast of the news from around the quadrant. He kept an eye on the broadcast while fiddling with his handset. He wasn't really paying attention to either, but he thought he might appear busy enough that he wouldn't have to talk for a little while longer.

"—six people died in the shuttle accident," said the newscaster over the speakers, "while the other four passengers, including the pilot, have been missing since the wreckage was found a day ago. Local authorities noted that the cause of the crash is unknown, with no clear signs of technical malfunction—"

"The cadets are in their bunks, Captain," said Squix, taking his seat in the navigator's chair to Dash's right. "Should I start making navigation calculations?"

"Mm-hmm," said Dash.

"That Washington kid sure knows a lot about…" Squix paused. "Stuff. Lots of stuff."

"Mm-hmm."

"When I showed her to her bunk, she told me all about how this model of ship was the second most widely used for cargo runs during the Precursor Wars." Squix flicked a few switches and turned on his navigation display. "Did you know that?"

The newscaster continued: "—the political climate around Drai's capital city has been in turmoil since the about-face from majority leader Skellen Arbo—"

"I didn't know that," said Squix. "Pretty interesting!"

The newscaster: "The Interstellar Alliance's governing council continues to argue over deployment of jump-chain technology on member worlds, holdings, and space stations throughout Alliance territory. The initiative, which has remained a subject of intense debate since its first proposal by the Human delegation from Earth nearly a decade ago, would add an extra layer of security in the form of planet-wide force fields powered by a large-scale remote reactor Hub orbiting IA Prime. If approved, the system would supplement the jump-beacon network that currently connects all Alliance worlds. But despite the security benefits the system would provide, many non-Human council members oppose the jump-chains initiative, arguing the technology could slow trade and travel, and could also have calamitous atmospheric and environmental impacts on planet surfaces. John-Dean Clifford, the Speaker for Earth in the council, defended the initiative during a recent meet-and-greet at his office on IA Prime."

The round, doughy face of Councilman Clifford filled the screen, his straight, white, smiling teeth gleaming as he spoke. His down-home, good-time accent reminded Dash of a pie that'd been left in the sun too long.

"Now, see, I don't know how they do things over on Rhyolar or Aphix or any o' those other planets," he said. "But where I'm from, we like a good fence. Good fences make good neighbors, and I tell you what, I want our member planets to be just a bit more neighborly—especially with these Frawgs flyin' around, tryin' to eat folks—"

Dash realized he'd been transfixed by Clifford's highly punchable face, so he looked away from the display and glanced at his copilot. While beginning his navigation calculations with one pair of arms, Squix started tapping some controls with another—depressurizing and retracting the docking tube—prepping the *Gremlin* for takeoff. The hiss of the docking tube releasing its atmosphere and the whir of its retraction back into the ship complimented the newscaster's monologue.

"You're watching 75X-GNN, Galactic News Network," said the anchor. "As more details arrive from the incident at the jump-drive manufacturing facility at Delta Pallas III, Alliance authorities still speculate at what might have transpired. Currently, investigators are theorizing on the causes behind the sudden destruction of the asteroid that housed the factory, as well as its jump-beacon, located nearby. Several government officials have speculated about the involvement of a cell of Frawg insurgents in the incident, though conclusive evidence to support those claims has yet to materialize. No survivors have been found since the facility's destruction was first discovered two days ago. When reached for comment this morning, Fleet Commander Gerald Sharp didn't mince words."

An older man appeared on screen, his silver hair cropped close to his head, the picture of military efficiency. "Our investigation is ongoing, but once again I ask that certain members of the governing council consider supporting the jump-chains initiative," he said, a weary kindness in his voice. "The threat posed by groups like the Frawgs has only grown in the years since the Forger War, and I know ordinary citizens throughout the

Interstellar Alliance would sleep better with the added security the jump-chains system would provide—"

Dash switched the broadcast off. He rested his chin on his hands and stared out the main viewport at the front of the cockpit. "What do you think made that girl ask that question?"

"Which girl?" asked Squix. "Oh, and which question?"

"Washington," said Dash. "When Kenzie asked if we should investigate the gift shop thing." He shook his head. "Investigate. Like that's a thing to do."

Squix tapped a tentacle on the console thoughtfully. Its suckers stuck and unstuck, filling the cockpit with a popping rhythm that would've been annoying if Dash weren't so used to it.

"I dunno, Cap," he said. "Guess she figured you were into that sort of stuff." He thought for a second more. "Maybe she's a fan?"

Dash shut his eyes and shook his head. A fan. Great.

The endorsement deals had dried up years ago. No one had invited him to a grand opening or a ribbon cutting in ages. And the sporadic royalties that came in from the book and the movie barely made a dent anymore. It was hardly enough to live on. These days, Dash's only reliable sources of income were taking on shipping and courier jobs and the cadet-immersion program.

He'd figured out that charging parents to have their kids help him load and unload cargo made more fiscal sense than hiring an actual crew. For the first few years of the program, the memory of the Forger War was fresh enough that he had no trouble finding new cadets. After all, what kid wouldn't want the chance to work with the famous Dashiell Drake, hero of Gantoid IV? Who wouldn't want to meet the man whose heroic feats helped put an end to the war and usher in a new age of prosperity for the Interstellar Alliance? Who could deny the offer of an authentic spacefaring experience at semi-affordable prices? Who wouldn't want to work with the guy whose name could easily improve the chances of acceptance for any potential cadet's application to the Academy?

As time went on, the answer to those questions turned out to be "lots of people." At first, Dash was kind of upset at how, with each tour, fewer cadets actually knew who he was. But it didn't take him long to feel relief at the lack of recognition. The downside, of course, was that signing up new cadets got harder and harder—resulting in the cost of "tuition" going lower and lower.

Having another fan on board was something Dash was not prepared for. And not particularly excited about.

At this point in his life, Dash just wanted to take whatever low-stress jobs he could find, get paid, and forget he was ever the most famous man in the Interstellar Alliance. Was that too much to ask?

Squix flicked a row of switches in quick succession. His calculations were done.

"Ready to depart Arcadia Station," he said.

Dash opened his eyes and sighed. He sat back in his seat and took the helm control with his right hand.

"What's our first stop?" he asked. As he spoke, he turned up the throttle, and the *Gremlin* began its trip away from the space station towards the nearest jump-beacon.

Squix reached out a tentacle and pulled a display screen close.

"We have enough fuel to make it to the Kembar Colony," he said. "They have some pretty good technicians there, I think. So we can probably get the docking tube's pressure valves fixed, maybe even upgrade the internal sensors like you mentioned."

Dash nodded as he flew the ship to the entrance lane of Arcadia Station's jump-beacon. There was a fair amount of traffic—which he'd planned to avoid, had it not been for the unexpected field trip to the medbay that kept him docked for an extra hour.

These jump-beacons—sort of like manned space-buoys—dotted the Alliance's territory. They gave ships safe, easy passage to and from each star system when they traveled through the galaxy via jump-space—the alternate layer of spacetime allowing ships to move faster than light without smearing their crews into paste. Before the Alliance implemented the jump-beacon network, traveling between planets was chaos. It was nearly impossible to know when ships would jump in or out, where they'd come from, or where they were going. Unpredictable, unregulated jumps among the galaxy's different civilizations was part of what led to the Precursor War nearly a hundred years ago.

But with that war's end came the formation of the Interstellar Alliance. And from that, came the jump-beacon network. The beacons were a sort of interstellar highway, since each one communicated with all the others throughout the network. When a ship traveled to another system, the journey was logged in the system, the destination beacon knew to expect a ship, and intergalactic commerce blossomed.

And that meant that people like Dash could always count on a job hauling crap from one planet to another. It made owning a functioning spaceship a more important quality than, say, having any discernible life skills.

Dash sighed at the thought of his rapidly fossilizing ship. And that led to thinking about the bank account he and Squix shared to run the business—and how it might actually be on the full side with three new recruits aboard.

"Did the cadets' tuition clear?" he asked, suddenly feeling bright.

Squix tapped and swiped on his display. "Yes!"

Dash smiled.

"Oh, wait."

Dash stopped smiling.

Squix tapped a few times on the screen. "Uh-oh."

"Uh-oh?" said Dash.

"Yeah," said Squix. "Looks like I spoke too soon about those sensors."

"Why?"

Squix tapped a few more times. "And also the docking tube."

"Um," said Dash, guiding the *Gremlin* in behind a blue Drook freighter as they headed toward the jump-beacon.

Squix tapped again. "It says here we have a negative balance in our account."

The ship lurched as Dash turned to his first mate.

"What?!" he yelled as he wrestled his ship back into its lane.

The cockpit speakers pinged, and a voice piped over the comms.

"Pilot of the Earther transport ship *Gremlin*, do not deviate from your course, or you will be ticketed and fined," crackled the voice of the beacon's traffic agent.

"What do you mean, 'negative balance?'" said Dash.

Squix turned green, curling and uncurling his tentacles reflexively. "Well, it looks like Arcadia charged us for another day's docking fees. For that extra time we were, uh, docked."

"Another day? We were docked for like an extra hour!" He switched on the comm dialer. "I'm calling Arnon."

"Arnon doesn't like you, Cap," said Squix.

Dash held the helm steady with his right hand while punching in the code for Arcadia's station manager with his left. "How do you know that?"

"He told me today while I was in his office, signing out our cargo," said Squix. "He said, 'I do not like your captain, Dash Drake.' I'm like ninety-nine percent sure he was talking about you."

"Well, I think he's a bug-eyed freak," said Dash, "but I can still do my job without screwing over everyone who breathes."

Arnon's voice buzzed through the speakers, his insectoid face already on Dash's hanging display. "And who is this 'bug-eyed freak' screwing over today?"

Dash closed his eyes and pinched the bridge of his nose. Then he smiled and looked at his screen.

"Hey, Arnon," he said, trying his best impression of a person who did not want to fly his ship directly into the sun. "It's Dash. Dash Drake. How you doing today, buddy?"

"You're calling about the extra day I charged to your account," buzzed Arnon. It was hard to tell when Aphids smiled, what with the mandibles covering their mouths. But Dash could hear the joy dripping in Arnon's voice.

"Yeah, I was kind of wondering about that, because—"

Arnon cut him off. "You signed an agreement when you docked saying you were aware that we charge a daily flat rate. You exceeded your reservation without notice, so we had to add a surcharge."

Dash attempted a good-natured laugh. When it exited his mouth, it distinctly resembled the sound of someone choking on his own rage.

"Well, sure, I know we went a little over, but we also had a medical emergency, as my ship's records clearly indicate," said Dash. "I know my doctor sent that over as soon as he activated his first-aid protocols."

Dash watched Arnon lean back in his chair in his office on Arcadia Station. Behind the Aphid was a computer display that read, "Medical Emergency Report: *Gremlin*."

"Oh, I'm sorry, I didn't get any report," said Arnon. The station manager clicked a few keys, and the report disappeared from the display behind him. He'd deleted it.

"You stinking, mantis-faced—" said Dash.

Arnon tapped his headset. "Sorry, what was that? You're breaking up, Captain."

Dash nearly missed his turn to keep up with the beacon traffic ahead of him, so he swerved hard to compensate and narrowly avoided hitting the craft to the ship's port side. A Crag coupe pulled up next to him to flip him off, just as the speakers crackled with the voice of the traffic agent once more.

"I'm warning you, *Gremlin*, stay in your lane or you'll be fined!"

"Maybe you want me to take over the stick, Cap?" said Squix.

"What'd I ever do to you, Arnon?" Dash pointed at the display. "Why are you giving me this crap today?"

"I think you suck," said Arnon without hesitation. "Your book sucks, your movie sucks, and that sandwich they named after you gives everyone on the station gas."

Dash considered this.

"Okay, all of that's true," he said, "but why are you giving me such a hard time *now*? I've docked at Arcadia dozens of times the last few cycles, and you usually keep your repellent personality to yourself."

"Earlier today my nephew was detained by Arcadia Station Security," said Arnon, the smile gone from his tone. "One of the cadets aboard your ship accused him of stealing merchandise from a gift shop."

Arnon blinked his eyes' outer membranes, then continued: "It was extremely embarrassing for my sister."

With that, the Aphid cut the connection, and the display went black.

Dash turned to Squix, who by this point had scrunched himself into little more than a ball with eyes.

"Kenzie Washington," he said.

Dash stared back out of the main viewport. The Drook freighter in front of them was next to the beacon and made its jump, blinking out of sight in a flash of bright red.

"Okay, *Gremlin*, you're cleared for jump," said the beacon agent over the comm. "Next time you come through here, keep the drunk flying to a minimum, huh?"

"We're broke," said Dash.

The *Gremlin*'s viewport flared bright red, and the ship was gone.

Taking Stock

4

Kenzie flopped onto her bunk and coughed. The smell of the mattress had suddenly wafted to her nose, cutting through the fading scent of lemons like a knife through butter. But in this case, the butter was lemon-scented air freshener, and the knife was a funky old bed.

It didn't matter. Kenzie flipped over, put her hands behind her head, and smiled. She looked up at the bottom of Jo's bunk above. Stickers and graffiti left by former cadets were scattered across the bed frame above her. She glanced over at Vor's bed, already piled high with scraps of metal and machinery he'd unpacked. Kenzie couldn't really identify any of it, though she suspected most of the parts used to live inside various more complicated devices.

She wasn't sure how her fellow cadets felt about her, but that was nothing new. She'd never really connected with other kids in school. She usually skipped lunch in favor of a protein shake and midday flight simulator sessions. And she was the youngest member of the computer programming club she'd joined in her Washington, D.C., suburb back on Earth.

It didn't much matter whether she got along with Jo and Vor. Kenzie wasn't aboard the *Gremlin* to make friends. She was here to get the experience she needed for her application to the Academy and to prove herself to—

An alarm from Kenzie's handset cut through her thoughts. She looked—it was a message from her dad.

"Love you, Kenzie," it read. "Hope you're having fun. Don't forget today's date."

Oh, yeah. That was today. She would've forgotten. She always did.

"Thanks, dad," she wrote back. She sighed and put her handset down on the funky mattress.

Kenzie sat up, reached under her bunk, and grabbed her purple and blue duffel bag, somewhat deflated now that her clothes had been stowed inside her locker. She fished around the bag until she found it: a round, black disk with a single button on its side.

As she lay back in her bed, Kenzie held the disk in her palm and just looked at it. She pressed the button and a holographic image of a woman with dark skin, the same shade as hers, hovered above.

No matter which angle Kenzie tried, her mother never met her gaze.

"That's a weird looking mirror."

Kenzie started at the sudden interruption as Jo entered their shared cabin. The disk fell from her hand and clattered onto the floor as Jo walked past.

Vor followed Jo into the room and reached down to pick up the disk.

"It's not, uh—it's not a mirror," Kenzie said, slowly swinging her legs around and sitting up on her bed. She was trying to play her sudden spazz attack off as purposeful. It didn't work. She reached her hand out towards Vor, who eyed the device closely. He put both hands on it, looking like he was planning to pry it apart.

"Vor!" snapped Jo at the base of the ladder to the top bunk.

Kenzie looked up and saw Jo make a motion in her direction with her head, her glittering eyes wide.

Vor conked himself on the head with his hand—"how silly of me," was how Kenzie interpreted the gesture—and leaned down to put the disk back in Kenzie's palm. Jo shook her head at her brother, who was already busying himself with the junkpile spread across his bunk on the other side of the room.

Kenzie clicked the button again. The holographic portrait hung in the air once more.

"This is my mom."

"Uh, neat," said Jo, either making a half-hearted attempt at interest or looking to set a record for sarcasm. It was hard for Kenzie to tell with her. "She's, like, way smaller than I would've guessed."

Kenzie was about to correct her, but then she second guessed herself and squinted at Jo instead.

"Yeah, I was obviously kidding," said Jo.

"I—I knew that," said Kenzie.

"No, but seriously, she looks just like you," Jo continued as she climbed the ladder to her top bunk. "Same eyes, same nose, same ears. Very boring."

Kenzie felt a flush creep into her cheeks. Compared to Jo—who had subtle, glowing patterns etched across her lavender-gray face and even glittering teeth—of course Kenzie was boring looking. She had dark brown skin, unremarkable brown eyes, and black, frizzy hair that she always struggled to tame. At least her mother knew how to do something interesting with her hairdo—her holo-portrait featured long, intricate, crisscrossing braids. Kenzie usually just settled for the two small poms at the back of her head like she wore it now.

Kenzie couldn't see Jo on the bunk above her, but she heard her tapping away on her handset, the clicks revealing that she was scrolling through her feeds—again. Despite apparently being involved in some conversation with other people halfway across the galaxy, Jo kept talking to her.

"So what's the deal," she said. "We've only just left the station and you're already homesick?"

"Not really," said Kenzie. "I, uh…I never knew my mom really. She—she was in the Forger War. She didn't come back."

"Uh-huh," said Jo's disembodied voice from above.

"Today's the anniversary of when my dad got the transmission that her ship was lost—"

"Wait, when?" Jo interrupted.

"It was, um—" Kenzie thought for a second, "—twelve years ago. Mom was an engineer in the Alliance Fleet. She and her crew were experimenting with different ways to get technological advantages over the Forgers, but, well, they never managed to. For a while my dad got messages from her every day. Then they just…stopped. The whole ship vanished. Destroyed, probably."

"*What?*" asked Jo, incredulous. "How could that even happen?"

Kenzie furrowed her brow. "We never really found out. Just…one day mom was sending messages, and then the next—nothing. She was just kinda—y'know, gone. And then it was only me and Dad. Well, whenever Dad's home from work. Which…isn't too often…"

"Ugh, that sucks," said Jo from above.

Kenzie thought about what Jo said, a warm feeling in her chest at connecting with one of her new peers. It *did* kinda suck, though—it'd been just her and her dad for years. It was hard to imagine her life at home being different. Kenzie cocked her head, looking at the hologram. Her stranger mother floated there, saying nothing. How could you look just like someone you never even knew?

"Anyway," Kenzie continued. "Dad just sent me a message. He reminds me every year, since I was so little when it happened."

"What?" said Jo.

"I said I was so little when it happened," repeated Kenzie.

"What do you mean?" asked Jo, sounding confused.

"My mom's ship?" said Kenzie. "Lost in the Forger War? I was two years old. I literally just—"

"He did?" said Jo. "He just told you he didn't like your etchings right to your face? Just like that?"

Setting the disk down on the mattress next to her, Kenzie pulled herself up, peeking at Jo on the top bunk. She was on her handset, talking to someone else, explaining her disgust at how rude some people could be. Jo didn't notice Kenzie looking at her. That made much more sense. The warm feeling in her chest went cold.

Kenzie sat back down and clicked the button. The image of her mother disappeared.

She glanced over at Vor. And to her surprise, he was sitting on his bed, staring straight at her, his glowing eyes wet. He sniffed once. Was he crying?

He lifted a hand at her, motioning for her to continue.

"Oh, uh, anyway," she smiled, "a couple weeks after that was Gantoid IV, when Dash Drake—well, when he basically helped the Alliance win the war." Kenzie turned toward Vor, her feet dangling off the side of the bed. "I still remember my dad telling me all about what a hero Dash—I mean, uh, Captain Drake…well…anyway, here I am. On his ship. This is gonna look great on my Academy application. And maybe he'll write me a recommendation! Pretty awesome, right?"

Vor nodded vigorously, and Kenzie felt a grin spread across her face.

"So what brought you guys here—" she said, before getting interrupted by a crackle from the comm-speaker embedded in the wall. Captain Drake's voice filled the tiny room.

"Cadets, report to the lift for your duty assignment," he said. "And someone bring me an aspirin from the medbay. Captain's got a migra—"

The comms clicked off, cutting off the last word.

"I gotta call you back," Jo said. Then she scoffed, "Great."

"Yeah," said Kenzie, looking at an equally excited Vor. "This is gonna be so great."

* * *

Captain Drake leaned against the wall inside the elevator looking like someone who wasn't up to the task of staying vertical. The cadets gathered on the opposite side of the lift.

The captain pulled the control lever, sending the elevator on its brief descent from the top deck to the bottom. "Hope you guys are good at math," he said.

Kenzie got excited. She *was* good at math.

This was what she'd been waiting for ever since she first signed up for the immersion experience. She couldn't believe she got a spot without being put on a waiting list or anything. And now, she was about to jump into some high-level mathematical computations for her hero.

The elevator door to the cargo bay opened with a deep rumble, probably a sign that the gears inside needed oil—or replacement. Kenzie looked around at the large, dimly lit cargo bay.

The lift was on the port side of the ship. When Kenzie stepped into the bay, she looked left and saw the large, copper-colored cargo bay doors, sealed during their journey through jump-space. To her right was the decidedly smaller, Human-sized door to the engine room. A few dozen crates were stacked haphazardly along the wall in front of her, along with two dinged-up, anti-grav pallets floating nearby. One was covered in stickers of bands from across the Alliance's territory—probably a gift from a former cadet, Kenzie guessed—while the other was missing half of its steering handle. Seeing the boxes arranged so roughly made Kenzie's teeth itch. And off in a corner was an oblong object, maybe about eight

meters across, three meters high, covered in a musty, faded tarp. Kenzie
figured it might be a small ship—probably a fighter—and a thrill went up
her spine as she guessed which one it was.

But she put that thought aside. The captain crossed the bay and
grabbed a canvas bag hanging on the wall. He reached in and handed her
and the other cadets small devices: drab, gray, older-model handsets that
hadn't been on the market for at least ten years. Vor looked at his hungrily,
turning it over and over in his hands. Kenzie could already imagine him
prying it apart to get at the wires and circuits inside.

Kenzie activated hers and saw that it connected directly to the ship's
internal computer, but not to the galactic network that dotted the
Alliance's star systems. The captain was trusting her with access to the
brain of the *Gremlin* itself. She could already envision the task at hand. An
analysis of ideal cargo weight distribution to maximize thrust when leaving
a planet's atmosphere. Plotting the most efficient navigational course
based on fuel reserves and their shipping contracts' deadlines. Whatever
she was about to do, it was going to be some high-level kind of amazing.
Her face hurt from smiling.

"So, this is called 'inventory,'" said Captain Drake, scratching the
back of his head.

Kenzie stopped smiling.

Inventory?

"Yeah, so, things, uh, didn't quite work out with our last cadet," he
said, a frown creeping onto his face. "Our current cargo load isn't really,
like, organized? That's where you three come in."

Jo let out a heavy, annoyed sigh. Dash continued.

"Scan each box with these handsets, tally up their contents, and
arrange them in order of destination. First destinations closer to the front
of the bay—" he said, pointing towards the big doors, "—last destinations
at the back." He jerked his thumb at the door to the engine room on the
other wall.

"Those crates must weigh like fifty kilos apiece," Jo said. "This is the worst." Her hand was on her hip, her mouth twisted into a sneer. Even though she'd hate to display such an unprofessional attitude in the presence of the captain, Kenzie couldn't help but feel the same way. But maybe Captain Drake had more in mind for this assignment than it seemed...

"Yeah, inventory pretty much *is* the worst," said Dash. "But there's an important reason I needed to give you this assignment."

Kenzie leaned in.

"Because I'm definitely not gonna do it," he finished.

Kenzie heard a loud pop to her right and looked over. Sparks shot from Vor's now-dissected handset, a spider's web of wires now all that connected the two halves together.

"Ugh, come on, man," said the captain. He took the broken handset and tossed it onto the floor, then reached into the bag and pulled out another, handing it to Vor.

"Don't break this one," he said, looking directly into Vor's face. Vor gave a quick nod, then a salute, and looked back to the discarded and apparently broken device on the ground. Then he wandered over toward the anti-grav pallets.

Dash called after him, "Don't break those either!"

"I told you before," said Jo. "He does this all the time."

"Yeah, but why?" Kenzie asked.

"I dunno, he can't help himself. He was always taking stuff apart at the house and sticking things together to make, like, super-machines. Sometimes they don't even blow up. Still, dad got kind of fed up with it all and signed him up for this program so maybe he'd, y'know, stop."

She fiddled with the handset the captain had given her. "His engineering teacher said he might even be a genius—if, like, he actually stopped and thought about what he was doing." Jo made a face. "Ugh, this thing isn't even on the network!"

"You don't need to be on the network for this job," Dash said, crossing his arms again. "The handsets are there to tally boxes and tell you where they're going so you can organize them." He pointed at the pallets. Vor was already poking at one, though Kenzie could tell he was making every effort to resist the urge to pull it apart and see its insides.

"We've got those anti-grav pallets for you to stack the crates, but I'm not gonna lie—doing inventory sucks."

Kenzie looked up and saw a grid-like track crisscrossing the cargo bay ceiling, along with a deactivated sensor array. She realized something was missing. It looked like a piece of hardware that used to run along that track had been removed.

"Doesn't this class of ship have a Built-In Load-Lifter?" she asked, pointing up.

"What's that?" said Jo, who'd started playing a game on her device.

"A robot that does inventory so people don't have to."

"We do have a Built-In Load-Lifter," said Dash, who leaned over to Jo's handset and turned off the game while she was in mid-swipe. "It's in the medbay. You met him an hour ago."

Kenzie squinted. "I did?"

"Yeah, he patched you up after you tripped. On that towel."

Kenzie's ears got hot at the memory of falling in front of the captain. "You mean Doctor Bill?"

"Built-In Load-Lifter Bill—that's the guy, alright," said Dash, walking into the elevator. "I installed a different program, swapped his lifting arms for medical probes, and suddenly I didn't have to pay to keep a doctor on staff.

"Besides," he said, turning to face them and grabbing the elevator's control lever. "If I had a robot lifting and organizing cargo, what would there be for you guys to do?"

He pulled the lever. The door slid shut with a rumbling thud.

Kenzie watched the elevator door, hoping it'd open again and the captain would spring out to announce it was all a joke. "I'm kidding!" he'd cry. "Of course I'm totally not going to waste your talents on counting boxes in a spaceship cargo bay! That would be silly, and plus, you're awesome."

But that didn't happen. All she heard was a disgusted "ugh" from the back of Jo's throat. The Crag was playing her game again, so Kenzie wasn't sure if her annoyance came from a bad swipe or the thought of stacking boxes for hours. And as Kenzie looked around the dingy cargo bay, her heart was making an "ugh" of its own too.

She pocketed the old handset she got from the captain and took out her own to start taking notes. This wasn't going quite how she'd imagined. Sure, she'd only been aboard the *Gremlin* for a day—well, less than a day— and she didn't expect to be taking a turn at the helm or anything. But counting boxes in a dimly lit cargo bay? What had gone wrong? Had she said or done something to offend him?

"I wonder what we did wrong," said Kenzie, thinking out loud.

"Nothing," Jo said, still playing her game. "I'm pretty sure getting his cadets to do inventory was always part of the captain's plan," Jo said.

"But it just…doesn't feel right," said Kenzie. "I mean, this is Dash Drake. Would he really take money from a bunch of kids and just have them do a bunch of grunt work?"

Jo looked up at Kenzie from her game. "Um…"

"Unless," Kenzie said, putting her hand on her chin. She looked at Vor, who was slowly riding the sticker-covered anti-grav pallet like a scooter around the cargo bay.

"What if this is all a test?"

"Uh," said Jo.

Kenzie smacked herself in the forehead.

"Of course this is a test!" she said, pounding her fist into her palm. "You said it yourself. This was 'always part of the captain's plan.' He wants us to step up and find an ingenious way to finish this work."

Jo's mouth went into a thoughtful pout.

"I'm pretty sure I don't I know what you're talking about."

"Think about it," said Kenzie, her voice getting louder as she got more excited. "We're in a room with helpful tech that's been strategically removed or disabled. Look up there," she said, pointing at the deactivated scanner in the ceiling. Jo's gaze followed her finger.

"That's a perfectly functional scanner that's just been turned off. Why? Because Captain Dash Drake wants us to rise to the occasion."

"I mean," Jo said. "I guess that's possible…"

"Work smarter, not harder," said Kenzie. "Drake, page four. I read the words myself."

Kenzie smiled.

"Trust me."

Pity Stop

Dash sat alone at the round table in the galley, the only light coming from his handset's glowing screen. He'd just finished cramming two candybars into his face, and he had no plans of stopping now. He unwrapped a fresh Earth Bar and took a bite, hoping the taste of nougat would help him forget that his life had started resembling a garbage fire. It wasn't working.

He scrolled through his social feeds, tapping on posts from people he barely knew or remembered from his former life. Oh, look, someone he went to high school with started a new job. Neat, that guy he shared a bunk with at boot camp got a new, top-of-the-line ship. Wow, that woman he'd dated for five months just had her second kid with that guy who looked kind of like Dash if you squinted but if you got closer and saw him he was actually way more handsome and his clothes were tight in the way that you want and not the way that Dash's were around his middle parts.

Plenty of his classmates were drafted into the Fleet when the Forger War broke out, just like he was. But none of them became galaxy-famous war heroes when they were still teenagers. Dash hadn't aspired to much before the war started, so he wasn't sure how to aspire to anything at all once it ended. Going from ordinary to extraordinary in an instant didn't help Dash figure out how to be ordinary again just a few years later.

Dash took another bite of his candybar and swallowed, barely tasting it. This cargo run was supposed to last for weeks…but he was also supposed to have way more credits in his account. Or, in fact, any credits in his account.

As it was, he would have to dip into his cash reserves to buy more fuel rods when the *Gremlin* arrived at the Kembar Colony in two days. Otherwise, they'd never make their first delivery, and they'd never collect their fee, and then they'd be stuck floating through space like a piece of trash ejected from the bowels of a luxury cruise ship ferrying a horde of fat tourists to their next destination who couldn't be bothered to think of how pointless and meaningless their lives truly were—

Dash shook his head and threw the Earth Bar onto the table in disgust.

There was a time when he didn't think about money because he had so much of it. But all the years he should've spent figuring out how to be a real person and pursuing a career were wasted on luxuries that had long since been sold or repossessed. All that was left was his ship.

Unfortunately, even that wasn't what it used to be. Cozy and marginally functional, the *Gremlin* kept getting older. The ship was slowly falling apart with each passing year. Meanwhile, the galaxy's ever-growing advancements in technology put Dash's operations even further out of date.

Then again, having an older ship had certain advantages. For instance, even though the *Gremlin* had been outfitted with a full complement of networked inventory systems when Dash bought it, he'd dismantled most of them. That way, when he brought new cargo aboard with each new contract, it wouldn't get scanned and logged within the Alliance's network. Sure, he'd have to manually file his cargo with each trip—but he only ever reported a fraction of it. That meant he wouldn't have to pay taxes or fees on the rest of it as he jumped from system to system. When the beacon crews saw how old his ship was, they weren't surprised by how little cargo he said he was carrying. It was one way he kept expenses down—or "passed savings on to customers," as he liked to think of it.

Still, his customers were getting harder to please. Dash got a harsh reminder of that fact at that exact moment, when his handset dinged. A new post appeared on his feedpage. It was Jonah: the snot who left his post as a cadet after one little rash. If Dash had a nickel for every rash he'd ever gotten on a cargo run, well, he wouldn't have many money problems, would he? Though, maybe he should really take the rash situation a little more seriously now that he thought about it.

Dash tapped the notification bubble and instantly regretted it.

"WRST PROGRAM EVR," he read. Jonah left the comment on Dash's personal feedpage, apparently ignoring the fact that his folks had gotten a full refund. He also wasn't the strongest speller.

"SUPR GROS SHIP TERIBEL CAPTIN," the post continued.

Dash ignored his better judgment and hit "reply."

"Sorry you weren't satisfied with the cadet immersion experience, Jonah," he typed. "Maybe someday you'll give us another chance, and we can change your mind."

Dash felt reasonably comfortable with his response and rewarded himself with another bite of candybar. His handset dinged, and another notification bubble appeared.

Jonah again. "ID NVR COM BACK UR SHIP SUKS."

Dash's mouth went tight as he composed his next reply.

"Sorry to hear you feel that way," he typed, the bile rising in his gut. "I'd like to point out that we provided your family a full refund. Thanks again for giving us a try."

He watched his handset expectantly. Within moments it dinged again.

"MY RASH WONT GO AWAY U SHUD BE ARRESTED."

Dash fumed. But before he could reply, he got a new notification on his handset—this time unrelated to his feedpage. It was the Interstellar Alliance's Tariff Authority. And they were fining him.

"You gotta be…"

He pocketed his handset and threw his half-eaten candybar into the trash, taking off for the cargo bay at a run.

* * *

When Dash looked through the open elevator door to the cargo bay, he didn't expect to see two anti-grav pallets driving themselves and stacking boxes up to the ceiling. So when he did, it was enough of a surprise that he forgot why he'd rushed there in the first place.

Kenzie called from the left, near the large cargo bay doors. "Captain Drake!" She waved, flanked on both sides by the Crags. For once, Jo wasn't staring at her handset. Meanwhile, Vor sat cross-legged on the floor, his head craned forward in fascination. Both Crags' eyes were locked on the mechanical ballet.

Dash walked from the open lift across the cargo bay, watching the anti-grav pallets stack box after box. Where once there was a mess of crates that he and Squix failed to organize, now sat rows of nearly completed towers of cargo.

"What did you…" Dash said, rubbing the back of his head. "Uh…do?"

"Pretty cool, huh?" Kenzie beamed as Dash joined the cadets. The pallet missing half its handle floated several meters off the floor and dropped another crate onto the stack closest to the cargo bay doors. Meanwhile, the sticker-covered pallet worked its way underneath a box near the entrance to engineering and ascended to drop it off on top of a stack in the middle of the room.

"So, we figured out pretty quickly you didn't actually want us to stack these boxes ourselves," said Kenzie

Dash looked over at the girl. "You did?"

"Yup," she said, smiling. "The other cadets and I devised a way to use the available equipment to our advantage. Vor," she said, turning to him, "rigged the busted old handsets you gave us into control systems for each anti-grav pallet."

Dash squinted and spotted the busted remains of the handsets he'd given the cadets wired directly into the anti-grav pallets' steering columns.

"And Jo—" she turned to her next, "—checked her feeds for friends or friends of friends who could find programs to automate the pallets. Took her about three minutes."

"It would've been faster if the pallets weren't so old," Jo said, still watching the cargo getting sorted.

"And I," she said, jerking a thumb at herself proudly, "wrote the program to connect them to the cargo bay's sensor array. So instead of us scanning each crate, one at a time, the sensors scanned all the cargo at once to do one single inventory, and then fed that data to the handsets attached to the pallets."

Dash looked up at the sensor array. Sure enough, it was activated and scanning.

"Pretty cool, huh?" Kenzie said again.

"You said that already," said Jo.

Dash turned back to Kenzie.

He pointed up. "You reactivated the sensor array?"

"Sure did," she said. "And it took a lot of creative hacking. Definitely wasn't easy!"

Dash rubbed half of his face as though he were trying to scrub it down to the bone. "It wasn't meant to be," he said. "When I turned that array off, I meant for it to stay off."

Kenzie's smile evaporated. "What?"

"Yeah," said Dash, leaning back against the wall. "Now I owe the Tariff Authority a lot of money." He closed his eyes and jammed his fists onto his forehead. "Money I do not have."

When he opened his eyes, he saw Kenzie looking at him with a puzzled expression. This kid.

"So you're saying this wasn't a test?"

"Only of my patience," Dash said.

The anti-grav pallets hummed and whirred as they floated around the cargo bay. Kenzie broke the silence.

"But if it had been a test, would I have gotten an A?"

Dash looked at her, but before he could answer, the ship started shaking violently. The crates—not yet secured—tumbled out of their stacks and into piles on the cargo bay floor.

The captain and the cadets struggled to maintain their feet as the *Gremlin* vibrated. Dash grabbed his handset and yelled over the din.

"Squix, drop us out of jump-space!" he shouted.

The Octopus's voice crackled over the handset's small speaker. "Which button do I push?"

Dash saw his navigator's tentacles waving nervously from his seat in the cockpit. "The big red one," Dash called back. "The same one it always is!"

"You know I get nervous when you yell at me!" Squix cried, flashing a defensive green.

The room shimmied less with each passing moment. Dash ran for the lift.

"You three," he said to the cadets. "Clean this mess—"

He turned and saw that the anti-grav pallets had already begun re-stacking the crates.

The cadets looked at him.

"Never mind." Dash turned and shut the elevator door behind him.

A minute later, Dash was in the cockpit, trying to get Squix to tell him just what he'd done.

"I didn't do anything!" Squix whined.

"Okay, then," Dash said, slumping into his chair. "What happened?"

Squix swiveled in his seat and started to mime his actions.

"I was sitting here. Just like this." He started pretending to flick switches. "Beep boop, click clack," Squix said as his tentacles waved over the control board, miming his typical motions. Dash balled his hands into fists. He felt like he might be getting an ulcer.

"And I was just running the numbers to see if there was a way to squeeze some more distance out of our current fuel reserves without needing to dip into our cash," he said. "And then the ship started shaking and I got scared and I didn't get to finish my last set of calculations and then I started thinking about how all that was separating me from space was one pane of glass but then I remembered that it was actually high-density astro-glass and—"

Dash put up his hand. "Okay," he said. Squix flashed a shade of yellow. "So it wasn't anything you did. But that doesn't help us understand what's going on."

Squix pointed at the helm console in front of Dash.

"What's that?" he asked.

The captain squinted and saw a little, blinking yellow light. He reached under his seat and pulled out the ship's manual, flipping towards the back.

"Check engine," he said.

* * *

"Drake?"

Dash sat up with a jolt. He'd fallen asleep in his seat in the repair shop waiting room. A wonder, considering the chairs seemed designed for people with knees in the back of their legs. The monitor hanging in a corner of the room had a news report on. Someone in a nice suit was droning on about escalating tensions with the Frawgs near a border somewhere. Dash jammed his left hand into his eye and rubbed. Why did the news always knock him out? He felt dumb.

"Captain Dash Drake, you still here? Your ship is ready."

He shook the sleep away and stood. Zrxx, the woman who ran the shop, called his name from the door to the repair bay. Wearing greasy coveralls, she was built like a tool shed, with a fine pelt of orange fur dotted with black spots. Two small, round antennae sprouted from under her red mane, but whether or not they served any kind of purpose was a mystery to Dash. He wasn't sure what species Zrxx was…or really even where in the galaxy he was.

After deciphering the mystery of the blinking dashboard light, Dash knew he needed help but had no idea where to get it. They were only partway to Kembar Colony, but this wasn't a part of the galaxy he'd really ever explored. This was jumpover country.

The *Gremlin* hadn't been anywhere near an inhabited world, outpost, or space station. Squix crunched the numbers, and it would've taken years reach the closest one if they'd relied on the ship's thrusters. They would've run out of food long before then.

And Dash wagered that waiting to starve to death would've been really annoying with these cadets. Well, one cadet in particular. She probably would've blown all the ship's food out of an airlock in an effort to conserve gas.

Despite the potential danger, the *Gremlin* took a quick, bumpy dip into jump-space to get within spitting distance of Purgamentum Orbis II. It was a detour from their original destination—but it was also the closest planet with a repair shop that might diagnose the ship's problems. The trip, brief as it was, nearly tore the ship apart. Dash's favorite coffee mug—a blue one with that funny robot from TV on it—had fallen off the helm console and shattered during the trip.

When they'd touched down on the landing strip, the maintenance hatch in the cockpit ceiling opened with a hiss. Dash poked his head out to breathe some fresh air—the kind of fresh air produced by an actual atmosphere—for the first time in months. Okay, well, maybe not "fresh" air, considering the skylines of junk and garbage heaps that surrounded the repair shop. But it was definitely air that didn't come out of a recycler.

But his moment of communing with nature was shortlived. Zrxx came out to greet them, directed the *Gremlin* to the nearest open repair bay, and thus began the long wait to get the thing fixed—and to get the bill. And now the moment was at hand.

"Here," Dash said, still groggy. He wasn't sure how long he'd been out, but he didn't see the cadets or Squix. "I'm right here."

He walked over to Zrxx and she led him into the repair bay.

"One of your landing struts was a little wobbly, so I reinforced it," she said as he followed her to the *Gremlin*.

"But a wobbly landing strut isn't why my ship almost shook itself apart, is it?"

They reached the ship and Zrxx pointed to a bump behind the cockpit.

"It's your jump shield," she said sighing.

Dash felt a ball form in the pit of his stomach. "Crap."

"Yeah," said Zrxx, pulling a rag from her pocket and wiping her hands. "You're actually really lucky you got here before the thing died completely. It's kind of amazing that you lasted as long as you did."

Dash nodded. Jump-space gave ships the ability to close great distances in very little time—but it wasn't exactly safe. Without the protection provided by a jump-shield, a ship would get torn apart when it entered jump-space. And anyone traveling on a ship without a working shield wouldn't fare much better. For instance, they might get headaches, suffer nausea, or lose consciousness. Or even explode. Or implode. Or any of the other plodes in between.

Really, jump-shields were high on the list of important components to be fully functional when it came to interstellar travel. And that made them expensive.

Dash gritted his teeth and asked. "How much do I owe you?"

Zrxx pulled out her bulky handset and started tapping away.

"Well, I got good news and I got bad news," she said.

In Dash's experience, that usually meant that there was actually just bad news and worse news.

"The good news is that you don't actually owe us that much," she said, handing Dash the handset so he could see the invoice for himself.

"But…?" he said, cocking an eyebrow at the suspiciously affordable bill.

"But that's because this was a patch job—and that's not what you need," she said. "I couldn't actually replace your jump-shield," she said. "That bucket of yours is pretty old, and I didn't have any spare jump-shields that were compatible just laying around. So I fixed up the one you have as best I could."

"How long will it last?"

"I hope it lasts forever!" said Zrxx laughing, her antennae bobbing as she chuckled. Dash just looked at her. She saw Dash wasn't laughing too, and her face quickly took a sober expression. "But you should probably get it replaced as quickly as you can. Seriously."

"Super," said Dash. "Okay, I'll be back in a minute to give you some credit chips."

"Chips?" Zrxx looked like someone had slapped her. "You're paying in cash?"

"It's been that kind of day," Dash said. "I just gotta go find my partner."

"You mean the, uh, um…" Zrxx looked off to the side, snapping her fingers to try and jog her memory. "The Squid?"

"Actually, he's an Octopus," said Dash.

Zrxx blinked. "What's the difference?"

"I'm not sure," said Dash. "But his name is Squix."

"That's weird," said Zrxx.

"That's nothing," said Dash, walking towards the door. "You should watch him eat."

He walked back to the waiting room, then outside. The sky was a bluish-green—or maybe it was greenish-blue—and the few standing trees were bare and covered in ash or soot. In the distance, Dash tried to look beyond the mountainous skyline of scrap, but all he saw was more garbage. Across the landing strip was the only other building he could spot: a squat little convenience store and refueling station.

Inside, the brightly lit store was stocked full of all the salty carbohydrates a space trucker could want as he stopped to buy more fuel and take a bathroom break. Despite how remote Purgamentum Orbis II was, there were still a few creepy people wandering around like zombies, buying decorative trinkets and commemorative knives, ordering coffee, or just giving each other weird looks.

Dash found Squix carefully deciding which snacks to buy, while the cadets were scattered throughout the store. Kenzie had managed to occupy Vor with an arcade game, but Dash half-expected him to stop playing at any moment and start taking the machine apart. Jo was in a corner on her handset again.

"Cap, I'm glad you're here," said Squix, pointing his tentacles at two packages with writing in a language he'd never seen before. "Should I get that one, or that one?" He tapped the bright orange one on the right, which had a label dotted with brown specks. "I think those are supposed to be bits of chocolate. Right?"

"Sure," said Dash. "Might as well roll the dice while we're here on the garbage planet. Apparently we barely survived getting here. How bad could mystery snacks be?"

Squix stopped considering his next meal and looked at the captain. "Barely survived?"

"There's good news and there's bad news," said Dash.

"So you mean bad news and worse news," said Squix.

"The *Gremlin* is patched up and ready to fly, and even after repairs, we still have a tiny bit of cash leftover. But we need to replace the jump-shield, and I mean yesterday."

Squix's eyes went wide. "The jump-shield? Oh, no."

He let go of the snack packages and sank onto the floor.

"Yeah," said Dash. "We need to make some serious money. Even if we finish our cargo run, we won't have enough to replace the shield. We gotta take on more work as soon as possible."

Squix took out his handset and started tapping. Dash heard the sound of shaking from the other side of the store and saw Kenzie holding Vor's arms, which were gripping the sides of the machine. He really hoped he wouldn't have to pay to replace a dissected arcade cabinet.

"We're actually pretty close to Technica Outpost, only a few hours in jump-space," said Squix. "I'm pulling up the info page…looks like Pendros is there for a little while."

"Pendros?" Dash thought for a second. "That could work. We've worked with Pendros before. I think he kinda likes me, right?"

Squix blinked at him. "Uh."

"We were even a week early with our last shipment!" said Dash.

"Didn't we damage one of the containers and lose half the product that time?"

"Of course not," said Dash, offended. Then, quietly, "We only lost a quarter."

"Oh."

Dash waved his hands. "Besides, Pendros probably doesn't remember that. He likes me!" He thought for a second. "I'm pretty sure he likes me."

Squix flashed yellow.

"I am reasonably sure he doesn't hate me," he said. "Send him a message. We're going to Technica Outpost."

Advanced Diplomatic Relations

6

Kenzie tapped furiously at her handset: "What do you mean, 'it vanished'?"

Seconds later, m0reez replied: "its just gon"

He didn't have time for correct punctuation. Or spelling. This was serious.

Sitting at a table in the food court aboard Technica Outpost, Kenzie was catching up on news from around the quadrant with one of her friends from her favorite feeds. Well, "friend" was maybe a bit strong. "Acquaintance" might be better. "Anonymous contact, data source, and sometime hacking rival" might be best.

And Kenzie wanted more data about this. Reports said a jump-drive facility at Delta Pallas III disappeared without a trace, which was a big story. And m0reez claimed to have heard something about the culprits through the interstellar grapevine.

"What do you think it was?" Kenzie typed.

"Nt sure," wrote m0reez. "But sum1 syng frwgs."

Frawgs? That was surprising—and it didn't sound right to Kenzie. Everyone knew the Frawgs made trouble and ate a person or two out on the fringes of Alliance territory. But ever since their homeworld was destroyed and the remaining Frawg tribes became galactic nomads and pirates, they'd never managed to organize enough to do much of anything. Certainly nothing like making a whole factory disappear…at least not without leaving a few body parts with telltale chomp-marks floating around to show they'd been there. And definitely not that far inside the Interstellar Alliance's territory, where the former factory had floated for years without any trouble.

But before Kenzie could think of any theories of her own, m0reez surprised her again—he asked a personal question. "Hows ur trip," he wrote.

"Pretty good so far," she typed back. "Working with Captain Drake is amazing. Pretty sure he'll write me an Academy recommendation."

"Uh-huh," wrote m0reez.

"We've stopped for supplies, and he's given me the responsibility of getting the ship's most important provisions."

Before she could write more, Kenzie's train of thought was interrupted by a stony tap on the shoulder.

"Hey," said Jo, standing next to Kenzie's table, a small crate under her arm. "Squix said you weren't answering. You get the toilet paper or what?"

Kenzie quickly tapped her handset's screen to close her chat with m0reez. That's when she saw the many messages Squix had sent her while she'd been chatting during her lunch break. On the table was a small Coke and an empty container that used to contain spaghetti and meatballs. The tall, red-haired woman in front of her in line kept raving about the spaghetti—that this was her third helping. Kenzie thought it was okay.

"Oh, hi Jo," she said, quickly pocketing her handset. "I got it right here." She patted the package stowed under her seat. The words on its front read "Insta-Paper! 200 Rolls! Just Add Moisture!"

"Cool," said Jo, already having switched from looking at Kenzie to her handset. "I'm telling Squix now."

Kenzie took a sip of Coke and surveyed the food court as Jo typed. People of countless species and limb configurations milled around, carrying trays piled high with steaming, gleaming glop offering approximations of intergalactic cuisine. A short woman covered in fish scales and wearing an orange visor stood a few feet away from Kenzie's table. She kept offering small paper cups of a foaming green substance— apparently free samples of "grack"—to passersby. Whether grack was a solid or a liquid, Kenzie wasn't sure.

The outpost's walls were composed of glittering tan rock, braced with thick metal pylons and girders. The ceiling on this level—the top floor, Level One—was similarly made of stone, having been smoothed out from when Technica Outpost's original builders hollowed out this asteroid. Instead of stalactites pointing down from above, there hung high-powered lights on thick black cables. But powerful as the lamps were, Kenzie still had the feeling of drinking soda in a deep cave somewhere.

Meanwhile, there were nine more levels below this one, each corresponding with different levels of commerce. The further down you went, the higher the amounts of money that changed hands.

Captain Drake was finding a job for the *Gremlin* on Level Two.

"Okay, Squix is freaking," Jo said. "He said he got the replacement piston for the landing strut that busted when we got here, and he wants us to meet him and the captain so we can install it while Dash keeps negotiating. Seriously, Squix is one of the weirdest Humans I've met. And you're all pretty weird already."

Kenzie condensed her garbage onto her tray, then tucked her package of Insta-Paper under her arm. "What do you mean?" she asked, carrying the tray to the nearest wastebin. She grabbed a small cup of grack as she passed the scaled woman, who gurgled her appreciation. "You think Squix is Human?"

Jo looked at Kenzie.

"You mean he isn't?" she asked, dumbfounded.

"No, he's an Octopus."

Jo blinked at Kenzie.

"Are you being racist?" Jo said. "I honestly can't tell, but it sounds like you might be saying something really offensive right now."

Jo turned and started walking. Kenzie jogged to catch up.

"I'm not being racist!" she said, panting slightly. "Have you ever been to Earth?" Kenzie asked, looking into the cup of grack as she walked.

"Nope," she said, wrinkling her nose at another Crag who was wearing the same outfit as her. Under her breath, she said, "gross."

"Okay, so, what do you know about Humans?" Kenzie tasted the grack with a little sip, fought a gag, then slurped down the rest. She always took the opportunity to try foods from other cultures. Even if they smelled like grack.

"Um, they're the dominant lifeform from Earth?" said Jo, rolling her eyes. "They're carbon-based? They supposedly put their intolerance of diversity and history of bigotry behind them before even engaging in the Precursor Wars? Guh, everyone knows that, Kenzie."

"Right, yes," she said, "but even though Humans are the dominant lifeforms, they're not the only sentient species. Squix is from a species that lived in Earth's oceans for millennia while Humans built civilizations on land."

Jo pondered this as the pair passed a stand selling aftermarket plasma torches.

"Is that why Squix has that metal thing on all the time?"

"His exosuit," Kenzie said. "It keeps him hydrated when he's not in his aquarium. And keeps him from leaving a trail of slime on the floor when he walks."

"Oh," said Jo. "Well, whatever. All you Earthers look the same to me anyway."

The pair kept walking, passing an Aphid trying to sell a Blob a jar of powder that he said would improve his overall texture and viscosity. Kenzie took a quick glance and saw the writing on the jar roughly translated to "baking soda."

"Hey, where's your brother?" Kenzie asked, noticing for the first time that Vor wasn't there.

"He wandered off somewhere near Level Four, I think," said Jo, waggling her hand vaguely.

"Level Four? Stuff down there's pretty flash. What's he doing there?"

"How should I know?" Jo looked at Kenzie. "He doesn't have a mouth."

Eventually, Jo led Kenzie to the lifts, where they went down one level and made their way to a room on the outpost's edge that held no shops or stands. It was filled with people from dozens of planets, all babbling at each other, looking to make deals. The room was dim, illuminated only by small lights placed on each of the cramped tables. A wet, dirty bar on the right side of the room dispensed drinks, while men and women in brown crew uniforms served them. If music played, Kenzie couldn't hear it over the chatter and arguments and the clinks of glasses.

One windowed wall offered Kenzie a view of the jump-beacon floating a few kilometers away, along with the line of spacecrafts waiting their turn to jump from the star system.

Kenzie couldn't help but watch the traffic move as she followed Jo towards a corner of the room: after each ship jumped, winking out of existence in a red flash, another ship jumped in with a red flash of its own. Away jumped a caravan of civilian transports, bringing settlers to colonies or tourists to alien civilizations they'd seen on broadcasts. In jumped a freighter probably loaded with spices and ship parts followed by a sleek-looking coupe stopping to refuel and to allow its pilot to empty the ship's waste system and maybe grab a coffee. Incoming crafts lined up to enter the outpost's hangar bay, and the life on Technica Outpost kept going, one deal at a time.

Seated at a table near the window's edge, Kenzie saw Dash, Squix, and a blue Skalorian, whose head tendrils were covered in dull-grey feathers. Kenzie hadn't read enough about Skalorians or Skalorian culture to know if the feathers were decorative or biological. And considering how upset Captain Drake looked as she approached, she figured she might not have the chance to ask.

"—remind Pendros that we were a week early with our last shipment," Dash said to Squix, though he was looking at the Skalorian.

Squix turned to the alien and spoke, his tentacles whirling and swirling, making patterns in the air. "Boo-la-la, ooganawaran et toto envaraldamor. Boo-ga?"

The Skalorian shook his head, tendrils striking one another, and made a clicking sound in the back of his throat.

"Boo-for-for nobordana frendorlaga bendava fodeep endava," Pendros said, his head tendrils making their own patterns around his face as he spoke. "Boo-ca-ca randolovo Captain Moron."

His tendrils punctuated those last words with stabbing motions towards Dash.

"He says, 'The shipment arrived early, but the cargo was still damaged in transit. A quarter of the total product leaked onto your cargo bay floor, and I barely broke even on the deal,'" Squix said to Dash. "Oh, and he called you 'Captain Moron.'"

Dash squinted at Squix. "Yeah," he said, "I got that last part."

Pendros started talking and waving his head tendrils again, Squix translating as he spoke:

"He says, 'Your reputation from the Forger War can only get you so far these days. If you want to ship my moolk, fine. Your rates are a bargain, and if you can actually deliver the full shipment, even better. But I'm not paying you any amount of the fee in advance. I will transfer the credits into your account after the cargo is successfully delivered. Not a moment sooner.'"

Pendros slapped the table after speaking his last word, then raised his eyebrows at Dash, a universal expression that asked if he understood.

"I need the advance, Pendros, so I can pay the docking fees to even leave Technica Outpost. I've had some," Dash's eyes darted at Kenzie, "unforeseen setbacks, and I just need a little to get over the hump."

"That's too bad," said Pendros through Squix, "but that doesn't affect me. I'm running a business, not a charity." His tendrils gestured toward the window at the jump-beacon. "In case you haven't noticed, there are many ships that can get my job done. I took this meeting because you are the cheapest and because I thought that movie they made about you was hilarious."

"It wasn't a comedy," Dash muttered.

"But the novelty of talking with a celebrity has long ago worn off. Good luck, Captain."

Dash slumped against the wall as Pendros rose from his seat.

Kenzie looked at the Skalorian and said, "What about the chalzz?"

Pendros stopped and looked at Kenzie, apparently noticing her for the first time.

"Chalzz?" he said.

Squix turned to Kenzie. "He says, 'Chalzz?'"

"What's chalzz?" said Jo.

Dash looked at Kenzie. "What are—why are you talking? Who said you could talk?"

Kenzie said to Squix, "Ask him if he's had any luck finding someone to ship all the chalzz crowding his storage unit."

As Squix translated her message, Pendros eyed her, frowning. He said something quickly, his tendrils curling in frustration.

"He says, 'How do you even know I have chalzz in my storage unit?'"

Kenzie took a sip of her Coke, which was getting progressively watered down as the ice inside the cup melted.

"Because you're here on Level Two talking to us about shipping moolk cheaply," she said, as Squix jabbered back at him, waving his tentacles frantically. "If you could process and ship your chalzz, too, you'd be down on Level Eight or Nine, making bigger deals with bigger shipping companies, not independent contractors like us who can only move small amounts of your less profitable product. You'd be too rich for us to even be in the same room if you could sell your chalzz."

Squix punctuated that last point with a few flashy tentacle waves and wiggles. Dash looked at his first mate, his hands gripping the table tight.

"Why," he said, pleading, "are you translating for her?"

Pendros ignored the captain's interruption. He sat back in his chair and laced his fingers together, the edges of his mouth curled into a hint of a smile.

"Human girl is smart," he said through Squix. Dash kept his grip on the table and stayed quiet as he saw Pendros's reaction. "She knows about chalzz, living byproduct of moolk."

Kenzie smiled back. "And I know that processing chalzz into a form that's easily shipped to the outer rim systems that eat it like popcorn is expensive. And that smaller producers like you take a loss on selling the live stuff to bigger processors. I've read all about the chalzz market."

"Oh my God, you are such a nerd," said Jo on Kenzie's left.

Kenzie ignored her. "We can ship what you have in your storage unit—the live, unprocessed chalzz that would fetch a hefty price when we reach the outer rim. But only if you agree to Captain Drake's request for an advance."

Dash spoke again. "Wait a second—"

"How will you keep the chalzz alive and healthy until you reach your destination?" said Pendros.

"No, seriously, hang on now—"

Kenzie answered: "We're a small crew, and we have lots of room in our cargo bay. We're more than equipped to deal with the chalzz and all its requirements as we go. We get our advance, plus ten percent of the final sale at market, and you get higher profits by shipping a gourmet product to the outer reaches of Alliance space."

"Kenzie, I really don't think this is a good idea," said Dash.

"Blorp," said Pendros, revealing a smile full of sharp teeth.

"Done," translated Squix.

Pendros turned to Captain Drake and grabbed his hand for an exaggerated shake, clearly modeling his behavior on what he'd seen in Earth movies. "I'm very excited by this new crewmember, Captain. I will have two-hundred kilos of chalzz sent to your ship in the docking bay within the hour. I'll even throw in some respirators for your crew."

"Respirators?" Jo said after she heard Squix's translation.

Dash looked at Kenzie as he replied to Jo.

"Living, unprocessed chalzz breathes oxygen and exhales dihydrogen-sulfide," he said, an edge to his voice that surprised Kenzie. "Better known on Earth as 'sewer gas.' It's both highly flammable and toxic if there's enough of it."

Pendros said something in Skalorian, waving a tendril in front of his nose.

"And it stinks," translated Squix.

"And, also, it stinks," echoed Dash.

Kenzie took another sip of her flat soda and turned to Pendros.

"So, are those feathers real?" she asked. "Or do you just like to look fancy?"

* * *

Captain Drake's arms were crossed as he leaned against the *Gremlin*'s hull. Kenzie noticed he crossed his arms a lot.

"Where's your brother?" he said to Jo, who was a few feet from him. As usual, she tapped on her handset.

"That is literally what I'm trying to find out, man," she said. "Uh, I mean, Captain Drake."

Two hours had passed since their meeting ended. Kenzie and Jo finished repairing the *Gremlin*'s damaged landing strut about thirty minutes earlier. As they'd worked, Pendros's automated drones loaded five large crates of living, chattering chalzz into the ship's cargo bay. Once there, the crates combined into a small, enclosed pen that let the chalzz—yellow, ovoid-shaped, six-legged blobs without any obvious orifices—roam around a bit. The other people in Technica Outpost's landing pad wrinkled their noses (or simply held their hands over their smell-holes) as the crates made their way into the ship. Even though the ship's cargo bay blast doors had since been sealed, people still gave the *Gremlin* a wide berth.

Kenzie sat on an empty crate. She looked up at the stars beyond the force field separating the landing pad from the open space surrounding Technica Outpost. The jump-beacon in the distance maintained its position over the asteroid, its growing line of outgoing ships stretching from the outpost and into the inky black beyond. She was only one day into her first mission in space, and she'd already brokered a trade deal with an alien species.

"Advanced diplomatic relations," she said to nobody. This was going to look great on her application to the Academy. She saw Squix walk down the gangplank from the cockpit to meet the rest of the crew on the landing pad's floor.

"We're ready to go, Captain," he said. "Doctor Bill hasn't mentioned any fluctuations in the air quality aboard the ship, so at least we know the air filters are working."

"Gotta get going if we want to get our cargo to its destination alive," he said to his first mate while looking in Kenzie's direction. "Plus, we have to make our delivery to the Motomondo System before our deadline, not to mention make the rest of our deliveries."

"At least the account's full again," said Squix, his skin flashing blue. "We've got even more in there than we did when we picked up the cadets."

The captain closed his eyes and held the bridge of his nose. "I know," he sighed. "I just wasn't counting on spending time tending to a cargo bay full of six-legged fart monsters. Colossally valuable, dangerous, and fragile fart monsters, at that."

When he opened his eyes, Dash was looking square at Kenzie. "But I think we're going to have to make another detour."

Squix let out a confused, "Huh?"

"Cadet Washington," he said, walking over to her spot on the crate. Kenzie felt her heart racing. This was it. He was going to give her a commendation. They were going to make a detour so he could pick up a special gift. He was going to invite her to take a permanent position on his crew right then and there. She'd have to decline, of course—she was only fourteen, and besides, she still planned on enrolling at the Academy. But maybe if he held a spot for her after she graduated—

"I have had absolutely enough of you," he said.

Kenzie's heart sped up—she was confused.

"As soon as we leave the Outpost, I'm going to find the nearest Earther colony and drop you off so your parents can pick you up."

"What—I...I don't..."

"You've cost me more money in a day than I ever thought I could lose," he said, his arms crossed again. "I cannot believe you."

"But," Kenzie sputtered, her mouth dry. "But the chalzz—"

"Is a headache I hadn't planned on dealing with," he said, cutting her off. "Suddenly I'm shipping live produce? I'm glad for the advance, but I would've found someone else to pay me up front. Now I'm locked in."

"But—"

"You're done. Fired," said Dash. "Look, I'll even give your folks a partial refund, but I can't take you anymore."

What…what was happening? Kenzie looked at Jo for support, but her bunkmate didn't seem to notice she'd just gotten fired.

Jo let out an annoyed grunt. "Where is he? He's not responding to any of my messages—"

She was interrupted by a chorus of screams from the other side of the hangar bay, followed by shouts in several languages that roughly translated to, "Look out!"

A small, two-person craft smashed into the floor of the hangar bay about a hundred meters away from the *Gremlin*, crushing another ship underneath it. Technica Outpost's emergency systems kicked in, throwing up a containment field over the crash and filling it with foam.

Kenzie looked up at the hangar's force field, checking to see where the craft might've come from, or what had caused it to smash into the floor of the landing bay. Maybe the pilot was drunk or tired, or maybe there'd just been a horrible malfunction.

Where only moments earlier there was an orderly line of outgoing traffic leading to the jump-beacon, instead, Kenzie saw dozens of ships scattered, flashes of red blooming in the starfield as crafts jumped in and out at random. Ships zoomed across her field of view, sometimes narrowly avoiding collisions with other vessels suddenly appearing in space, sometimes not avoiding collisions at all. Small pieces of debris from crashes bounced harmlessly off the force field, too small for the outpost's sensors to register them as ships or let them pass through the field.

Behind the chaos, the jump-beacon was in pieces. It produced rapidly spinning fragments of metal. The beacon's corpse blossomed with small explosions, produced by its damaged engines and its compromised artificial atmospheres. The balls of fire quickly bloomed and were snuffed out by the vacuum of space.

With the beacon gone, ships in transit to Technica Outpost could only guess at where they should exit jump-space, and ships leaving had no idea when or where they should make their departures. It was, in short, a catastrophe.

"Well," said Dash as he ran back up the gangplank into the cockpit, "that's not super good."

Rescue

Dash burst into the cockpit and dove under the helm console. He heard metal twisting and crunching as the floor of the outpost's landing pad was bombarded, the *Gremlin* vibrating with each new impact. Every few moments, more spacecrafts collided with the asteroid as they popped out of jump-space blind.

After reconnecting a few dangling wires, a new sound entered the cockpit: a sturdy hum, signaling the activation of the *Gremlin*'s combat shields. Dash had disconnected them years ago after realizing how much power he could save without them. Considering he didn't make a habit of getting into fights—and that he never hauled anything much worth stealing—he preferred shaving off a little overhead and making sure the ship's hull could take a smack or two if he ever needed to beat a hasty retreat. Now, however, the combat shields would be the only thing protecting the ship inside the hangar. Of course, the shield wasn't as strong—or reliable—as Dash would've liked. It'd only take a few collisions for it to fail and leave the hull exposed again.

He bonked his head on the helm console's underside as he reemerged, then massaged his forehead while looking out the viewport at the pandemonium. Other ships glowed with newly activated combat shields. Some simply took off, willing to take their chances in space, where ships continued to blink into existence at random. Meanwhile, people on the ground pushed and shoved each other as they ran to escape the scene.

He flipped a few switches on the main console, then ran down the gangplank to the landing pad. Squix, Jo, and Kenzie took cover under the *Gremlin* amid the carnage. Dash retracted the gangplank with his handset.

"Okay, we have to get Vor, and we don't know where he is."

"He hasn't answered any of my messages," Jo said quickly, panic in her voice. Dash noticed that this was the first time he'd heard her display an emotion that couldn't be categorized under "bored" or "annoyed."

Kenzie spoke next. "I have an idea. I can try to ping his handset using the outpost's network." She was surprisingly calm considering that Dash had just fired her. And that spaceships were literally raining down all around them. "That way even if he doesn't respond, the device will."

Dash nodded. That sounded smart. "Do it."

"But it might be tough with all the emergency messages being broadcast right now," she said.

"Okay," said Dash, checking his laser pistol's charge.

"Also, I have to hack the outpost's security protocols to do it," said Kenzie.

"Alright," said Dash, re-holstering his gun.

"Also, I've never done it before," said Kenzie.

"It's also really, really illegal," chirped Squix to Dash's left.

"It's also really, really illegal," said Kenzie, looking at Dash expectantly. Apparently she didn't want evidence of the hacks traced back to her personal handset.

"Here," said Dash, tossing her his handset. "Go nuts."

Kenzie's eyes went wide, and she set to tapping away on the device.

"In the meantime, let's head to the security office on Level Five. I know someone down there who might help us find Vor so we can get the hell out of here."

"Does it make sense for all of us to go?" said Squix, tentacles wiggling with anxiety. "Shouldn't some of us stay here in case he comes back?"

Another ship slammed into the ground twenty meters away, sending debris and scrap bouncing to and fro.

Dash winced.

"If Vor comes back, the Doc will let him in and let us know. But I'm not getting separated from anyone else until we're outta here."

Dash saw the stairwell in the southwest corner of the landing pad. Three ships were parked between the *Gremlin* and the steps leading to the asteroid's lower levels, which would hopefully protect them until the outpost's defenses finally kicked in. He took off in a crouching jog, the crew following close behind. They joined a group of Marvinians who were huddled together under a domed civilian transport.

"Who do you know in security?" asked Squix before they could trot to the next ship in the bay.

"Lucy Reese," said Dash, looking up through the bay's force field as ships continued to appear in the starfield above. "We used to date. Move!"

Another ship plummeted into the landing pad, just moments after the crew bolted from beneath the transport and reached the underside of a small two-person coupe. The ship bounced off the combat shield of a parked freighter and shot back out of the bay's force field at a strange angle, spinning out into the blackness of space.

"You dated Chief Reese?" said Squix, rubbing the top of his head with a tentacle. "When?"

Dash kept his gaze trained above him, waiting for more signs of carnage.

"Like three years ago," he said. "We kept the *Gremlin* here for an extended repair."

Squix curled a tentacle thoughtfully.

"I remember you went out the night after we arrived. But you came back an hour and a half later and locked yourself in your room." He pointed at Dash. "Then you stayed on the ship for the next week watching reruns of that one show with the funny robot."

"I love that show," said Kenzie, still tapping at Dash's handset.

"Okay!" said Dash, looking from the force field and back to Squix. "We went on a date. One date. And I drank some wine and some got up my nose. And I sneezed and she was wearing white, okay?" Another ship collided with the asteroid's exterior, rocking the landing pad.

"But I do know her, and she can help us," he added. "Probably."

Dash took off running for the last ship, a light supply van, but stopped in his tracks as the tail half of a vessel sailed down from above, smashing into the van's hull and exploding. He felt a flash of intense heat until another containment field jumped up from the landing pad's floor and swallowed up the wreckage. The crew ran around the containment field and headed straight for the stairwell, which by this point was crowded with people escaping the carnage. As they made their way down, Dash heard the emergency alarms finally sounding in the landing pad itself, for whatever good it would do now.

* * *

As Dash, Squix, and the cadets emerged on Level Five, they were greeted by wide hallways lined with obsidian walls. Contemporary lighting fixtures hung tastefully from the ceiling. The floor was made of some of the nicest imitation redwood Dash had ever seen. Potted plants with wide, purple fronds and thick trunks lined the halls, spaced about a meter or so apart.

It was a display of opulence he hadn't expected, since his business had never taken him below Level Three. Even when he'd gone on his one date with Lucy, she met him at the nicest restaurant on Level Two, so he'd never actually had the chance to see where she worked.

"Uh, pretty sure her office is down here," Dash lied, and he led his crew through the hallway towards what he figured was the asteroid's center, fighting through the throngs of people who'd escaped the chaos of the landing pad above.

As the panicking civilians funneled themselves through the corridors, he started noticing more of Technica's Human security officers corralling people into separate rooms, usually reserved for the level's more sensitive business dealings. At one point, Dash reached out and grabbed Jo's hand when it looked like she was being swept up into one of these little groups. He didn't want to lose one cadet while searching for another one.

About halfway down the corridor, a security officer clad in the outpost's grey-green uniform stepped in to block the crew's way. Dash juked and maneuvered around him and continued on his path.

Dash craned his neck and talked as he walked past, saying, "Sorry, we'll be right back in just a minute, just have to discuss logistics with Chief Reese."

Before the puzzled security officer could respond, they were already out of his reach. The officer returned to directing less important folks into business rooms. Dash had learned long ago that acting like you knew where you were going usually meant people wouldn't bother you along the way. Eventually the herd of people thinned to the point where he and his cadets were alone in the hallway.

He saw in the distance that the hallway opened up into a large atrium, the end-point for four other hallways feeding in from other directions. At its center was the windowed security office, which had a 360-degree view of its surroundings.

From his limited time with Lucy, Dash learned that the glass itself was capable of providing a view of rooms and hallways throughout the outpost. So even if a security worker was watching events unfold two levels below, it still looked like she was staring straight ahead through transparent windows.

He fell into a quicker trot, hoping to close the gap between him and the office.

"Hey, Captain Drake," said Kenzie from behind him. She jogged up to meet him holding Dash's handset out to show him something.

Before he could see what Kenzie wanted, something caught Dash's eye. He could make out more distinct shapes of who was in the security office. Sure enough, there was Lucy. She'd gotten a shorter hairdo since the last time Dash had seen her. She was surrounded by what looked like security personnel in some pretty heavy-duty armor…red armor…

Dash stopped short where the hallway met the atrium and dove behind one of the large, exotic-looking potted plants.

As Squix emerged from the hallway, Dash grabbed him by a couple tentacles and pulled him down beside him, motioning for Kenzie and Jo to get low behind the plant too. The wide, waxy fronds of the purple tree-thing all but obscured the view to the security office.

Jo was the first to attempt to talk.

"What—"

"Shhhhh!" Dash pinched the air with his hands like a crab.

Kenzie tried next.

"Why are we—"

"I said 'shhhhh!'" Dash yell-whispered.

Squix's skin flashed purple with fear.

Dash glared at him.

"Why are we hiding behind this plant?" Jo whispered.

"And why are we all whispering?" whispered Squix after tapping his exosuit's volume button.

"Look." Dash said, as he pulled the fronds apart to offer a better view of the security office.

In the center of the room sat Lucy Reese, a woman in her mid-thirties with brown hair and a gray-green uniform and jacket befitting the head of Technica Outpost's security force. Her arms were crossed and her jaw was set. She did not look happy.

And around Lucy stood three figures clad from head to toe in angry crimson armor, etched with hard lines and angles, outfitted with holsters for weapons and technology that Dash didn't have names for. The fronts of their helmets were comprised entirely of dark face plates. Not a centimeter of skin showed through the powered battlesuits.

"Those are Forgers," whispered Kenzie.

"But that's impossible," hissed Jo.

No one had seen any Forgers for twelve years—not a single one. Not since the end of the war that was named after them.

"Is she…are they holding her captive?" said Squix.

Kenzie didn't hesitate. "We have to rescue her." She started to get up from her crouch, but Dash put out a hand and grabbed her arm.

"Wait," he said.

Kenzie's eyes went wide.

"But we have to—"

Dash pinched Kenzie's face with his hand and turned her back toward the security office. "Look!"

Lucy stood and started yelling in the faceplate of the Forger directly to her right. Amazingly, rather than pushing his captive back into her seat, the Forger actually took a step back at her outburst.

"That is not what I expected," said Jo.

"Cap," said Squix, "how can they be here? I thought they left Alliance territory after the treaty? After, you know…Gantoid IV."

Dash winced, then sighed and shook his head.

"That's exactly what they were supposed to have done. But I guess it's kind of hard to know if your enemy has really left if you don't know where they come from in the first place."

Jo shot him a sideways look.

"You mean the Alliance really doesn't know where the Forger homeworld is?" she hissed. "I thought that was just something the conspiracy psychos said on all the feeds."

"I know the Governing Council likes to say it's classified, but as far as I could tell while I was still with the Fleet, they never figured out what star system the Forgers came from. Or where they went when they left. They were just...gone."

The four were silent for a moment. A Forger to Lucy's left started in on her, jabbing his finger into her face. She flinched but was otherwise undeterred.

Dash leaned over to Squix. "Hey, do you think you could do your thing over there?"

Without another word, Squix tapped a button on his exosuit and extricated himself from his apparatus. He flattened out and his skin became red-brown to match the floor. If he hadn't known where to look, Dash would've thought Squix had disappeared entirely. He saw a flurry of movement as the Octopus—the size of a small watermelon—ambled down the hallway towards the security office, a blur of nearly imperceptible motion. Dash could see the tiniest dribble of ink on the patch of floor he'd just left. Even though he couldn't talk without his exosuit, Squix didn't have to say anything to let the captain know he was scared.

Jo whispered, "What's he doing?"

"He's gonna see what the hell is going on down there while Kenzie finishes hacking the outpost's security network to find your brother."

"Yeah, about that," Kenzie said, and she pulled Dash's handset back out. She held it up for him to see. "I was about to say, I got in, but I couldn't ping Vor's handset anywhere. It's like..." Kenzie looked anxiously at Jo. "...like he's vanished off the outpost."

Jo furrowed her brow, the etched lines in her face glowing a dull purple against her lavender-gray skin.

"No, he's still on the outpost," she said. "I would've gotten a ping on my handset if he'd left or if his handset was destroyed or something. Our dad turned on the Buddy Feature before we left home. He's kind of a control freak, actually."

Jo thought for a second and turned to Kenzie. "When I can't find someone on my feed, it's not because they don't exist, it's just that they're not on the social network. And we know he's still got to be on the outpost—so is there maybe a way to see if there's an area of the outpost's network that's turned off right now?"

Kenzie smacked herself in the forehead. "I should've thought of that. 'Every spot is a weak spot if you use the right tools against your foe,' Drake, page 68."

Dash frowned at that. Kenzie started tapping on Dash's handset again.

"I can echolocate using my indoor mapping app in conjunction with the outpost's security nodes," she explained.

"What did she just say?" Dash whispered at Jo.

"Something smart, I think," Jo replied.

Suddenly Squix's exosuit started moving and Dash yelped before putting his hands over his mouth. His first mate reappeared, a splotch of wood grain remaining on his skin from his camouflaged reconnaissance mission. The Octopus gasped as the exoskeleton rehydrated him.

"They're...looking for something," he croaked. "A crystal? They think...it's supposed to be on...the outpost..."

Dash leaned in.

"And Lucy? How is she—"

"She's...one of them..."

Dash sat up straight and looked back at the security office.

"Got it," Kenzie said. "There's blank space just a few doors from the security office along that corridor," she pointed down the hallway slightly to the office's left. "It's a dark spot matching the dimensions of the other rooms, but it doesn't show up when I try to map the level."

Dash peered down the hall and saw it clear of people and security personnel, then looked back to the security office where Lucy and the Forgers continued arguing.

"Jo, Kenzie," he said, grabbing the rim of the tree's pot, "help me lift this thing."

The three of them carried the potted tree-thing slowly in front of them through the atrium, rotating it to keep themselves obscured. Squix walked along with the rest of them, though he wasn't helping carry the plant. Dash figured he was still too tired from his trip into the office and didn't want to put any more strain on him. As they carried the heavy pot across the atrium, Dash could feel his body wanting to give out, sweat making his jumpsuit stick to his back. He wished he'd worn a lighter jacket, but Technica's environmental controls had always run on the colder side.

After a few minutes of slowly walking the plant through the open atrium, they finally reached the entrance to the other hallway. They lowered the pot and Dash slumped, panting, onto the floor beside it. His arms felt like jelly. The Forgers hadn't noticed them—that was some good luck, at least. And good luck made Dash suspicious.

"What are they watching in the security station?" Dash asked Squix, panting.

"Footage of the other levels," said Squix. "All the monitors are in use."

"So they can't see into the atrium?"

"Nope."

Ah. That was more like it.

"The room we're looking for is over there," Kenzie said, pointing down the hall.

The crew crept a few meters along the now-deserted corridor and found a door that wouldn't open, no matter how many times they hit the button. Kenzie stepped in and punched a few commands into Dash's handset and, after a soft 'click,' the door swished open.

"Hey," said Dash, "how many laws have you broken with that thing today?"

"Only a few," she said, tossing the device back to the captain. He caught it and slipped it in his pocket as they entered the room.

Unlike most of the other rooms on Level Five, which they'd seen filled with scared civilians, this room was empty. In place of people, there was just a mess. A workbench and desk on the left side of the room were covered in wires, circuitboards, a shopping bag, and data chips, among other spare bits of tech. The shelves on the right were lined with red Forger helmets and ammunition clips. All four walls were plastered with half-completed equations, photos of Humans, Crags, Aphids, Drooks, Marvinians, and a dozen other species, along with schematics of Technica Outpost that someone had scribbled on.

"So," said Jo. "A crazy person hangs out in here."

Dash heard a banging sound coming from the wall opposite the entrance door. Amid the wall's coverings, he spotted one blank patch about twenty centimeters wide. Kenzie must've noticed it too, and she put her hand there.

The wall slid away, and there on the ground sat Vor, hands cuffed behind his back, his already line-etched face sporting what looked like some new cracks and craters around his left eye, which was swollen and bloodshot.

Jo yelled, and she threw her arms around her brother. He winced in pain at the family reunion but still buried his head into the crook of his sister's neck.

"Vor," said Dash, "what happened to you?"

Jo and Vor both turned to look at the captain.

"Oh, right," he said. "You still don't have a mouth."

Squix piped up. "Not that I'm not happy to see you, Cadet, but we should probably leave now before someone shoots us all!"

"I second," Kenzie said.

Dash gestured to the door. "Motion carries. Let's go. We'll take your cuffs off on the ship."

As they started to leave, Vor stomped his foot to get their attention. Everyone turned to look and saw him motioning his bruised head at the shopping bag on the tech-covered workbench.

Dash sighed and grabbed it.

"Great, first no mouth," he said. "Now no hands."

* * *

By the time they returned to the landing pad, the scene had changed. The room still shook, likely the result of a few ships jumping in without the benefit of a beacon and colliding into the asteroid. But the hangar's blast doors above had finally sealed shut. Instead of the starfield filled with debris and ships narrowly avoiding collisions, all Dash could see when he looked up was the giant metallic shutter sealing the room tight. Meaning that, at the very least, Dash could cross "getting crushed to death by falling spacecrafts" off his current list of concerns.

In its place, he added, "getting killed by mysterious alien death-soldiers."

A few clusters of Forgers, three to a group, clad head-to-toe in their severe red armor, patrolled the landing pad. Meanwhile, all the civilians who'd been cowering under parked ships were gone, either having taken off or been herded into rooms on the lower levels by outpost security.

The containment fields sealing up the crashes on the pad's floor had been dropped while the crew rescued Vor. Piles of wreckage smoked everywhere Dash looked.

But the *Gremlin* wasn't one of them. The combat shields had either managed to stand up to the impacts of incoming ships, or it had simply never been struck. Either way, Dash was just happy to see his ship in one piece. Of course, how they'd get the *Gremlin* out of there was a question for Future Dash.

He pulled out his handset and tapped a few commands.

From his position peeking out of the stairwell doorway, he saw the *Gremlin*'s gangplank drop from the cockpit.

Dash, Squix, and the cadets broke for the *Gremlin* during a gap in the Forgers' patrols. Despite their stealth up to this point, the sound of two Humans, two Crags, and one Octopus running up a gangplank was just too loud to ignore. As Squix ducked into the cockpit, blaster fire started to erupt from the Forgers around the bay.

Dash took his seat in the pilot's chair as Squix started the engine warm-up sequence while also plotting their exit course from the outpost. The sound of blaster bolts being absorbed by the ship's combat shields rang around them.

"Vor, get to the medbay," Dash barked. The handcuffed Crag left the cockpit running. "Kenzie, you and Jo get to the engine room and see if you can't get our jump-drive online faster."

"Do what now?" Jo asked.

"Shouldn't I try to hack the blast door open?" asked Kenzie.

Dash swiveled in his chair and looked at the two of them for a half-second.

"New plan," he said. "Kenzie, stay here and hack the blast door open." He tossed her his handset again. "Jo, let's go down to the engine room and see if we can't get our jump-drive online faster."

Jo followed Dash aft from the cockpit towards the engine room at the rear of the ship. As they ran, Squix's voice piped over the *Gremlin*'s speakers.

"Cap," he said, "there's some kinda broadcast coming in over the outpost's system."

"Pipe it through!" he yelled as he opened the door to the engine room.

He heard Lucy Reese's voice next, clear as a bell.

"—assure you that when we arrive at our destination, you will all be treated well, despite being prisoners of war."

Dash cursed under his breath as he climbed down the ladder onto the engine room's lower deck.

"Do not be afraid," Lucy's weirdly calm announcement continued. "We are that much closer to reclaiming that which is rightfully ours: the star systems and resources that belong to the Forgers, which your government denied us and claim for themselves as part of the Interstellar Alliance. Fortunately, once the Forgers have crushed the Alliance, we will negotiate your safe return to your homes, though you will all be citizens of our merciful regime."

Dash ran behind the engine room's reactor cores and started unhooking cables and tubes from the two smaller power stations on either side of the main reactor, which had its own series of connections snaking down into the ship's engine conduits.

"Until then, you will be given the honor of working for the betterment of our glorious empire. Prepare for dimensional jump in five minutes." With that, Lucy's voice cut out with a click.

"Wow," said Dash, pulling more cords out of the power stations. "She really sucks, huh?"

"Basically," said Jo, watching from the main engineering console.

Dimensional jump. What did that even mean? Dash wished he'd paid more attention when he'd heard the term thrown around when scientists appeared on the news, or, more realistically, on late-night talk shows. All he could guess was that it was sort of like traveling through jump-space—only instead of going from point A to point B, you were traveling from point A to…another dimension? Somewhere on the other side of…reality? Would that be, like, point A-squared? A-cubed? A-whatever-came-after-cubed?

Once again, Dash wished he were smarter so he could understand what, exactly, was going on. No time for that now.

"Okay!" Dash said, clutching the disconnected tubes and cables to his chest. "I need you to open up the engine's operating system and reroute power that would've gone to our subsystems into the jump-drive as I plug each one into our engines."

Jo started tapping on the console. "Which subsystems did you disconnect?"

"Nothing more important than the engines right now," he said. "Water reclamation, long range sensors, primary weapons—"

The ship gave a small shake. Squix's panicked voice came over the comms.

"Taking fire, Captain!"

"—and combat shields," said Dash as he ran to the engines' main power conduits.

"Fighters deployed inside the hangar," said Squix. "Taking evasive maneuvers!"

The ship lurched as Squix piloted it off the landing pad floor.

"Aren't weapons and shields, like," Jo asked, eyes wide with alarm, "kind of important right now?"

"In theory, sure," said Dash as he lifted the panels to expose the connectors. "But we're one ship on an asteroid filled with who-knows-how-many people who want to shoot at us, which will be jumping into—if I'm not mistaken—*another dimension* in four minutes. If we don't get outta here, shields and weapons won't really help much."

"Gotcha," said Jo. "I've got the operating system online. One problem: I have no idea how to reroute power."

Dash searched through the tubes and cables bundled in his arms.

"Just think of it like social feeds," he said, finding a thick green cable and holding it between his shoulder and neck. "As each new node attempts to come online, instead of letting it be friends with the subsystem it's supposed to match, tell it to make friends with the engines instead."

"Oh," she said, poking at the console. "Okay."

He hoped the simplified user interface he'd installed on the operating system would make sense to her. After all, he couldn't make heads or tails of the standard issue interface that the *Gremlin* had when he bought the thing. This new interface was advertised as "idiot proof." So far, he'd managed to prove that claim true by living this long. He made a mental note to reach out to the company that made it for a possible endorsement deal.

The ship shook again as he plugged the green cable into the engines. Jo dragged her finger from one end of the console's display to the other, and the engines started humming happily.

"Oh, cool," said Jo.

He plugged the rest of the cables and tubes in his arms into the engines, and Jo didn't miss a single connection. When he finished, he started climbing the ladder back up to the top deck. He talked to Jo as he climbed.

"There are straps mounted on the wall behind you," he said as he pulled himself up each rung. "Put them over your shoulders and keep watch on the console to see if any of those connections drop. I'm gonna need you to keep them connected until we get out of here."

"You mean *if* we get out here," she said, strapping herself in.

"Yes, that is what I meant. Thank you, Jo," Dash called down to her as he reached the top of the ladder.

As he got to his feet, the ship shook as it took another blaster bolt. Dash remembered that the last time he'd paid for repairs to the hull, he'd argued to use a competitor's coupon. He prayed the mechanics didn't skimp on the job in retaliation.

Back in the cockpit, Kenzie had her face buried in Dash's handset. Squix sat in the navigator's chair, still plotting their jump course. With two spare tentacles, he was reaching over to the helm controls on his left, attempting to pilot the ship and keep out of the firing arcs of the Forger fighters pursuing them inside the sealed landing pad. He was doing the job of two people at once, and doing both jobs pretty badly.

"What's the situation?" Dash asked, sitting in the pilot's chair and taking the helm.

"Jump-drive is operating at a hundred and forty-six percent," said Squix, the mix of alarm and relief unmistakable in his voice. "Ready to jump in two minutes."

"How long until the outpost makes that dimensional jump thingie Lucy talked about?"

"One minute, thirty seconds," said Squix.

"Wonderful," he said as he rolled the *Gremlin* away from his pursuers' line of fire.

"Blast doors should open…" said, Kenzie, giving the handset a few more taps, "…now."

True to her word, the main blast doors in the landing pad started splitting apart in the middle, revealing the chaos in the space around Technica Outpost.

"Thank you, Cadet," said Dash. "Remind me to give you a promotion if we don't die or get sucked into another dimension."

"Am I still fired, Captain?" said Kenzie, finally remembering to strap herself into her seat.

"Let's table that conversation for—" Dash looked at Squix's console and saw the timer, "—roughly fifty-eight seconds."

Dash flipped the *Gremlin* towards the newly established exit and gave his thrusters full power. The ship rocketed out of the landing pad at full speed, enemy fighters in hot pursuit.

A harsh beeping from Dash's helm console suddenly filled the cockpit, and he rolled the *Gremlin* hard to port. He narrowly avoided another ship popping in from jump-space with a red flash. His tactical display told him it collided with one of the Forger ships that was pursuing him, though there were still seven or eight angry red dots closing the distance.

"What was that beeping?" Kenzie asked.

"You don't know?" Dash smiled. "You told Squix that they used this model of ship during the Precursor Wars—" Dash rolled the ship starboard to avoid a floating piece of fuselage. "—which was before the Alliance formed and set up the jump-beacon network."

The console beeped again. Dash checked his screens, then pulled hard on the helm. Dash sank into his seat as the *Gremlin* rocketed upwards, evading yet another ship's sudden entrance from jump-space.

"That alarm used to tell pilots when a ship was about to jump in," said Dash, pushing the helm in and diving the *Gremlin* back down. "They don't put them in the newer ships anymore."

After his evasive maneuvers, Dash had positioned the ship in such a way that the asteroid comprising Technica Outpost filled the main viewport. Surrounding the rock was what looked like a giant metal belt, an accessory that definitely hadn't been there when the crew arrived earlier that day.

"Huh," said Kenzie. "So that's what a dimensional jump-drive looks like." He spared a quick glance to her seat behind him and saw Kenzie holding up his handset, taking a picture. Apparently *she* knew what "dimensional jump" meant. She was so annoying.

"Forty-five seconds to the *Gremlin*'s jump, Captain," said Squix, his skin a bright, constant purple. "Fifteen seconds to Technica's jump!"

"No time for sight-seeing," he said, adjusting the helm to move into the right heading for the jump Squix had calculated. Only...the controls weren't responding.

"What—" he started, until he was interrupted by a crackle of the comms.

"Hey Captain..." It was Jo in the engine room. "I rerouted some more power so we can make the jump even sooner."

Dash saw the angry red dots behind the *Gremlin* getting closer to the center of his tactical screen.

"Six seconds to jump," cried Squix, his tentacles wiggling. "But maneuvering thrusters are gone, and we're on the wrong heading!"

"Thanks, Jo," said Dash.

"Two seconds!" cried Squix.

The alarm on his console started to beep.

The metallic ring around Technica Outpost glowed red, then green.

Dash slapped the jump button and everything went dark.

Spinning Out

Kenzie woke up.

The cockpit was dark, lit only by the flashing colors of jump-space swirling and roiling in the viewport, and the dull glow of Captain Drake's display screen. It hung down at an odd angle just above his slumped form.

She felt like she'd been asleep for a week, but the cockpit's chronometer showed that only a few hours had passed. She unstrapped herself and approached the helm console. To her right, Squix blinked into wakefulness.

"I'm hungry," he said, his exosuit's speaker crackling with interference. "And dizzy."

Kenzie's head spun as she looked at the captain's display, its support arm having come partially loose from its perch, exposed wires peeking out where they shouldn't. It was still connected to the ship, but tenuously. The screen flickered as cables struggled to maintain their connections with the rest of the *Gremlin*. Kenzie shook her head, trying to knock the fuzz from her brain. That made her dizziness worse, but it helped her become more alert. She turned to the captain, whose eyes were shut, and saw a big purple welt had formed on his forehead.

The display's readout indicated that the ship was quickly proceeding on its course through jump-space for somewhere called "NAVIGATION ERROR." Either that was a star system Kenzie had never heard of or, more likely, their nav-computer was busted.

"I think we're in trouble," she said. She pointed at the display.

Squix swiveled his eyes at the screen and squinted. His skin flashed purple with fear when he saw.

"We're definitely in trouble," he said.

"What should we do?"

Squix sunk deeper into his exosuit. "I, uh, I think…" His eyes darted to Dash, motionless in his chair. Kenzie waited. "I think the captain usually handles things like this."

"What's he done before?" Kenzie asked. "How many times has this happened?"

"Zero," said Squix. "Zero times."

Kenzie looked at the helm console.

"I'm gonna drop us out of jump."

A tentacle shot out and grabbed Kenzie's hand.

"But you don't even know where we are," said Squix. "We didn't plot this course! And the navigation computer is completely dead!" He tapped a few buttons and got only angry buzzes. "We could— we could drop out of jump-space inside a star, or get sucked into a singularity, or get eaten by one of those space whales I've read about—"

"The longer we stay in jump-space, the further we get from…" Kenzie looked out the viewport again. "…from anywhere."

"I…I don't…"

Kenzie gripped the console to steady herself and slapped the big red button.

The *Gremlin* shuddered as the viewport flashed red, then black. The stars in the sky whirled as the ship tumbled end over end. It was hard to tell as the ship spun, but it looked like there were more than just stars around them. Blurred shapes whizzed past the viewport. Or maybe blurred ships.

Kenzie grabbed the helm and yanked up, trying to pull the ship out of its spin. But nothing happened—maneuvering thrusters were still dead.

Kenzie hit the comm button and raised the engine room.

"Jo," she said into the microphone. "Jo, are you awake?"

The comm stayed silent. The shapes-that-were-maybe-ships zipping across the viewport grew with each pass.

Kenzie yelled. "Jo!"

"I'm…" Her voice was thick. "I'm here."

"You need to reroute power back into the helm controls." Kenzie watched as the ships took longer and longer to leave the viewport with each spin as the *Gremlin* hurtled towards them. "Hurry!"

"Reroute…" said Jo over the comms. "I need to…reroute…"

"I can't watch," cried Squix, his tentacles shielding his eyes.

"Get me that power, Jo!"

Another pause. It was only three seconds, but Kenzie felt every one of them like a year.

"Got it," said Jo.

Leaning over Captain Drake, Kenzie took the helm. The maneuvering thrusters fired, and the ship's spin slowed, then ceased altogether. The *Gremlin* stopped a moment later, resting about half a kilometer from a hulking space cruiser hanging lifeless in the void. Faded, blocky letters spelled out a word on the ship's hull, but there wasn't enough light, and the *Gremlin* was at the wrong angle for Kenzie to see it all. Still, something about it was familiar.

The electronic speaker in Squix's exosuit echoed with the sound of panting. He stared straight ahead at the dark ship in front of them, his tentacles reflexively curling and uncurling as he breathed.

"That was the worst."

"That was amazing!" Kenzie said. The Octopus's eyes swiveled at the cadet. She felt the smile plastered across her face but couldn't do anything about it. She brought up a mental checklist of her accomplishments over the last twenty-four hours and penciled in "advanced problem solving with computer interface" and "crisis and resource management during an emergency." Her self-congratulations were interrupted by Squix.

"Cap!"

"Oh," said Kenzie. "Right."

The captain was still slumped in his chair, his head lolling to the side. Kenzie checked and found a weak, but consistent pulse.

"Come on," she said, digging her hands into Captain Drake's armpits. "Let's get him to the medbay."

Squix peeled himself out of his chair, then grabbed the captain's legs with two of his tentacles. They hauled him out of his seat and started waddling towards the exit, Kenzie leading the way by walking backwards. Dash groaned softly as Kenzie hit the door button with the back of her head. The exit to the hallway slid open with a "woosh."

How could Kenzie have forgotten? Here was the captain of the ship, lying unconscious in his own chair right under her nose, and she totally blanked. She blew it.

The pair carried Dash through the corridor toward the medbay. Kenzie once again smacked the door-open button with her skull.

"We should probably get some automatic doors," said Squix sheepishly.

"Yeah, probably," Kenzie answered, looking over her shoulder at the medbay behind her. The captain moaned something that sounded like "phumfrfterm."

Kenzie saw Vor laying on a bed with a healpac strapped to his swollen eye. He blinked his uncovered eye lazily—he'd only just woken. His arms were still cuffed behind his back.

Doctor Bill slid along his track on the ceiling, waving his arms frantically.

"Why didn't you answer my comms?" he asked, concern and genuine annoyance competing in his voice. "I've been calling the cockpit for hours!"

Squix leaned over Captain Drake's body and cupped his exosuit's speaker with a spare tentacle, tapping the volume control button down with the other.

"The captain usually has the medbay on mute," he whispered to her.

"What was that?" asked Bill, crossing his instruments.

"The captain's unconscious," said Kenzie, directing herself and Squix to an empty bed. They placed Dash onto it and Doctor Bill zoomed over and started scanning.

Moments later, Jo appeared in the doorway to the medbay. Her skin was grayer and duller than usual, lacking its usual crystalline glint. She looked like a rock in need of polishing.

"I just barfed," she said.

"Where?" asked Kenzie as Jo hobbled to another empty bed and lay down.

"Engine room."

Vor rolled over so everyone could see his cuffed hands. He gave his sister a weak thumbs up.

"Someone should probably clean that up." Squix flashed brown.

"Don't worry," said Jo, "it's mostly gravel."

A hatch opened in Doctor Bill's back and another scanner arm extended out, reaching to where Jo lay with her arm over her eyes. Kenzie walked to the wall and dimmed the lights. She leaned against the supply closet door.

"How are you two feeling?" Bill asked, his screen angled towards Kenzie and Squix.

"Hungry," said the Octopus. "And woozy. But mostly hungry."

Kenzie thought about it for a second.

"Yeah, me too," she said, realizing she was famished.

"Everyone's symptoms are consistent," said the doctor, folding his instruments behind his back. "Unshielded exposure to jump-space. It wreaks havoc with biological organisms."

Kenzie smiled as a weight lifted off her chest. That must've been why she'd forgotten about the captain being unconscious. She wasn't a bad cadet—just horribly injured. What a relief!

"Cadet Washington, I have some protein supplement rations for you, Jo, and Squix in the supply closet there." Doctor Bill waved an examination probe to her left. "There should also be a nutrient injection for our mouthless friend here."

Kenzie found the supplies, then passed Squix and Jo a bar each. They devoured them quickly, while she tucked one into her pocket for later. She quietly administered the injection to Vor.

"That's not all," Bill continued. "The captain has suffered a blunt trauma to the head."

"His display came loose," said Squix, his mouth full.

Bill folded his instruments in front of him, placing one end on his digital face's chin. "That's not surprising. We're lucky the ship stayed in one piece at all during our time in jump-space."

"Jrmfshds bokkn," the captain mumbled from his bed.

"What did he say?" Jo asked, staring at the ceiling.

"I think," said Squix, "it was 'jrmfshds bokkn.'"

Kenzie stood up straight. "Did he say the jump-shield's broken?"

Squix pointed a tentacle at her.

"That was it," he said.

"Is that bad?" asked Jo.

"Exceedingly," said Doctor Bill. Behind him, Vor slid off his table and slowly walked backwards to a tool drawer, opening it with his still-cuffed hands.

"We got it patched up before docking at Technica," said Squix. "But we definitely still need a replacement. And I bet all the lasers didn't help much."

Kenzie had forgotten all about that. They'd just survived a potentially deadly brush with one of the galaxy's most feared warrior forces. An alien warrior force that managed to steal an entire asteroid outpost and enslave all the people on it using dimensional jump technology that had only been theorized in the journals she read between periods in ninth grade. And they were searching for something—a "crystal," apparently, and she was one of the only people in the galaxy who even knew about it.

This was incredible.

This was amazing!

And then, like a punch to the gut, she remembered: she'd been fired.

Or had she? When the crew searched for Vor, she'd proven herself an invaluable asset. She hacked her way to his location and opened the hangar bay doors so the *Gremlin* could escape. The captain even said she'd get a promotion if they lived. Though, suddenly it seemed plausible that maybe he wouldn't…

"Is he gonna make it?" she asked trying to keep the worry out of her voice. "Is he gonna…die?"

"Nut-ded!" yelled Captain Drake from his table, suddenly staring at her, his eyes wild. "Not…dead. I…Inut…notdead! Parsnip."

"I revived him," said the doctor, wiggling his left probe. "We needed more information about the ship's condition."

"Magician," said Dash, looking at Doctor Bill.

"Unfortunately, it seems the blunt head trauma has rendered my efforts moot."

"Hrgh," said Dash, closing eyes. He put his hand to his forehead. "Blap."

A gout of flame erupted on the other side of the medbay. "Holy cow!" Squix cried, flashing purple then red.

Vor had set fire to his examination table with a surgical laser he'd grabbed from the tool drawer. It was hard to tell from across the room, but Kenzie surmised he'd been in the process of cutting through his cuffs. He didn't do too bad considering he'd been beaten, suffered a jump-space-related trauma, and had both hands restrained. Then again, he set fire to the medbay. He probably couldn't have done much worse, actually.

Doctor Bill slid along his track on the ceiling and sprayed a jet of fire suppression foam at the conflagration. Once the fire was out, Vor nodded his thanks at the doctor. Then he went right back to laser-cutting through his cuffs.

Jo weakly slid off her table and walked over to her brother. "Here," she said. "Let me help."

"Plalp," said Dash, who'd watched the whole thing.

Squix was a dull, sickly greenish purple and trained his wide eyes on the captain.

"So what do we do now?" The Octopus consulted his handset. "I'm getting all kinds of damage reports from the ship's systems. And those are the ones our crappy internal sensors can detect—we have no idea what else might be wrong with the *Gremlin*. Do we even know where we are?"

"Arrrrh," Dash said.

Apparently no one knew how to respond to that. The room was silent except for the sound of the surgical laser cutting through Vor's cuffs. Kenzie put her hand on her chin and thought.

"I'll be right back," she said, and she sprinted to the cockpit. She had a hunch, but there was only one way to discover if it was right.

She leaned over Squix's console and checked the short-range sensors. Kenzie saw just what she'd expected—a mess of static featuring all the tell-tale signs of ion distortion flooding the area.

Satisfied her hunch was turning into honest-to-goodness-proof, she hopped into Dash's chair and swiveled around to the helm control. With a slight lurch, the *Gremlin* slowly flew backwards, away from the giant, dead cruiser. She'd spent hours in the flight simulator after school, but somehow piloting a wide, old cargo ship didn't quite feel the same way.

Kenzie angled the *Gremlin* starboard, then port, then a little more starboard. In the quiet ship, she heard its maneuvering thrusters firing— distant but unmistakable vibrations from each side of the *Gremlin* as she piloted into the right position.

There. She could read the letters on the cruiser that had almost crushed her and the rest of the crew to death not ten minutes earlier. Kenzie sat back and admired the word, a self-satisfied grin plastered on her face. Kenzie saw a small blue-brown planet in the corner of the viewport and sighed.

She pushed herself out of the chair and sauntered back into the medbay. When she walked through the doorway, everyone was looking at her—even Vor, who only had one eye not covered with an oversized medicinal eye patch.

Kenzie put her hands in front of her, pinched shut like two quiet sock puppets.

"The *I.E.S Valor*," she said, opening her hands and spreading them apart dramatically.

She was aiming for "fireworks." It's possible she landed somewhere near "jazz hands."

Dash blinked at her.

"Vlar?" He stuck his pinkie in his ear and twisted like he was trying to unclog his brain.

"The *I.E.S Valor*," Kenzie said again. "That's the megacruiser floating outside."

"You mean the ship we almost crashed into?" Squix said.

"We almost crashed?" said Jo, more than a hint of panic in her voice. Vor, whose hands had been freed while Kenzie was in the cockpit, gaped at the Octopus while rubbing his wrist.

"What?" he said, turning a slightly embarrassed yellow. "I said 'almost.'"

"The *Interstellar Earther Ship Valor* played a decisive role in the Precursor Wars, protecting a convoy of civilian vessels as they journeyed out of the Sheaffer star system. The *Valor* held the line and kept attacking Aphid forces at bay while the civilians escaped, at the cost of the crew's lives. The Aphids decimated the system's habitable planets, and Earth never recovered the *Valor* after the war's end. She's floated here in space, right where she died, for almost a century."

The room was silent.

"Isn't that great?" Kenzie asked.

Dash squinted at her.

"Uhhhh," he said.

"You said it, Captain," Squix added.

"Guys, we know exactly where we are," Kenzie said, pounding her fist into her palm. "The sensor distortion pattern in this space sector confirms it. It's consistent with the aftereffects of the ion weapons used during the *Valor*'s Last Stand."

"How do you even know all this?" interrupted Jo.

"What?" Kenzie felt her face flush. She scratched the back of her head. "I like documentaries."

Jo twisted her mouth and raised an eyebrow. Kenzie pressed on.

"The point," she said, regaining her composure, "is we know we're in the Sheaffer system, not too far outside of Alliance territory. And the *Valor* was built around the same time as the *Gremlin*."

As Kenzie walked to the center of the medbay, she felt the crew watching her, waiting for her next words. She had their undivided attention. A thrill went up her spine as she prepared to lay it all out.

"This is our three-part plan," she said, looking from Squix, to Jo, to Vor, to Doctor Bill, and finally to Captain Drake. "One: we dock the *Gremlin* with the *Valor* and start a salvage mission to secure the parts necessary to repair the jump-shield and the nav-computer and whatever else we need to replace. Two: we repair the *Gremlin*. Three: we rendezvous with the Alliance Fleet and relay the intel we've gathered on the enemy. And then we join the fight."

Jo's face pinched. "Fight?"

"Yes," said Kenzie. "The Forgers are back. They blew up a jump-beacon. They stole an asteroid and captured everyone on it—except us. And they're searching for a crystal—" She put her hands on her hips. "—and we're the only ones who know about it."

When Vor pounded a nearby table, it startled everyone. Kenzie jumped, ruining her dramatic pose.

He fumbled around, looking for something. Finally, he grabbed a nearby handset and started typing. Moments later, Jo's handset dinged.

"Vor says, 'the Forgers were searching for someone on the station,'" she read.

Vor nodded vigorously, then apparently regretted it as he held his head in pain. He shook it off and resumed typing. Jo read as her handset dinged with each new message.

"'I was down on the lower levels shopping for supplies for my special project" *ding* "when I heard some guys talking about dimensional jump" *ding* "and I was like wow that's crazy I've only ever read about that so I knocked on the door to see who it was" *ding* "and then the Forgers grabbed me and hit me and cuffed me and then they put me in that closet" *ding* "and then they started talking about how the ship carrying the person they were looking for had just landed" *ding* "and they were going to make their move" *ding* "and I was afraid" *ding* "like really scared" *ding* "that they were going to break all my stuff.'"

Vor put his handset down and held his face in his hands, clearly upset at the memory of almost having all his purchases nearly broken. Jo put her arm over his shoulder.

"So they were searching for the crystal," said Kenzie. "And also for a person?"

She looked at Dash.

"You," she said.

He scratched his nose. "Me?" he said sheepishly, forming an actual word for the first time since waking up. Besides "parsnip" and "magician," of course.

"Lucy Reese knew you," Kenzie said, her hand back in its thoughtful place on her chin. "And you're famous throughout the galaxy as the man who turned the tide in the Forger War. They were looking for you, Captain."

"I don't—" He rubbed his eyes with the heels of his hands. "I don't really feel up to this conversation right now."

Doctor Bill slid over to him and started scanning.

"You're recovering well enough from your injury," he said. "But I still don't want you out of bed for several hours."

"Right," said Kenzie. "I'll head to the cockpit and prepare to dock our ship with the *Valor.*"

Kenzie turned and started to walk out of the medbay.

"No—nope."

She turned and saw Dash had crossed his arms. She'd learned by this point that usually meant he was about to tell her something she didn't want to hear.

"The doctor said you need to stay in bed," she said.

"Yeah, and that's why we're gonna stay put, right here," he said. "There's no way I'm letting you fly the *Gremlin* and…" He nearly choked on his next word. "…dock with a derelict megacruiser."

"Okay, so Squix will do it," Kenzie said, waving an arm at the first mate. He appeared to be trying to make himself as small as possible in his exosuit.

"Uhm," said Squix.

"No, Squix isn't doing it," said Dash, shaking his head slowly. "No one's doing it. We are not docking with the *Valor*. It's a nice idea, but no one's in any condition to start exploring a ghost ship."

"Then how—"

"Don't you worry about how," said Captain Drake, scowling. "We— ugh…" He put a fist to his head, clearly still in pain. "…we barely escaped the outpost in one piece. And I feel like someone dropped a television on my head."

"Actually, Cap'n…" Squix started to say. Dash cut him off.

"I'll think of something," he said. "If we find any cracks or holes forming in the hull, we have a whole stack of breach shields and patch kits in the cargo bay supply closet to seal 'em up. And we have enough food to last us a while if we have to wait for a tow—but we're going to wait. You're…" He sighed. "You are no longer fired, okay? I dub thee re-hired."

Vor clapped from the other side of the medbay. He looked around and saw no one else joining in the applause. He quickly stopped.

"But it's just out of the question," Dash continued. "There could be anything on that cruiser—booby-traps, alien bacteria, pirates. You said yourself our short-range sensors don't work here, so we can't know what we're getting into. There is no way the *Gremlin* is going to dock with that ship," said Dash. "So don't ask again."

Kenzie felt a weight in her stomach. Tears welled up behind her eyes, but she held them back, knowing the captain was only looking out for his crew's safety—for her well-being.

But she just couldn't do nothing while her crew needed her. And while the galaxy was under attack.

"So what can I do to help?" she pleaded.

Captain Drake got a weird look on his face—like he was fighting a grin. Kenzie figured he must've felt proud of her for not giving up in the face of adversity.

"Where'd we put those respirators Pendros gave us?"

* * *

"Here comes another one," said Jo, her voice muffled by the respirator strapped to her face. She pointed to Kenzie's left. "Get it!"

Breathing heavily through her own mask and fogging up the transparent eye-shields every time she exhaled, Kenzie gripped the long handle of her brush. She dipped its head into the bin of gray-green glop to her right inside the air-sealed enclosure pen. A yellow, six-legged chalzz brushed past her leg, and as it walked in front of her, she smeared the goo onto its backside. If it enjoyed its nutrient bath, she couldn't tell. It just kept shuffling, blending in with the rest of the herd, becoming indistinguishable from the others as it absorbed the goop into its body.

She and Jo were each armed with brushes while Vor and Captain Drake recovered from their injuries in the medbay. Squix, meanwhile, was still assessing the extent of the damage to the *Gremlin*'s systems.

With all the excitement around their escape from Technica Outpost, Kenzie forgot all about the deal she'd struck with Pendros. It had seemed like such a good idea at the time. But now that she was breathing through a mask to avoid choking on the chalzz's toxic fumes, covering their backs with mineral-rich sludge designed to keep the profitable creatures living and walking and wiggling and stinking...

Well, she was starting to have second thoughts.

"Come back here!" Jo said from across the pen. Kenzie saw another chalzz scooting away from her fellow cadet. It was oblivious to the fact that, without these nutrients, it would eventually shrivel into a mustard-colored husk and die.

Jo muscled her way through the ankle-high herd, trying to slap some dripping nutrient-goop on the escaping chalzz. Kenzie could tell at a glance what was about to happen, and yet it was all too quick for her to actually stop it.

After only four steps, Jo slipped on some slime that had dripped off her brush-head.

"Agh!" Jo yelled as she hit the ground, butt-first.

From her seat on the floor, Jo looked around the pen. Chalzz scampered to and fro, their tiny feet making tracks as they wandered through the puddles of glop.

"I liked it better when we were being shot at," said Jo.

"Yeah," said Kenzie. "That was great." She propped the head of her brush on the floor and leaned against the handle.

Jo got to her feet and started flicking the slime off her jumpsuit.

"What if we dumped the bin onto the floor and just let them absorb that stuff through their feet?" Jo asked.

"Nope," said Kenzie. "It only works through their backs."

"Well, can't we, like, whip up some gizmo to make this go faster? Work your computer mojo or whatever like before?"

Kenzie looked around the pen and saw only chalzz and a Jo-shaped smear from where she'd landed on the deck.

"There's not really anything in here for me to, uh, 'mojo,' unfortunately," she said. Kenzie took the shaft of her scrub brush back into her hands and started spinning it absentmindedly. "Besides, even if there were something I could use to make this go faster, the captain said if I did, he'd toss me out the airlock."

"Right," said Jo. "There's that."

Kenzie was still kicking herself about how things went down in the medbay. Her plan had been so solid, hadn't it? The *Gremlin* was in rough shape, but the *Valor* was right there, ready for a salvage operation. Sure, with Captain Drake and Vor out of commission, they were a crew of three. And with Squix's overwhelming and all-consuming anxiety, more like a crew of two. And with Jo's general apathy and disinterest in anything beyond her handset, more like a crew of one.

But still! Kenzie knew that docking with the *Valor* and stripping it for parts was the best way to get their ship back into fighting shape. And she couldn't deny the appeal of floating around on an actual relic of the Precursor Wars either. What a field trip that'd be! How great would her application essay be with that kind of anecdote? The Academy might even grant her early admission after the *Gremlin* dealt with the Forger threat, whatever it turned out to be. Whatever they wanted with that crystal. Whatever they wanted with Captain Drake...

Kenzie thought about all the questions raised by the escape from Technica Outpost, about how she'd get back to Alliance space and find answers. And then she remembered Captain Drake telling her, in no uncertain terms, that the *Gremlin* would not be docking with the *Valor*.

She looked back at the nutrient bath as another chalzz waddled past her. Her heart sank and she sighed, fogging up the eye-shield again.

"Come on," she said. "Let's finish up."

"Wait." Jo put out her hand and stopped Kenzie from walking to the nutrient bin.

"Uh," said Kenzie.

Jo cast nervous glances behind each shoulder, despite knowing the rest of the crew was about as far as they could get from "those stinking fart monsters"—as Captain Drake called them. Then, much to Kenzie's surprise (and growing awkwardness), Jo dropped down to one knee.

Kenzie had known when Jo was going to slip and fall a minute ago. She had no idea what was about to happen now.

Jo gave a heavy sigh. "You saved my brother's life," she said. She was avoiding eye contact.

"I guess so," said Kenzie nervously.

"In accordance with the traditions of Rhyolar, the orb of my birth, I pledge my life to yours so I may repay you for the debt my family owes." From her kneeling position, Jo bent into a deep bow. And stayed there.

A moment of silence passed.

"Okay," said Kenzie. "Uh. Neat?"

Jo spoke, still staring at the ground. "Now you say, 'I accept your pledge.'"

"Oh," said Kenzie. "Um, I accept your pledge."

Jo stood and grabbed her scrub brush. "Great," she muttered. "Now let's finish this so I can save your life someday or something."

Kenzie watched Jo carefully wade back through the herd and smear more paste on their backs. Unsure of what to say, she decided to join her.

A little under an hour later, the two exited the pen into the rest of the cargo bay. Next to the pen holding the chalzz sat the magnetifically stacked cargo boxes she and the other cadets had organized shortly after they'd left Arcadia Station the day before.

And off in the corner sat the small fighter—still under that musty, faded tarp. The same one she'd noticed when she'd first walked off the lift and into the cargo bay, right before Dash had tasked them with doing inventory. She was tempted to walk over, take that tarp off, and see what she knew was underneath with her own eyes.

But when Kenzie took off her mask, all thoughts of mysterious, legendary relics of old wars were forgotten. Her clothes reeked. She hadn't counted on the smell following her out of the pen.

Jo gagged slightly as she removed her own mask. It was the first sound she'd made since—

Kenzie shook her head, both to clear her mind and her nostrils. Jo had pledged a life debt to Kenzie? She still couldn't believe what had actually happened in there.

She knew a little about Rhyolar culture. Of course, she knew a little about the cultures of every member planet in the Interstellar Alliance. But more than that, she'd also read adventure novels set on Rhyolar. While she couldn't really depend on those stories for accuracy, her research showed they had their roots in the Crags' actual way of life.

Even though they were a spacefaring species with technology rivaling her own planet's, Crag society shared a lot in common with that of medieval Earth. Questing, conquering warriors owing fealty to long-reigning monarchs, political intrigue at court with shifting alliances, and deep bonds between warriors who saved each other in the heat of battle or from the clutches of some vicious rock monster. All this, with the added cool-factor of laser guns and spaceships. It made for great stories, and those traditions had survived mostly intact on the planet for thousands of years.

And yet, Rhyolar's culture started to change significantly with the close of the Precursor Wars and the formation of the Interstellar Alliance. In just two generations, the influence of the other member planets throughout the IA made Rhyolar's courtly culture appear out of step. Jo and Vor—with their etched faces and technology obsessions—were proof enough of that shift.

That's part of what took Kenzie by surprise. Jo was hardly beholden to the traditions of her planet. Or even all that interested in them at all, really. And now, just like that, Kenzie held a life-debt from Jo.

Did this mean they were friends now?

"Does this mean we're friends now?" asked Kenzie.

"Pfft, I guess so," said Jo as she picked caked bits of nutrient paste out from the soles of her boots. "You're still pretty weird."

"Hey," Kenzie said, getting defensive. "Should you even say that to me? That I'm weird? I mean, that whole thing in there…"

"What," Jo said, jerking her thumb at the pen. "The life-debt?"

"Yeah," said Kenzie.

"Gimme a break," said Jo, shaking her head while she went back to scraping the gunk out of her boots. "I owe you a life-debt. That doesn't mean I have to, like, kiss your butt or whatever."

"But you do have to protect me?"

"Sure, I guess," said Jo. "I dunno. I haven't really thought about it. Mostly I know that when I got back home, my dad would've been super pissed if I hadn't done the debt thing after you saved Vor. He's nuts about that kind of stuff."

Kenzie walked over to the supply closet and stowed her mask inside. The smell wafting from her jumpsuit was dissipating, though its internal odor-control nodes were probably going to need changing by the end of the day. But her mind was already a few steps ahead of that—she started to understand exactly what Jo's pledge meant. And the opportunity at hand.

"So," she said, shutting the closet, "you have to protect or save my life for the debt to be cleared."

Jo was already back on her handset, scrolling through her feeds. "Why are we still talking about this?"

"And that means," she said, walking across the cargo bay, past Jo, past the pen, "you have to stick with me when I do things that might get me killed."

Jo stopped scrolling through her feeds. She looked up, locked eyes with Kenzie. Her mouth was twisted into a scowl, the etch-marks on her face glowing a dull purple.

"Why." It didn't sound like a question.

Kenzie finally ambled over to the covered spacecraft in the corner and pulled off the tarp with a whoosh.

Underneath was the small, two-person fighter that Captain Dashiell Drake had made famous at the battle of Gantoid IV: a classic Mark 6 Dart. Its blue and silver stripes had dulled with age, but otherwise, it was exactly as she remembered it from the photos in all the books.

"Never do something dangerous by yourself when you can bring a friend," she said. "Drake, page 76."

Bad Medicine

In his dream, Dash was sitting in his captain's chair. The cockpit slowly filled with water. His ankles were wet, then his knees, then his waist, as he absently pushed different buttons on his helm console to try and figure out how to end the rising flood. Squix, not in his exosuit, lazily swam by.

"Maybe you should try flying instead of sinking?" he said as he curled and uncurled his tentacles above the water's surface.

"What?" said Dash. He was soaked up to his chest.

"Or maybe you could ask her?" Squix pointed behind the captain as he swam away.

Dash swiveled around, the water now up to his neck. He saw Kenzie floating—above the water, rather than on top of it. Even though the water was nearly up to the top of the cockpit, she still had plenty of flying room above the deluge.

She opened her mouth to speak—and instead squeaked. Like a dog toy, but worse.

"Uhh," said Dash.

Kenzie opened her mouth again. More squeaks. A long, prolonged squeal. Her face remained perfectly peaceful.

The water was gone, and Dash looked around. The cockpit was gone too—just empty space. He looked back at Kenzie, who was only several meters away now, flying away backwards. She opened her mouth one last time.

A piercing, high-pitched squeal jolted Dash out of his Doctor Bill-prescribed nap. He woke with a jump to find himself lying on his medbay bed. Gripping the sides to keep from falling out, he looked over to see Vor, sitting on his own exam table on the other side of the room. His head was down, focusing on the various parts and pieces in his lap, the empty shopping bag from Technica Outpost crumpled next to him. Dash also thought he noticed more than a few pieces of scrap metal and busted technology that Vor must've fished out of the cargo bay's garbage compactor. Dash didn't realize Vor knew where the garbage compactor was. Though, considering he hadn't gotten the chance to empty the thing since he'd picked up the cadets, the Crag was probably spoiled for choice when it came to fresh tech-garbage to use for his...whatever it was.

Vor turned a knob and the squeal filled the room for two seconds, going from annoying to ear-splitting. Dash glared at him. Vor didn't seem to notice. He turned another knob in the pile of gizmos in his lap and the noise returned for two more seconds, going from merely ear-splitting to brain-melting.

Dash cleared his throat.

"Say, buddy," he said, gritting his teeth into something resembling a friendly grin. "You mind maybe not doing..." Dash thought for a second. "...whatever it is you're doing?"

Vor kept his head down, apparently not having heard Dash. Then he put a single finger up in the air—one moment, he was telling the captain.

Before Dash could say anything, Vor turned another dial and the sound of a dolphin being pushed through a cheese grater filled the room once more. Dash stuck his fingers in his ears, and Vor twisted a tube clockwise. The sound got worse. Vor tried counter-clockwise. The dolphin started losing consciousness. Finally, the squeal disappeared entirely, making the room feel suddenly empty.

Then Vor looked up and gave Dash a thumbs up. There was a pause—Dash took the fingers out of his ears and gave a thumbs up back. Then the Crag set back to work, and the medbay was, for the moment, silent again.

Dash exhaled hard through his nose and then felt woozy. He brought his hand to his forehead and massaged the place where the big purple welt had been. Doctor Bill's treatment had reduced the swelling into nonexistence, but his body still told him there was something amiss. The bruise may have been gone, but Dash still felt like he'd been traversing at inconceivable speeds through an extra-spatial portal where the normal rules of physics don't quite apply and then gotten bonked on the head with a large piece of equipment. Because he had.

More than that, Dash's body ached from running through Technica Outpost and carrying gigantic potted plants for no good reason. Considering most of his daily routine typically involved sitting and sometimes talking, it was a wonder he managed to survive the experience at all. Escaping homicidal armored alien invaders was bad enough. Having to exercise while doing it was even worse. He'd been resting in the medbay for hours, but he was just as sore as ever.

He saw Doctor Bill in the corner, apparently sorting and reorganizing medical supplies or something equally tedious.

"Hey Doc," he called. "Got a second?"

Bill's screen flipped around and he rode the track in the medbay's ceiling to Dash's bed. His digital face looked bored, with a hint of displeasure around the corners of his pixelated mouth. In short, the usual.

"What can I do for you, Captain?" he sniffed. He wasn't used to having patients in the medbay for this long. When his services were required, he would usually set a broken arm, dispense a few stimulants, or just spray anti-inflammatory gel where necessary. But with two crewmembers injured, Doctor Bill probably felt positively crowded.

"What's my diagnosis?" asked Dash. He figured he was as eager to leave the medbay as Bill was to be rid of him.

Doctor Bill extended a scanning probe and waved it around absentmindedly.

"Based on these readings, it seems that you are, medically speaking," he consulted the results of his tests, "annoying. Let me know if you need a second opinion."

Dash rolled his eyes, then immediately regretted it, as it sent a new wave of pain through his skull. Doctor Bill slid away, but the captain could still hear the scowl in his digitized voice.

"I've already told you—" Doctor Bill flipped his panel to shoot an angry look at Dash, then flipped back. "—you need to rest for at least a few hours. If you don't take it easy, if we don't monitor your vitals constantly, you could do some serious damage to your brain. And I've seen your brain in scans. It can't take anymore setbacks."

The doctor scooted back to his corner of the room to busy himself again. Dash balled his hands into fists and tried thinking of something, anything, he could say back to this egomaniac of a reprogrammed cargo-lifter.

Then he remembered the magic words. And he smiled.

"Doc," he called again. "One more thing?"

Doctor Bill flipped around and slid back to his bed.

"What could you possibly still—"

Dash interrupted him. "I wanna watch TV."

"What? I—"

Doctor Bill's digital face disappeared, suddenly replaced by an old police drama from Dash's childhood. He'd installed a unique command phrase to override Doctor Bill's programming for when he got a little too snotty. Until Dash was done with him, he wasn't a doctor. He was a television.

Dash pulled out his handset and used it as a remote, flipping through shows being broadcast throughout the Alliance's galactic network. A teen drama featuring interspecies love quadrangles. An Aphid dating show to select a new Brood Queen for a politically weak clan in their planet's industrial district. That show with the funny robot.

Dash wasn't sure what he wanted to watch—or really that he wanted to watch anything, so much as he just wanted to forget his troubles for a while.

That's why the universe picked that moment for Squix to walk into the medbay to discuss all of the *Gremlin*'s new problems.

Squix's eyes were buried in his handset as he approached Dash's bed. "Cap, I got the damage report if you're ready." He looked at the captain, who'd stopped flipping channels when he got to that commercial for life insurance showing old people walking down a sidewalk holding hands.

"Ugh, perfect," Dash sighed. "That's totally just what I need right now."

"Great!" Squix said, beaming his damage report onto Dash's handset. The remote control's buttons disappeared and were replaced with a long checklist of malfunctioning systems and weak spots on the hull. He was about to tell Squix that now, in fact, was not actually a great time for him, when the television caught his attention.

"—back to our top story today, the sudden disappearance of Technica Outpost." On the screen, a Human woman with well-sculpted hair stood on the bridge of a vessel swarming with Alliance scientists and Fleet personnel. Behind her, the viewport showed a starfield littered with debris and destroyed vessels…and a big empty space where Technica once floated.

Dash knew the scene pretty well, considering he and his crew had just escaped with their lives only a few hours earlier.

He swiped Squix's damage report away from his handset's display and brought the remote buttons back to raise the broadcast's volume.

"It's unclear what caused the destruction of both the outpost and the jump-beacon formerly stationed at the site," the reporter said, "which has led to the devastation behind me. However, the disaster here has drawn comparisons to a similar incident from earlier this week, when the asteroid Delta Pallas III, along with the jump-drive manufacturing facility within, was also mysteriously destroyed without warning or any evident cause."

"Hey," said Squix. "Weren't they talking about that on the news the other day?"

Dash vaguely remembered hearing about the jump-drive factory as the *Gremlin* was leaving Arcadia Station, right after they'd picked up the cadets.

The reporter continued. "For now, the Alliance's scientists and the sector's authorities are looking to uncover answers. Leading the investigation is Commander Gerald Sharp, who held a press conference earlier today."

Onto the screen flashed Commander Sharp standing at a podium in what looked like a briefing room. His hair was all right angles, and his Fleet uniform looked as impeccable as it had the last time Dash saw him on TV. Standing next to him was another man in a Fleet uniform with dark skin, wide brown eyes, curly black hair, and an apparently semi-permanent smile.

"The parallels between what happened at Technica Outpost and at Delta Pallas III are difficult to ignore," he said amid the typing of reporters and the clicking of floating camera-drones. "While it's possible the cause of Technica's destruction may have been accidental, our investigation has found evidence pointing to the involvement of a hostile alien force."

Dash muttered, "You don't know the half of it."

Commander Sharp continued: "We have reason to believe that Technica and Delta Pallas were both targeted by a violent cell of Frawgs who have been working their way through Alliance territory in recent weeks, taking advantage the holes in this sector's security."

"They really *don't* know the half of it, huh?" said Squix.

Dash groaned.

Sharp kept talking, motioning to the man next to him. "Lieutenant Ravi Sidana and his science team here on the *IAS Concordance* are combing through the wreckage for clues as to what's transpired here, and we'll be sending smaller investigative teams to follow within the hour."

The broadcast switched back to the reporter on the bridge of the *Concordance*.

"Miraculously, some members of Technica Outpost's senior staff managed to escape," she said, "and are talking with investigators at this very moment."

As she spoke, photos of people wearing Technica's uniforms appeared on-screen—among them Lucy Reese, the outpost's security chief.

Dash got goosebumps. Squix had said Lucy was working with the Forgers. No, that she *was one of them*, he'd said. Was she brainwashed? Was the woman they saw in the security office on the Outpost even Lucy Reese at all? Or was she some kind of replicant pod-person? He wasn't sure if he should be thinking about finding ways to rescue her or keep running from her.

The newscast cut back to the anchors at their desks. A woman with blue lipstick spoke directly to the camera.

"And the destruction of Technica Outpost brings more sad news. The Alliance lost one of its heroes today: Dashiell Drake, hero of Gantoid IV."

"Uhh," said Dash.

"Hey," said Squix. "That's you!"

The screen cut to 12-year-old footage of Dash's appearance at a parade with Alliance Grand Chancellor Gork—right after the end of the Forger War. The expression on his face was technically a smile, but Dash remembered it as feeling something like quickly sitting down in an eel-filled ice bath. Gork's face was as unreadable as any other Aphid's, but he'd been nice enough to Dash.

"Drake single-handedly turned the tide of the Forger War when he discovered a network of cloaked dronecraft the enemy had deployed throughout Alliance territory. Those drones acted as energy conduits, providing greater firepower to the Forgers—until Drake's discovery, that is, which provided Alliance forces with the intelligence necessary to detect them, repel the invaders, and send the Forgers back to their own territories in the deep reaches of space."

The news report cut to a scene from *The Glory of Gantos*—that dumb movie they'd made about Dash and his fateful discovery. The actor playing him, some showbiz idiot, pushed out his jaw bravely as he stood his ground to his superior officer.

"I'm telling you," yelled fake Dash, pointing at his commander handsomely, "those drones are out there feeding the enemy with raw power!"

"Dammit, Ensign Drake," replied the wrinkled old commander with a heavy accent that betrayed years of good breeding, "you just don't know when to stop playing the damn hero!"

The anchor's voice spoke over the movie footage.

"While movie producers dramatized Drake's legendary exploits for box-office profits, the real Dashiell Drake had a somewhat more complicated legacy."

"Uh oh," said Squix.

"After living off of royalties and endorsements," the newscaster continued, "Drake settled into a life as the proprietor of a cargo shipping service."

A file photo of the *Gremlin* appeared on-screen.

"Along the way, he began providing what he called a 'cadet immersion experience' to prospective applicants to the Alliance's Fleet Academy."

The screen cut to what looked like space station security camera footage. There was Dash from something like five years earlier—he remembered that particular bad haircut—pointing at a broken shipping crate while lecturing a former cadet whose back was to the camera.

"The Academy's admissions director told us the immersion program's actual effect on increasing a cadet's chances of admission was rarely significant. But it did prove to be a routinely popular service among Alliance students looking to earn extra credit or to simply stay occupied during breaks from school."

"Hey," said Squix. "She said we were 'popular!' Not bad!"

"However, in recent years its popularity has waned."

"Nuts," said Squix.

The screen cut to a face that literally made Dash feel sick: Jonah. And he still had that rash.

"Captain Drake is a creep, and his ship is a pile of junk," he said, flecks of spit forming in the corners of his mouth. He scratched a nasty looking red bump on the side of his nose. The interview was mercifully short, as the feed cut to another familiar face, though one significantly less nauseating: Zrxx, the orange-furred mechanic from Pergamentum Orbis II.

The anchor's voice spoke over the on-screen footage of the mechanic's face. "Additionally, Drake had fallen on hard times recently."

"Yeah, he stopped here just the other day, was having trouble with his ship's jump-drive," said Zrxx to a reporter just off-camera. "His ship was really beat up, and he paid for everything in credit chips, so I guess he wasn't doing so hot. I didn't recognize him at first—I thought he'd be taller."

Her pause was a heartbeat, but it felt longer to Dash.

"And, y'know…thinner," she added.

Dash's hands instinctively went to his midsection, and he held himself protectively. He was not having his best moment.

The broadcast cut to another photo of him from the end of the Forger War. Better haircut, thinner, still not that tall. The anchor spoke over the image.

"Despite these recent hardships, it's impossible to deny Dash Drake's important impact on the Alliance and its current prosperity."

Suddenly the round, fleshy face of Councilman John-Dean Clifford filled the screen.

"Terrible, terrible tragedy what happened with Drake," he drawled. Looking at him, Dash felt the urge to throw up. "I met him once and he was a hell of a guy—hell of a guy, that man."

Dash had never met Councilman Clifford.

"In the wake of this terrible loss, I'll be chatting with my fellow council members about the jump-chains initiative. I'm sure Mister Drake would've wanted the Interstellar Alliance to be as secure as possible."

Dash sneered until the politician's face disappeared from the screen, replaced by that of the desk anchor.

"Wherever he is, hopefully Drake has finally found the peace that eluded him for so long."

The broadcast cut to a sharp-dressed Crag man who flashed a glittering smile.

"And now, sports! The Novarr Ice Spiders have taken a beating lately, as their division rivals haven't let up—"

Dash clicked off the broadcast. Doctor Bill's face appeared in its place.

"Gracious," he said, with an expression a few hairs away from sympathetic. "That was embarrassing."

Then he slid along his track back to the other side of the room to continue sorting medical supplies.

Dash leaned back on his bed, not realizing he'd actually been hunched forward as the broadcast played. He lay there, staring at the ceiling while the sounds of Doctor Bill sorting supplies and Vor's tinkering filled the room.

Squix spoke first.

"Hey, look on the bright side...they said you're dead!"

Dash looked at his first mate. "I'm gonna need you to unpack that for me."

"Well, think about it," said Squix, bringing a contemplative tentacle to where his chin would've been. "We know the Forgers are looking for you, right?"

Squix and Dash looked over at Vor, who—still working on his project—nodded in agreement.

"So if all the broadcasts say you're dead, doesn't that mean they won't be looking for you anymore? Or any of us?"

Dash's eyebrows crowded together.

"I mean…maybe?" he said. "There was a whole squadron of fighters chasing after us at Technica Outpost."

"And then Technica Outpost zapped itself to another dimension!" Squix raised three tentacles triumphantly. "None of those guys know if we made it out of there alive before they jumped away too, right?"

"That's true," said Dash. "We may have actually gotten a break on that."

"We were bound to get one eventually," said Squix.

Dash exhaled as the knots in his belly untied just a little. Maybe Squix had a point.

And with that in mind, Dash's options for addressing Squix's long list of necessary repairs suddenly got a lot shorter. He couldn't send messages to anyone for help, and he couldn't put out a distress call and hope someone might stumble by to lend him a spare jump-shield. If there was a chance that the Forgers actually thought he and his crew were dead, then he'd be stupid to give them the chance to think otherwise.

And that meant someone else besides Squix had a point: Kenzie.

Dash breathed again. The knots loosened a bit more.

He hated to admit it, but he couldn't really deny it anymore. Kenzie was right about docking the *Gremlin* with the *Valor* and stripping it of whatever spare parts they could find. They could patch themselves up in this ghost town of a sector, then jump to someplace safe until they figured out their next move.

In only a couple days, Kenzie had proven herself to be one of the brightest, most capable cadets he'd ever brought aboard the ship. And those times she'd messed up? She'd still been trying to do the right thing. It's not like she'd been making his life hell on purpose, willfully doing things she knew she shouldn't.

Kenzie was a good kid. Why, Dash even thought he'd let her take control of the helm to dock the *Gremlin* and lead the salvage operation. She'd certainly earned it.

He looked at Squix and smiled.

Squix took a small, frightened step back in surprise.

Dash pulled out his handset and patched into the cargo bay's comms.

"Hey Kenzie, wanna come on back up to the medbay?" he said. "I have some good news for you."

Silence.

"Kenzie, do you read me?"

Nothing.

"Cadet, do you copy? Kenzie? Jo?"

Dash heard his handset ding. He saw a new message…from Vor. Who was sitting across the room.

He looked up at the cadet—who met his gaze—then looked at his handset and opened the message. Two words.

"They left."

He looked back at Vor. "What do you mean, 'they left'?"

Another ding. Dash looked at his handset again.

"Buddy system," read the message. Jo and Vor's father had set it up so that if either of them left the network they were both accessing, the other would know. Apparently it had kicked in, and this was Vor's way of sharing that information. The knots in Dash's belly were back, in an all new configuration. Like a sheepshank or a tugboat hitch or something.

"Uh, Cap?" Squix said. "If this activity log from the cargo bay is right—I mean, um, we've taken a lot of damage, so it might not be accurate because sometimes the computer gets all goofy when we're running too many programs anyway—"

"Squix."

"Well, uh, it looks like the cargo bay made an unexpected, um, drop-off?" said Squix, turning bright yellow. "Because it opened an hour ago and a ship flew out of it."

"A ship flew out of it?" Dash repeated, unable to process the information. "What—how—what ship flew out of—"

Then it clicked. He closed his eyes and pinched the bridge of his nose.

"No," said Dash. "They didn't."

They Did

After rocketing out of the main doors of the *Gremlin*'s cargo bay, Kenzie only spent about ten minutes flying Captain Drake's legendary Dart how she'd always imagined she would. Loop-de-loops, barrel-rolls, and simply opening it up at full-throttle…it didn't matter that the ship pulled a little to the left—okay a lot to the left. And it shuddered like an earthquake for exactly 3.4 seconds every time you opened up the throttle, probably because of the many years it spent under a tarp. Still, it had been just like Kenzie's dreams.

No, better. This was real.

But after those ten minutes, Kenzie gritted her teeth and got down to business. She had to get back to her mission. She had a job to do.

"I'm gonna throw up soon," said Jo from the Dart's rear seat.

That was another good reason, Kenzie noted. It'd be hard to get all the gravel out of Jo's spacesuit.

Kenzie set the Dart down on the *Valor*'s hull near one of the megacrusier's many jump-shield generators. In the emptiness of space, there was no gravity, so Kenzie activated the fighter's magnetic clamps to hold it in place. Likewise, she and Jo activated their magnetic boots and slowly Frankenstein-marched to the jump-shield generator.

Soon, the two of them pried off the hull plating, detached the generator—a smooth oval pod made of titanium and high-density carbon fiber—and stashed it in the small storage compartment behind the fighter's cockpit.

When they finished, Kenzie spotted a nearby maintenance hatch. There was no power from the *Valor* to help them open it, but there also wasn't any power keeping it closed. She found the panel hiding the manual release lever and, with Jo's help, threw it open and entered the megacruiser.

The corridors inside were dark—they lit their way with helmet-lights and handlamps. The generators had been deactivated for decades, so there was no life support, no artificial gravity, and clomping down the corridor with magnetic boots would've doubled the salvage mission's length. Kenzie and Jo were basically still floating through the void, only now with walls and doors they had to pry open.

In minutes, Kenzie and Jo found the astrogation room and forced the door open. Inside, a large operations console and a gigantic screen covered an entire wall. This was where Earther officers plotted the *Valor*'s course from system to system, all with the help of its nav-computer— now nearly a century old, and probably a good fit for the equally ancient *Gremlin*.

"Ugh, gross," said Jo, her voice crackling over the comms in Kenzie's helmet. Kenzie turned and saw Jo's light trained on a small picture on the wall of a Human woman in a bikini. "Why's she so lumpy?"

Kenzie thought for a second.

"It's a mammal thing," she said.

Jo made a face. "I'll pretend to know what that means," she said.

Before she could feel too self-conscious, Kenzie turned, reactivated her boots so she'd stay in place, and connected her handset to the nearest console. Despite there being nearly a hundred years of technological advancements between the *Valor* and Kenzie's handheld computer, the console sprang to life and began booting up.

"How are you doing that?" asked Jo.

"What do you mean?"

"I thought this ship was, like, broken. Or something."

"Oh," said Kenzie. "Well, even though the ship's generators aren't powered up, my handset's battery is strong enough to power the console. So now I can access the ship's diagnostic functions and memory banks to see what parts should be in this room."

"Uh-huh."

"Actually," Kenzie smiled, "a lot of people don't know this, but the main reason the *Valor* stopped working was because its computer core was too badly damaged in the battle."

"Plus all the holes that got shot in it," said Jo.

"Right," said Kenzie. "But a few of the important systems still work—or they would if it had a functioning computerized brain to connect everything."

"But *you* know this," said Jo.

"I, uh, read a lot."

"Uh-huh."

"Anyway," Kenzie said, looking her handset's readout. "Looks like this is the right place."

She disconnected her device and started tearing the console apart with gusto. She tossed parts to Jo, who caught them in null-gravity and stuffed them in a bag they'd brought.

Kenzie gave one particularly stubborn circuit board a futile yank, then another. The wires connecting it to the long-dead navigation console were taut.

"You can't disconnect it?" asked Jo behind her.

"I don't have the right tools—it's wired right into the guts of the ship," Kenzie said, unclamping her right magnetic boot from the floor and bracing it against the console. She pulled as she spoke. "I didn't, ngggggnh, really have time, ngggggggggggnh! to packaghghhhg!"

Kenzie pulled with all her might, and the wires finally snapped. Kenzie started flailing, her right foot coming loose from the console, her left boot still magnetically attached to the *Valor*'s floor. The lack of gravity made it hard for her body to determine which way was "down," even with the added bonus of being in a room with a specific top and bottom.

A moment later, she reattached her right foot to the floor and stopped waving her arms. Hands on her knees, she let out a long, slow breath. Then she stood and looked at Jo.

"Got it?" she asked.

"Nope," said Jo. She pointed up.

The room wasn't especially big, but neither of the girls were tall enough to easily reach the circuit board floating in a corner, its wires trailing it like a flat, mechanical jellyfish.

"One sec," said Kenzie. She touched a pair of buttons embedded in her jumpsuit's gloves, detached both boots from the floor, and started gently floating up. She squeezed her fists in a specific motion, and fired the maneuvering thrusters embedded in the lining of her suit.

She flew up towards the errant circuit board—but couldn't help showing off for her friend. She somersaulted before reaching the top of the room, then clamped her boots to the ceiling. Up was now down. To her, Jo was upside down and standing on the ceiling. She exaggerated a casual strut over to the part and grabbed it, then gently flung it down—or was it up?—to Jo below-above her.

"Pretty cool, huh?" she said.

"Yeah, sure," said Jo as she grabbed the part, her face failing to mirror the smile Kenzie felt on her own.

Kenzie put her hands on her hips. "C'mon, Jo! How are you not loving this?"

"Oh," said Jo, her voice thick with irritation over their shared comm channel. "You mean how am I not loving stomping around a creepy old ship in the middle of nowhere after I helped you steal the captain's little shuttle thing?"

"First of all," said Kenzie as she flew back towards Jo. "We didn't steal it. We borrowed it—to help fix the *Gremlin*. And it isn'a shuttle—" she flipped again and clamped back onto the floor. Up-down became regular-down again. "—it's the Dart. His legendary fighter craft. The one he used to help end the Forger War. It's important."

"If it was so important, why didn't we tell the captain?" asked Jo, the tips of her fingers pressed to her helmet. "You know how he gets when you—"

"That's exactly why," said Kenzie, cutting her off. "I know how he gets, because he's incredibly protective of his crew. He doesn't want anything bad to happen to us, so I removed that problem for him. Now he won't have to feel guilty about us doing this. Besides, he said the *Gremlin* wouldn't dock with the *Valor.*" Kenzie crossed her arms. "And now it won't have to."

Jo scoffed. "I was going to say, 'you know how he gets when you do crazy things he doesn't want you to do.' Y'know, like when he fired you?"

Kenzie shrank. She hadn't thought of that. "I, uh…"

"I mean, seriously." Jo shoved the bag full of parts into Kenzie's hands. "I know I pledged save your life or whatever, but I didn't think you'd make me have to actually do it. At least not within ten minutes. Like, why do you even—why are you even like this?"

For a moment, the only sound between them was the crackle of static over their shared comm channel. Kenzie's face felt hot.

"I'm…" she started. "I'm not good at being…normal. I—"

Jo put up her finger. Kenzie thought she was going to yell at her, but instead she said, "Do you hear that?"

Kenzie frowned. "Hear what?"

Jo waved her finger in Kenzie's face. "Shh!"

Kenzie stared at Jo, who looked like she was trying to see into the back of her own skull. Finally, she locked Kenzie's eyes.

"There's someone else here."

* * *

Jo had heard the telltale crackle of comm chatter and interference from another network. Well, telltale signs to a Crag, a race with better hearing than most others in the galaxy. And especially to a Crag who spent lots of time on the phone.

After scanning the local networks—on an unpowered ship like the *Valor*, there shouldn't have been *any* networks aside from the one Kenzie and Jo shared to communicate—the pair discovered that the dead, empty megacruiser they'd been stripping for parts wasn't as dead or empty as they'd thought.

Kenzie and Jo crept down a few corridors and discovered the hangar bay filled with a crew of Frawgs, their bulbous green faces barely fitting inside their helmets. Three bumpy, bulgy gunships were being prepped to launch an attack—against the *Gremlin*.

"—ammunition loaded," croaked one over the comms Kenzie and Jo were eavesdropping on. "Fuel reserves at half, but should still be enough."

"Have the ship's computer systems cross-check your data," said another disapprovingly. Kenzie figured that one might've been the Frawgs' boss.

There was a pause and then a strangely familiar, automated voice flooded the comm channel. "Fuel reserves at fifty percent. Conditions acceptable."

"How many you think are in there?" said another Frawg. It was hard for Kenzie to tell which ones were talking. "More than the last ship we caught? With fatter prey? I'm hungry."

The computer with the familiar voice chimed in again. "Scans of lifeforms in target vessel inconclusive due to interference." This time, Kenzie finally placed it—that sounded a lot like Doctor Bill. The Frawgs' ships must've had computers outfitted with unmodified versions of Bill's artificial intelligence program.

"There should be enough for all of us," said Boss Frawg, an edge of irritation creeping into her voice. "We're all hungry. But this isn't just about lunch."

"Yeah, it's about leftovers for breakfast tomorrow too!" A storm of throaty, croaking chuckles filled Kenzie's helmet. Through the window separating their hiding spot in the control room and the pirates in the hangar, she saw the Frawgs shaking and convulsing with laughter as they worked.

Kenzie tapped her handset with her thumb and the sound cut out. She'd switched back to per private channel with Jo.

"Okay," Kenzie said. "We should probably call the captain now."

"Right?" said Jo. "This is really bad." Jo looked back through the window. "Do you think they know we're here? That we flew the Dart onto the *Valor*?"

Kenzie thought for a second. "Probably not," she said. "There's tons of ion interference out there messing with the sensors, remember? That means they're relying on visuals to know what's going on out in space. Unless someone was watching the *Gremlin* every second, they probably didn't see us leave."

"Plus, you were flying ridiculously superfast," said Jo.

"Yes," said Kenzie. "Also that."

Kenzie tried connecting with the comm systems on the *Gremlin* but wasn't having any luck. Three signals sent, three bounced messages back. She couldn't tell what the problem was. What she could tell, though, was that they were running out of time. Most of the Frawgs had boarded the trio of ships, and the few remaining on the hangar deck made last minute supply runs before their launch.

"I can't get the *Gremlin*'s signal," she said to Jo.

"Let me try," she said, pulling out her own handset. Jo apparently only needed a few taps and swipes to figure it out. "The Frawgs' comm channel's blocking us—it's too strong for us to jump onto the *Gremlin*'s network. There are too many of them connected." She let out a big breath. "We can't warn the captain about the pirates."

Pirates—that gave Kenzie an idea. She had a plan.

"I have a plan."

"Of course you do," said Jo. "What is it this time?"

"So, they're pirates, right? They hijack ships, take what they want. Well, we can do that too."

"Huh?"

"Let's hijack their comm channel," said Kenzie. "And I know how we can really mess with them."

Jo raised an eyebrow.

Kenzie poked at her handset for a few seconds, then she spoke.

"Warning!" said Kenzie. But the voice coming through the speaker in Kenzie's helmet was all Bill, complete with his exhausted, annoyed attitude. She'd hacked into the Frawg's comm channel and tapped into Bill's vocal subroutines. "Multiple safety hazards detected! Catastrophic system failure imminent!"

Kenzie pointed at Jo to give it a try.

"Warning! Coolant leak flooding the…" Jo stopped talking for a second. She was thinking. "…flooding the plasma…manifolds. Stop launch operations…right now!"

Jo looked at Kenzie. Kenzie just shrugged. Her improvisation did the trick.

The Frawgs spilled from their ships to find the coolant leak. And the plasma manifolds. Those weren't a thing. Now it was Kenzie's turn again.

"Primary thrusters disengaged," she said, hearing Bill's voice in her ears. "Unstable fuel additives detected. Drain fuel tanks and replace with uncontaminated combustibles."

The Frawgs were frenzied, running around the hangar bay, bumping into each other, flipping switches on and off, and generally being idiots. Two of them even started dumping the fuel out one of the ships.

Kenzie was thrilled. She looked over at Jo and was happy to see she was finally smiling, too.

"Communications network is generating monumentally unsafe levels of electromagnetic interference!" yelled Kenzie. She barely kept from laughing. "Disengage all comm channel connections immediately!"

She saw half the Frawgs touch their helmets and cut their comms out. The croaking voices piping through Kenzie's helmet speaker suddenly dropped in volume. The other Frawgs who didn't cut their comms were too busy looking for coolant leaks and plasma manifolds and draining fuel out of the second ship to heed this latest warning.

Kenzie gave a nod to Jo, who started tapping on her handset. She'd hoped enough Frawgs had broken their connections to the communications network to let them get a message out to the *Gremlin*.

A new voice—Boss Frawg—cut through the panicked croaks remaining in the channel.

"Computer, check fuel systems for unstable additives," she said.

Before Kenzie could say anything, the actual computer responded: "No abnormal additives detected. All systems normal."

Half the Frawgs running around the hangar bay stopped losing their minds. And the ones who'd disconnected from the comms network were confused enough at why the others had stopped panicking that they started slowing down, too. One more Frawg—taller and sleeker than the others, and with colorful, almost tribal-looking accents of green, red, and purple smeared across its spacesuit—emerged from the third ship, the one that hadn't yet been drained of its fuel. Boss Frawg.

"Stop it, you morons!" she yelled. She pantomimed to the others who couldn't hear her, putting out her hands and then pointing to her helmet—she was trying to tell them to reconnect to their shared channel. The other Frawgs just mimicked her, putting their hands up, pointing at their own helmets. Boss Frawg shook her head, exasperated. The rest did their best to imitate her.

This was going pretty great.

Then something bad happened.

"—come in! Cadet, come in! This is Dash broadcasting on all channels, attempting to reach the *Valor*, please respond!"

The good news was that Kenzie and Jo had clearly gotten enough Frawgs to disengage from their network to connect with the captain. The bad news was that all the Frawgs on the *Valor* suddenly heard Dash's broadcast—and knew she and Jo were there.

Boss Frawg turned to the window separating the hangar bay from the control room where the girls were hiding and locked eyes on Kenzie. The rest of the Frawgs, still mimicking their leader, followed suit.

"Now would be a good time to leave," said Kenzie.

She turned to look at Jo, but she was already gone, having fired her suit's thrusters and taken off towards the door that opened to the main corridor, the bag of nav-computer parts forgotten and floating in zero-G where she'd been moments before.

Kenzie grabbed the bag and kicked on her own thrusters, following Jo out the door. Her spine electrified as she heard Boss Frawg yell over the comm channel, "Get them!"

Kenzie switched on the private comm channel and found that Jo had already contacted the captain and was filling him in.

"—it's full of Frawgs and they were getting ready to attack you but we messed them up kind of so we're heading back to the Dart now," Jo said, her words tumbling out quickly.

Kenzie chimed in, making sure Captain Drake heard the good news. "And we've got a replacement jump-shield and nav-computer parts!"

"Great," said Dash over the comms. "Maybe the Frawgs will send that stuff over after they murder you."

She rocketed through the corridor with the bag of parts, the lack of gravity making her feel like she was flying straight up, even though, according to the ship's layout, she was flying horizontally. She looked down, back at the door to the hangar bay control room. Three Frawgs spilled out and fired their own thrusters to chase her. And either their thrusters were pretty good, or hers were junk, because they were gaining on her.

The access hatch they'd used to enter the ship was only a few meters away, and Jo was nearly there ahead of her. Kenzie had to go faster. Or make the Frawgs go slower. Or both.

She overturned the bag of nav-computer parts and opened it, tossing it away. A mess of bulky circuit boards, chips, and wires bloomed out below her. The Frawgs reacted instinctively, flinching away from the onslaught of ancient technology. Their suits' thrusters sent them in awkward directions, while Kenzie's were made all the more effective now that she wasn't as weighed down.

When she reached the hatch, Jo had just finished prying it open. They scrambled out and, after clamping their boots to the *Valor*'s surface, shut the hatch behind them.

As they clomped back to the Dart—not risking using thrusters in open space, for fear of spiraling out into the infinite nothingness of the void—Dash piped in over their channel.

"Hey," he said, the usual mix of fear and irritation in his voice, "You said you 'messed up' the Frawgs, right?"

"Kind of," said Jo unhelpfully. "We said we 'kind of' messed them up. Why?"

"Because a ship just launched from the *Valor*, and it's definitely shooting at us!"

"Oh, nice!" Kenzie said, relieved. "That's awesome."

Dash shrieked. "*What?*"

"There's only one after you," said Kenzie, reaching the Dart and climbing into the cockpit. "When we found them, there were three ships preparing to attack. That means the other two we got them to disable are still busted."

There was a second of silence as Jo clambered into the seat behind Kenzie.

"Oh," said Dash. "Uh…thanks." He clicked off the comm channel.

Kenzie started the Dart's engine, and moments later they disconnected from the *Valor*—just as the hatch opened and three angry Frawgs flew out.

Kenzie laughed and opened up the throttle. She did one more barrel roll—she figured she'd earned it. She wasn't sure when she'd get to fly the Dart again. As a fighter craft, it was better equipped for battle and speed than anything the Frawgs were throwing at Dash and the rest of the crew. Considering she was about to fly back to the *Gremlin* and start shooting cannibal pirates away from her friends, she wanted to enjoy the experience while it lasted. Between the tricks she'd done when she first launched from the *Gremlin*'s cargo bay and this one last spin before turning to save the captain, this excursion had exceeded her wildest dreams.

"Seriously, I'm gonna be sick if you keep—" said Jo behind her, followed by a long, low urping noise, and the sound of tiny rocks hitting glass.

"Sorry, Jo," said Kenzie smiling. "I keep forgetting."

"Ugh, it's getting up my nose," said Jo.

"We'll head back and blast those Frawgs now. Hold on to—"

Before Kenzie could finish her thought, an unfamiliar buzz filled the comm channel, while a red light she hadn't noticed before started flashing. She leaned in and examined it closely. Uh-oh.

She raised Dash on the comms. "Captain?"

"Little busy right now, Kenzie!" Behind his voice she heard laser fire striking the *Gremlin*'s hull, along with the sound of tentacles gripping and releasing the console. "Are you gonna get back here any time soon?"

"Probably not, actually," said Kenzie.

"What?" said Jo.

"Why?" Captain Drake demanded.

"Because," said Kenzie, wincing. "We're kind of sort of…out of gas."

Scoop

Dash spoke slowly. "Not sure I understood that, Kenzie. Say again?"

"We're pretty much out of fuel. We're about thirty meters away from the *Valor*, and we only have enough for one really short burn. We can't get to you. You need to come pick us up."

Dash looked at Squix. The Octopus, working frantically at his own console, was a deep shade of angry red.

"How could you be out of gas?" said Dash. The *Gremlin* shook as it took another blast. "You didn't fly the Dart that far, right? You only went, like, a few hundred meters."

Silence.

"Right?" asked Dash. "Right, Kenzie?"

"Well…"

"What do you mean, 'well'?" A light ignited on Dash's console—Squix had finished calculating a new escape vector for the *Gremlin* to follow to try and shake the Frawgs. Dash flipped a row of switches, and he jammed the stick forward, sending the ship diving. The *Gremlin*'s engine roared as the maneuvering thrusters fired in alternating patterns, making their flight path as unpredictable as possible.

"Kenzie, what'd you do?"

"I mean, I only did a few loops and spins," she said over the comms. "I didn't think there was so little gas in the tank!"

"Why would I keep a full tank of gas in a ship I never use?" Dash yelled. He checked his display to clock the enemy's position, saw the same interference preventing the sensors from working the last ten times he'd checked them, then hung a left. The ship veered port, the engines pouring on the heat again.

"Really?" Kenzie asked. "You never fly the Dart? Ever?"

"I don't think this is the conversation I want to have right now, Kenzie!" Dash killed the engines and pulled the helm, sending the *Gremlin* into a three-sixty rotation. Without sensors, he couldn't track the Frawgs. But with this move, he'd sacrifice some speed to get a fix on his pursuers. The dark, hulking body of the *Valor* loomed into view on the right side of the viewport, then out again. He caught a glimpse of the Frawg ship approaching…

…and something else, further back. He couldn't see it clearly enough to make it out. Maybe the Frawgs launched another ship after all?

The *Gremlin* finished its spin, and Dash let it go a few more degrees to throw the aliens off. He punched the engines full throttle, and the ship lurched onto a new vector.

"Frawgs pursuing at eight o'clock high, Squix!"

"Got it." Squix began calculating another escape pattern.

"Kenzie," said Dash. "You're sure the Frawgs only launched one ship?"

She didn't hesitate. "Positive. The other two ships' fuel tanks were emptied, and we've got eyes on the *Valor*'s launch bay from here. Why?"

"I thought I saw something…but maybe…"

He shook his head. "We need to get you back to the *Gremlin*."

"What do you want us to do, Captain?" Kenzie asked.

"Oh, so now you want to follow orders?"

"Definitely, yes," said Kenzie.

Jo cut in. "Can't you get us with, like, a tractor beam?"

"We don't have one of those," said Dash.

"Well, why not?" she challenged.

"Because they're really expensive!" he said. "I've never been chased by pirates while trying to rescue teenagers who stole my spaceship before!"

"Borrowed," corrected Jo.

Dash groaned. This was a new challenge for him—and he was pretty much clueless as to his options.

"What about a scoop?" said Squix, still working on a new evasion plan.

"A scoop?" said Dash.

"What's a scoop?" asked Kenzie over the channel.

"Well," said Squix, "when I used to haul freight with Marvo—you remember Marvo, Dash—we'd pick up extra work from ships that couldn't finish their jobs. So they'd subcontract out to us. It was actually a pretty good—"

A blaster bolt whizzed past the viewport.

"Squix!" Dash cried. "What's a scoop?"

"Okay, so, we'd meet clients at certain coordinates. To save time, they'd dump their cargo while they were still in transit, and we'd open our cargo bay doors and match velocity to reduce the impact when we'd, y'know, scoop it all up."

"Isn't that, like, really dangerous?" asked Jo over the comms.

"Incredibly!" said Squix. "But Marvo actually had some pretty slick inertial dampeners in his cargo bay to suck the speed out of whatever we picked up. As long as whatever was in the shipping containers wasn't too fragile, it usually worked okay."

"You do realize," said Jo from the Dart, "there are two living, breathing people in this ship who would probably get smeared into jelly? Right?"

"I mean," said Squix, suddenly unsure. "You might...not?"

Kenzie spoke up. "If the Dart were to match the *Gremlin*'s speed at the last moment, that would minimize the force of the impact."

"That's true," said Squix, rubbing the top of his head with a tentacle. "The Dart's own combat shields could help dampen the force of the impact too."

Jo spoke next. "I'm not a big fan of this 'force of the impact' thing you guys keep saying."

The *Gremlin* took another hit, this one penetrating its shields and striking the hull. The ship shuddered violently, and sparks flew from the consoles. Dash ducked instinctively, hoping his screen wasn't about to come loose again. He'd only just barely gotten it screwed back into the ship.

"Okay, we're doing it," said Dash. "The sensors don't work, so Squix—follow their comm signal to home in on the Dart's location."

A few button taps later and Squix was done. Their location and distance from the *Gremlin* appeared on Dash's display, which still hung at an odd angle. His head throbbed at the reminder.

Dash patched into the medbay, and Vor, still tinkering with his purchases from Technica Outpost, suddenly blinked onto his display.

"Vor," he said. The boy looked up, startled. "You ever seen a breach shield generator? Things that seal cracks in a ship's hull?"

Vor nodded.

"Down to the cargo bay's supply closet, we've got a whole stack of 'em, like ten. I need you to scatter them all over the bay and set them to activate at their highest frequency. We're picking up your sister. And we're not stopping to do it."

Vor's eyes went wide. Not with disbelief, but with pure excitement. Dash suspected that if Vor had a mouth, it'd be grinning stupidly.

"And I need you to do it in the next—" Dash looked at his chronometer. "—five minutes. Maybe a five-and-a-half, tops. Got it?"

Vor gave a quick salute and switched off.

"Squix, start calculating," Dash ordered.

"Aye, Cap," said Squix, whose skin alternated between blue and purple.

"Kenzie, standby for Squix's data about heading and how hard you'll need to burn and when to start."

He punched the *Gremlin*'s throttle as far as it would go.

"We're gonna scoop you guys up," said Dash.

"Eep," said Squix.

"Cool!" said Kenzie.

"Ugh," said Jo.

"Oh, and hold on tight," Dash continued, "this is gonna be bumpy."

While the *Gremlin* flew at full-burn, Dash knew they'd have to rely on speed alone to shake the Frawgs pursuing them. Still, he did a few rolls, arcs, and weaves for good measure. A few stray shots zoomed past the ship as he flew, but there were plenty more that struck true. More shots than he felt confident the ship could handle if they didn't take more thoroughly evasive maneuvers soon. But he couldn't do much of anything until his cadets were aboard so he could plan his next move.

"Calculations finished," said Squix. "Data sent!"

Dash watched the simulation Squix had calculated play out on his display, along with a countdown timer at the top of the screen. If Kenzie followed Squix's directions, she would point the Dart in the same direction as the *Gremlin*. When Dash gave the word, she'd start burning and nearly match his velocity, so they'd be going almost the same relative speed. The *Gremlin* would close the distance to gobble them up into the cargo bay—and at the last second, the Dart would use the rest of its fuel to fly as fast as the *Gremlin*. After that, it'd be "safe" for the Dart to land in the cargo bay, while the breach shields, and the shields on the Dart, cushioned the impact so the smaller ship wouldn't tear through the wall to the engine room, collide with the reactor, and kill them all.

At least, that was the theory he'd been working from for the last four minutes.

"Data received, maneuvering into position," said Kenzie. "Ready to execute on your mark, Captain."

Dash saw a new window appear in the corner of his display and he tapped it. Standing in the center of the cargo bay, Vor held his handset while spinning around, making Dash dizzy for watching. The translucent blue-green bubbles of energy generated by the breach shields surrounded him.

"Great, good, now please leave before your sister and her friend smash a spaceship into you," said Dash.

Vor rushed into the lift and closed the connection.

The timer clicked down to nine, eight, seven…

Dash smacked the button to open the cargo bay doors.

Six, five, four…

"Oh man oh man oh man," muttered Squix.

Three…

A bright speck in the viewport quickly grew into the blue and silver of the Dart, its rear thruster housings still dark.

Two…

A blaster bolt sailed by, missing the Dart by a meter.

One…

"Ready," said Dash.

Zero.

"Now!"

The Dart's thrusters roared to life, and the small fighter stopped growing larger—or, more accurately, it nearly matched its speed with the

Gremlin in an instant. The dead, hulking megacruiser sailed out of view below them as Dash and Kenzie flew towards the inky void together. A blue-brown planet loomed in the distance.

Kenzie's calm-yet-excited voice came through the speakers in the *Gremlin*'s cockpit. "Cutting engines in three…two…one…"

The fire blasting out of the Dart's rear thrusters snuffed out, and Dash angled the *Gremlin* just right so it'd be in position to scoop up the cadets…

A blaster bolt struck home again and the *Gremlin* shuddered. Out of the corner of his eye, Dash saw his display flash red. The ship was knocked out of alignment. He nudged the helm ever so slightly, correcting his heading, correcting again, correcting for another overcorrection, and holding his breath as the Dart disappeared from view. It was underneath the cockpit now…

The ship shook viciously. At first Dash thought they'd been hit with another blaster bolt, but the rumble below his feet told him the Dart was probably bouncing around the cargo bay like a pinball. The breach shields appeared to have kept the Dart from careening through the wall to the engine room. Dash knew this, since the *Gremlin* wasn't in the process of exploding.

He slammed the button to shut the cargo bay doors.

He glanced at Squix. "I really hope Kenzie and Jo didn't die just now."

They Didn't

12

The Dart's combat shields collided with the breach shields scattered throughout the bay, bouncing from one to the next like a stone in a rock tumbler. Then Kenzie thought of Jo and immediately felt guilty for thinking about rock tumblers. Was that like a meat grinder to a Crag? Or did they use rock tumblers the same way Humans used nail files, to sand away life's rough edges? Did Crags even have rock tumblers? She'd have to ask Jo after this was over.

Clearly Kenzie's thoughts were pretty confused as the Dart spun and rolled around the cargo bay. Soon, the fighter skidded to a stop along the floor. The rock was done tumbling.

Kenzie looked around the Dart's cockpit saw no major dents or dings. She patted her arms and legs—no immediate signs of breaks or fractures, though she knew she'd be sore later. But right now, she didn't even feel nauseous.

The sound of gravel hitting glass came from behind her again.

Jo hadn't fared quite as well.

"You okay?" she asked, unbuckling her restraints.

"Eyeuughh," was Jo's only response.

Kenzie opened the Dart's cockpit and stood to help her friend. The Crag's visor revealed a pile of tiny rocks lining the bottom of her helmet. Jo wasn't really cut out for space travel.

The readout on the arm of Kenzie's jumpsuit showed safe oxygen levels in the cargo bay. The *Gremlin* might've been old, but its life-support systems worked fast. She helped Jo from her seat and onto the cargo bay floor. Once out of the Dart, Jo lay down, splayed out like a starfish.

"I'll just stay here a while," she said.

"We gotta go help the captain," said Kenzie. She removed her helmet, then helped Jo remove her own helmet, managing to keep the teeny rocks from spilling everywhere.

"I can probably help from down here," said Jo, her eyes closed.

The ship shook with another blaster bolt hit. Things were maybe not going so great in the cockpit.

"Kenzie, Jo, status!" It was Squix on the cargo bay's speakers. "Are you guys alive?"

Kenzie stepped over a thick cord connecting two humming breach shields together and ran to a control panel on the wall. She tapped the comm button.

"We're here, and we're okay."

"Oh, phew," said Squix. Kenzie figured he'd have turned blue right about now. "The captain wants to tell you something."

Kenzie brightened.

"You're fired," said Dash.

Kenzie deflated slightly.

"Get up here," he continued.

"Coming," she said.

She stepped back into the center of the cargo bay, climbing through the web of thick cables connecting the breach shields lining the walls. The cables all snaked back into a port in the wall separating the bay from the engine room. Kenzie had overheard Captain Drake giving Vor orders to prepare the bay for their arrival—but she didn't think Dash had expected him to connect the shields into the ship's reactor itself.

And it was brilliant work. The shields were placed nearly perfectly, and between the power of the reactor and their fine-tuned frequencies, the cargo bay wasn't much worse for the experience. Even the chalzz pen was still sealed tight, though the cargo stacks had lost six or seven boxes during Kenzie and Jo's dramatic entrance. The fallen crates were scattered on the floor, and one had sprung a leak. Something orange oozed out— but that was a problem for later.

Kenzie helped Jo up, and they walked to the lift, the ship vibrating and bucking under their feet. She wrote a few more lines on her Academy application in her head: successful application of emergency salvage techniques; contact with hostile alien species; advanced application of physics and propulsion systems.

She smiled.

"Any landing you can walk away from is a good one," she said. "Drake, 102."

"Oh, shut up," said Jo.

The pair met Vor in the lift. The brother-sister reunion played out just as it had when the crew found Vor in the Forgers' workshop on Technica Outpost—only this time it was Jo's turn to be hugged into submission. Moments later, he quickly hugged Kenzie too.

In the cockpit, Jo and Vor took chairs behind Squix, while Kenzie took her seat behind the captain, who looked pretty sweaty. In fairness, he'd had a rough couple days.

The stars in the viewport whirled as Dash piloted the *Gremlin* furiously. The large blue-brown planet she first saw when she discovered the *Valor* grew larger by the moment as the ship flew further from the megacruiser's final resting place.

Squix kept feeding the ship's computer new escape vectors, causing the main and maneuvering thrusters to fire in patterns unpredictable enough to keep the Frawgs from scoring too many hits. But based on how often the ship shook and shimmied from blaster fire, it didn't appear to be going super well.

Kenzie knew what she had to do.

"I gotta refuel the Dart and go back out there," she said to the back of the captain's head.

He barked out a laugh, but he didn't seem to think anything was actually funny.

"Are you kidding?" said Squix.

"You're insane," said Jo, slumped in the next chair.

Vor gave her a thumbs down.

Kenzie stuck out her chin. "I can take them!"

Dash sighed, his shoulders sagging.

"I'm sure you probably could," he said. "But that's not happening. One of my goals with this gig is to make sure all cadets live to the end of the trip—"

He threw the *Gremlin* into another dive. Kenzie's stomach lurched.

"—no matter how determined some of them are to do otherwise."

Kenzie bit her lip. She kept forgetting how selfless he was.

Jo spoke up. "Okay. What about weapons? We have guns on this thing, right?"

Dash's shoulders unslumped.

"Oh, yeah," he said. "It's been so long since I've needed them, I forgot we—"

"—don't have them," Squix interrupted.

"What?"

"Sorry," said Squix, turning green. "It was in the damage report. From before. Did you read it yet?"

Dash's shoulders reslumped.

"I knew I forgot something," he said. Vor stood and ran from the cockpit. Dash didn't notice.

"I'm open to suggestions here," said the captain.

"Have we considered just talking to the Frawgs?" asked Squix. "Maybe we should find out what they want. Maybe we could give it to them!"

"They want to eat us," said Jo.

Dash threw an exasperated hand into the air. "Oh, of *course* they do!"

"I retract my suggestion," said Squix.

"Kenzie," said Dash, sparing her glance. "I need you to tap that creative weirdo juice right about now."

"What?" she said.

"Look, I don't know how your brain is wired, but you have…unconventional ideas. I need one now. One that doesn't involve you actually leaving the ship again, and one that might actually get us out of this not exploded."

"Or eaten," added Squix.

"Or eaten," agreed Dash.

Kenzie swelled with pride. This was her moment. Finally. She was ready.

She leaned forward. "We have to get down to the old colony," she said, pointing at the blue-brown planet growing in the viewport. "And I know just how we can —"

"Look out!" Squix cried, as an angry, angular Forger ship rocketed into view from below. It barreled straight at them.

The captain pulled up and the *Gremlin* veered away from the threat. He pitched the ship port, then starboard.

"Well," said Dash through gritted teeth, "I guess the Forgers don't watch the news after all…"

"Where'd they come from?!" said Squix, tentacles flailing. He was practically neon pink.

"I think," started Dash, before letting out a heavy sigh. "I think I spotted them earlier. After the Frawgs started chasing us, I saw something in the distance."

"How'd they even find us way out here?" asked Jo, clearly freaking out. Kenzie had a theory.

"They must've sent scouts after us when we left Technica," Kenzie reasoned. "They saw our heading when we jumped away, and now they've found us."

"Well this is just great," said Dash, cutting main thrusters and throwing the *Gremlin* into another spin so he could see who was chasing them now. "This is just—"

Through the viewport, they saw the Forger ship dominating the Frawgs, delivering precise blaster strikes against the pirate vessel.

"—great?"

The *Gremlin* completed its revolution, and Dash pointed it away from the scene of the battle. He kicked on the thrusters.

"Why are they attacking the Frawgs?" asked Jo. Kenzie didn't hesitate with her answer, still kind of annoyed at having had her big moment interrupted.

"Maybe we're more valuable to them alive," she said. "Could be there's a reward for us…and how can you claim a reward if all you've got is a bunch of spaceship bits? They need proof, and that means taking us prisoner."

"Beats getting eaten," said Dash.

The display hanging above his head sprang to life. Suddenly, Dash's usual ship-system datastreams were replaced with Vor standing amid dusty consoles. He was patching in from the weapons control room, where tangles of sparking cables snaked about the room.

Kenzie and the others watched as Vor pointed to a nearby tactical display, which, under the dirt and grime from years of disuse, was surprisingly not-broken-looking. Vor had gotten the other two ships in the tactical system's sights.

Squix checked his console's readings. "Full power to the weapons?"

"Fire!" yelled Dash, punching a fist into the air.

Vor slammed his free hand onto a big green button under his tactical display.

The long-dormant laser turret mounted on top of the *Gremlin*'s hull suddenly roared back to life. The *Gremlin* bucked to one side as the cockpit walls hummed.

Kenzie saw the fight break up on Vor's display as a green beam of energy slashed between the two enemy ships. A moment later, the Forgers went after the Frawgs again. The two ships shrank as the *Gremlin* escaped, apparently forgotten in the heat of their battle.

"Fire!" yelled Jo.

"Yeah, fire!" echoed Dash, who angled the ship toward the planet.

"No, I mean fire!"

Dash looked back at the display—sure enough, Vor's console had produced a small flame. He tried batting it out with his hands.

"Uh, no more power to the weapons," reported Squix.

The display's connection to the weapons room went dead. Jo unstrapped herself, grabbed a fire extinguisher, and ran from the cockpit.

"Well," said Dash, sitting back in his chair. "Next stop, the abandoned ghost colony on that planet right there."

"Think anyone's down there?" asked Squix.

"Probably not," said Kenzie. "The Aphids turned the colony into a wasteland."

"Whatever we find down there," said Dash, "it's got to be better than these stupid pirates."

More Pirates

Dash had started to relax as he piloted the *Gremlin* through the planet's atmosphere, heading for the ruins of Sheaffer Colony so they could search for abandoned tech or supplies. A place that used to have so many people—there had to be something salvagable, right?

The interference that had rendered his ship's sensors useless in space wasn't an issue down here on the planet. As he scanned the planet's surface, suddenly four flying security pods—each roughly the size and shape of a hippo, but considerably faster and pointier and also with guns—appeared on his scope and started shooting.

"Okay," said Kenzie from behind him. "So I guess there's more pirates here."

"You think?" Dash yelled as he jerked the ship hard to port.

The Frawgs' tribal colors—green, red, and purple—covered the pods, and throaty croaks and grunts filled their comm traffic. Great—more of these guys. Dash didn't think the pirates were happy to see visitors. Or maybe they were really happy. Cannibal space pirates were tough to read like that.

"Where'd they come from?" cried Squix, his tentacles whipping frantically across his control console. "I thought you said this planet was deserted!"

"It was," said Kenzie in her seat. Dash looked back at her and saw her typing at the computer console to her left. "Uh...looks like it's not anymore."

"That's not super helpful," said Dash.

The ship shook as its combat shields partially absorbed the pods' blasts. Dash's vision blurred as his seat vibrated. Looking out his viewport, he could see the ruined landscape of the former Sheaffer Colony. Under a slate gray sky, burned out husks of collapsed buildings and houses sprawled out below—rubble surrounded by dirt, ash, and scraps of grass and shrubs. In the distance he saw the shape of what looked like a mountain riddled with dark cracks.

He flew the *Gremlin* into the ruined city's heart, hoping to lose his pursuers among the skeletons of buildings jutting out from the ground. Twisting around a crumbling highrise, diving under a highway overpass, Dash did all he could to shake them. He wasn't having much luck––the Frawgs simply flew above the city and shot at them from further away. There was no obvious place to hide and regroup.

Dash punched a few buttons on his console, and the weapons control room appeared on his display. Well, it was supposed to be the weapons control room—it was hard to tell, because of all the smoke.

"Jo," he said, sending the ship into a spin to throw off the pods' targeting systems. Blaster fire whizzed past the viewport.

The cadet's head came into view, fanning her hand in front of her face to clear away the haze.

"Yeah," she coughed.

"Status?" said Dash.

"Uh…" She looked behind her and gave a half-shrug. "Not currently on fire."

"Not currently?" asked Squix.

"Yeah," said Jo. "We were on fire. Now we're not." A jet of foam sprayed out behind her, as Vor appeared with the extinguisher she'd brought into the room minutes earlier. "So, pretty much not on fire. Currently."

While trying to dodge another barrage of blasts, Dash veered a little further to the left than he'd wanted. The *Gremlin* clipped the side of a building and nearly spun out. Dash wrestled with the helm and kept the ship aloft. He spoke through gritted teeth. "I don't know if you noticed, but we're being shot at."

"What, again?" she said.

"Sounds like she didn't notice, Cap," said Squix.

Dash ignored him. "I need you and Vor to get the weapons back online."

Vor dropped the fire extinguisher with a loud clang. His mouthless face, covered in soot, filled the display. He flashed Dash a double thumbs down, shook his head, and cut the connection.

"Guess that's a no," said Squix.

"I should help them," said Kenzie.

"Stay here and try to use our computers to disrupt their weapons," said Dash. "Is that a thing you can do? Do one of those things!"

Before Kenzie could answer, Squix cried out in surprise.

"Whoa!" he said, flashing green. "Sensors getting a huge energy spike from…there." He pointed a spare tentacle toward the mountains in the distance.

"That makes sense," said Kenzie. "This colony was one of Earthspace's biggest quadronium mining operations. Before the formation of the Interstellar Alliance, of course."

"Of course," said Dash, pretending to understand why that detail should've been obvious.

As they flew closer, Dash discovered that what he'd thought were cracks in the rock face was actually a web of metal platforms and cables. It was a mining rig—with a dark opening in the center.

"Kenzie," he said. "Quadronium mines—big tunnels or small tunnels?"

"What?"

"The tunnels!" Dash repeated. "Big or small? Quick!"

"Uh, um," Kenzie stammered, "big?"

"Hope you're right." Dash aimed the ship for the opening.

"Oh boy," said Squix.

"Hey! I have an idea!" yelled Kenzie. Dash glanced backward and saw her plug her handset into the computer console. "If I connect my echo-locater program to the ship's external sensors, we can map the mine!"

"I told you to hack those pods, not—" Dash started. The black mouth of the mine grew larger in the viewport as the *Gremlin* rocketed towards it. "—actually, yeah. Do it."

More blaster bolts whizzed by as Dash bobbed and weaved. A few struck home, and the ship shook each time. After the fifth hit, a warning light flashed on his console.

"Shields are gone!" Squix cried. "Our butt's in trouble!"

"We took too many hits back in space," said Dash. "If we can't shake these things soon…"

Kenzie typed at her station. Dash wasn't sure what connecting the program to the ship's sensors entailed, but he figured he probably wouldn't understand if he asked her to explain it. So he didn't.

"Almost there," she said.

The ship was nearly inside the mountain's maw, and blaster bolts struck all around the mining equipment lining the cave's entrance.

"Kenzie…" said Dash.

The dark of the mine swallowed the *Gremlin*. Dash saw on his scope that the pods were still on their tail.

Squix shouted: "Look out!"

Dash looked up and saw a vast rock wall filling the viewport. He grabbed the throttle and pulled it all the way back, killing the ship's forward propulsion. He tapped a button on his console and maxed out the braking thrusters to keep the ship from turning into jelly. Pushing the helm as hard as he could, he angled the ships' nose down and pushed the throttle back up again, switching the braking thrusters off simultaneously.

The *Gremlin* rocketed down into the mine like a bullet fired from a gun. Dash sunk into his chair while the ship's outer hull scraped against the mine wall.

One of the pods wasn't as lucky. Dash saw the red dot disappear from his scope as it slammed into the wall and showered debris down on them. The other three fired their own braking thrusters in time and pivoted to keep up the pursuit.

A few more taps from Kenzie's keyboard. "Connected!"

"Scanning," said Squix.

The tunnel that brought him into the mine was big after all—just big enough for Dash to avoid smashing the *Gremlin* to bits, as long as he didn't make any wrong moves. After a half-kilometer, Dash saw the tunnel curve to the left and jerked the helm to follow it. The ship only briefly bottomed out, and he paid for his mistake with his spine.

"Hull integrity at eighty-five percent," said Squix, trying and failing to keep calm.

Dash saw dozens of paths open before him, each potentially helping them escape the pods—or leading to a dead end, where he and the rest of the crew might become smears of goo. He looked up at his display and saw Kenzie's program was working. He had a detailed view of the tunnel network, its various crisscrossings and intersections. He had plenty of information to choose a path. Too bad he had no idea where to go.

The three dots on his scope were getting closer.

"I've got multiple signals from ship transponders about two kilometers away," said Kenzie behind him. "At least two-dozen, all different makes and years."

"There are *more* ships in here?" cried Squix.

Dash noticed the collar of his jumpsuit sticking to his neck. He was drenched with sweat.

"Which tunnel do I take?"

Kenzie poked her head over his shoulder and pointed to a spot through viewport.

"That way," she said. "Third tunnel from the right."

Dash aimed the *Gremlin* right for it.

"And this will take us away from those signals?" asked Dash.

"Nope—we're heading right for them."

Squix's tentacles stood out straight in panic. "What?!"

Dash looked at her. "Kenzie!"

She didn't miss a beat. "Trust me, Captain."

The *Gremlin* rocketed through the third tunnel from the right.

"Not much choice now," said Dash, trying to keep his anger in check. He'd have time to yell at her later. Probably.

Kenzie sat back in her chair, and Dash heard her tapping at her console. Squix started navigating beside him.

"Left here," he said, "now a right…quick left and the tunnel dips down some more."

Dash followed the cavern's twists with Squix's help. With each turn, he glanced at his scope and saw the three pods keeping pace.

"Got one," said Kenzie, clacking at her console.

"Got one what?" said Dash.

"A Frawg pod."

Dash glanced at his scope: one of the red dots suddenly turned green.

"Kenzie? What—" He looked back and saw something weird on her console's screen. It was the *Gremlin*—its rear, at least. "Is that us?"

"Yup," she said. "I'm controlling one of their ships." Then she added, "This is so cool."

Dash turned frontwards and veered the ship up to keep from slamming into an outcropping of rock. He heard Kenzie type a series of commands.

"Uh," said Kenzie suddenly. "Whoops."

Dash looked back at his scope and saw the green dot stop in midair—forcing a collision with the red dot behind it.

Suddenly, the entire cavern shook. Rocks and rubble fell from the cave's walls as the *Gremlin* zoomed toward a fork in the path. Dash jerked the helm right to avoid a boulder falling from above.

"Was that an explosion?!" Squix cried. He turned back to the viewport. "Is the cave exploding? Agh! Left!"

Dash veered left, then looked back at Kenzie's console and saw the display was static.

"So," said Kenzie. "Looks like the colonists didn't strip this mine of all of its quadronium."

"And you forgot to mention it's explosive," said Dash.

"Yes," she said. "Also, I broke my Frawg pod. And possibly this computer console."

Dash looked up at his display and saw the cavern they'd just traversed was now blocked off behind them—the explosion had caused a cave-in. The one red dot left was stalled, but Dash saw it resuming its pursuit via a different path.

Still, at least he finally had some distance so he could plan his next move. Though, as it happened, Kenzie had already done that for him.

"Over that way—make this next right," she said, leaning over his shoulder again.

Squix shook his head. "My map says the exit's this way—we hafta take a left!"

"Don't go left," Kenzie insisted. "The pod will catch up to us before we make it out," she said. "Take this right, toward the transponders!"

Dash looked at Squix. Squix shrugged four sets of shoulders.

"Trust me!" Kenzie said.

He flew right.

The tunnel sloped downward and widened out. Soon, the *Gremlin* flew into a large cavern without any immediately apparent exit, except for the way they'd just flown in. On the ground sat a sea of old ships—about two dozen of them. They'd all seen much better days.

"It's a graveyard," she said. "This is where the pirates take whatever's left of the ships they capture." Kenzie pointed to a bare spot on the edge of the heap while using her other hand to enter commands on her handset. "Down there." Then, out of the corner of his eye, Dash saw her talking into her handset. "Keep quiet a minute, okay?"

"Me?" said Dash. "Or Jo?"

"Both," said Kenzie. "Everyone."

Dash set the *Gremlin* down with a thud. Kenzie pocketed her handset then reached over him and quickly entered commands on his console.

"Hey!"

"Shh!"

He heard a hiss come from the rear of the ship—she'd just released the *Gremlin*'s spare coolant into its reactor.

"Why are you—"

Before he could finish, Kenzie grabbed the large ignition dial handle in the center of the console between him and Squix. She clicked it counterclockwise with a loud *clank*, and all the lights went dark. Dash's display was blank. The deep, constant hum of the ship's engines was gone. Kenzie had turned off the ship's reactor entirely.

"Quiet," she whispered.

Dash looked around the darkened cockpit. He was about to ask what was supposed to happen next when it happened.

Through the viewport, Dash saw a single beam of light emerge from the mouth of the pitch-dark cavern. The last remaining Frawg pod.

He looked at Kenzie, but her large brown eyes—made nearly black by the ship's darkness—were fixed on the hovering pod.

Dash turned back to see it looming over the ship graveyard, sweeping its light along each long-dead vessel's hull. He felt a tap on his shoulder—Kenzie. She put a finger over her mouth, then pointed to the space underneath his console. Without waiting for a reply, she folded herself underneath and hid. He and Squix followed.

Moments later, Dash saw the light from the pod illuminate the cockpit in an eerie white glow. His already quick heartbeat grew even faster. His pulse thundered in his ears.

How had he gotten here? Hiding in the dark, in a ship graveyard, on some forgotten planet overrun with pirate cannibals... How did this become his life?

After an eternity, the light moved away. Dash contorted and peeked out over his console. The beam of light slowly flew out of the cavern.

Dash let out a breath he hadn't realized he was holding. They were safe.

Then, there was a loud bang. Dash almost fell over—someone was knocking at the cockpit door.

Kenzie grabbed the ignition dial and clanked it clockwise. With the reactor humming again, dim light shone in the cockpit once more.

The cadet ran to the door and opened it to reveal Jo, her usual annoyed expression firmly in place.

"Are we dead yet?" she asked.

Dash slumped in his seat with a whump. He sighed.

"Not currently," he said.

Extras

14

Huddled together outside the *Gremlin*, Kenzie and the rest of the crew activated the small rescue lights embedded into the shoulders of their jumpsuits. Usually those lights were meant to help identify lost crewmembers during rescue operations in space. But they were pretty handy for rooting around busted old spaceships in a dark cave too.

The lamps provided small circles of light, revealing only some of the broken vessels around them. Outside those circles: total black. The walls of the cavern were effectively invisible. Amid the ocean of darkness, Kenzie felt like her crew was a small raft of light. If any of them strayed too far, they might all drown in the underground night.

The cavern felt damp and cold on Kenzie's skin, though all she tasted was the stale, recycled oxygen of her respirator. While the planet was habitable, sensors found all kinds of noxious stuff floating in the cavern air, from quadronium dust to microscopic xephu spores. Doctor Bill was excited to hear about those. He told them that, if inhaled, the spores would make their lungs turn inside out. So Kenzie packed a few extra respirators, just in case. Squix didn't even need one, since his exosuit let him breathe from built-in tanks of water while he was on land.

On her handset, Kenzie scrolled through the list of ships the *Gremlin*'s sensors had identified when they entered the cave. "Okay, I see a few salvage possibilities. The problem," she said, looking at the others, "is we actually need a lot of stuff, and that means we need to hit a lot of ships."

Captain Drake waved an oblong, cracked piece of machinery with a tail of frayed cords. "Think we'll be able to find a replacement for, uh, this?"

Vor leaned in for a closer look. Squix's light pointed off into the distance—he looked worn out and wasn't paying attention.

"What is that?" asked Jo.

"I don't know," said Dash. "I think it's, uh…" Dash rotated it in his hands. In the dim lamplight Kenzie saw his hands were covered in something dark and viscous. "I think it's an oily…flange. Thing."

There was a pause while everyone waited for him to continue.

"Look, the ship told me it's broken, so I figured if I brought it with me, we could, y'know…"

Another pause.

"Find another thing. That looks like *this* thing."

Kenzie put her hand on her chin. "Pretty sure that's the jump-phase stabilizer." She scrolled through her list. "There are a few ships here that might have what we're looking for."

That's when *it* happened.

It didn't matter that she and her shipmates were marooned inside a highly explosive mine, pursued by cannibals in flying, laser-shooting pods, and on the run from an evil race of alien warmongers with a mysterious and dangerous plan they knew little to nothing about, and that everything hinged on some kind of enigmatic and probably very powerful crystal something-or-other that she and the rest of the crew were no closer to discovering.

No, in that moment, Kenzie wasn't worried about any of that. She simply felt joy.

Because *it* happened.

Captain Drake said five words. The most perfect words:

"Alright, Kenzie. Lead the way."

Then Jo kind of ruined the moment.

"What? Really? Her?"

"Uh, yeah," said Dash. "Why not?"

"Well, aren't you, like, the captain?"

Dash coughed.

"Yeah—I mean, yes," he said. "I'm, y'know. Delegating. It's a thing captains do. Right Squix?"

"Huh?" said Squix, turning his light toward the captain. "Sorry, I wasn't listening."

Dash sighed, closed his eyes, and went to pinch the bridge of his nose. His fingers hit the clear respirator mask instead, instantly smudging it with the oil on his hands.

"Oh, come on," he said, his eyes crossing as they focused on the smears in front of his face.

"Don't worry, Captain," said Kenzie, reaching into her satchel. "I brought extras."

* * *

For two hours, the crew collected nearly every part they needed. There was no shortage of battered cargo ships littering the junkyard—they were apparently a favorite target of the Frawgs, with their combination of valuable goods they could sell and the hard-working crews they could eat. Kenzie tried not to think about the crewmembers that staffed these ships and how they ultimately wound up devoured at some kind of communal pirate luncheon. Instead, she tried focusing on the task at hand.

They'd salvaged a new laser energy matrix for the weapons systems, a sturdier pair of reactor induction coils, a few replacement motherboards and grandmotherboards for malfunctioning consoles, a few tanks of shield gel, and even a jump-phase stabilizer. They'd found that last part in the lower decks of an Aphid cargo carrier with a missing back half. When they did, Dash just tossed the old stabilizer onto the floor. It landed on the deck with a loud clang that made the captain smile.

That left one item on their list: a nav-computer to replace the one they'd fried in their escape from Technica Outpost. And also the one Kenzie had thrown at the pirates chasing her and Jo on the *Valor*. She never realized nav-computers could be so much trouble.

Kenzie checked her list and found a nearby Alliance shuttle that might be a good match for the *Gremlin*'s systems.

She waved her handset above her head, its light a signal in the darkness.

"Almost done, guys," she said. She pointed at the shuttle a few meters away and started walking. "That's the one."

"Finally," said Jo. "I can't wait to get back to, like, civilization."

"Yeah," said Dash, following Kenzie out of the cargo carrier. "This trip needs to end."

Kenzie, a few steps short of the shuttle's hatch, stopped in her tracks. "What?"

Dash walked past and put his hand on the hatch's handle. "I said, 'this trip needs to end.' I need to get you kids home already."

Kenzie ran to catch up to Dash and faced him in front of the shuttle entrance. "What do you mean? We're supposed to be on the *Gremlin* for two weeks."

"Uh-huh," said Dash.

"It's only been—" Kenzie thought a second. She couldn't remember the last time she slept. All this faster-than-light travel and running for their lives was confusing. "How long has it been?"

"Exactly," said Dash. "Long enough. Your parents are all probably freaking out. I mean, they said on the news that we died."

"But—um—I mean," said Kenzie, her gaze darting around in the darkness in search of an argument. "I mean, we've still got missions to complete."

"We do?" said Squix, who'd caught up to Dash and Kenzie at the shuttle.

Jo and Vor joined them.

"I'm pretty sure we actually don't," said Jo.

"Yeah, we do! We've got that cargo to deliver, plus we need to get the chalzz out of the cargo bay while it's still alive," she said, listing each item on her fingers.

"I wouldn't say those are 'missions,' *per se*," Dash interjected, crossing his arms.

Kenzie continued, undaunted.

"Then there's figuring out what's going on with that crystal the Forgers want, figuring out why they sabotaged the jump-beacon and stole Technica Outpost—"

"Stop right there," said Dash. "Just stop."

Kenzie put her hands down.

"Look, I know you've been having a great time with all this—" Dash waved a hand in the air. "—craziness. I get that. But those aren't missions. Half of those are just, y'know, jobs. And the other half aren't even any kind of anything."

"But the Forgers are after us," said Kenzie. When she heard her own voice, she was disappointed at how much it sounded like whining.

"Which is all the more reason to get you back with your folks and cut this trip short. Getting shot at by aliens and high-speed chases aren't really my usual scene. I'm kinda out of my depth here."

"But—but—" Kenzie stammered. "You're Captain Dash Drake! You're the hero of Gantoid IV!"

Dash scrunched his face like he'd just sucked a lemon.

"Ugh, don't remind me," he said.

Kenzie tried to think of what she could say next when Dash opened the hatch and walked into the shuttle's dimly lit cockpit. Kenzie followed, about to launch her next argument, but she lost her train of thought as soon as she laid eyes on what was in front of her.

It was a man, cuffed by the arm to a console in the shuttle's cockpit. Thin with dark skin, he had wide brown eyes, curly black hair, and he wore the uniform of an Interstellar Alliance lieutenant.

On the other side of the cockpit sat another man, cuffed to another console by the arm. This one wore a tattered jumpsuit that wasn't from the Alliance. More puzzling, however, was his face: equally divided between green flesh and silver metal, a small patch of white hair atop his head. He was asleep.

The Alliance lieutenant looked up as they entered, and his face broke into a smile.

"Captain Drake!" he said, beaming. "You've come to rescue me!"

Dash blinked at him.

"What's that, now?" he said.

Ravi and Twince

Dash stared dumbly as the crew filed in behind him, crowding the doorway as they took in the scene themselves.

Jo sighed and shut the hatch. "Now, who's this guy?"

"I knew it," the Alliance officer continued. "I just knew you were alive. When I detected that old reactor's energy signature, I knew it had to be yours. I knew you couldn't be dead! Who else but the daring Captain Dash Drake would fly a ship with such an antiquated reactor?"

Dash felt his mouth twist, and he crossed his arms.

"Who—" Dash looked at Kenzie, cleared his throat, then looked back at the officer. "What are you doing here? Who are you?"

"Oh, how rude of me," said the man, smiling. "I'm Ravi—Lieutenant Ravi Sidana, science officer on the *LAS Concordance*. I followed your ship's energy signature from the former site of Technica Outpost. And I've found you!"

"Well, technically," Squix said, taking his place next to Dash, "we found you."

"Of course," said Ravi, nodding and using his free hand to pretend-smack himself in the forehead. "You have found me! And I'm grateful for that and excited for you to help me get out of, well, this."

He pointed at the metal tube surrounding half his left arm and effectively kept him stuck to a console.

From the other end of the cockpit, the half-metal man stirred and quietly grunted. He blinked his non-mechanical eye as he shook off the last remnants of sleep. His other eye—a cybernetic prosthetic—pulsed and glowed red as he regained consciousness.

He'd been so surprised to find these people—any people—in the belly of a semi-abandoned quadronium mine, Dash hadn't gotten a good look at them. But now that he actually took a moment to see this other man, a flash of white-hot anger washed over the back of his head.

It couldn't be. Not *this* guy.

"Ah, and this is my friend—well, not actually my friend, more of a co-prisoner sort of thing; it's a little embarrassing to tell you the truth—"

Dash interrupted Ravi, narrowing his eyes at the other man.

"Twince."

"Drake," said the half-metal man. Dash noticed Squix felt similarly about the unexpected reunion. He'd turned a shade of bright red and put two tentacles on what would've been his hips.

"Fantastic," said Ravi. "You know each other!"

"Oh, I know Twince alright," he said, turning to the cyborg. "I thought I recognized your unique stink when I walked in here."

"You're wearing a gas mask, Drake," said Twince.

"That's—" Dash exhaled hard, then took off his respirator and handed it to Kenzie. "Shut up." He turned to Ravi while the crew stowed their own respirators. "What are you doing here with *that* guy? What are you doing here at all?"

"It's a funny story," said Ravi, smiling, "I was dispatched as part of an investigative task force to determine the causes Technica Outpost's disappearance. Things are pretty crazy back in Alliance space, let me tell you. The Governing Council held emergency meetings to put new security measures in place in star systems across the galaxy. They're finally moving forward with the jump-chains initiative to increase security on all member worlds. Force fields, large-scale energy consumption, a remote reactor hub orbiting IA Prime, and a tremendous expansion of the Alliance's authoritative powers on member planets…"

Ravi sighed wistfully.

"Really, I was reading about it shortly before we arrived here, and the broad implications for limiting individual worlds' ability to regulate their own security measures sounds terribly fascinating—"

"Uh, lieutenant," Dash interrupted. He gestured at Twince, who had an expression on the non-metal half of his face that said he'd heard about these terribly fascinating new developments more than a few times already.

"Ah, yes," said Ravi, grinning. "Anyway, while I was investigating the jump-beacon explosion and the disappearance of the outpost, I happened across our mutual friend floating in an escape pod, unconscious! I checked Alliance records, seeing that Mr. Twince here has a bit of a- -"

Dash interrupted. "Reputation for assaulting people, damaging their vessels, and stealing their cargo?"

"—checkered past," said Ravi, still smiling. "So naturally, I brought him aboard with plans to take him into custody. That's about when I detected the energy signature from your reactor, followed it to this sector, and, well…"

Ravi waved his one free hand in front of him, implying that, yes, of course, they knew exactly what happened next. Dash assumed he meant, "and then some pirates disabled my ship and took us prisoner."

"How come they didn't eat you?" asked Kenzie.

"A wonderful question," said Ravi. "They said I was 'too skinny.'" He did an air-quote with his free hand.

"Can you believe that? Finally, this slight frame pays off!" Ravi chuckled. "They promised to stuff me full of food to fatten me up before I'm to be devoured. So, I've got some meals to look forward to, eh?"

Everyone looked to Twince.

"I don't taste good," was all he said.

"Shocker," said Dash, rolling his eyes. "Kenzie, Vor, get Lieutenant Sidana out of that thing. Squix and Jo, salvage that nav-computer so we can leave already."

Kenzie gestured toward Twince, who was looking at her. "What about—"

"Nope," said Dash, shaking his head.

Kenzie approached Ravi while Vor grabbed a multitool from his pocket. She furrowed her brow and bit her lip nervously as she tapped a few commands on her handset.

"Try it," she said.

Vor jammed his multitool into the cuff that held Ravi's left arm. Vor twisted and strained, putting his foot up on the console to try and get some leverage, but the cuff didn't budge.

"Hey, good try," Ravi said, still smiling. "You'll get it soon!"

Dash spent the next ten minutes watching Kenzie trying to hack the cuff's software with no luck. She explained the problem: it was a hodgepodge of Alliance security programs crossed with whatever malware the Frawgs had cooked up in their demented IT labs. Every time she circumvented one security measure, another appeared and locked her out again, meaning she'd have to start over from scratch.

Vor, meanwhile, did everything he could to break through the cuff's hardware. But considering his skill for taking stuff apart, this piece of technology presented a major challenge. It was a tangle of metal and wires, not to mention electrodes and needles connected to some kind of toxin. It was a puzzle, and a particularly dangerous one. If Vor had a mouth, Dash imagined it'd be cursing.

Meanwhile, Jo was only a few meters away, and she actually was cursing—a lot—as she and Squix tried to free the shuttle's nav-computer from its housing. It wasn't going well.

"Seriously, this is not helpful," Jo said toward the rear of the cockpit. "Instead of pointing at things and telling me to pull it, why not, like, actually help me pull?"

Squix turned green, then red, and waved three tentacles frantically. "These are delicate—they're not for pulling! And pointing is what they're really good at!"

"Gimme a break," said Jo.

"I don't even have a skeleton! You're made of rocks! Why is this even an argument?"

As they bickered, Dash leaned against the far wall, his arms in their usual crossed position.

He wanted to keep his attention focused on Twince.

And Twince just looked back at him. The staring contest went on for a while until Dash broke the silence.

"You owe us fifty-thousand credits." Dash leveled a finger at him. "You jerk."

Twince grinned. "Send me a bill."

Squix piped up from the rear of the cockpit. "We did!" Then, quieter, "That guy is the worst."

Dash glared at Twince. The cyborg just shook his head.

"You lied to us. And you almost killed us," Dash continued. "Do you have any idea how much damage you did to my ship?"

"Oh, stop whining," Twince said with a sneer. "You knew who you were dealing with when you took the job. Besides, you didn't die."

Dash curled his lip and felt his eyebrows slam together. "I'm only allowed to be mad if I die?"

"Pretty much," said Twince.

Dash pinched the bridge of his nose. It was practically involuntary.

"What were even you doing at Technica Outpost?" he demanded, waving a hand in the air.

"Just looking for a job, same as always," said Twince. "I was on Level Three, trying to contact one of my old buyers."

"Was it Joey Rats?"

"Maybe," he said. "Why?"

"He owes us sixty-thousand," said Dash, leaning back against the wall again. He shot a look at Kenzie. "And I really could've used the money."

"If I may interject," Ravi said gently. "I have reason to believe that our mechanical acquaintance may not be telling the truth. In fact, he may have actually had something to do with Technica Outpost's disappearance."

"And I'm telling you—again—I didn't," Twince spat. "I'm looking for my buyer and suddenly the place starts shaking, everything goes bananas, there's crazies in red armor everywhere rounding people up. So I haul my butt into the nearest escape pod."

The green half of Twince's face went pale while his red eye narrowed to a pinpoint.

"I'm tellin' you—it was the Forgers," he said.

Ravi laughed, shaking his head. "I'm so sorry. Here he goes again about the Forgers."

Still smiling, he used his free hand to mime his mock-panic. "Ah! The Forgers! The Forgers blew up that jump-beacon! The Forgers made the outpost disappear! The Forgers raised fuel prices and they've infiltrated the government!"

"Actually," said Kenzie, who looked from Dash to Twince to Vor and back to Ravi, "the Forgers did kinda do all that." She paused for a second, reconsidering. "Well, the first two for sure. We were there."

Ravi's eyes went wide—and he finally stopped smiling. "Really?"

"I told you," said Twince. He nodded at Kenzie. "This kid gets it."

Ravi looked at Dash.

"Yeah," Dash sighed, looking at the ceiling. "He's telling the truth. For once."

"Incredible!" Ravi said, his smile returning. "That's wonderful news—well," he gestured at Twince, "wonderful news for you. It appears our civilization may once again be on the brink of annihilation. But you're in the clear, Twince!"

Twince trained his glowing red eye at the once-again-grinning Ravi. "What a relief."

"That's not all," said Kenzie. "The Forgers figured out some way to achieve dimensional jump." Vor looked up from Ravi's cuff to nod at him. Once more, Dash felt like the dumbest person in the room.

Ravi's smile disappeared again, this time replaced with a look of genuine puzzlement. "What?"

"It's true! That's how they took Technica Outpost," Kenzie said, her voice's pitch rising with excitement. "They've been chasing us ever since—we just got away from a Forger scout that followed us here from Technica, same as you. They're after us. Us and some crystal."

"A crystal?" asked Ravi.

"Not this again," said Dash. This was the last direction the conversation needed to go in.

Kenzie punched new commands into her handset as she talked. "We're not sure where it is, or even what it is, but we know they're looking for it, so it must be important."

"The crystal," Twince whispered from his seat on the other side of the cockpit. "It can't be…"

The cyborg's gaze fixed on the cadet.

"What d'you know about the crystal?" Twince said. Dash heard a sound not unlike panic in his voice.

"I—I don't really know much," she stammered.

"The Forgers," Twince continued, "they're looking for it? You said they're looking for the crystal—but that means they don't know where it is yet, right?"

Vor stopped working and stood up straight, looking from Twince to Kenzie and back again.

"I guess not…" said Kenzie.

Twince looked at Dash.

"You have to take me with you," he said.

"Uh-huh."

"I'm serious, Drake. I can take you to the crystal."

"I don't want to go to the crystal," said Dash.

"You know what it is?" asked Kenzie.

"It's an artifact of immense power," said Twince.

"Stop talking," said Dash to Twince.

"And you'll take us to it?" asked Kenzie.

"Stop talking," said Dash again, this time to Kenzie.

"I will—just get me out of this," said Twince.

"Shut up!" Dash yelled as he marched toward Twince. "You," he said, jabbing a finger in the cyborg's face, "stop annoying my cadet. She has a hard enough time focusing on tasks I give her as it is."

Next, he pointed back at Kenzie.

"You. Get Ravi out of that thing. And stop talking to this dummy about—" Dash did a voice. "—'artifacts of immense power.'"

Suddenly, Kenzie's eyes lit up, almost as if a switch went on in her brain. Dash had grown to recognize that look. It usually offered a fifty-fifty chance of either ruining his day or saving his butt. He wondered which side of the coin this one would land on as she put her hand on her chin.

"Power…" she said. "Immense power…"

"Uh?" said Dash.

Kenzie looked at Ravi.

"You're breathing right now," she said.

"I am," he replied, then took a deep, theatrical breath. "It's literally what I was born to do." He smirked. "That's a little science officer joke."

Kenzie looked up, then pointed at the lights, which cast a dim glow throughout the shuttle's cockpit.

"The lights are on," Kenzie said.

"I think Kenzie's broken," yelled Jo from the rear of the cockpit.

"Ravi," continued Kenzie, "when the Frawgs captured you, did they damage your shuttle's reactor?"

"No," he said. He started counting on his free hand's fingers: "Only my shields, my hull, my engines, my primary weapons, my secondary weapons, auxiliary sensors…" Ravi stopped and realized he'd have needed his other hand out of the cuff to keep counting. He shook his head wistfully. "Wow, sounds like we really took a beating there! I am not good at fighting pirates!"

"But the reactor wasn't damaged," she said, "and it's still online."

Dash was getting frustrated. "What are you getting at, Kenzie?"

Kenzie started tapping away excitedly on her handset again.

"Sorry, sorry…it's just that every time we try and hack the cuff, we come up against two blocks—one from the Alliance and the other from the Frawgs, right Vor?"

Vor's eyes went wide as he picked up on Kenzie's thought. He nodded vigorously. Not for the first time since meeting Kenzie, Dash felt dumb.

"So if we cut the power from the reactor, I'm pretty sure the Alliance shuttle's software can't stop us from hacking our way in anymore."

"Won't we suffocate when you turn off the reactor?" asked Twince. "It's keeping the life support on."

Kenzie reached into her bag and produced two more respirators.

"I brought extras."

It Grew Back

16

Once everyone's respirators were in place, they were ready. Kenzie looked around the shuttle cockpit one last time to double-check—the shape of the cockpit itself was more rounded and smoothed than the *Gremlin*'s, with soft whites and grays instead of the tans and browns she'd gotten used to over the last few days. Kenzie switched on her jumpsuit's light. It was about to get pretty dark.

She tapped a few commands into the main control console at the front of the cockpit, just about the center point between the captive Ravi and Twince. She took hold of the ignition dial—a bit smaller and more discreetly designed than the one in the *Gremlin*—and turned the reactor off.

The low, nearly imperceptible hum that had filled her ears since she entered the shuttle quickly faded into nothingness. Its absence felt cold and empty.

Kenzie glanced at her handset, and she liked what she saw. Instead of two layers of security blocking her from accessing Ravi's cuff, she only saw the one made by the Frawgs. And when left on their own, the Frawgs, it just so happened, weren't the most gifted software engineers. And they were no match for her.

She turned to Vor, who consulted his own handset. "You seeing what I'm seeing?"

Vor nodded vigorously.

It only took a few short commands for Kenzie to crack the Frawgs' security protocols. She looked up as the cuff around Ravi's arm hissed, clanged, and—somewhat distressingly—warbled. After about ten seconds of noises, Ravi took his left arm out and flexed his hand, almost as though he were making sure his fingers were still attached. They were.

"Good, you're out," said Dash from the starboard side of the cockpit, nearer to Twince. "Squix, you got everything we need?"

"Yup," said Squix, holding the new nav-computer circuit board.

"We would've had it sooner if you'd helped," said Jo, sulking beside him.

"I did help!" said Squix defensively. "I showed you all the pulling spots!"

"Okay gang—let's scram," said Dash. He turned to Twince and smiled without his eyes. "Well, Twince, goodbye. And don't think it hasn't been a little slice of heaven…" He turned to walk toward the hatch, then turned back. "…because it hasn't."

Kenzie saw the blood drain from Twince's face—well, the green half of his face.

"Captain," she said. "We're not…we're not just gonna—"

"Yes," he said, turning to face her. "We are 'just gonna.' We're outta here."

"We're leaving him here to die?" said Kenzie, putting herself between the captain and the cyborg.

"I should be so lucky," said Dash, crossing his arms. "But he never did what I wanted him to anyway, so I doubt he'll start now."

"Go to hell, Drake," said Twince from his corner.

"You first, jerk!" Dash yelled over Kenzie's shoulder.

"Captain," started Kenzie. "Dash—"

He held up a hand. "Look, I know you think this is harsh. And…well, it is. But this is no worse than how that metal-faced creep left me and Squix a couple years back. In fact, it's kinda better."

Kenzie's eyes went wide. "How could this be better?"

Dash looked up, thinking.

"Okay, it's not better at all, actually," he conceded. "But seriously, this guy is the worst. Trust me, he'll con his way out of this. Guys like him always find a way to worm out of trouble."

"Classic," said Twince with a low, angry chuckle. "Classic Dash Drake. Opportunity staring you in the face, chance for a huge score. And whattya do? You walk away."

"Yes," said Dash. "This is me walking away. Bye!" He turned and walked toward the hatch.

"Say so long to the crystal," said Twince. "And say goodbye to your Interstellar Alliance if the Forgers get it."

"Ooh," said Ravi, massaging his wrist. "That does sound bad."

Dash wheeled on Twince. "Why are you still talking?" He looked around the cockpit exaggeratedly. "Why can no one hear me? Am I speaking Marvinian or something?"

"It's definitely English, Cap," said Squix.

"Thank you, Squix," said Dash.

"He can't really be, like, *that* bad, can he?" asked Jo.

"Actually, he's pretty terrible," said Squix. "See this?" He held up a tentacle on his left side. "He tore this tentacle right off my actual body. Just threw it out the airlock."

"Uh," said Jo. "I'm looking at it right now."

"Yeah, well, I mean, it grew back," said Squix, flashing bright red. "I'm an Octopus. But it still really, really sucked."

"See?" said Dash, gesturing at Squix's not-gone tentacle. "He's a scumbag. Not to be trusted. I know this guy, Kenzie. Let's go."

"But—but maybe he really can show us where the crystal is," pleaded Kenzie. Her heart was thudding.

"I'm not interested in the crystal, Cadet," he snapped, emphasizing her low rank on his ship. "I'm not interested in the Forgers. I'm not interested in whatever they're planning, and I'm definitely not interested in *him*." He punctuated that last word with a stabbing fingerpoint at Twince.

"But—but—" Kenzie's mind raced. Sure, Twince seemed dangerous, but he was just one man. And he had important secrets that could potentially save the Alliance and stop the Forgers from executing their plan...whatever it was. Then she remembered.

"What about page ninety-four, and I quote, 'Saving lives is dangerous business, but it's the only business I—"

"Would you shut up? Just—just stop it with that!" yelled Dash. "I didn't even write that book!"

Kenzie felt like she'd been slapped.

"What..." she said, "what do you mean?"

Dash closed his eyes and shook his head slowly.

"Just..." He sighed. "Nothing. Never mind. C'mon. We have to go before the Frawgs find us here. I was just getting used to the idea of not being someone's lunch."

Kenzie's head spun. He didn't write the book? How could that be? It had his name, his face, right on the front. Why would he...

Then Kenzie pieced it all together. She realized what was really happening here. Dash was desperate—as desperate to leave Twince here as she was to take him aboard the *Gremlin*. He wanted so badly to protect his crew from this man who'd once hurt him and his best friend and his ship that he'd do anything, say anything, to do just that. Even lie about not writing his book.

Kenzie's heart started to hurt a little. He was being noble, willing to look petty to protect his crew. But she knew by now they were more than just a crew. They were becoming a family.

And Kenzie had helped Dash stay alive ever since she'd come aboard. She negotiated the chalzz deal with Pendros, she'd hacked them out of Technica Outpost, and she helped them escape the Frawgs. She wasn't done helping yet.

She turned to Twince.

"You swear you know where the crystal is?"

Twince looked up at her, staring her straight in the eye.

"I swear."

"What are you doing?" said Dash.

"You swear not to hurt any of us?"

"Kenzie—"

"I swear," said Twince.

She turned to Captain Drake.

"Trust me," she said.

She took out her handset and entered a few commands.

"Kenzie, stop this, now…"

Twince's cuff hissed, clanged, and warbled. He freed his right arm and rubbed his fingers.

Dash unholstered his laser pistol and leveled it at Twince. Kenzie gasped and took a step back, then another, getting herself out of the potential line of fire.

"Captain?" It was the only word her brain could muster.

"Whoa," said Jo. "I forgot he even had that."

This wasn't good. Kenzie knew he didn't like Twince…but would he really shoot him? Didn't he realize she had this under control?

"Stick your hand back in that—that thing," said Dash, waggling the pistol at the cuff.

Twince looked from his hand to Dash, narrowing his bio-eye. His other narrowed to a small, red point.

"You wouldn't," Twince hissed.

"I would," said Dash.

"You won't."

"I will!"

"He might!" Squix whispered loudly.

Twince turned and slowly walked toward Dash.

"Um, what are you doing?" asked Ravi, his voice unsteady.

"Go ahead," said Twince, stalking forward. "You're the big war hero, right? Hero of Gantoid IV?"

The cyborg stepped right up to Dash, just a few centimeters between him and the pistol's barrel.

Twince stared Dash down.

"C'mon, Drake," cooed Twince. "Do it."

No one said anything for what felt like a long time.

Finally, Kenzie broke the silence.

"Captain," she said. "Please."

Dash kept Twince's gaze. He lowered his gun, holstered it. He turned, walked to the hatch, and left.

"Thanks kid," said Twince, grinning like a cat. "Now, which way to that pile of crap you call a ship?"

* * *

The walk back to the *Gremlin* was quiet. Nobody spoke as the crew, plus its two new guests, walked from the shuttle and wended their way through the dark cavern. Jo and Vor led, followed by Twince, Ravi, Squix, and Kenzie at the back. Dash wasn't in the pilot's chair when the rest of the crew arrived. Kenzie assumed he was in his quarters.

When Squix raised the gangplank to the *Gremlin*'s cockpit, Ravi turned to him.

"So," he said, "where's the brig?"

Squix rubbed his head with a tentacle.

"The what?"

"You know, the brig," said Ravi. "Where you keep prisoners on a ship. Because—well…"

Ravi leaned over, winked, then conspiratorially pointed at Twince, who leaned against the rear wall watching everything Ravi did.

"They don't have one of those," said Twince.

"Hey, shut up you!" said Squix, briefly flashing red.

He turned to Ravi. "We don't have one of those."

"Containment field? Stasis pod?"

"No," said Squix.

"What about restraints? Manacles? Handcuffs?"

"Oh, we have those!" said Squix.

"Where are they?"

"They're in the medbay. We, uh, cut them apart with a laser."

Ravi's head cocked to the side, like a dog hearing something he couldn't understand.

"I'll just see myself to my bunk," said Twince as he exited the cockpit. "Don't worry, I'll lock myself in."

When the door shut, Squix said, "Man, I hate that guy."

"You don't have any way of keeping him from roaming free?" asked Ravi.

"We're not really…equipped for that kind of thing," said Squix. "We're not in the habit of taking prisoners."

Kenzie quickly changed the subject.

"Vor, why don't you head up top and get started on repairs?" she said. "I'll get out there with you in a minute—I just wanna grab something from my bunk."

Vor pulled his respirator back on, shouldered his tool bag, and walked toward the small circular maintenance hatch in the cockpit's ceiling. He paused, then walked over to Kenzie and surprised her with a small hug. Then he turned back, grabbed the bag full of replacement parts, and climbed up the retractable ladder to the top of the *Gremlin*.

Kenzie walked out of the cockpit and passed Dash's door. She paused there and thought about knocking. She didn't.

She sat on the bed back in her bunk. She put her elbows on her knees and just sat there, staring at a chipped tile in the floor.

What was happening? At every turn on this trip, Kenzie showed she was just as capable, just as brave, as Dash had ever been. Maybe Twince had bad blood with Dash and Squix. But he was their first clue to figuring out where they could find the crystal the Forgers wanted.

And the crystal sounded like it was exactly what she was afraid of— if the Forgers got their hands on the powerful artifact, it could spell disaster for the entire Interstellar Alliance. Why would Dash pull a gun on someone with information that valuable?

Kenzie decided to stop thinking and start doing. Time to help Vor with those repairs. The sooner they were underway and back in space, the sooner they could find the crystal. She'd just have to prove herself to Dash one more time.

She stood to go, hefted her bag filled with respirators, when suddenly her handset dinged. A new message from Dash.

"Meet me in the galley," it read. "We need to talk."

Kenzie's stomach did a backflip. She couldn't tell if she was nervous or relieved. But she didn't hesitate.

When she opened the door, Dash was sitting at the table, looking at his own handset. He looked up and rolled his eyes as soon as he saw her.

"You wanted to see me, Captain?" she asked nervously, dropping her bag in the corner.

"Actually, no," said Dash. "I didn't. I'm meeting Squix in here."

Kenzie was more confused than ever.

"But—" Kenzie held up her handset. "I got a message from you…to meet you in here?"

"Looks like you were wrong," he said. "Again."

The door opened and in walked Ravi, followed by Jo.

"Where are they?" said Ravi.

"How long you've been hiding these from us?" said Jo.

Dash's eyes went wide. "What're you—where are what?"

Jo scoffed, then opened cupboards and drawers. "Kenzie told me there's cookies in here."

"I didn't—" Kenzie began.

"I'll check up there," said Ravi, reaching into a high cabinet. "First I get rescued by Captain Drake, then I get cookies. I love this ship!"

Dash turned to Kenzie. "Did you tell them we had cookies?"

"No," she said.

"Everyone," said Dash, jumping up and knocking over his chair. He ran to the exit. "We have to get out of here—"

The door opened to reveal a metal fist, which collided with Dash's face. Everyone in the galley turned in time to see him crash onto the floor.

Twince stood in the doorway. He held Squix, squishing the Octopus with his powerful fingers in a way that hurt Kenzie just to look at it.

With both hands, he ripped Squix from his exosuit, then tossed him into the galley, where he landed onto Dash's chest with a wet thud. The cyborg crumpled the exosuit into a compact ball of scrap, its internal water tanks bursting with a pop. He casually flung it over his shoulder into the hallway behind him.

He leaned against the doorway and smiled, leveling a finger at Kenzie.

"You should've listened to your captain, kid," he said. Then he turned to Dash. "And you should've shot me when you had the chance."

The Hero of Gantoid IV

Dash, his right eye throbbing and swelling shut, his hands shaking, scrambled through the galley's cabinets and found the water pitcher. In his rush to pull out the large glass carafe, he accidentally knocked its side against the cabinet. He cursed under his breath, simultaneously at himself and with relief that the pitcher hadn't cracked or shattered.

He put it in the sink, taking extra care now not to hit it against the metal faucet. After it was filled with water and he'd poured the full contents of the galley's salt-shaker into it, he set the pitcher carefully on the counter top and waved Jo over.

She hurried to the counter and carefully dropped Squix into the water with a "ploop."

Dash leaned over and watched his friend slowly open his eyes. Squix looked around, disoriented. After a moment, he stuck two tentacles together into a ball, then poked the tip of one up through it. Thumbs up.

Dash exhaled and sat on the floor.

Squix swirled and spun in the pitcher, taking in his new surroundings. Without the exosuit—which not only kept him hydrated, but kept him from suffocating out of water—Squix couldn't talk to the rest of the crew. There was no way to know how badly Squix was hurt when Twince crushed him and tossed him into the galley.

That said, Dash didn't have any trouble knowing exactly how *he* felt: sick to his stomach. That was partly because, even now, with their captor having long since exited the galley, he could still hear the guy's voice.

As soon as Ravi tried and failed to reopen the door, Kenzie used her handset to try hacking into the *Gremlin's* computer to unlock it. But she wasn't up against the usual kind of security programs or firewalls—she was trying to hack her way through Twince himself. And he was taunting her directly.

"Give it up," said Twince, his voice needling Dash's eardrums through the handset's tiny speakers. "You're pretty good, but you're not as good as me. As long as I'm sitting at this console, I control this ship and its computers. And that means you don't."

"Why are you doing this?" she said. "You—you said you wouldn't hurt us! You swore!"

"I sure did," he said, a laugh lurking behind his words. "And you believed me. Really, I think there's a lot of blame to go around on this one."

Dash lay on the floor, halfway under the table, and closed his eyes. He was so tired. And his face hurt from getting punched by a cyborg.

Kenzie seethed—he heard it in her voice. "So this means you won't even tell us where the crystal is, will you?"

Kiddo," said Twince, "I don't know nothin' about any kind of crystal. Sounds like a buncha crap to me, to be perfectly frank. But you sure did want it. Honestly, I almost feel bad."

"Almost," said Dash from his position on the floor.

He let out a dry laugh. "That you, Drake?"

"Get bent, Twince."

"That's the spirit."

"Excuse me…" That was Ravi. Dash heard his ever-present smile. "Twince, please don't do this. Think of all we've been through together!"

"Uh, yeah," said Twince. "I have."

"I saved you when you were floating out in space!"

"You captured me against my will, then got me taken prisoner by a bunch of Frawgs in the middle of nowhere," said Twince.

"Okay," said Ravi, "but we had some good times, right? Shared a few laughs?"

"No," said Twince, "we didn't."

"So you won't let us out?"

"Nope."

"Well," said Ravi. "I tried."

"Where's my brother?" That was Jo.

"Last I saw, he was up top, making repairs. Soon as he's done, we're taking off and getting away from this rock. Don't think I'll be letting him in before lift-off, though. Sorry you won't get to say goodbye."

Dash wasn't too surprised by that. But he felt bad when he heard Jo gasp. She didn't say anything else. No one did. Twince let that moment hang before continuing.

"Figure Captain Drake will earn me a nice little chunk of credits if I turn him over to that Forger ship you saw. Maybe they're still looking for you. Or maybe I'll just blow the airlock on all of you once we break the atmosphere. Haven't really decided yet."

Then he laughed. "Enjoy those cookies, though!"

His voice disappeared, replaced with hissing static.

"Hello?" said Kenzie. "Hello?! Come back! I'm not—" Dash heard the handset clatter to the floor beside him. She grunted in frustration.

Dash opened his eyes. "You guys know there's definitely no cookies, right?" he said, sitting up.

He looked and saw Jo, her purple eyes rimmed with red, glaring at him.

"Sorry," he shrugged from his position on the floor. He said it again as he climbed to his feet: "Sorry."

He opened the freezer and took out a package of frozen peas, then stuck it against his bruised eye. The cold stung, but in a good way. Then he grabbed a chair and sat down, leaning on his free elbow at the table.

Kenzie stood at the sink, looking down at Squix in the pitcher, keeping her back to the captain. Dash jumped a little when she spun around to face the others.

"Okay," she said, steel in her eyes. "Our handsets don't work. We can't hack our way out of this room. We need a plan. What about the door's manual release lever?"

Ravi, excited, piped up from behind Dash, standing near the tricrowave. "I tried it earlier!"

Kenzie leaned back, her face impassive.

"It didn't work!" Ravi concluded.

"Okay, manual release lever is off the table."

Dash saw her gaze land on him.

"Gun," she said.

"What?"

Without answering, Kenzie strode to Dash and unholstered his laser pistol.

"Hey!" was all Dash could say before she marched to the door and fired.

A small beam of yellow energy erupted from the gun—and barely singed the door.

Kenzie looked at the pistol and read the letters printed on its side.

"Crunger Killer?" she read.

"It's for pest-control," said Dash sheepishly.

Jo glared at Dash. "You were gonna shoot Twince with that?"

"Hey, you ever been shot with one of those?" Dash pointed back at the pistol. "It hurts. A lot."

Kenzie dropped the pistol on the table in front of Dash. She surveyed the room and spotted something up near the ceiling.

"Air duct," she said.

She hopped up on a counter and pulled the magnetic vent cover off the wall. She poked her head inside. Dash could see from his seat that her shoulders—already narrow for a fourteen-year-old girl—were still clearly too wide to fit through.

"Get down, Kenzie," he said, sighing.

She tried pushing her way into the duct. "But I might be—unf—able to—rggh—shimmy down—"

Jo chimed in. "You won't fit, Kenzie." Her voice dripped with discouragement.

Kenzie pulled herself out of the duct and slammed the vent cover back on. She sat on the counter, her legs dangling over the edge, not touching the floor. Her dark, frizzy hair poked out at all the wrong angles.

"Okay, the vent's out." She looked at Dash. "What now?"

Dash blinked at her. "Now? Now we probably wait to die. Or get sold to the Forgers. Both sound pretty bad."

Kenzie cocked an eyebrow.

"What'd you do last time?"

"Last time?"

"When Twince tangled with you before. You guys came out of that in one piece."

There was a splash, and everyone in the galley turned to see Squix waving one of his tentacles out of the top of the pitcher, a flash of red rippling through his skin.

"Okay, well mostly one piece," Kenzie conceded. "How'd you get out of it? What are his weaknesses?"

"Well," said Dash, "he doesn't shower a lot, so he has a hard time getting dates. Other than that, you got me."

"But how'd you beat him?"

"We didn't," said Dash. "We didn't beat him. At all."

Dash took the frozen peas off his numb, swollen eye and dropped them onto the table. He leaned back in his chair.

"We'd agreed to share the profits of our cargo—some crates filled with Draibor spice—since Twince had connected us with his buyer. Only, he wouldn't give us the name or info on how to reach said buyer, so we had to take Twince with us. Couple days after we set out, I wake up to alarms. There's a reactor leak and a hole blown in the cargo bay. Squix is down there, missing a tentacle, and Twince is gone. So's the cargo. Figure he and someone else set up a side deal so they'd just steal our cargo directly—cut me and Squix out and keep all the money."

Dash breathed out through his nose. Kenzie leaned in.

"And then what?"

"And then," Dash continued, "we patched the hole in the cargo bay and called for a tow. The end."

"That's it?"

Dash waved a couple fingers in the air. "Pretty much."

The silence lingered for a few seconds.

"But you were going to track him down later, right?" she said. "Bring him to justice?"

"I…I guess?" said Dash. "I mean, he owed us lots of money. And he stole our cargo. And also I hate him. But I think you might be missing the—"

"So what was your first move after you fixed the ship?" she said. "You activated a tracking chip you'd planted on him?"

He shook his head. "No, I didn't plant a tracking chip on—"

"Or you ran a cross-check of the sale of large quantities of Draibor spice in or around nearby star systems to get a fix on his likely whereabouts?"

Dash considered this. "That...probably would have been a good idea—"

"You called in some favors with your contacts in law enforcement from your days in the Fleet and gathered a posse to chase him down and flush him out—"

"Kenzie," Dash interrupted. "We called the cops and went on to the next job. We never saw Twince again until today."

Kenzie just blinked at him.

"You didn't do anything?"

"No."

"But you're the hero of—"

Dash put up both hands and stopped her. Enough was enough.

"I'm not," said Dash. "I'm not the hero of Gantoid IV."

Kenzie's eyes saucered. Her face's expression said what her mouth couldn't: *What?*

Dash looked at the floor. Time to come clean.

"That day—that battle at Gantoid IV. That was my very first deployment. Just turned eighteen and got drafted. Before that I was just some...some guy. Some loser who'd graduated from high school and still lived at home. But the war was on, and I got the notice on my handset to report for duty, and..."

Dash ran his hand through his hair and noticed how greasy it felt.

"Anyway, this was the first time I'd ever actually flown anything that wasn't my mom's van. I didn't even have a secondary gunner in the rear seat—we didn't have enough soldiers for a full deployment. They just grabbed anyone with a pulse and dropped them in a Dart. We were escorting a medical supply ship and stopped to refuel. Our convoy came out of jump-space, and a Forger armada was there, waiting. Right in front of us."

"I love this movie," Ravi murmured to Jo.

Dash ignored him.

"There weren't a lot of enemy ships," Dash continued, "not by the standards of other battles around the sector. But the Fleet could hardly ever put a dent in them. Not before our guys got blasted to bits. The Forgers' weapons were just unbelievably powerful. So when I saw them, I knew what I had to do."

"Listen to this," Ravi said to Jo. "This is the part where he discovers the cloaked energy drone feeding power to the Forgers."

"I turned my ship and ran," said Dash.

There was a pause.

"I was not expecting that," said Ravi.

"My fighter was on the front line, and I couldn't face the Forgers," Dash said. "And I couldn't just go the other way—the Alliance Fleet was behind me. So I angled my nose down and flew as far as I could while my jump-drive recharged.

"That's when I clipped the Forgers' drone. I thought I was under attack, so I just started spinning and shooting everywhere. I didn't...I didn't have any idea what the hell I was doing. And that's how I discovered—and destroyed—the Forgers' secret drone.

"The Forgers' weapons dropped dead. We won the battle, and the Alliance's scientists analyzed my sensor data later. That's how we found the energy network they used to beat us every battle. The Forger War was over within months, and I was never deployed in combat again.

"The movie—it was never my story. Not the real me. And I had a ghostwriter for the book. I can't write a book. I can't..."

He laughed once. "I can't do much of anything."

He put his hand on the bag of frozen peas, cold and damp from condensation. He slid the package onto the floor, where it landed with a wet thud.

Dash realized he'd never told story that to anyone. Part of him felt a tremendous weight he'd never noticed had finally been lifted off his chest.

He finally looked up and met Kenzie's gaze. That's when another part of him—specifically his stomach—felt the twisting, wrenching sensation of guilt suddenly flaring to life.

She was looking at him like a smear of bacteria on a microscope slide.

He could only think of one thing to say, so he said it: "I'm sorry."

Kenzie cocked an eyebrow at him and said just one word.

"Oh."

"I was not expecting that either," said Ravi.

Anesthesiology

It was like she was seeing Dash for the first time.

Captain Dash Drake. Technically he looked the same as always—and yet, somehow, Kenzie saw so many details she'd never noticed before. His sandy brown hair was thinning a bit at the top and colored with more salt than pepper. He had deep, significant frown lines around the edges of his mouth. He looked a little chunky.

How did she never notice any of that before?

"You," said Kenzie, her numbness barely ebbing. "You're a liar."

"I, uh…" said Dash, looking at the bag of frozen peas he'd knocked onto the floor.

"You're a liar," repeated Kenzie, waggling a finger at him. She hopped from the counter. She felt energized.

"I swear I'm telling the truth," Dash replied.

"No, I'm sure you are," she said. "Now. But you lied. You lied about who you were. You lied about everything. You're a fraud."

"Well, only kind of," said Dash, his eyes meeting hers. "And mostly by accident."

He cocked his head awkwardly. "And I didn't technically lie…I didn't make that movie, and I didn't write that book—"

"Your name is on the front!" said Kenzie, her hands clenched into fists. "It's—it's your face on the cover!"

"…I liked to think of it as more of an 'endorsement' kind of situation," said Dash, shrugging sheepishly. "I mean, look at this." He grabbed the bag of peas from the floor. Scooting across the front of the bag under the logo was the robot from TV. "You don't think the robot actually made the peas, right?"

"That's not funny," said Kenzie.

"I'm not trying to be!" Dash's unswollen eye went wide. "I'm just, y'know, I'm just saying…"

Dash sighed and put the peas back on his swollen eye.

"What would you have done, Kenzie?" he said. "What would you have done if you were me? What if you were thrown into a situation and you just   they said you saved everyone, but you knew you just got lucky? The one time in your life you were unbelievably lucky, and people said you literally saved all of humanity? What should I…" He trailed off.

Kenzie barely heard him. Her face was hot. "Don't you—don't you get it? I wanted to be like you!" The words tumbled out—words she didn't realize were there. "Everything…everything I did was to be more like you!"

Dash blinked at her. "You can still be like me."

"Not this you! The other you! The good you!"

Dash's face pinched at that.

"Who am I supposed to be now?" Kenzie said.

"You can be Kenzie Washington," said Dash. "She's…she's already pretty good…"

If she had heard Dash say that a week, a day, an hour earlier, Kenzie would have felt her life was complete. Now, all it did was throw a little water on the fire inside her chest. And she hated that those words could even do that much.

She turned and sat in a chair on the other side of the table from Dash. Kenzie kept her eyes locked on the table itself. She noticed that, this close, it was easier to spot the plastic table's fake woodgrain than when she'd been a meter away. Did Dash choose the table after he bought the *Gremlin*? Or did it come with the ship? Her mind spun. She couldn't concentrate.

Kenzie looked away from the fake wooden table and stared at the off-white tile floor and its scuff marks, not knowing what to say—what to think.

"Uh, so—" said Jo. "My brother? He's on the ship's hull, and we kinda need to save his life. Again."

"Again?" said Ravi. "Does this happen a lot?"

"Only since we started hanging out with these guys," said Jo.

Kenzie closed her eyes. Jo was right. Time was running out. They needed to retake the ship before Twince could power up the *Gremlin* and leave Vor to die. He was in trouble. They all were.

She shook her head hard, clearing the crazy thoughts from her mind. No time to feel sorry for herself.

Was there some way to damage Twince's cybernetic implants? What if she could overwrite his program with something else, like an artificial intelligence…no, that couldn't work. Not from the galley, at least. Twince had locked her handset out of the ship's computer anyway. If she even wanted to try that, she'd have to hardwire directly into his systems. Maybe if they managed to escape the room—but for now, computers were the wrong approach. She grunted with frustration.

"Kenzie?" asked Jo tentatively.

Kenzie looked around, searching for what she might've missed. They were locked in the galley, but there had to be some way out. Something Twince hadn't accounted for.

"Don't outfight your enemy," she said to herself, remembering her former favorite book. "Outthink him."

Dash coughed. He looked uncomfortable. Good.

Kenzie couldn't outhack Twince—not when he was half-robot. Those tricks wouldn't work against someone whose every waking thought was connected directly to the ship's computer.

But…what if he wasn't awake? He was a cyborg…only half-robot. Even without his cybernetic enhancements, he was still a living thing.

Kenzie looked at Squix, spinning slowly in the pitcher. Without his exosuit, he wouldn't stay hydrated. Wouldn't survive long in the air. Squix was vulnerable.

Twince—he still needed to breathe, Kenzie realized. Just like in the shuttle. Twince was still vulnerable, just like Squix. Just like all of them.

Kenzie spotted her bag in the corner—the one she'd brought with her to the galley before Twince locked them inside. It was filled with respirators.

A light switched on in her head.

"Ravi," she said, turning to him.

"Yes!" he said. Despite their desperate situation, a genuinely enthusiastic grin appeared on his face. He was just happy to be there.

"What are the effects…" She picked her handset up off the floor and checked her notes. "…of dihydrogen-sulfide on biological organisms?"

"Dihydrogen-sulfide," repeated Ravi, looking up at the ceiling, thinking. "Ah, you mean sewer gas!"

"Yes," said Kenzie.

"You mean in addition to it smelling like farts?"

"Yes," said Kenzie.

"This is a seriously fascinating gas! It has so many effects. Let's see…" Ravi started marking symptoms on each finger. "There's nausea, headaches, irritability, dizziness, and, of course, slight conjunctivitis, which we typically refer to as pink eye—"

"Can it knock you unconscious?" Kenzie asked.

"Oh, most definitely!" said Ravi excitedly. "It's incredibly dangerous, not to mention unpleasant. On account of the fart smell, of course."

"Of course," said Dash, rolling the eye not covered with a bag of peas.

Ravi continued. "All it takes is prolonged exposure in enough concentration."

"What if it's pumped into a small, airtight room?" said Kenzie.

"That'd do it," said Ravi.

"Perfect." Kenzie leapt from her seat and clambered back onto the counter top and grabbed the air vent off the wall.

"This again," Dash sighed. "You won't fit, Kenzie."

"Not me," Kenzie snapped as she tossed the vent cover onto the floor. It landed with a clattering clang that made the others jump.

She pointed at Squix. Squix goggled up at her from inside the water pitcher.

"Him."

* * *

No one was sure Squix fully understood the mission Kenzie laid out after Dash scooped him out of the water pitcher. It looked like he'd been banged up pretty bad when Twince ripped him out of his exosuit and threw him into the galley.

But the Octopus gave a little salute with one of his right tentacles, and his skin turned blue, then bright red.

"What's that mean?" asked Kenzie as the crimson Squix squirmed along the counter top.

"Blue means he's pleased," said Dash, giving Squix a handset, "and red means he's really, really pissed."

"Captain Drake," said Ravi, smiling as always. "I see you've got a bit of a green thumb!"

Dash looked at him.

"Wha—?"

"Those," Ravi said, pointing to a shelf with a row of dead or dying houseplants. They weren't really green. They were mostly brown.

"Oh," said Dash. "Those."

"Yeah," said Jo from the corner. "Not so much."

"I wonder—might you have a spray bottle handy?"

"Ah, uh, yeah. That cabinet," said Dash, pointing.

Ravi opened it and, sure enough, next to two small cookpots, both covered in a thick layer of dust, there was the spray bottle, completely devoid of moisture. The lieutenant filled it with water, then handed it to Squix, who grabbed it with a spare tentacle.

"Here," he said, "take this with you."

As Squix wiggled the spray bottle in the air, Ravi addressed the rest of the crew.

"My roommate at the Academy was an Octopus," he said, "and we used this trick when we pulled the old 'Octopus-under-your-desk' prank. You see, the Octopus' gills pull oxygen from water and transfer it into the bloodstream. However!" He punctuated this word with his finger. "If an Octopus can keep its skin moist while out of the water, its body can still carry out a small amount of the gas exchange necessary to keep breathing! Isn't that amazing?"

"Huh," said Dash. He looked at Squix on the countertop. "Why didn't we ever think of that?"

Squix shrugged.

Dash picked Squix up and carried him to the air vent. Kenzie looked and had trouble reconciling how small the Octopus really was when he wasn't in his exosuit. He was about the size of a watermelon, and fit in Dash's arms like a squishy, damp baby. With tentacles.

Not only that, but she also kept forgetting that Squix basically had superpowers. In addition to being able to change color and camouflage himself, he had no skeleton—his body was extremely malleable and could squeeze into just about any space.

Even still, Kenzie didn't like that she'd basically volunteered Squix for this job. But he was literally the only one with a hope of even attempting it.

Dash climbed onto the countertop and lightly pushed Squix into the vent. Kenzie watched as the tentacles carrying the spray bottle and handset disappeared within.

In minutes, Squix had crawled nearly a third of the way through the ductwork. Kenzie was a little surprised at how quickly he moved—and getting a little sick while she watched the camera feed streaming from his handset. Every few meters, the entire view swerved as he took another turn in the ducts or dropped lower toward the belly of the ship.

At the halfway point, he hit a junction separating the top deck from the bottom. There were six different paths he could take: four that would take him to either the cargo bay or the engine room, which shared the bottom deck, and two that would take him to spinning air turbines, which pumped the ship full of oxygen.

"Which way should he turn?" asked Dash, who watched Squix's progress with Jo and Ravi on another handset.

Kenzie looked at Dash. "What?"

"Which way should he turn, Kenzie?"

"Wait—don't you know?" asked Kenzie.

"This is your plan!" said Dash.

"Yes," said Kenzie, her face getting hot again. "And this is your ship. How should I know which way he's supposed to go?"

Suddenly, the *Gremlin* started to hum in a very faint but familiar way. The floor vibrated as the hum grew to a gentle rumble.

Twince was warming up the engines.

Kenzie saw Squix's eyes suddenly come into view on her handset, the view shaking. The look he gave them said what he couldn't. Hurry.

"Okay," she said. She couldn't let herself get angry again. Time to…make a totally random guess. "Try the second one from the left?"

"Are you sure?" asked Jo.

"No," said Kenzie. "But I've got a two-thirds chance of being right."

"I like those odds!" said Ravi, who everyone ignored.

Squix started crawling again, this time a little faster. It was even harder to tell what was going on now because of the ship's vibrations and Squix's hurried pace, not to mention the fine mist of water forming on the camera from the spray bottle.

Seconds later, however, the loud whirring from the handset's speakers told Kenzie everything: she'd given Squix the wrong directions.

It was hard to tell, but it looked like Squix was dangling over the spinning air turbine, attached to the wall of the duct by a couple of sticky tentacles. She saw the spray bottle fall down the shaft and burst against the spinning machinery.

"Oh, God," said Dash on the other side of the room. A pang of guilt stabbed Kenzie's chest.

"Get—get out of there!" Kenzie said into her handset.

The handset shook as Squix climbed back out of the turbine shaft. Kenzie imagined that his tentacles were braced against each side of the duct. It couldn't have helped that, without the bottle, Squix was now effectively holding his breath until his mission's end…and probably for longer than that. A few seconds passed and he was back in the junction point and heading for the next path over.

The floor of the *Gremlin* vibrated more intensely as the engine's warm-up sequence entered its next phase. Kenzie silently thanked Dash for owning such an old, crappy ship that took so long to start.

Kenzie saw Squix finally encounter a vent cover. A bunch of his tentacles came together and punched the cover off the duct, revealing the cargo bay below. There was the Dart, parked askew next to some fallen crates, just where she'd left it. And off to one side was the sealed up chalzz pen.

"Okay, Squix," Kenzie said. "Almost finished. On the side of the pen there's an airlock release lever. You need to pull that."

She watched as Squix quickly crawled along the ceiling, his suckers going into overdrive to work against gravity and keep him up there. Step, step, step, step—until he hung directly over the lever.

Kenzie's stomach lurched as Squix fell down a five-meter drop. Jo, watching with Dash and Ravi, let out a yelp.

But he didn't hit the ground: he reached out a pair of arms and grabbed the lever, breaking his fall. That had to hurt.

Squix tossed the handset on the ground, so she could only see some of what happened next: The Octopus braced himself against the side of the chalzz pen with four arms while grabbing the lever with the other four. With what she imagined to be a significant strain of his mollusk muscles, Squix threw the switch and opened the door.

Squix fell to the ground, leaving the handset where it lay. Kenzie and the rest of the crew watched him grow smaller in their displays as he ambled weakly toward the Dart. He inched his way up the fighter's landing strut, crawling around its hull, and into the cockpit. He tapped a few buttons and closed the hatch, sealing himself off from the rest of the cargo bay.

Moments later, the chalzz began exiting the pen.

The little six-legged creatures that fetched such a hefty sum in the gourmet food market really only ever did two things: walk and stink. And, as it turned out, that stink was a particularly potent toxic gas.

Kenzie looked at the others and put her handset on the table, pulling her respirator over her face. Dash, Jo, and Ravi did the same.

The handset sprang to life with Twince's half-green, half-metal face.

"What's that smell?" he said.

Double Trouble

Being unable to afford a newer ship was usually a sore point for Dash. Not today.

The tremendous amount of dihydrogen-sulfide already built up in the pen dispersed into the cargo bay, along with all the chalzz, too. The toxic gas flooded the *Gremlin*'s air system.

On most ships, the life support system would easily filter the gas out. The internal sensors would've detected the gas's source, locked down the cargo bay immediately, and there'd be little to no danger of anyone suffering any health risks because of runaway fart monsters.

The *Gremlin* wasn't like most ships. Its internal sensors had needed replacement for years. And its air system was really good at pumping gas, usually oxygen, throughout the ship quickly. But it wasn't anywhere close to sophisticated enough to filter most stinks out, much to Dash's constant frustration. Hence the Crunger Killer pistol.

It didn't take long for the cockpit to flood with sewer gas. Twince lost consciousness—and, more importantly, his control over the ship's computer. Kenzie tapped a few commands into her handset, and the door to the galley slid open moments later.

Kenzie, Jo, and Ravi ran to the cockpit to deal with the passed out cyborg. Kenzie said she'd had an idea she wanted to try. Dash still wasn't sure where he stood with the cadet, so he didn't ask for details. Instead, he rushed down to the cargo bay with the water pitcher. Squix had never been out of his exosuit for this long, and Dash was worried.

When he opened the Dart's cockpit door, Dash saw Squix lying in the front seat, unmoving. His eyes were open, but that didn't mean much—octopuses didn't have eyelids. He cradled him in his arms and dropped him into the pitcher, then bolted up to the medbay on the top deck. The dim light of the corridors, usually a comfort, now filled him with anxiety. Each running footstep, clanking against the metal deck plating, echoed and rang in his ears.

Doctor Bill started complaining immediately upon Dash's entrance.

"I thought you'd forgotten about me," he said. "I couldn't access the rest of the ship's systems—why was I locked out of the computer?"

Bill slid across the room and got a closer look at Dash's bruised face through the respirator faceplate.

"Did someone punch you? Did they get it on video?"

"I'll fill you in later—Squix is hurt," Dash said, putting the pitcher onto the nearest examination table.

Doctor Bill said nothing and set to work, inserting his medical probes into the pitcher to determine the extent of the damage. A few seconds passed.

"Why don't you head to your quarters, Captain?"

Doctor Bill was being polite. That was never a good sign.

"I really think I should stay—"

"I'll call you as soon as I have news, Captain," he said, producing a new set of tools and instruments as he removed the probes from the water. "Let me work."

Dash took another look at Squix, floating in the water. Then he turned to leave the medbay. He was halfway to the door before Doctor Bill called after him.

"Captain," he said. "If we could restock our supply of sodium chloride, that would be a great benefit to our cephalopod friend."

"Sodia-what?" said Dash, furrowing his brow.

"Salt," said the doctor. "Squix's extended time out of his suit has depleted his body of salt. We were running low before we embarked on this trip, and I believe that we'll need more for him to fully heal."

Dash nodded. "We'll make a pitstop," he said. "Thanks."

The doctor returned to his work and waved a med-probe in acknowledgment.

When he entered the cockpit, Dash saw the still-unconscious Twince surrounded by Ravi, Jo, and Kenzie. A steady banging noise came from the outer hull.

"What's this butthole still doing on my ship?" Dash said, gesturing to the sleeping cyborg.

Now that he was closer, he saw a cable running from the back of Twince's head to Kenzie's handset, with another cable connecting her handset to a nearby computer console.

"What—what are you doing?" he said, walking over to the main control console. He cut the cargo bay off from the rest of the ship's air supply and unlocked the top hatch for Vor. "Are you hacking Twince's *brain*?"

"Kinda, yeah," said Kenzie without looking up.

The small, circular maintenance hatch in the ceiling cycled open, and the banging stopped. Vor peeked his head into the dark cockpit and waved his hand like asking a question—what the heck took so long to open the hatch?

Dash looked at Ravi, who who was smiling at the cadet.

"Were you going to, y'know, stop her?" he said.

"I thought about it, but I really wanted to see where she was going with this," he said. Vor, his annoyance forgotten, dropped into the cockpit with a clang, closed the hatch, and mosied over to watch. Jo put her arm around him.

Ravi continued. "Cadet Washington presented an interesting experiment that promises remarkable results. Our Mister Twince has been enhanced with machines and computers from head to toe. And yet his mind and personality have the consistency of a rotten mango," he said. "Scientifically speaking, of course."

Before he could raise more objections—and before he realized he just could unplug the cables—Kenzie was done.

"And that should…do it," said Kenzie with a final tap.

Twince's one biological eye fluttered, while his cybernetic implant grew from dull to bright red. Dash backed away, his hand reaching for the blaster usually at his hip. And which was still in the galley, of course.

The cyborg sat up and looked around with confusion and alarm in his face.

And then he spoke. The voice was different and yet, terrifyingly familiar.

"Captain?"

Dash's stomach dropped.

"Bill?"

"This is most…most interesting," said Twince with Doctor Bill's voice. "I'm in the medbay, tending to Squix, but I'm also—I'm also sitting in the cockpit?"

Twince—or was it Bill?—stared straight ahead for a moment. The doctor's artificial intelligence was scanning the cyborg's memory files. He turned his head and smiled at Kenzie, while the cable running from his skull yanked her handset away, sending it clattering onto the floor.

"There's two of me!" he said, grinning with Twince's mouth.

Dash shuddered. Kenzie had taken the one man in the galaxy he hated more than anyone and somehow managed to make him even worse. He sighed to himself. Yeah—that sounded about right.

"You're only seeing double because you're both connected to the ship's computer," Kenzie said excitedly. "That'll stop once you're unplugged—then you'll be two distinct people."

Dash ignored Kenzie's explanation of her latest monstrosity.

"Vor," he said. "Did you finish repairing the jump-shield?"

Vor nodded.

Kenzie walked to the main console—the one she'd broken when they were escaping from the Frawg pods earlier.

"Weapons are still offline, this console needs patching up," she said. "The rest of the repairs aren't done."

"Can we jump home?" said Dash.

"Yeah," Kenzie answered.

"Good enough. Lieutenant Sidana, prep the ship for takeoff and get us off this rock," he said. "Then set a course for the nearest convenience store once we're back in Alliance territory."

"Ooh," said Ravi, wincing. "I am not super good at the whole flying thing. Which, as you may remember, is kind of how I ended up here in the first—"

Dash put his hand on Ravi's shoulder, cutting him off. "Can you fly the ship?"

"Legally?" said Ravi, clasping his hands together. "Sort of."

"Great," said Dash. "I'm going to bed."

* * *

Dash sat on his narrow bunk, eating a candybar. He thought about scrolling through his feedpage, but decided he'd rather settle for staring at a stain on the opposite wall. He was disappointed to discover it had roughly the same effect as his feedpage anyway: both made him feel like a speck of crap in a sea of empty, pointless nothingness. But he went with it anyway. His still-swollen eye throbbed as he chewed.

Over the last few hours, the *Gremlin* had traveled through jump-space to finally re-enter Interstellar Alliance territory for the first time since fleeing Technica Outpost. Ravi brought the ship out in the Soo-Nok system, which consisted of a few small, uninhabited planetoids, a smattering of moons, and automated service stations that resupplied ships traveling around the Alliance's edge.

The ship docked with one such station and Dash's handset pinged. Now he could order a new batch of supplies right from his bunk. What he liked most about these automated stations was the ability to avoid talking to or otherwise interacting with anyone. Even the artificial intelligence running the station was programmed without anything resembling a personality.

After he completed his order, the station dispatched a small, floating supply pod—filled with fuel rods, snacks, some toothpaste, and more sodium chloride to aid Squix's recovery—into the *Gremlin*'s docking corridor, where Dash assumed one of the cadets would receive it. With that done, he messaged Ravi asking him to set a course for Motomundo, so they could finally make the first of their deliveries. Hopefully his clients wouldn't notice how delayed he was.

As he mulled just how late the delivery would be—Dash had lost track of how long it'd been since this whole mess started—his door chime rang. He ignored it.

It rang again.

"I'm sleeping," he said.

The door slid open. Kenzie stood there holding her handset. She'd hacked the lock.

"Of course," said Dash.

Kenzie didn't walk in, just stayed outside the doorway.

"We got the delivery pod and put everything away," she said. "We refueled the Gremlin…and the Dart."

"You get that salt to the doctor?" asked Dash. "The real one—not Frankenbill."

"He said he wants to be called 'Twilliam,'" said Kenzie.

Dash made a face.

"Yes," she continued. "Doctor Bill said Squix should be okay soon."

"Good." Silence hung between them for an awkward three seconds.

"Captain—" Kenzie started, then paused, and started again. "Dash, I just wanted to…"

Dash just looked at her.

"I'm sorry," she said. "I'm sorry I lost my cool back there. And I'm sorry about—" Kenzie let out a heavy sigh. "—I'm sorry about letting Twince come aboard. I'm sorry about Squix. I'm sorry about everything."

Dash took a bite of his candy bar.

"Thanks," he said.

"And, for what it's worth, I think you were right. About before."

"Gonna need you to be more specific on that one, Cadet," he said.

"I mean about the trip—needing to end." Kenzie looked at the floor. "Maybe it's best if we all just go home."

Dash wasn't sure if he should feel surprised or angry or guilty or relieved at that. Mostly he felt numb.

"Does this mean," Dash said, crumpling up the wrapper to the candy he didn't realize he'd finished, "you're giving up on finding it? The crystal?"

Kenzie looked back at Dash, steel suddenly in her eyes.

"I think—"

Before she could finish her thought, the ship shook like it had been struck. By something big.

Kenzie grabbed the door jamb for balance, while Dash fell out of bed. The dirty clothes on the floor cushioned the impact a little.

"What the hell—" he said, struggling to pick himself up off the ground.

By the time he stood, Kenzie was already halfway to the cockpit. Dash followed.

Before she reached the door, it opened, with Ravi striding out.

"Captain," said Ravi, with an exaggerated grimace, "I have some not great news."

Jo and Vor popped out of the cadets' bunk and joined the hallway huddle.

"What's going—what happened?" asked Jo. "Did we hit something?"

"Not exactly!" said Ravi. "Just as we undocked from the supply platform, we actually ran into a little trouble. As I was plotting a course to Motomondo, I noticed another ship on the scope getting much closer to us than I would've expected, though, you know, I wasn't sure about the etiquette for coming and going from an automated service station because, as I've mentioned, I don't really do a lot of flying—"

The ship shook again. Dash and the others steadied themselves against the wall.

"Ravi!"

"Oh, yes, so anyway—do you remember that Forger ship you said you'd encountered earlier?"

Dash's eyes went wide.

"Are you kidding me?" he said.

Ravi nodded, his face scrunched up. "The ship appears to have followed us from the Sheaffer System, and it's been launching some kind of projectiles at us, and I'm not really doing a good job at evading them."

"Projectiles?" Dash sputtered as the *Gremlin* rolled under his feet again.

"Also, I probably don't need to remind you how I've repeatedly mentioned that I'm not very good at flying. Really, I'm more of a science-knowledge, data-analysis kind of guy—"

"Outta my way," he said, shoving Ravi and running into the cockpit. He heard Kenzie's boots clomping after him.

He took his seat—not bothering to move it into the position he liked, which Ravi had altered—and slammed on the throttle. The ship surged forward just as Kenzie plopped herself into the copilot's chair.

"Jump-drive primed, plotting course now," she said, tapping at the console.

"Raise combat shields," Dash yelled.

"Can't—the Frawgs drained them just before we entered the quadronium mines, remember?"

He did remember—now.

Dash cursed and jerked the helm to port, then starboard, then port again. He checked his scope and saw those "projectiles" Ravi had mentioned; the Forger ship was firing something at the *Gremlin*, but they weren't missiles. He wasn't sure *what* they were, but he knew they weren't good. He saw another whatever-it-was lurch out, and he threw the ship into a spin. The projectile's trail stopped dead, then suddenly snaked back into the Forger's ship, like a lizard's tongue. What was this thing?

"Course plotted," said Kenzie, no fear in her voice. For a moment, Dash marveled at how capable she was at only fourteen and after all they'd been through in such a short time. He'd have to tell her how remarkable she really was—if they lived through this latest crisis, of course.

"Engaging jump-drive in four seconds," said Dash, his heart beating faster when he stabbed the switch on his console. Three seconds…two…

The ship shuddered again—one of the projectiles had struck home in the aft section of the ship.

"Hull breach, engine room!" yelled Kenzie. His console buzzed angrily. "Engine's losing power!"

Dash checked his scope: instead of flying back into the Forger ship, the projectile was actually connected to the *Gremlin*. Whatever that ship's weapon was, it had punched a hole in his ship, and was draining their power. The ship slowed to a crawl.

Before he could think of what to do next, the *Gremlin* jerked backward, the cockpit shaking violently. Dash nearly fell out of his seat.

"Main reactor power is…power is gone," said Kenzie.

The lights died in the cockpit, his scope and displays blanking out. A moment later, auxiliary power kicked on, and the dim, orange emergency lights activated. Kenzie looked hazy, like something out of a dream, bathed in the orange glow that signifed their imminent doom.

Seconds passed. Then—another huge shudder as the ship collided with…something.

From the open cockpit door, Jo stuck her head inside.

"You guys, I think you better—"

The telltale sounds of the airlock corridor extending to meet another ship echoed through the hallway and into the cockpit. Dash flung himself out of his seat. Again, Kenzie's boots clomped in pursuit.

The outer airlock door cycled open with a whir. Dash reached for the laser pistol he'd once again forgotten to retrieve from the galley. He cursed.

He crept to the hallway intersection leading to the airlock. He poked his head around the corner to look down the corridor. Out of the corner of his eye, he saw that Kenzie had joined him, having apparently grabbed a big wrench from the cockpit's toolkit. Moments later, they were joined in the hallway by Ravi, Jo, Vor, and Twince—Bill—Twilliam—whatever he was.

The inner airlock cycled open with a woosh. There stood a Forger, at least two meters tall, its harsh red armor glowing in the dim light. Dash couldn't see a face behind the dark glass faceplate in the Forger's helmet.

As the armored, alien intruder lumbered into his ship, Dash felt every step in his bones. The sleek, terrifying helmet swiveled, analyzing its new conquest. Maybe it was gathering data, scanning for lifeforms, figuring out an effective way to subdue, capture, or simply kill everyone aboard.

Dash looked down and saw Kenzie looking back up at him. She nodded at him…and he suddenly realized with horror that she actually wanted to attack this thing. A towering Forger with deadly weaponry and advanced armor. With a wrench.

She put four fingers up and started counting down. Dash shook his head vigorously. His swollen eye throbbed with a dull pulse of pain.

Before Kenzie made it to one, however, Dash saw in his peripheral vision that the Forger had actually stopped walking down the corridor. He turned to look at it—moments later, he saw something that, as far as he knew, no living person had ever seen.

"Greetings," said the Forger, its voice a rumbling, artificially enhanced growl. It pushed a button on its wrist. There was a soft hiss, and the helmet retracted to reveal a face.

In the helmet's place was the head of a young, apparently Human woman, framed with short, red hair. Her green eyes—there was a nasty looking scar over the left one—spotted Dash and Kenzie crouching at the corner. The woman smiled and spoke.

"I am Commander Yera Crystal."

The wrench fell out of Kenzie's hand and onto the floor with a loud clang.

"Oh, come on," said Dash.

Crystal

The ship's corridor was silent as Kenzie and the rest of the crew gaped at the woman standing before them. Bathed in the dim emergency lights, she looked Human—standard green eyes of a Homo sapien, no distinguishing extra-terrestrial features or biology. And yet, she wore the armor of the Forgers. This was the crystal? This person who'd punched a hole in the *Gremlin*, drained the ship's power, and forced her way aboard? Kenzie's head felt stuffed with cotton. This didn't make any sense.

After another moment, Crystal spoke again.

"Take me to your weapons room, so we may negotiate the terms of a new alliance."

"What's that now?" said Dash from behind the corner.

Crystal's eyes went wide with wonder at the sound of Dash's voice. "Is that...truly you?"

No one said anything.

Crystal spoke again. "Captain Dashiell Drake?"

"I, uh...yes?"

Crystal crossed her arms on her chest and bowed deeply.

"You honor me with your presence," she said to the floor. "When I came here, I dared not imagine you would greet me personally. I am humbled."

Kenzie looked up at Dash. Dash looked down at her. A confused grimace flashed on his face, his swollen eye twitching once, his shoulders rising into a pained shrug. Kenzie didn't know what to do next, and apparently Dash didn't either.

Ravi whispered, "Perhaps you should step out there and say hello?"

Dash looked back at Ravi apprehensively. Then he nodded and took a step out, edging around the corner. He spread his hands apart in a gesture that looked to Kenzie like a cross between "we come in peace" and "please don't kill me."

Crystal didn't move as Dash's boots tapped across the metal floor.

Dash stopped in front of her, hands still in the air.

"Hi," he said. "Hello there."

Crystal glanced up at him, then straightened and spread her own arms, apparently mirroring Dash's gesture.

"Please," she said. "Allow me to honor you in the presence of your ship's guns so we may discuss our non-aggression treaty. Then, we shall join forces and crush our enemies as one."

"Soooooo…" said Dash. "I don't know what you're talking about."

Crystal's face broke into a confused smile.

"What do you mean?" she said.

"What do *you* mean?" said Dash, tilting his head at Crystal for emphasis.

"I have been following you since the abduction of Technica Outpost," she said, slowly lowering her hands. "I saw you escape my people, and I knew our destinies were intertwined. You and I will fight the treachery of the Forgers and disrupt their plans."

"Your people," said Dash, finally lowering his hands too. "But you look—you're a Human."

"Yes," said Crystal.

Jo peeked her head out from behind the corner.

"But," said Jo, "you're a Forger."

"Yes," said Crystal.

"Well, this is just getting absurd," said Twilliam. He stopped cowering with the rest of them and left, walking down the corridor toward the medbay.

"So, are we not going to negotiate?" said Crystal. "You would prefer the traditional duel for dominance?"

"No!" Dash's hands went back up. Crystal's hands went up too, mirroring his. "No—we don't—I don't—what the hell is going on? Who are you?"

"As I said, I am Commander Yera Crystal, of the Second Hellstrom Legion," she said. She balled her right hand into a fist and beat it once across her heart. The collision made a clank; Kenzie saw Dash flinch. "I have seen through the lies and propaganda of my people and sought to join your quest to defeat the Forgers in righteous battle."

"Okay, that's..." said Dash, lowering his hands again. "That's interesting. Only, that's not really..." Dash glanced at Kenzie, then shifted his gaze back at Crystal. "Okay. So the first thing that would be great, since we're, apparently, not trying to kill each other, is if you'd release whatever it was that you shot into my ship. Let's—let's start there."

"You mean the drainer cable," said Crystal. She tapped control buttons built into one of her armored gauntlets. The ship shuddered slightly, and a moment later Kenzie heard the reactor click on. The dim emergency lights went out, and the regular corridor lights activated. Kenzie squinted at the sudden brightness. "There. It is done."

"Great, that's just—just great," said Dash. "Cadets, could you maybe put on some helmets, and go see about that hull breach? I know we've got breach shields and patch kits down in the cargo bay."

"You mean the cargo bay that's filled with poisonous gas?" said Jo. There was a pause as Dash chewed his bottom lip.

"Yes," he said through gritted teeth. "I imagine the helmets would come in handy for going in there too."

"Are you, uh, sure you want us to leave right now?" It was the first thing Kenzie had managed to say since Crystal had boarded. The woman's eyes met hers as she spoke.

"Not entirely," said Dash. "But, it's probably a good idea…"

Kenzie slowly walked down the corridor toward the cadets' quarters, where her helmet was stashed in her locker. She walked slowly enough so she could still hear Dash as she crept away. Jo and Vor followed closely behind, apparently trying to listen too.

"Now, my uh, my 'quest to defeat the Forgers'?" he said tentatively as Kenzie, Jo, and Vor left. "That's…not really my quest, *per se*. But I'm still not totally…I just don't…did they abduct you or something? During the war?"

"Who?" asked Crystal, genuinely puzzled.

"The Forgers," said Dash. "Did they—I mean, were you abducted by the Forgers during the war?"

"I don't understand," said Crystal.

Dash grunted in frustration. She and the other cadets were halfway down the hallway. Ravi spoke next.

"What the captain is wondering, I believe, is why a Human would be wearing the armor of a Forger," he said.

"I—I don't…" said Crystal, sounding confused.

Kenzie stopped in her tracks. She didn't want to miss a word.

"You mean you don't know?"

"Don't know *what?*" said Dash, the impatience oozing from his voice. Kenzie strained to hear.

"Forgers *are* Human," said Crystal.

* * *

"What did she mean," said Kenzie as she, Jo, and Vor clomped through the cargo bay, gathering the scattered breach shields. "Forgers are Human? Forgers can't be Human."

Vor glanced at Kenzie and shrugged.

"Ew, get away from me," said Jo, nudging a wiggling chalzz out of her path as she walked.

The cargo bay was a ruin. Between the strewn inventory crates, the Dart having bounced around the space like a pinball, a huge puddle of orange goop, and the wandering, stinking Chalzz…

Well, it was pretty much a disaster.

Kenzie spotted a breach shield and bent to pick it up, adding it to her bag.

"I'm serious guys," said Kenzie. "It doesn't make any sense!"

"I guess?" said Jo, pushing another errant chalzz out of the way as she scooped two breach shields resting underneath the Dart's nose. "I mean—she looks like a Human to me."

"No, that's just my point," said Kenzie, dropping her bag onto the ground with a thunk. She put her hands on her hips. "The Forgers have crazy technology…powerful weapons and defenses that would've won the war if Dash hadn't—"

Kenzie stopped herself mid-sentence. Jo and Vor turned and looked at her.

"Well, they almost won with that technology, is my point," said Kenzie, grabbing her bag and setting back to work. "And they were using it against Humans. How does that work? Why would they use their weapons to hurt their own people?"

"I mean, isn't that basically what all wars are?" said Jo.

"Huh?"

"Like—think about all the wars on Earth before your planet developed space travel," said Jo, kicking a chalzz that wasn't in her way but seemed to annoy her. "Wasn't that just Humans hurting Humans anyway?"

Kenzie hadn't thought of that.

"I hadn't thought of that," said Kenzie.

"Anyway, I think that's all of them," said Jo, handing three more breach shields to Kenzie. "C'mon, let's patch the hole."

She started walking toward the door leading to the engine room until Vor jumped in front of it, barring her way.

"Ugh, what?" said Jo, taking a step back.

Vor waved his hands at Jo. Then he pointed to the airlock hatch to the left of the cargo bay doors on the other side of the room.

"We can't open the door to the engine room," said Kenzie. "It's been depressurized."

"I don't know what that means," said Jo.

Kenzie's eyes went wide. "Didn't you take a space travel training course?"

Jo scoffed. "I thought this 'cadet immersion experience thing' *was* my training course."

"If you open that door, everything in the cargo bay will get sucked into the vacuum of space."

"Oh, well, let's not do that then."

Vor shook his head at his sister, then strode to the hatch at the other end of the cargo bay. Kenzie and Jo followed. He cranked the wheel open and the metal door swung out, revealing what looked like a tiny little room—and another door identical to the one Vor had just opened.

Kenzie followed Vor inside, and Jo kept pace with them, albeit more hesitantly. Kenzie was constantly surprised at how little Jo knew about space travel. Didn't she know how airlocks worked?

Vor tapped some controls on the inside of the airlock, and moments later the air was being siphoned out, signaled by a loud hiss. A red light hanging above them flashed to green, and Vor spun the wheel on the outer door. A dizzying and immense starfield greeted them.

Kenzie took a deep breath and felt her mind go clear. Finally—some time to think.

She and the other two cadets began trudging across the ship's hull, their magnetized boots keeping them from spinning out into the vast, beautiful nothingness. Kenzie's perspective shifted as she walked across the *Gremlin*'s starboard side, the lack of gravity sending a thrill up her spine.

Halfway to the ship's stern, Kenzie started thinking hard about what she'd just been through.

They'd survived a Forger attack. Not only that, they'd made personal contact with a Forger. In the entire history of the Interstellar Alliance, no one had ever managed to converse with one and live through negotiations. No one had actually seen what was under their helmets—and apparently, Humans were under there. What did that even mean? How could the Forgers be Humans?

An image of her mom flashed into her mind, the same one she carried with her on that holographic disk. Her mom, who was lost in the Forger War. And now here was Kenzie, repairing damage done to her ship by a Forger—and she was a little ashamed to realize that mostly what she felt was curiosity. She knew she should feel fear or maybe even anger. But Kenzie figured that after the blowup in the galley, while Twince was trying to kill them, she'd used up all her anger on Dash. Even thinking about Dash didn't do much—there was just a numb ache in her mind where thoughts of the captain used to be. It was confusing.

The three cadets walked down the sloping curve that brought them to the ship's stern. There, in roughly the center of the *Gremlin*'s butt, was a giant, person-sized hole exposing the two-story engine room to space. The metal of the hull was split and curling inward, having suffered the puncturing effects of Crystal's…whatever it was.

Kenzie walked to the lip of the hole and peered inside, shining her light on the reactor itself. There were clear scuffs and scratches where there hadn't been before. More signs of the mysterious Forger tech Crystal had used to bust into the engine room and temporarily suck the ship's power dry.

Reaching into her bag, Kenzie grabbed two breach shields, then took another just in case. She handed them to Jo as Vor floated into the engine room through the hole. After tucking the three breach shields under her arm, Jo looked around for her suddenly absent brother. Kenzie pointed toward the gap in the hull, where Vor floated, waving and waiting.

"I knew that," said Jo over the shared comm channel. She followed him in.

Vor activated one of the shields and moved it toward the hole's bottom, then motioned for his sister to hold the shield in place. As Jo and Vor plugged the gaps in the oddly shaped opening, Kenzie took out her patch kit— a folded nanocarbon blanket—and unfurled it, draping it over the gap. It followed the new contours of the breach shields. And when Kenzie activated the material, the blanket went from flexible and foldable to rigid and rock-hard, forming a new skin for the outside of the *Gremlin*.

The patch, of course, wouldn't be as strong as the actual hull of the ship, but it would last until the *Gremlin* could get more meaningful repairs. Still, Kenzie wondered about what kind of tech could literally punch a hole straight through the hull. The destructive effects of missiles and other explosives were easy to explain. Blaster bolts, sure—those were powerful energy beams that could rip matter apart at the molecular level. But what kind of weapon could do this, and then manage to siphon energy from the reactor too?

Kenzie activated her comms. "Exterior patch in place," she said. "Go ahead and put your patch on, Vor."

There was a brief pause. Jo came on the line.

"He gave you a thumbs up," she said.

Kenzie smiled.

"Thanks," she said. "I'm gonna go...check something out."

"Uh-oh," said Jo. "Are you about to do one of those things that'll make the captain mad?"

Kenzie thought for a second, realizing how nearly everything she'd done since meeting him had apparently annoyed Dash in one way or another and thought about how now that mattered to her less than ever.

"Probably," said Kenzie.

She released her magboots and activated the small thrusters built into the lining of her jumpsuit. She piloted around the bend toward the *Gremlin*'s port side—where Crystal's blood-red Forger battlecruiser was docked. It looked like an angry, poisonous insect, all sharp angles and points. Its crimson paintjob said one thing: stay away. Kenzie ignored that warning, of course.

As the ship grew larger in her field of view, Kenzie thought about how many other people must have had such a close view of a ship like this—and how few of them probably lived after the fact.

Kenzie flew closer and closer to the battlecruiser, angling herself towards the Forger ship's bow while flying along its underside. It was thick with armor plating, which itself was covered in dents, dings, and scuffs. Leftover signs from battles long past, Kenzie supposed.

Near the front of Crystal's ship sat a row of mounted blaster turrets—all very dangerous looking. And on its port side, something that looked like a powerful winch with a barbed, bulky something on the front of it. Some kind of dense battering ram, near as Kenzie could tell. That must've been what broke through the *Gremlin*'s stern. But how did it manage to suck the power from the ship's reactor?

Kenzie flew in for a closer look—and pulled out her handset. If she could connect into the Forger ship's computer systems, she could figure out how the device worked. All she had to do was hack her way in—and she'd gotten plenty of practice hacking Forger computers on Technica Outpost. Kenzie started tapping at her handset. Within moments, she'd breached the computer's security, and she started downloading its schematics.

And that's when the ship's turrets suddenly sprang to life, and swiveled to aim directly at her face.

What Do You Know?

Dash crossed his arms, scowling at Ravi and the Doctors Bill. He felt doubly annoyed as he tried to figure out which Bill he should focus his scowl at.

"What do you mean, 'she's Human'?" he said.

"The results are entirely conclusive, Captain," said Ravi, his eyes glued to his handset. "There are some very small, fascinating discrepancies in her DNA that may be the result of genetic engineering, or perhaps a few hundred years of divergent evolution—really, I'd love more blood samples to work on later..."

Crystal, who'd patiently endured Ravi's and Bills' three-pronged exams for the last quarter hour while sitting on a center table in the medbay, raised a gloved hand and removed the thin analysis probe from her mouth.

"I already told you I was Hum—"

Twilliam pushed the probe back in, cutting her off.

"Keep that in there, please," he said, as Doctor Bill raced along his track to the front of the room, leaving his other patient, Squix, to float unconscious in a tank against the far wall.

"Yes, my scans indicate that our armored friend is, in fact, fully Human," he said. "As I was explaining—"

"Excuse me, but they were *my* scans, and *I* was the one explaining it—" interrupted Twilliam.

"Oh, not this again," said Doctor Bill.

"Yes, this again, because I've had about enough of your condescending—"

"If they're *your* scans, they're still *my* scans—"

"Not when I'm using *these hands*—"

Crystal spat out the probe and stood,

"Agh, shut up!" she yelled, the sudden ferocity in her voice taking Dash by surprise.

She pushed both Bills out of her way as she walked toward the end of the room. Doctor Bill swung back and forth in the aftermath of Crystal's shove.

"By the great Forge, are they *always* this annoying?"

Dash pointed at the still-swinging Doctor Bill. "That one is." Then he pointed at Twilliam. "That one's new, but also probably yes."

"Hey!" said the Bills.

Crystal wheeled around and locked eyes with Dash, who stepped backward.

"Captain Drake—please, enough! I need your help."

"Okay," said Dash, patting the air nervously. "Alright, just—hold on. I'm still trying to figure out your whole, uh, deal."

Crystal sighed and sat, though this time further from either Bill. They both crossed over to her with scanning instruments anyway.

She cocked an eyebrow. "My deal?"

"Well," said Dash, "Technica Outpost gets stolen by Forgers and we escape, a Forger ship pursues, and then you punch a hole in my ship, board it by force, say you want to negotiate a treaty and that our 'destinies are intertwined,' and—to top it all off—you tell me Forgers are Humans, which is bonkers, since the Forgers are *aliens* that declared war on the Interstellar Alliance twelve years ago."

Dash turned to Ravi. "Did I get just about everything?"

"Yes," he said. "That was pretty much all the big ones."

"Ah," said Crystal. "That."

Crystal walked to the room's center.

"When I was a young girl, a member of the Forger warrior caste, training as a soldier in the High Smith's service, I learned that the sins of the Interstellar Alliance were great. That its mongrel people, living across the dimensional divide, had taken what was rightfully ours. That the worlds and moons and stations comprising the Alliance should all fall within the High Smith's control. Its inhabitants were thieves and usurpers."

She turned to Dash.

"Captain Drake was the worst of them all —a cunning and evil man who would stop at nothing to see the Forgers debased and destroyed."

Dash grimaced, anticipating a smack.

"All lies."

The words hung in the air before she continued.

"In truth, our Empire, crumbling and overextended, never had any claim to your worlds. But because we shared DNA with the Humans in the Alliance, our High Smith decided your worlds should be his to command and control.

"Have you ever made a choice that led you down one path that changed everything? Mercy given to one enemy, a blaster shot that missed by centimeters—one action, one pivotal moment that made a world of difference?"

Ravi, who'd been with him in the galley when he'd revealed that he'd once saved the galaxy entirely by accident, glanced Dash's way for the briefest of moments.

"Uh, kinda," said Dash.

"Sometimes," continued Crystal, "these decisions, these moments, create ripples in time. And so, hundreds of years ago on your Earth, something happened. One person assumed power, while another did not. Their names would mean almost nothing to you, Captain Drake, as neither had a lasting effect on your world, and civilization unfolded according to the histories you know.

"But on *my* world, my Earth, the opposite happened. A different person assumed power. He changed his world and set in motion the events that led to the Forger Empire.

"Like you," she said, motioning to Dash and Ravi, "I come from Earth. But on the other side of the dimensional divide, we call it Forger Alpha. For centuries we have marched across our galaxy, seizing worlds and resources and exhausting them until nothing is left. And that is why our High Smith hates you and everyone you've ever known. Because your world is what ours should have been. That is why the Forgers declared war on the Alliance all those years ago—and why the High Smith has been planning his revenge ever since our defeat.

"Since the end of the Dimensional Conflict—what you call the Forger War—I have proven myself in battle time and again, quelling rebellions within our Empire, keeping order and obedience throughout our worlds. I was ordered to lead a battalion in our latest incursion into your dimension and came to Technica Outpost to serve under the direction of the woman known here as Lucy Reese. I was to execute her will, whatever it might be."

Crystal paused and shut her eyes.

"But I could not. And do you know why?"

No one spoke.

"Because of noodles," said Crystal

Everyone continued to not speak.

Crystal looked around the medbay, a grave expression on her face. It was as if a dog had just stood up and asked for help putting on a necktie. Finally, someone popped the balloon of silence.

"Did you just say 'noodles?'" said Twilliam incredulously.

"Indeed, green-machine-face," said Crystal. Her eyes took on a faraway look as she beamed with joy at the memory. "It was a dish you call 'spaghetti and meatballs.' The intensity of its flavor, the sensation of each bite—it was too much for me to bear. Being in Technica Outpost's food court, eating the various noodle dishes that came from your Earth, sampling the many cuisines from all around your galaxy—tasting the sumptuous flavors that represented the freedoms that came from living without the tyrannical boot of the High Smith crushing the windpipe of expression and creativity…"

Crystal sat down, overwhelmed.

"All my life, I'd eaten a simple nutritional paste that came in two flavors. Can you imagine an entire life consuming only two flavors?"

"What were they?" asked Ravi quietly.

"Vanilla…and plain."

"How awful," said Ravi, his voice cracking.

She stared at the floor, looking almost ashamed.

"It was enough for me to live and grow strong. But as I discovered the food that flourished in ways our culture could never hope to produce because of the High Smith's thirst for control and conformity…I discovered that everything I'd ever known had been false.

"I researched and read, and I learned that your Alliance valued the exploits of Captain Drake and saw him as a great warrior."

Dash coughed.

"And when you escaped from the Outpost when so many did not, I discovered more lies I was expected to believe. I read reports Reese had filed from years earlier. They said you were nothing more than an incompetent, overrated figurehead posing no threat to anyone at any time."

Dash frowned.

"It was clearly more propaganda designed to hide the truth and keep my people slaves. I monitored Technica's sensors and watched as a handset belonging to Captain Drake broke through locked doors, sowing chaos and fighting for justice and freedom in the face of the Forgers' plans."

Dash was confused for a moment, until he remembered...the handset belonging to him that had so inspired Crystal—Kenzie was using it. It was all her.

"You inspired me," she continued. "Your brave deeds drove me to disobey orders, to betray my culture and civilization—to fight for justice and freedom and noodles for all.

"I tracked your ship, yes," she continued. "Because I need you, Dash Drake, Hero of Gantoid IV. I know the strengths of the Forgers' technology. I also know its weaknesses, how to circumvent defenses, where they are vulnerable, where to strike the killing blow."

"Help me, Captain Drake. Help me stop the High Smith's plan to steal your worlds from you—just as it stole Technica Outpost—and leave the Alliance in ruins."

Crystal looked around the room, waiting for a response. What she got was mostly stunned silence. After another moment, Dash spoke.

"So...what's their big plan?"

"They have machines," said Crystal. "Machines large enough to transport huge amounts of mass through the dimensional divide—"

"Right," said Dash, putting up a hand. "I know all about those. We saw one when we escaped Technica. You followed us from there, right? What I want to know is how they plan on deploying those on the Alliance's planets. And how many planets. And which planets."

Crystal's eyes took on a flash of panic. "The Forgers have high ranking agents who've infiltrated the Alliance," she said. "They—they are instrumental in getting the machines into place at the target worlds."

Ravi spoke up next.

"But what worlds?" he said, smiling gently. "What agents? Do you know who we're looking for? Or where?"

"No," said Crystal. "I…I don't…"

Ravi continued to press her. "Are they infiltrating the Interstellar Alliance's Governing Council? On each of the worlds themselves, like Lucy Reese did on Technica? Are they in the Fleet?"

"I…I do not…" Crystal heaved a frustrated sigh. "I do not know these things. I thought you—thought you knew…" She trailed off.

Dash pinched the bridge of his nose. His swollen eye throbbed once, a stab of pain piercing his face. More nonsense. More craziness. When could he get back to his stupid life?

"There's a whole galaxy full of planets and territories and citizens," he said. "You come here and want to negotiate a—a partnership or team-up or something, but you don't even know what we're looking for.

"But I—"

"How is that helpful? At all?"

Crystal stammered. "I—I don't know…"

"What *do* you know?"

An armored fist smashed down onto an examination table. Dash felt the floor vibrate.

Crystal bellowed. "I know battle!"

"Excuse me!" said Doctor Bill, racing over to Crystal on his track. "I'll thank you not to—"

Her face a mask of rage, Crystal grabbed Bill's rectangular body with both hands and wrenched him from the ceiling, his surprised, digital scream going tinny as his power connection with the ship was severed. Dash jumped back instinctively.

A moment later, Crystal's expression went blank—just as Bill's digital face went dark as well. Holding the rectangular former doctor in her hands, Crystal suddenly looked embarrassed.

"Sorry," she said. Crystal gingerly placed Bill's unpowered body onto the exam table with a gentle clack. "I didn't, uh...sorry about that."

Dash saw that his own hands were raised in a defensive position. He saw out of the corner of his eye that Ravi and Twilliam had taken similar poses. He lowered his arms slowly, his gaze locked on Crystal.

"Now—just calm down a second," he said in his most soothing voice.

"Yes, the captain doesn't mean to be so aggravating," said Twilliam. "He just has a way with people. And that way is bad."

"Not helping," said Dash.

Crystal apparently saw Dash and the others treating her like a wild animal and closed her eyes, her head shaking slowly.

"I am not...I am not accustomed to conversations such as these," she said. She let out a big breath and opened her eyes. "I know only a few things in my life, Captain Drake. I know how to follow orders, and I know how to give them to the soldiers under my command."

"And you know battle," said Ravi.

"Not helping," said Dash again, this time through gritted teeth.

Crystal barked out a short, rueful laugh. "Yes. Yes, those are the things I know. How to defect from my people, how to gather allies, make plans, and crush the High Smith's mad schemes...these things are new to me. And they are hard."

Crystal picked up Doctor Bill's inert, rectangular body and shoved him back into his place along the track on the ceiling, plugging him back into the ship's power. His digital scream picked up where it had left off moments earlier. She let go and his body swayed slightly. He stopped screaming and looked around the room with his digital eyes.

Before he could say anything, a horrible siren—a skull-splitting whoop—erupted from Crystal, filling the room with chaos again. Dash covered his ears.

"Agh!" Bill cried, covering his digital face with his skinny metal medical probes and scooting away on his track to safety at the rear of the room.

Crystal tapped a few buttons on her armored gauntlet and the noise stopped.

"My ship," she said, her face grim. Without another word, she strode from the medbay, the door wooshing shut behind her.

Dash didn't even stop to think before he pulled out his handset.

"Kenzie," he said over the comm, "what'd you do?"

* * *

The door to the lift opened to reveal the cadets, still wearing their helmets. Kenzie leaned against the wall. Her posture said "tired," and her smell said "cargo bay" and also "fart monsters." She'd just been through an ordeal. Dash immediately started yelling at her.

"What the hell were you thinking?"

Jo and Vor slunk down the corridor toward their bunks. As they stalked away, Kenzie pulled her helmet off, a sneer already on her face.

"Oh, thanks for asking, I'm fine, Dash," she said, stowing her helmet under her arm. "Just a little shaken up after a Forger battle-cruiser aimed its guns at me after I patched the hole in *your* ship."

Dash noticed how Kenzie emphasized the word "your," but he didn't take the bait. When Kenzie breached the Forger ship's computer with her handset, it alerted Crystal in the medbay—who, in response, remotely swiveled her ship's turrets at Kenzie's head. If the cadet hadn't been so quick at hacking into the weapons to shut them down, she wouldn't be there flinging her attitude at him now.

"Don't give me that," said Dash, "like I should be grateful you stuck your face directly in front of some deadly super weapons. Like you did that for my benefit!"

"But that's just it," said Kenzie, scowling. "I did do that for your benefit! Don't you want to know what just ripped the hull to pieces?"

"Yeah, but I could've just asked Crystal what it was," said Dash.

"So did you?"

Dash felt his ears get hot. He didn't think to ask. That probably would've been smart.

"Well…no, but—"

"Whatever," said Kenzie, shaking her head. "Just tell me the plan."

"Plan?"

"What are we gonna do?" she asked. "How are we gonna stop the Forgers?"

He blinked at her.

"We're not," he said.

"What?"

Dash looked around the corridor to see if they were alone, then stepped closer and spoke quietly.

"Crystal is *nuts*," he said. "She ripped Bill out of the ceiling in the medbay, she's smashing stuff up. Her ship is punching holes in ours, and she's aiming weapons at you. She's dangerous. And she doesn't know anything. She doesn't know anything about…anything."

Kenzie cocked her head to the side.

"But she said she wanted to join our quest," she said. "She's been following us since Technica Outpost. Why?"

"She thought we had information, that we had a plan," he said. He was suddenly tired and sat on the corridor's floor. "That's why she's been following us. And the Forgers were never after us—just her. The 'crystal,' and the person Vor heard them talking about on Technica…it was always her."

"But why…" Kenzie paused, trying to process this new information. "Why would the Forgers be looking for her on Technica?"

Dash surprised himself by laughing.

"Because she didn't show up for work." He laughed again, bitterly. "A lady with severe anger issues and a thing for pasta decides to take a sick day, and my life gets flushed down the toilet."

"Pasta?"

Dash sighed, then grunted as he forced himself to his feet. "I'll tell you later. Anyway, thank you for patching the hull. Seriously." Dash stretched, then turned to walk down the corridor to the cockpit. "Once we say goodbye to Crystal, we'll plot a course back to Alliance space and get you back home."

"No," said Kenzie. "I don't think that's a good idea."

He turned back at the cadet, noticing her face looked hard as stone. And that was saying something, since two of his cadets were literally made of rocks.

"Come again?"

"Crystal may not have a plan, but she's still a Forger," said Kenzie, hands on her hips. "There's never been a Forger who's switched sides. And we know they're plotting against us. They're trying to steal our planets!"

Dash ran his fingers through his hair nervously. "What—how—what do you even expect us to do about that?"

"I don't know!" said Kenzie. "Something, though. We have to do *something.*"

"Look, I'll grant you that we—we have information. Information is good."

"Knowledge is more powerful than any weapon," said Kenzie.

"Yeah—that's a good way of putting it."

"It's from your book."

"Oh, uh," Dash stammered. "We can, uh—Ravi! We can have Ravi contact the Fleet, and Crystal can rendezvous with them. They can take it from here. Ravi even said they're working on those—those—what're they called? The security things?"

"Jump-chains," said Kenzie.

"That's them. The jump-chains will protect the planets. Hell, the Alliance probably already knows about all this! They're a massive, intergalactic government! They know things. But for the first time in what, days? We can finally get back to our lives. I can make my deliveries and get back to my life."

Kenzie got a pitying look in her eye that made Dash want to run the other way.

"What life?" she said softly. "You're a coward."

"Uh-huh," agreed Dash. "And that's not even—"

Crystal suddenly burst through the docking tube next to the lift.

"Incredible!" she shouted, looking at Kenzie. She scooped up the cadet in a bear hug, and Dash winced watching her get crushed in the Forger's grip.

"I am very impressed, Mackenzie Washington," she said, putting her down. "Not many people would risk their lives by looking into the barrel of a Forger's guns."

"Yeah," said Dash. "Kenzie's definitely not like many people."

"You're not mad?" said Kenzie, gazing at the armored lunatic looming above her. "Since I messed with your ship and stuff?"

"I am furious!" said Crystal with a manic smile. Kenzie flinched. "My anger is only superseded by my awe. I have met few living souls brave enough to approach a fully armed battlecruiser unprotected and met none who have survived such an encounter. You are very, very clever, Mackenzie."

She gently wagged an armored finger at her, still smiling. "Though cleverness isn't worth much if it gets you killed."

"That's what I keep trying to tell her," said Dash.

Crystal put a hand on Kenzie's shoulder. Her knees buckled slightly at the weight of Crystal's gigantic, armored gauntlet.

"Regardless, our righteous quest to defeat the Forgers and save your Interstellar Alliance will surely be triumphant."

"Uh, about that," said Dash, spreading his hands like he was opening a book. "I've been thinking that we're maybe not the best people for the whole 'righteous quest' thing."

Crystal's face fell, and she took her hand back.

"I do not...understand," she said.

"See, it's kinda like—I mean, our ship is very—we've got these cadets, and we really gotta get them back home—I'm sure if we get in touch with the Fleet you can meet with them..."

"You do not want to..."

"It's not so much that I don't want to, uh, Crystal," said Dash, tapping the tips of his fingers against each other nervously. "I'm just not really in the best position—right now—to start a, um, new quest."

He glanced at Kenzie who watched him with a kind of smug curiosity. Man, he hated her.

"Your warrior's flame," said Crystal slowly, "is extinguished."

Dash snapped his fingers.

"That's it," he said. "Extinguished flame. That flame's extinguished and, y'know, what can you do?"

Crystal nodded knowingly. Kenzie rolled her eyes.

"You must take time, regroup, rest," said Crystal. "Every battle takes its toll. And the condition of your ship is, indeed, appalling."

"Hey," said Dash.

"I will leave you shortly," she continued, opening and reaching into a compartment in her gauntlet. She retrieved a small, high-tech-looking cylinder with a couple buttons on it. Dash wondered if it might be a bomb.

"Take this communicator," she said, "and call me when you have delivered your charges to safety. When you are ready. Meanwhile, I will gather forces to my side. When we meet again, we shall have our own army."

Dash took the device, still not convinced it wouldn't explode. "Great," he said. "So—yeah. I'm gonna…I'm just gonna go now."

He waved at Crystal.

"Bye."

Dash spun on his heel and left Kenzie and Crystal in the corridor. He marched to the medbay to check on Squix.

"How's the patient?"

Doctor Bill, still shaken up from his encounter with Crystal, swiveled nervously to face Dash.

"Oh!" he said, his digital face looking startled. It took a moment for it to relax into its usual condescending sneer. "I, um, he, yes…Squix is faring much better and should be able to resume duty soon."

Over the next few minutes, Bill showed him some of the readouts on the medical displays near Squix's tank, pointing out the various ways his first mate's vitals had improved since his adventure through the *Gremlin*'s ventilation system. There were a lot of numbers, charts, and graphs.

"That's good—good to hear," nodded Dash, pretending to understand what Bill was saying. "And your other half? Where's Twilliam?"

"Hopefully as far away from here as possible," said Doctor Bill, back to his old self. "I cannot stand that green-skinned abomination. He is insufferable."

Dash bit his lip.

"I know what you mean," he said through a cough.

A small rumble shook the *Gremlin* slightly, the physical effect of Crystal's ship undocking from his and leaving his life. Finally.

"I'm getting us out of here," said Dash, walking toward the door.

"Please see that you do, Captain. I can't imagine spending another moment anywhere near that armored barbarian. Never in all my life have I—"

Dash didn't hear the rest of Bill's complaints as he left the medbay.

He walked back to the cockpit, dimly lit and empty, and sat in his chair. He looked at the communication device Crystal had given him, turning it over in his hand a few times.

Then he reached under his console, opened the garbage chute that fed the trash compactor, and tossed the device in. Dash heard it ping and pong its way down to the *Gremlin*'s belly, and he let the door to the chute slam shut with a clang. Gone.

A newfound feeling of relief and hope filled his chest. Sure, his cargo would be late, but he'd been late before. Yes, the *Gremlin* had never gotten so beaten up in so short a time, but she still hung together—and even late cargo paid for repairs. And the chalzz in the cargo bay were still alive, and that was worth a bit of cash all on its own.

He plotted a course for Motomondo, the jump-drive spinning up with power. Maybe when Squix was up and about again, they could take a break at that diner he liked—the one with the good gravy fries. That'd be a nice way to feel like things were back to normal. And he and Ravi could provide their intel to the Alliance Fleet's top brass so they could do…whatever it was they would do to deal with the Forgers. Whatever they decided, it wouldn't be his problem anymore. He could finally get back to his life—such as it was.

Dash felt a weird sensation on his face. After a second, he realized he was actually smiling. It had been a while.

He picked up the intercom.

"Listen up, everyone," he said, his voice echoing back to him through the speakers positioned throughout the ship. "We're getting back to work. We're heading straight for Motomondo to make our deliveries, and then we can make arrangements with your parents to have you picked up at the nearest Alliance outpost.

"We've been through a lot together, and I just wanted to say…"

He paused, wanting his next words to really matter.

"…that once I drop you off, I hope I never see any of you again."

He clicked off the intercom and thought for a second. He clicked it back on.

"Nothing personal," he added, then clicked it off again.

The stars in his viewport went blurry as the ship began entering jump-space, then a flash of red. They were on their way.

It wasn't until about halfway to Motomondo that Dash found out that Kenzie, Jo, and Twilliam weren't on the ship anymore.

Stowaways

22

After the fitful sleep that came with hiding out on Crystal's battlecruiser overnight, Kenzie started doubting her decision to leave the *Gremlin*. Part of it was coming to realize that her ideas weren't always particularly well-received by her travelling companions. Another part was that in leaving the *Gremlin* behind, she'd consciously abandoned Dash, Squix, Ravi, and Vor—and over the last few days they'd all more or less benefited from her presence aboard the ship.

At this moment, however, having woken up in the cramped cargo compartment in the Forger vessel's belly, Kenzie felt uneasy about stowing away for a different reason. Mainly because of the small army of security drones pointing several aggressive looking guns at her, Jo, and Twilliam.

"Uh, Kenzie," said Jo. "Those robots look kinda mad."

Kenzie frowned and slowly sat up. "I guess Crystal knows we're here."

One of the security drones—it looked like a floating traffic cone covered in spikes and guns—clicked angrily and waggled a blaster, the momentum causing it to bounce in mid-air on its hoverpad. "Intruders! Raise your hands, claws, or any other appendages not used for locomotion above your heads. You are coming with us."

"Well, this is just wonderful," said Twilliam, putting his hands in the air, his red eye glowing. "I'm so glad I let you talk me into coming with you."

"Why *did* you come with us?" asked Jo.

"Are you joking? The first chance I had to get away from Captain Drake, and you're wondering why I took it?"

The trio filed out of the cargo compartment and followed the half dozen small, floating drones down the corridor.

"But aren't you still, like, technically on the ship?" said Jo. The lead robot opened a door to a medium-sized room that had force fields embedded in the walls.

"That's not me. That's that other me—and he's almost as bad as Captain Drake. I'm—well, I'm someone else. And I won't be contained."

With the push of a button, the lead drone revealed small, closet-sized compartments behind the force fields.

"Get in that cell!" It pointed a gun at Twilliam menacingly.

"Yessir," Twilliam muttered as he shuffled into the nearest one.

Kenzie hesitated for a moment, then ran her palm over her pocket, feeling the conforting weight of her handset there. She walked in and the drone reinitialized the force field—a blue-green haze of energy separating Kenzie from the rest of the brig. As the drone-patrol hovered out and left the three of them alone, Kenzie heard a clang from the left side of the room.

"Agh!" yelled Twilliam.

"Are you okay?" asked Kenzie as she risked a touch of the force field with her finger. Her hand bounced back as it zapped her.

"No, I—I can't seem to…" said Twilliam, suddenly mumbling. "I'm on the floor and I—I can't move half my body!"

Kenzie pulled out her handset. It was dead.

"Dampening field. These holding cells kill anything with an artificial power source. Your cybernetic implants won't work while the field's up."

"Wonderful," said Twilliam with a bad case of mush mouth. Twince must've had implants in his jaw.

"So, wait," said Jo. "I can't check my feeds while we're stuck in here?"

"I don't think so," said Kenzie.

"I hate this," said Jo, a pout in her voice.

"*You* hate this?" cried Twilliam. "I can't even move!"

Kenzie shook her head to clear her mind as the two bickered through the wall between their cells. She looked around the room, giving herself a moment to take in the design elements in the Forger battlecruiser.

In so many ways, the vessel was similar in its design and layout to the Earth ships that she'd known. After all, if Forgers were Humans, the races had societal, as well as biological, similarities. Doors were roughly Human-sized, and seats were built for people with their knees in the front. She couldn't say the same for every ship she'd ever been on, since so many different alien races populated the Interstellar Alliance.

In fact, even most modern Earth ships had a few accommodations for people from other planets so everyone could function in relative comfort: ramps and hanging baskets for non bipedal organisms; vapor canister refill stations for anyone who didn't breathe oxygen. Kenzie had never really thought about the presence of those kinds of details before, and they were conspicuous by their absence here.

There were some other differences too. The Forgers' sense of style had more sharp, angular points, and an obsession with the color red. Polished, decorative spikes sat atop most doorways, and Kenzie didn't see anything resembling seat cushions. That could've had more to do with the fact that she and her friends were in holding cells, of course, but she didn't recall seeing any padding on the ship since sneaking aboard the day before.

Kenzie pondered the Forgers' interior decorating habits for an hour or so, until she realized she still had no idea how to escape the cell. She'd searched for hidden access panels and found nothing. And the force field was, well, forceful. She couldn't figure out how to disengage it or break through—not without possibly frying her nervous system in the process.

"Well?" said Twilliam. Could you hurry up and get us out of here? I'm discovering I'm apparently claustrophobic."

"You were stuck in the medbay your entire life," said Jo from the next cell. "How are you figuring this out now?"

"The medbay was much bigger," mumbled Twilliam.

"I...I don't know what to do," said Kenzie, shaking her head. "I don't know how to get us free if my handset's dead."

"Well," said Jo. "That's a new one."

Kenzie stepped back and leaned against the wall, closing her eyes. Was she only as good as her handset? Without her trusty device, could she do much of anything? She'd never realized just how much she'd relied on technology to get herself out of—and, not unrelated, *into*—trouble. Now that she was stuck in that cell, who was she? Just a fourteen-year-old girl in over her head.

She shook her head again.

"No," she said, softly to herself. There was a way out. Just because she didn't see it right away, that didn't mean she couldn't find it eventually.

"Sometimes patience is your most valuable tool. Drake, 212." she said, quoting again from her once-favorite book.

"What?" said Jo.

"Nothing," said Kenzie, smiling.

A little while later, the door to the brig finally swished open. Kenzie leaned forward and looked through the blue-green force field of her holding cell. A person in full Forger armor, sealed-in from head to toe and complete with its faceless helmet, strode into the room. Even though she couldn't see her expression, Kenzie knew Crystal probably wasn't happy.

"I'm not happy!" she bellowed, her voice distorted and vaguely horrifying as it was amplified through the helmet's voice modulator. "You have already breached my ship's security once. And now you have stowed away without my knowledge nor consent."

Crystal drew a particularly terrifying blaster rifle from behind her back and leveled it at Kenzie. Even with the force field up, Kenzie felt her already quickly beating heart speed up a few ticks.

"Given that I have just failed to ally myself with Captain Drake, one of the Empire's greatest enemies, I can only conclude that you still view me as a foe and that you three are here as spies, meant to gather a tactical advantage for a later attack—"

Kenzie held up her hands, patting at the air.

"Whoa! No, we're not—we're not here to spy on you," she said. "We're here to help you. You know, on your quest."

"My quest? But your commanding officer denied me, sent me away. Why would he send you in his stead?"

"He—he didn't."

"You defy your commander's orders?" Crystal's distorted voice held no small degree of contempt…and a hint of confusion, Kenzie realized. This was the moment.

"Well, we—we decided to help you. We rebelled against him in order to, uh, right a grave injustice. We're…we're like you."

Crystal said nothing. Kenzie saw herself reflected in the blank, mirrored mask of Crystal's helmet, though her face was stretched and curved along its contours. As the silence drew on, Kenzie wondered whether she was about to be zapped into powder. Not quite how she'd pictured this moment. She figured that her death would involve more last-minute spaceship battles, maybe a dramatic, heroic explosion and self-sacrifice—and less staring down the barrel of an advanced, super-gun.

Without warning, Crystal holstered her rifle and pressed a button on her wrist to retract her helmet, revealing a smiling face streaked with wild-eyed tears. She tapped the button in the wall and removed the force fields keeping Kenzie, Jo, and Twilliam in their cells—then walked toward Kenzie, arms outstretched. Kenzie took a surprised step back as Crystal scooped her up into a bear hug, just as she had on the *Gremlin*.

"My quest," Crystal whispered, as Kenzie felt her vital organs squishing against her ribs.

Suddenly Kenzie remembered Dash's insistence that Crystal might not be entirely reliable in the sanity department. At the time she'd dismissed him, figuring he was just looking out for himself. Now she wondered again if stowing away on Crystal's ship was really that good an idea after all.

After what felt like an eternity, Crystal dropped Kenzie onto the floor. Kenzie's knees wobbled for a moment, but she managed to keep herself from collapsing into a heap.

"Come," she said. "You and your companions must now learn about this ship and what duties you will perform while you serve under my command."

"Duties?" scoffed Jo.

"Serve?" said Twilliam with the same tone of voice.

"Indeed," said Crystal, nodding. "A ship such as this usually has a compliment of ten. The vessel has suffered in their absence. You three will have to suffice."

Kenzie gulped. Crystal had mentioned she wanted to build an army to fight the Forgers. Apparently they'd just been conscripted.

Crystal led the three of them from room to room, proudly explaining the various functions and capabilities of each system housed within. The weapons control room, for instance, was far more powerful than the

Gremlin's—and also hadn't recently been on fire, which was another plus. The weapons were capable of unleashing significant force upon anyone unlucky enough to get in their way. Kenzie thought back to that tense moment as she floated just meters in front of those guns a day earlier.

The shield control room, the engine room, the enormous, pulsating reactor core, the small hangar bay of reconnaissance shuttles that, too, were armed to the teeth. Crystal beamed proudly as she gave the tour and described, in great detail, how each of them would be expected to operate and maintain the ship's systems as she hatched her plan to fight back against the Forger Empire. Kenzie made a mental note to herself that Crystal hadn't yet actually explained what that plan might be—another fact she realized with some annoyance that Dash had pointed out to her yesterday.

Finally, they ended their walkthrough in the cockpit, which had room for only a pilot and copilot. It was much smaller than the *Gremlin*'s, surrounded by armor plating and backup shield generators to protect the people inside controlling the vessel. That was probably because of the battlecruiser's focus on, well, battle.

Part of Kenzie's curious mind thrilled at the advanced tech that came from a whole other dimension. She was itching to examine every button and switch, every console and circuit. But she couldn't help but feel sad at how uninviting the cockpit seemed, with its generally aggressive and utilitarian style. Sure, it made sense for a race of violent, extra-dimensional warriors.

But couldn't it have been just a little…cozier?

"…and finally, this cleans the viewport," said Crystal, pointing at a small green button on the main console. "Any questions?"

"Yeah," said Jo. "What's this thing called?"

Crystal's eyebrows scrunched. "It's called the viewport wiper."

"No, I mean the ship," said Jo. "Does the ship have a name?"

Crystal's eyebrows remained scrunched. "No," she said. "Why should my vessel have a name, Rock Girl? It is just a tool. Does the carpenter name her hammer? Does the doctor name his scalpel?"

"I used to call my scalpel 'Mister Cutty,'" said Twilliam.

"That's amazing," said Jo.

Kenzie looked at Crystal. "I think what Jo means is that this ship isn't part of the Forger armada anymore. It's more than a tool, right? It's a symbol. You're using it to lead a revolution. And symbols should have names."

A smile spread across Crystal's face as she nodded in understanding.

"Yes," she said. "Now I see. A name. A name befitting a great war vessel."

"Exactly," said Kenzie.

Crystal thought for a moment. Then: "What about the *Orzo*?"

"The what?" said Jo.

"The *Orzo*," repeated Crystal. "As I explained to your Captain Drake, I was inspired by the Alliance's vast selection of noodle dishes to rebel against the Empire and embark on my sacred quest. I tried orzo shortly after the spaghetti and meatballs and found it particularly engaging."

Pasta. Kenzie remembered Dash saying Crystal had a thing for pasta. Oh, boy.

"We'll, uh, we'll talk about the name later, but that's a—a good start," Kenzie said.

"Thank you," said Crystal. "It *is* good."

"But what are we doing first? What's the first item on our quest to fight the Forgers?"

"We raise an army," said Crystal.

"Great. How?"

Crystal didn't say anything for a moment. Then Kenzie saw a realization fill the Forger's eyes.

"The Frawgs," she said.

"What?" said Jo

"Are you crazy?" said Twilliam, a greater hint of Twince creeping into his voice.

"I have bested the Frawgs in combat," said Crystal, seemingly referring to when she chased the Frawgs away from the *Gremlin*. She tapped on the wrist-mounted console built into her armor. "Therefore, they will bend to my military superiority and join our cause—willingly or by force."

Kenzie's scalp itched. By force?

"By force?" she asked.

"Indeed, Mackenzie. I am setting a course back to the Sheaffer system and sending a message to inform the remaining Frawg forces of our approach."

"You're telling them we're coming?" asked Twilliam incredulously.

"That sounds like a bad idea," said Jo.

Crystal looked from her wrist and smiled at Jo.

"Do not question me and expect it to end well for you, Rock Girl."

Jo's eyes went wide, but she clamped her mouth shut.

"Prepare the ship for jump, then load and prime all weapons," said Crystal. "We are going to negotiate."

* * *

Crystal sent her invitation to negotiations by simply blasting a message through space to the Frawg tribal encampment in the Sheaffer system. In the message, Crystal demanded they meet her on one of the planet's bigger moons to discuss their impending subjugation.

And that if they refused, they were cowards, and deserved a slow agonizing death at her hands.

So, yeah, it was not a great start.

Kenzie wasn't having much luck trying to talk to Crystal about it either.

"We're just going to jump back and land on that moon?" she asked from the copilot's chair.

"Yes," said Crystal beside her as she entered the coordinates into the *Orzo*'s nav-computer.

"Won't the Frawgs have time to get there, set up an ambush, and gain a significant tactical advantage over us while we're on our way?"

"Yes," said Crystal.

Kenzie's mouth went tight. "Are you sure you want to do that?"

"Yes," said Crystal, activating the ship's jump-drive. The cockpit vibrated slightly, and the viewport flashed red as they entered jump-space.

Crystal stood and turned to leave the cockpit. Kenzie followed.

"But don't you think that—"

Crystal wheeled around, snarling.

"By the Forge, would you stop your incessant prattle?" She smashed her armored gauntlet onto the wall with a great clang. "If you questioned your former commanding officer this much, I cannot understand why you still draw breath."

Kenzie bit her lip and didn't say anything. Crystal's gaze lingered on her for a moment longer and then the Forger smiled serenely, which Kenzie found a bit more frightening than her snarl.

"We will be fine," she said. "I am the superior warrior. I have trained to achieve unrivaled tactical and command expertise. This is a fact. They will swear allegiance to my cause—or face my wrath."

Crystal turned and left the cockpit. The door whooshed closed behind her, leaving Kenzie staring at its polished metal surface.

A few minutes later, Kenzie found Jo and Twilliam below decks. Crystal had ordered them to clean out the ship's torpedo tubes in the weapons room. Jo had commented that they already looked clean, but Crystal commanded they scrub them anyway.

"Well, we're going back," said Kenzie, sitting on one of the many crates of missiles.

"Oh, cool," said Jo, who tapped at her handset, "so we're gonna be eaten soon, right?"

"I mean, I hope not," said Kenzie. "But...yeah. Probably."

"This is so annoying," said Jo, her eyes going wide as they stayed glued to her device's display.

"What, getting eaten?"

"No, I can't get onto any networks," said Jo. "Fix it." She flipped her device to Kenzie, who caught it after a couple juggles. It only took a moment for her to see what the problem was.

"We're blocked," she said. "The ship must have a dampening signal—makes sense for a military vessel. No way for unauthorized signals to get in or get out."

Kenzie tossed the handset back to Jo.

"Ugh. I may as well be dead," she said. "I hope I die before you anyway. I'm never gonna hear the end of it from my dad if I somehow get away but you still get chomped."

"I'll, uh, try to cower behind you," said Kenzie.

Twilliam, who was scrubbing a completely clean torpedo tube threw his rag onto the floor and put his hands on his hips.

"I only got this body yesterday," he hissed. "And now some stupid Frawg's going to eat it? This is just great."

"Actually, Twince said he didn't taste good when we first found him," said Kenzie.

"Yeah, maybe too much metal in there?" added Jo.

"Oh, so now I'm not good enough for Frawgs to eat?" scowled Twilliam. "I just can't win." He picked up his rag and resumed scrubbing.

Kenzie rolled her eyes. She felt a pang of sympathy for Dash at having to work with Bill for all those years.

Jo looked at Kenzie.

"So, what's your plan?"

Kenzie smirked just a little.

"What makes you think I have a plan?"

"You always have a plan," said Jo, shaking her head. "And considering how screwed we are right now, I figure it might even be a good one this time."

Kenzie's smirk twisted into a pout. "I have good plans!"

"You mean like sneaking aboard the ship of a crazy woman with too many guns and a noodle fetish?" said Jo. "Was that one of the good ones? I lost track."

Kenzie considered this. "Okay, good point," she said. "Anyway, this time it's a good one for sure. And that's because it involves…" Kenzie paused for dramatic effect and turned to Twilliam, who had his back to her as he scrubbed. "…you."

Twilliam didn't say anything.

"Twilliam? I said it involves you. We need your help to make my plan—"

"Uh-huh," he said, interrupting Kenzie mid-sentence and continuing to scrub without turning. "Think I'll pass. I've had about enough of people telling me what to do on this ship. And the last ship. Really, on any ship."

He stopped scrubbing and turned to face Kenzie and Jo.

"You know, really, maybe ships are the problem for me. All my life, I've been flying from one place to another, never putting my feet on the ground…and look where it's gotten me? No, I think this is the last ship for me, girls." He went back to work. "Once I finish scrubbing that madwoman's torpedo tubes, I'm getting off at the next place with solid ground and staying put."

Kenzie looked at Jo, who rolled her eyes.

Kenzie pulled out her handset and extended its connection cable.

"Sorry about this, Twilliam," she said. "I, uh, I saw this in your code back on the ship, but I wasn't sure that I'd ever..." Kenzie sighed. "I wanna watch TV."

Twilliam managed to squeak out a "What—" before he froze and tipped over onto the floor.

And then she plugged her handset into the back of his skull.

"This is kind of messed up, Kenzie," said Jo.

"Yeah, well, we don't have a ton of options right now," said Kenzie. "Trust me."

* * *

Hours later, they arrived, setting down on the surface of the Sheaffer system's largest moon. As the *Orzo* extended its landing struts, Kenzie looked at the copilot station's scope and tracked a baker's dozen of small- to medium-sized Frawg ships stationed about half a kilometer away from their landing site. The welcoming committee.

"Come, Mackenzie Washington," said Crystal, unfastening her restraints. Her helmet was in place, distorting her already-booming voice into a monstrous Forger growl. "Let us build our army."

Kenzie's stomach did a flip as she looked at Crystal through her own helmet's visor. She pushed herself out of her seat and followed her out of the cockpit.

Jo was waiting for them in the hangar bay, her helmet on and ready for the airless moon.

"Where is your metal companion?" asked Crystal. "Does he share your disinterest in following orders?"

"He's, uh—" Jo stammered.

"He had to power down," interrupted Kenzie. "He recently upgraded his operating system, and there are some firmware updates that need to get installed."

Crystal's inscrutable helmet stared Kenzie down. Kenzie stared back, wondering if Crystal knew what firmware was.

"That sounds important," said Crystal after a few seconds. "He will stay on the ship and miss our moment of triumph."

Crystal reached into a storage locker on the wall and pulled two deadly looking pistols and hip holsters out, handing them to the girls without a word.

"Uh, thanks," said Jo.

It felt pretty heavy, though Kenzie also realized the moon's reduced gravity would likely remedy that, making it easier for her to handle and fire. Then she remembered she had no idea how to use a Forger-made pistol. She buckled on the hip holster and just put the gun away.

"What about those?" said Jo. Kenzie looked and saw Jo pointing at a compartment embedded in the hangar bay's wall. A row of vacant Forger suits of armor—just like Crystal's—hung within, standing shoulder to shoulder. "Can we wear those?

Crystal turned her head to the armor

"Those," she rumbled, "are Forger battlesuits. You must train for years to even learn the proper respect for the suit. It is capable of providing full life support and advanced rocket propulsion, as well as a complement of offensive and defensive measures. Wearing the suit is like being encased inside a small, fully armed battleship. The suit would kill you in five minutes."

"So that's a no?" said Jo.

"Correct. That's a no," said Crystal, turning and walking to the front of the hangar bay. "The pistols should suffice. Simply follow my commands, rely on your previous battle training, and all will be well."

Kenzie and Jo exchanged a look.

"Door, this is your commander," barked Crystal. "Open—now." The small airlock built into the front of the hangar bay swung open, then shut behind them after they'd filed inside, and then began the depressurizing sequence. Kenzie couldn't help but marvel: Crystal was so used to giving orders she even did it to her own ship. She could've just pushed a button and gotten the door to do the same thing.

Soon, they walked out onto the moon's surface. The door shut with what would've been a clang or a thud, had there been any atmosphere for sound to travel through. Instead, it simply vibrated the small, retractable gangplank beneath Kenzie's feet.

Crystal marched with purpose—and an overall lack of gravity—toward the thirteen hostile ships waiting for them. Kenzie and Jo kind of did a low-gravity bouncing shuffle behind her.

After they'd gotten some distance from the ship, Kenzie checked her handset. The countdown timer had six seconds left, and Kenzie turned her head to look back at the *Orzo* as she walked. Moments later, the hangar bay door flopped open, landing onto the surface with a puff of moon dust and a small rumble under her feet. Kenzie chanced a glance back at Crystal, who didn't break her stride.

An oblong reconnaissance shuttle drifted lazily out the hangar and left the moon behind just as casually as if it was off to an afternoon lunch date. The *Orzo*'s hangar bay door closed back up. Kenzie felt her heartbeat quicken as the reconnaissance shuttle became just a dot, joining the rest of the stars that shone down from above.

"Why did we land so far away?" asked Jo over the comms.

"Intimidation," said Crystal. "It is a valuable weapon."

Kenzie watched as Frawg footsoldiers spilled from their ships to await their arrival and saw what she meant about intimidation, though probably not quite how she meant it.

Ten minutes later, the trio stood in the center of a hastily constructed landing platform. It was a simple sheet of matte black nanocarbon that provided a firm, flat surface for the Frawgs' ships to land on. Surrounding them were Frawg foot soldiers in their greenish-brown armor. While only a few had guns on them, they were all covered in in various improvised

spikes or claws. The Frawgs all looked much pointier than the last time
Kenzie had seen them.

Just when it looked as though they'd been surrounded by hostiles on
all sides, yet another Frawg emerged from the biggest ship on the landing
pad. This one stood about a head taller than the others and wore armor
slathered with accents of green, red, and purple tribal paint.

Kenzie recognized her: it was Boss Frawg—the smart one. Uh-oh.

Boss Frawg pushed a button on her wrist. Suddenly the comms in
Kenzie's helmet crackled to life with the sound of quiet, throaty squawks.
Now they were all sharing one communication channel.

"I am Chief Katak," croaked the woman Kenzie formerly thought of
as Boss Frawg. "You have trespassed on our territory multiple times,
injured my people, destroyed our ships, and taken our property."

"Yeah, and we were gonna eat that property!" said one of the
assembled Frawgs. The comm line filled with croaks of aggrieved
agreement that blurred the line between laughter and anger. After a
moment, Katak lifted her hand for silence, and she got it immediately.

Kenzie saw Katak's bulbous eyes narrow through her helmet's visor.
The chief extended her long, slender arm and pointed accusingly at
Crystal.

"And now you have the temerity to return here and demand
allegiance."

Crystal took a step forward, and Kenzie was shocked to see a number
of the Frawg soldiers cower in response. Turned out intimidation tactics
were a two-way street.

"Your allegiance is mine, by ancient right," said Crystal, her voice
booming over their shared comms. "I have bested you in combat, and I
claim your lives as my spoils!"

"I do not recognize your claim," Katak spat back, her hand now
clenched into a fist.

In that moment, the dozens of Frawg soldiers, standing in a circle around Kenzie, Jo, and Crystal, all shifted into a crouched stance. Kenzie thought it might be best described as "ready to pounce."

"These 'negotiations' are over," said Katak.

"This is just foolishness," said Crystal, her voice booming over the shared comms. The response from the Frawgs was a lot of throaty hissing. That was what Kenzie suspected the Frawgs did before they got ready to eat people.

Crystal gave a distorted sigh, then said, "Alright girls, basic attack pattern alpha-nine."

Jo turned to Kenzie, a look of total befuddlement on her face. Kenzie returned the expression.

"Execute!" yelled Crystal. She did an acrobatic-looking tumble and rolled away, pulling her blaster rifle off her back in one fluid motion and started firing. The Frawgs scattered as Kenzie and Jo stood back to back and fumbled their pistols out of their holsters.

Kenzie chanced a look at the stars for any sign that her plan might have worked and didn't see anything to encourage her faith. With her hopes dashed for the moment, she tried figuring out how to get her gun's safety switched off.

Crystal continued her series of tumbles and her volley of plasma bolts at the running Frawgs. "Girls!" she called over the comms. "Alpha-nine! Execute!"

"What are you talking about?" pleaded Jo, whose pistol wasn't cooperating enough to even come out of its holster.

Kenzie thought she might have found the right buttons to make her pistol fire, when she suddenly felt her arms press up against her ribs, and all the breath was squeezed out of her. The pistol fell from her hands and tumbled silently to the ground.

She looked down to see she was bound by a glowing energy rope. Looking up, she saw that Jo and Crystal were similarly captured.

Crystal growled incoherently over the comms as she twisted and struggled against the bonds. The armored Forger toppled onto the ground, a great plume of moon dust puffing up from the impact.

"Alpha-nine! Alpha-nine!" Crystal boomed. "It's a basic battle maneuver! They teach it to children!"

"We didn't—ngh—we didn't go to Forger school, you psycho!" Jo said, still on her feet but struggling with her own restraints.

Crystal groaned with disgust as she rolled around, trying to get free. "It's no wonder you were practically conquered by the Empire during the war…"

Kenzie didn't try to muscle her way out of her restraints—she was held too tight, and there was nowhere to run. They were surrounded. She looked back up at the sky, hoping she'd see what she was looking for.

Katak sauntered toward them slowly, hands on her hips.

"For years, the Interstellar Alliance has marginalized us, pushing us out to the fringes of civilization, forcing us to scrounge and scrape for resources, for food. Frawgs are accused of plotting against the Alliance, of wreaking havoc in your territories, of snatching your children in the night, and cooking you for our supper."

"Well," said Kenzie, meeting Katak's gaze. "Don't you, y'know, do that? Eat people?"

"Yes," said Katak. "We're carnivores. And we're starving."

"You're telling me," said one of the Frawgs over the shared comm channel.

Katak continued as though she hadn't been interrupted.

"Before the Forger War, the Frawgs had colonies throughout the Interstellar Alliance—on brutal, wild, inhospitable worlds." Katak turned to the ring of soldiers around them. "We were forced from our homes—driven out! No one even wanted our worlds where we lived peacefully. The planets were destroyed, and we were cast into the blackness of space, adrift and alone. And now? We hunger!"

The Frawgs all croaked in unison. "We hunger!"

Something was itching at the back of Kenzie's brain, but she couldn't quite put her finger on it. The war...destroyed worlds...

"Wait a second..." she said to no one in particular.

"We sought the Alliance's protection!" cried Katak. "We wished to join and become a part of Interstellar society!" She turned and leveled a finger at Jo and Kenzie. "But your leaders shunned us. Your politicians, your news feeds called us savages. We were turned away—left with nothing. And now? We hunger!"

The Frawgs were closing in, creeping inward, tightening the circle. They cried as one. "We hunger!"

Something clicked in Kenzie's mind.

"Oh," she said. No one noticed.

Katak stalked around the three of them, a predator circling its prey.

"No habitable world to call our own. No resources so our culture could thrive. Or survive. No food! No food! *No food!* So now..."

The Frawgs surged forward and screamed. "We hung—"

The ground erupted around them, Frawgs flying this way and that, moon dust billowing upward like a thick gray fog.

Katak and the rest of the Frawgs howled over the comms as blaster fire rained down from above. Moments later, the dust cleared enough so Kenzie could spot Jo. The Crag glared at her through her helmet's faceplate, her annoyed expression illuminated by the internal heads-up-display.

"Okay, fine," said Jo. "Maybe that was a good plan."

"Just in the nick of time, right?" said Kenzie, trying to keep her voice light and free of the anxiety that came with almost being eaten by an army of hungry amphibian people from outer space.

"Barely," said Jo.

Her arms still tied, Kenzie crouched and duckwalked to where she thought Crystal lay on the ground, feeling around for the bound Forger with her feet. When the toe of her boot struck something hard and metal, Kenzie gave Crystal's shoulder another good whack.

The Forger's head swiveled up at Kenzie, and she wondered just what kind of expression the red helmet's mirrored visor hid from view.

"Come on," said Kenzie.

Crystal struggled to her feet without the use of her arms. Once the Forger managed to stand, Kenzie began bounding back toward the *Orzo*. She hopped a meter or so off the ground with each step, thanks to the moon's reduced gravity. Crystal and Jo followed behind.

As they made their way out of the cloud of moon dust, Kenzie finally saw it: hanging low in the black sky above was the *Valor*, full of holes, and looking every minute of its hundred years as a derelict megacruiser. It continued firing its barrage of blaster bolts down on the scattering Frawgs, who were more interested in retreating to their own ships than pursuing the three fugitives.

Twilliam's voice crackled through on the comms. "What am I doing?" He sounded upset. That made sense since he'd woken up after having autonomously plugged himself into an ancient megacruiser, following Kenzie's preprogrammed directives. "Why am I doing this? What have you done to me?"

"Sorry, Twilliam," said Kenzie, huffing and puffing.

Kenzie had uploaded a new program into his memory, directing him to seek out the *Valor* in a reconnaissance shuttle, and then to use his own computerized brain to replace the megacruiser's damaged computer core. Kenzie felt kind of bad about what she'd done…taking over people's brains was a bit of a new horizon for her in terms of the various schemes she'd been cooking up since she first arrived on the *Gremlin*. Still, it was hard to argue with the results.

She ruminated on Twilliam, the *Valor*, and the direct role she'd played in turning what had once been a stuffy, sometimes-nice medical robot into a giant, floating weapon. She was lost in thought—and she didn't see

Katak, who'd managed to catch up with them during their escape, until it was too late. The Frawg chief sprang out from behind a rocky outcropping and surprised Kenzie, causing her to trip over her feet and fall to the moon's dusty surface.

Katak wasted no time to take advantage of the vulnerable Kenzie and pounced, hissing over the still-shared comms. Kenzie tensed, bracing to be torn apart and exposed to the cold void. But then, the Frawg was tackled mid-leap by a blur of color—Jo collided with Katak and knocked her away from Kenzie, smashing the chief into the rocks she'd hidden behind moments earlier.

Kenzie struggled to her feet and carefully shuffled to the two crumpled forms nearby. The Frawg was knocked out—good. Jo was awake, but injured—not good.

Kenzie saw a claw-shaped slash on Jo's jumpsuit. The suit's emergency self-repairing functions were already knitting it back together, but Jo had been cut and exposed to the vacuum of space. Even if her rock-hard skin protected her more than Kenzie's flesh, Jo was hurt, bad. Peering through her visor, she saw a wild look on Jo's face, with a spiderweb of cracks around her left eye.

"Can you—can you move?" said Kenzie.

"Huh?" Jo looked at Kenzie as if she'd just noticed her there. "I—yeah, I think so."

Jo started twisting and writhing on the ground, trying to stand, but failing. A moment later, Crystal's towering red form arrived. The Forger carefully walked to the Frawg that lay on the ground, and then she kicked Katak as hard as she could. The chief went flying, rocketing away as though she'd just remembered she was late for an appointment.

Crystal leaned over and, with Kenzie, nudged Jo to her feet. Kenzie felt an awful weight form in the pit of her stomach as she saw Jo panting and wincing with pain.

"I think the debt's paid," said Kenzie, chancing a half smile.

"Ugh, finally," said Jo. Her annoyed attitude hadn't been injured in the attack.

The three resumed their low-gravity march back to the ship.

"Mackenzie Washington," said Crystal as they had nearly reached the *Orzo*. "You and I will have words."

"Fine," said Kenzie, feeling a mix of anger and guilt. Both were different flavors of the same kind of burning in her guts. "Threaten me when we're back in the ship. It doesn't matter."

"Doesn't matter?" Crystal said, incredulous. "It doesn't—"

Kenzie cut her off, tired of Crystal's righteous warrior routine. "No, it doesn't matter what you have to say to me."

"And why not?"

Because," said Kenzie, "I figured out what the Forgers are doing and how they're doing it."

Resurrection

As Dash handed over the signature pad, Andrew squinted at him.

"Wasn't this shipment of bolts supposed to be here days ago?" he said, taking the pad.

"Yes," sighed Dash, crossing his arms.

"And aren't you dead?" said Andrew, pressing his thumbprint to accept the cargo.

"That's your *second* question?" said Dash as he snatched the pad back from the warehouse's director of receiving.

"Well, we really needed those bolts, man," said Andrew, grabbing the anti-grav pallet and guiding it into the warehouse. Dash turned and walked back toward the ground transport where Ravi, Vor, and a recently recovered Squix waited.

The skies of Motomondo's second largest port city had a foggy yellow hue, the smell of oil and metal floating wherever you walked. The streets were filled with transports of all kinds—here, everyone had their own ride. Citizens on the planet drove wherever and whenever possible, and it showed in the designs of the vehicles they rode at all hours. At one intersection, Dash waited a full five minutes before getting the walk signal, and he still had a hard time crossing without being squashed by a speeding, purple landcruiser with flames painted on the side and whose driver clearly had no regard for the planet's few traffic laws. Motomondons were obsessed with horsepower, even though none of them had ever seen a horse.

When Dash finally reunited with Squix, Vor, and Ravi, he was famished from the ordeal of just living through crossing the street, not to mention wrangling the loose, crawling, stinking chalzz back into their pen. Soon, the four of them sat at a table at an uncrowded restaurant situated about halfway between the warehouse and the landing pad where the *Gremlin* was parked. The few patrons ate quietly—some of them probably playing hooky from their jobs here in the warehouse district, or they were owners or managers of smaller factories talking business. A screen hanging in the corner droned with the monotone of the local news.

Dash ate his cheeseburger sullenly, his nearly healed black eye twitching and itching as he chewed.

He wasn't having a great day.

When they'd first arrived in the Motomondo system, the traffic clogging the entry lanes near the planet's jump-beacon was unbearable. An arrival that had always taken about fifteen minutes suddenly took several hours—all because some stupid politician approved some stupid infrastructure project that took up the whole stupid planet.

Things didn't feel much better as he started making deliveries. This was the first time he'd managed any deliveries at all since the arrival of the cadets—two of whom he'd lost to a bloodthirsty warrior woman from another dimension who was also literally a crazy person. Thinking about calling their parents to let them know what happened gave him indigestion.

The only consolation, he thought, was the fact that Kenzie and Jo's parents probably believed he and the kids were all already dead. And so, Kenzie and Jo's actual aliveness would feel like a vast improvement, despite Dash's inability to perform even the minimum requirements of his temporary guardianship. That was the good news.

"Good news" was a relative term in Dash's mind at that moment. That's why he started spitballing ideas for a career now that his days running a moderately successful cadet immersion program were pretty much over.

"What about construction?" asked Dash, eating a fry from the basket in the middle of the table. "I like working with my hands."

"—delays of nearly two hours for new arrivals as the project gets underway—" said the television.

"You have that bad back, Cap," said Squix, pointing at Dash. His tentacle quivered, though if it was from Vor's hacked-together patch job on his exosuit or a lingering effect of Squix's injuries, Dash wasn't sure. "And also, you're not strong."

"That's true," said Dash, twisting his mouth. "What about—uh, what about being a chef?" He inspected his cheeseburger for a second. "I love food."

Ravi took a thoughtful bite of his sandwich. "A chef..."

The sound of the newscaster filled the silence.

"—provided much needed economic relief to Motomondo, as it's created temporary jobs for many of the planet's unemployed or underemployed workforce—"

"Can you cook?" asked Squix, interrupting the newscaster and tucking a shaking fry into his mouth on the underside of his exosuit.

"Kind of," said Dash. "Sort of."

Vor, who was working on that device he'd put together from parts he bought at Technica Outpost, looked up and shook his head.

"Oh, shut up," said Dash, even though Vor didn't say anything since he didn't have a mouth. "You don't even eat."

Vor nodded slightly and made a face that said, "that's true," then went back to tinkering with his device.

"—after recent events throughout the Alliance, opposition to the initiative has nearly evaporated—" said the television.

"Well, I don't know. Maybe I could just reenlist with the Fleet."

Ravi laughed, his mouth full of half-chewed chicken salad. Then he looked up to see Dash glaring at him.

"Oh, you're serious?" he said, eyes wide. "I don't know…they might not take kindly to, uh—" Ravi coughed. "—how you accidentally left two kids with a Forger warrior. So maybe…"

"Yeah, okay, I got it," said Dash. He took another bite of his cheeseburger. This sucked.

"This sucks," said Dash, grabbing the last fry. "Vor, get us a refill?"

Vor looked up at the empty basket in the center of the table, shrugged, and took it to the front of the restaurant along with his bizarre invention. It was a mish-mash of tech—some of it made with stuff he'd bought on Technica, some of it clearly rescued from the garbage—all strung together to form some kind of ring, about half a meter around. Dash still had no idea what it was.

"Hey Ravi, you're a science guy," Dash whispered as Vor wandered off to the bar for more fries. "What's that thing he's working on?"

Ravi blinked at him. "I haven't got a clue," he said. "I assumed you knew."

Before Dash could respond, he was suddenly distracted by a voice that made his brain curl up into a ball.

"—obviously we're pleased, pleased as punch," said Councilman John-Dean Clifford. "This is a big win for everyone in the Interstellar Alliance, from Rhyolar to Earth to Aphix and all the way back to the itty-bitty worlds in between. I can say personally that Grand Chancellor Gork is thrilled we've finally come to a decision on this one."

Dash looked up in time to see Clifford's round, fleshy face disappear from the screen. What he saw next on the news broadcast was, much to his surprise, even more nauseating.

"What," said Dash, lifting his hand to point at the screen, "the hell." Ravi and Squix swiveled in their chairs to look at the display themselves.

On the screen was a Human newscaster sitting at a desk, his suit pressed, his hair impeccably coiffed. Behind him hung a graphic showing the planet Motomondo—the planet Dash and his crew were on at that very moment.

And around Motomondo was what looked like a giant metal belt.

"—despite the difficulties brought about by the preparations to make the project a reality, the actual installation of Motomondo's jump-chains will be completed by day's end," said the anchor. "When the governing council holds its activation ceremony on IA Prime tomorrow, the jump-chains surrounding this planet, as well as all Alliance worlds, will go live, remotely powered by the reactor hub orbiting the Interstellar Alliance's capital world. The initiative's longtime proponents say that once the switch is thrown at the ceremony, the jump-chains will provide some much-needed peace of mind to citizens throughout the galaxy."

Dash stood up, hands on the table. His chair crashed to the ground.

"What the hell?!" he repeated, this time much louder. Diners around the restaurant gave Dash some annoyed glances but otherwise ignored him. Clearly this restaurant regularly had people yelling at TVs during lunch.

"Holy crap," said Squix, eyes glued to the television.

"Captain Drake," said Ravi, smiling nervously. "I had no idea you were so...emotionally invested in the jump-chains initiative."

"*Those* are jump-chains?" said Dash, who felt his eyes bugging out of his skull as he looked from the television to Ravi and back again. "Those—*that?* That thing?"

"Holy crap," said Squix again.

"Yes, Captain," said Ravi, patting Dash's hand with a mix of concern and condescension. "I received a dispatch this morning from my ship's executive officer, Commander Sharp, that he'll be at the activation ceremony tomorrow." He frowned. "Actually, I was wondering if you could drop me off at the nearest transportation terminal—"

Dash grabbed Ravi's face, pinching the lieutenant's cheeks and mouth into a pucker and forcibly turned him back to the television.

"*That* is the same thing the Forgers used to steal Technica Outpost!"

Dash let go of Ravi's face. The science officer's wide brown eyes went wider.

"Holy crap," said Ravi.

"We gotta—we gotta get out—we gotta—" Dash stammered as he started plotting the fastest way back to the *Gremlin* in his head.

He was reeling. The jump-chains were supposed to protect against invasions. But the Forgers had somehow managed to…what? Take over the jump-chains project? Fool the Interstellar Alliance's governing council into using their planet-stealing machines instead? Could they figure out a way to get to IA Prime—to warn them? Would they believe them?

"If we run," he said, picking his chair up and pushing it back under the table. "If we run, maybe if we find a ground transport, we can be back at the ship in thirty—"

"Uh, Cap?" said Squix

"We have to—" said Dash. He took a nervous chomp of his cheeseburger, then clutched it tightly in his fist as he started pacing, babbling with his mouth full. "Ugh—we have to find—I don't remember—we have to—"

A light went on in Dash's mind, and he started breathing faster.

"Kenzie! Kenzie will know—"

"Cap," said Squix again. "I think—"

"Captain Dashiell Drake," a sickeningly familiar voice interrupted from the other side of the room. "Put the burger down, and put your hands up."

Dash looked up and saw Lucy Reese surrounded by a security detail.

"You're under arrest for crimes against the Interstellar Alliance," she said, smiling.

Dash put his hands up and let the burger go. It hit the floor with a wet plop.

Dash sighed.

"I liked it better when I was dead."

* * *

Dash immediately noticed one thing after he was locked in a containment cube with only his head sticking out of the top. A person's nose can get really, really itchy.

Immobilized in the tiny box, it didn't take long for Dash to start trying to rub his face against the cube's surface. Unfortunately, his neck wasn't as flexible as he would've thought, and he had a heck of a time scratching the itch. So he was a bit distracted when, after an hour of fruitless neck strain, an angry voice blared through the small speaker embedded in the ceiling.

"Prisoner 4001, prepare for a visitor."

Lucy entered the dimly lit holding cell, the door sliding open with a municipal whoosh.

"What took you so long?" she said.

A confused Dash sniffed in response, hoping it could help scratch the itch and also prompt her to elaborate. It did neither.

"What?" he said.

"I've been waiting here for you," said Lucy, folding her arms as the door swished shut behind her.

"I'm pretty sure," Dash said, sniffing again, "that I don't know what you're talking about. I've been sitting here with the worst itch on my nose, like, all day. Waiting for *you*." Dash sniffed one more time. "You jerk."

"I've been stuck on this backwater planet, Drake," said Lucy, sauntering toward his containment cube in the center of the room. She leaned forward, her slate gray eyes boring into his. "I've been here for days, waiting for you to show up in your crappy little ship so I could arrest you and move on with my life."

Suddenly, Lucy raised a hand toward Dash's face, and he flinched. Much to his surprise, she reached over and gently scratched his nose.

"Thank you," he said.

"Don't—the High Smith's going to execute you on Forger Alpha in a few days."

"Oh," said Dash. Then, "Why?"

"He hates you," said Lucy. "So, so much. Ever since Gantoid IV. Your 'act of heroism.' I mean, there's gonna be a lot of work to do once we steal the Alliance's planets at the ceremony. Tons. He thinks cutting your head off with a laser sword on TV would really motivate everyone to do a good job. I told him it was pointless—you're a complete fraud. Anyone with two working eyeballs could see that after spending five minutes with you. I figured it out pretty quick during that date we had. Which totally wasn't a date, by the way. It's been officially logged in my file as an undercover fact-finding operation."

Dash chewed on that for a second.

"Well, uh…okay," he said. "Thanks. I guess."

"Sure. I tried convincing him you're an idiot," she said, pacing around the cube, walking behind Dash to where he couldn't turn his head to see her. "I really did. I mean, I didn't want to wait around here for you to finally show up. But when he saw the logs from Technica Outpost—saw that not only had you been there when we took it, but that you also managed to escape…well, he just wouldn't take no for an answer. He really, really hates your guts, Dash. A lot."

Dash didn't really know what to say to that.

"Sorry?"

"Whatever," said Lucy, who by this point had circled back within Dash's field of vision. "But here's the thing. I don't hate you. I don't like you, and I don't understand how you convinced anyone you were anything more than a total and complete doofus. But I don't believe being stupid should be enough justification to get you killed. So even though I know the High Smith would be happy to cut your head off himself, he wouldn't necessarily be too upset if you, say, 'died trying to escape'." She did air quotes. "You know what I mean?"

Dash raised an eyebrow.

"No," he said. "I don't."

"I'm saying I can let you leave—and live—if you tell me where she is."

Lucy put her hands behind her back.

Dash frowned.

"Her who?"

"Where is Crystal?"

"Oh," said Dash. "Her."

"You know her."

"Unfortunately."

"Let me guess," said Lucy, smiling joylessly. "She was pretty nuts, wasn't she?"

"Oh, not really. Not unless you call an obsession with death and noodles nuts," said Dash, squinting at Lucy. "In that case, yeah, I'd call her totally pistachios with a few pecans thrown in for good measure."

Lucy's laugh was like sandpaper.

"I'm not surprised," she said. "The warrior caste—well, they don't always manage to keep their minds in one piece, y'know? A few tend to crack under the pressure. All the conditioning, training. A few years ago, one of my sub-commanders had a psychotic break and became obsessed with flamingos. Glued pink feathers on his armor, always stood on one leg. So, we hunted him down through the ship and shot him—funniest execution I ever saw."

Dash's face pinched, not sure how he should react to that particular story.

"Of course," she continued, "none have ever gone quite so far as your friend Crystal."

"She's not my friend," said Dash.

"Well, then you won't mind telling me where we can find her."

"If she's so crazy, why do you even want her?"

There was sudden steel in Lucy's eyes.

"In the history of our civilization, no Forger has ever betrayed the empire and lived," she said. "Crystal was under my command. An example must be made."

Dash suddenly had an idea. It was a weird feeling.

"Okay. Just let me go to the *Gremlin*. She gave me a communicator. I'll call her to come out here."

Lucy shook her head, rolled her eyes.

"We're not letting you leave. Just tell me where the communicator is—I'll have someone go get it. Your hunk of junk is already in the hangar."

This escape plan already wasn't working. How'd Kenzie do this, like, every minute? "You stole my ship, too?" asked Dash incredulously.

"I impounded," said Lucy, jabbing a finger towards Dash, "the ship of a criminal." Her patience was wearing thin. She wasn't alone in that. "Enough. Do we have a deal or not?"

Dash thought. He didn't have much love for Crystal; she blew a hole in his ship, kidnapped his cadets, and, whether she knew it or not, had been a tremendous pain in his butt for a while before he even met her. Here was his chance not only to cause *her* some trouble for a change, but to save his own neck, too. It was a tempting offer.

But Kenzie and Jo were with her. And Twince—Twilliam—whatever he called himself. And Lucy probably wouldn't think twice about killing them while getting to Crystal. And who was to say Lucy would let him go now, even if he helped her find them anyway?

No. For once Dash could do the right thing. Better yet, he could do the right thing by doing nothing. And he was great at doing nothing.

"Drake," said Lucy.

"Sorry," said Dash, letting out a sigh. "No deal."

Lucy turned and opened the door to the cell.

"You really are an idiot, Drake."

She left and the door whooshed shut behind her.

Once his heart stopped racing, Dash felt a lead weight drop in his guts. His nose still itched, but he didn't really care.

He was going to die. His head would be cut off with a laser sword, executed by the High Smith of the Forgers. Would it hurt? Probably, though he didn't know enough about laser swords to really know for sure. One thing Dash was sure about was that the news would probably run that awful memorial package about him again when word got out that he'd been killed a second time. He wondered if he could die of preemptive embarrassment first and spare himself.

Dash was deep in morbid thought for hours when an unfamiliar robotic voice piped through the tinny speaker embedded in the cell's ceiling.

"Captain, you okay?"

Dash looked up at the ceiling, scanned the room, and saw nothing.

"…hello?"

The speaker talked again. "Captain, it's me!"

Dash pouted.

"Do I know you?"

"Hang on…"

The door to the holding cell opened and there stood Vor, armed with a blaster rifle. His face was surrounded by a mess of tech and cables.

"Captain!" said Vor, apparently able to talk now. His voice crackled with electricity and distortion. Dash was surprised by how young Vor sounded. "I saw them taking you and the others while I was getting more fries. I'm busting you outta here!"

"Holy what," said Dash, staring in disbelief. "You can talk now?"

Vor pointed at the bundle of junk strung together where the ruin of his mouth used to be.

"Special project," he said. "Check it out!" He turned his head and pointed out the cables embedded in the back of his skull.

"Agh!" said Dash.

Vor walked to the containment cube and plugged his handset into it. "Here," he said, tapping in some commands. "Learned a trick from Kenzie."

Dash looked at the handset, which blinked with lines of code he couldn't follow. Nothing happened.

"Uh," said Dash.

The rocky eyebrows on Vor's face furrowed, and he gave the cube a single, solid kick, shaking Dash to his bones.

"Ow, hey!" he said.

The cube finally hissed and opened like a flower. Dash felt his arms and legs screaming in pain as he tried to stand. He braced himself against Vor as he slowly got to his feet. As painful as it was to stretch out, it was also probably the second best feeling Dash had ever experienced. The first best was when he scratched his nose.

"Come on," said Vor. "Let's get the others."

Vor led Dash out of the cell, and he didn't see any Forgers posted at any of the doors in the detention block.

"Where are all the guards?"

The mass of tech that was Vor's new mouth curved into a creepy smile. He pointed at it, then punched a few buttons on the techno-maw itself.

"I got a few cool tricks now," he said with a deep voice that suddenly sounded very familiar. It boomed and crackled with unbridled fury. It was exactly how Crystal sounded when she'd had her Forger helmet on.

Vor flipped another switch and continued, this time without the added special effects. "I convinced the guards there was a coolant leak in the plasma manifolds."

"Is that a thing?" asked Dash as they walked down the hall.

"Nope," said Vor. "Learned that one from Kenzie, too. 'Don't outfight your enemy. Outthink him.' Right Captain?"

That stupid book.

"Uh...yeah," said Dash.

"I know you're sore, but we need to hurry."

Dash realized he'd stopped moving, and was rubbing his own tender back. "Sorry," he said and formed back up with Vor. He followed along closely as they hustled through the winding corridors of the prison, one drab, slate hallway after another. Fifteen minutes later, Squix and Ravi were freed from their own cubes, and the four of them ran into the detention center's deserted ship hangar. The *Gremlin* was there waiting for them, and they clambered aboard.

The four of them settled into their seats and fired up the *Gremlin*'s engines, the familiar hum of the reactor comforting Dash more than he'd expected. Until he looked up through the viewport and realized they had a problem.

"Uh, we have a problem," he said. "The hangar doors are closed."

Vor smiled with his machine-mouth. "Another trick from Kenzie."

He tapped on his handset, and the doors in the hangar's roof slowly parted. Seconds later, the hangar's deafening alarm filled the cockpit.

"And that's another trick from Kenzie," said Dash as he pulled up on the helm. The ship took flight toward the now-open hangar doors.

"We got company, Cap," said Squix at his console, plotting out an escape route. Dash peeked at his scope and saw a mass of red dots bearing down on him from behind.

It was the security forces of Motomondo, converging on the *Gremlin* as it left the planet's surface, blaster fire whizzing by and occasionally hammering the ship's rear hull. A blaster bolt struck home, and Dash's seat vibrated. The lights dimmed, then flickered—that wasn't good. Dash wasn't happy about how familiar this kind of scenario had become lately.

"Shields…holding?" said Ravi from his station, a little confused.

"Jump-route plotted!" said Squix at Dash's side.

"Are things actually going right?" said Dash. He smashed the jump button. The viewport flashed red and they were gone.

Dash saw the swirl of colors roiling outside as they barreled through jump-space. He swiveled around in his chair and looked at his crew— what was left of it at least.

"Did we actually just escape?"

Squix, Ravi, and Vor all looked at each other and then back at Dash.

"Apparently," said Squix.

"Great job, team!" said Ravi. "So! Now what?"

"Now," said Dash, "we have to find Kenzie."

Guile

24

"I have attempted to contact Captain Drake," said Crystal, her booming, helmet-altered voice shaking Kenzie's seat. She placed the communicator onto the console. "He does not answer my calls."

"But you're gonna dump us anyway?" asked Kenzie.

Crystal turned away from Kenzie and stared out the viewport. "Correct. You have proven unworthy of trust. I cannot build an army with soldiers who cannot follow."

"You can't build an army at all."

"Silence. Enough of your gibbering. You should be able to follow that order, even if you cannot understand simple battle tactics."

"I saved you—I saved us all," said Kenzie. It was like talking to a red, person-shaped wall.

"That is why I have allowed you to live. However, I anticipate your imminent departure from my company. Your appearance displeases me, and I no longer wish to gaze upon it."

Kenzie gave up. "Okay," she said, curling her lip. Crystal had quickly transformed from a fearsome military commander into a whining teenager. But now that it had happened, Kenzie knew she didn't have much time.

Crystal had set a course through jump-space for Motomondo, the *Gremlin*'s last-known destination, planning to dump Kenzie and Jo and make them Dash's problem once more. The *Valor* followed close behind with Twilliam plugged in as the megacruiser's reluctant brain. And Jo lay in her bunk, hurt and hanging on as best she could after the rudimentary patch job from the *Orzo*'s medical robots. They were built only with knowledge of Forger physiology. When it came time to treat Jo's injuries—and the excruciating poison that Katak had apparently dosed her with—the robots provided the medical equivalent of an indifferent shrug.

Her friend was stable, but suffering—and it was Kenzie's fault. So, she had to take over the ship.

Kenzie swiveled her seat away from Crystal, pulled out her handset and quietly entered her Forger hacking commands, hoping Crystal wouldn't notice. Moments later, she finished.

The cockpit went dark and a red light flashed around the main display screen.

"What…" said Crystal as she looked up. Two words appeared on-screen, which she read aloud. "Intruder detected?" She turned to Kenzie. "In jump-space…?"

Kenzie's eyes went wide.

"How's that possible?" said Kenzie.

"The Frawgs," said Crystal, her armored hands clenched into fists. "It must be. They are…more formidable than I believed."

The leader of Crystal's security drone force appeared on-screen, the spiky, floating traffic cone looking as aggressively obedient as ever.

"Report."

"An unknown entity has infiltrated the ship, Commander!"

Crystal hunched forward in her seat. Kenzie imagined her face was seething with rage.

"Where."

"The holding cells, commander!"

"Contain it," said Crystal, standing. "I shall deal with the scum."

She lumbered out of her seat and out the cockpit door, Kenzie following close behind. One lift ride and a stride down the hallway later, the two stood at the entrance to the brig. Kenzie heard the security drone barking orders through the metal door.

"Door! This is your commander. Open—now."

The door slid open obediently, and Crystal combat-tumbled into the room. The security drone, its own weapons drawn, hovered out of the way to let Crystal in. Kenzie ran in behind her, peering over her shoulder.

"Where…?" said Crystal as she gazed into the empty holding cell that had kept Kenzie prisoner the day before. She stepped inside to inspect the empty space.

Kenzie hit the panel on the wall and the force field activated, blue-green light forming a hard energy barrier between herself and Crystal. A second later, Crystal's armored form crumpled onto the floor with a thudding clang. The dampening field had taken effect, and Crystal's powered battlesuit was rendered inert.

"What is—what is the meaning of this?" she yelled, struggling to move, her voice muffled by the helmet on her head. Without her powered armor to amplify her voice, she sounded like someone with her head stuck in a pickle jar.

Crystal slowly lifted her hands and pried the helmet off, the unpowered armor weighing her down like a pile of boulders, and the automatic helmet retractor no longer functional. She twisted to glare at Kenzie, looks of anger and confusion fighting for dominance on her face.

"Drone!" yelled Crystal. "Attack her!"

The drone, hovering behind Kenzie didn't move.

"Drone!" repeated Crystal. "This is your commander!"

"Drone," said Kenzie quietly. "Go to your charging station."

"Aye, commander! You order! I obey!" The cone drone hovered out of the room.

"What…why…"

"I have bested you in combat," said Kenzie. "Therefore, you will bend to my military superiority and join my cause—" Kenzie folded her arms and stared Crystal down with what she hoped was an intimidating look. "—willingly, or by force."

"You dare…you dare claim the right of mastery over me?" Crystal sneered at Kenzie. "You dare claim to be my superior in battle…"

Kenzie's eyes darted around the room, suddenly unsure. "Uh…yes?"

"This was no battle, Mackenzie Washington. This was cowardice!"

Kenzie thought about how to respond.

"Was not," said Kenzie.

"Was so! Was so was so!" Flecks of spit formed at the corners of Crystal's mouth, the scarred skin over her left eye flushing red with anger. "Tell me! Tell me how! Tell me how one so puny and weak could claim to have bested a warrior so fierce without ever striking a single blow? Tell me! How? With what technique? With what weapon? Tell me!"

Kenzie squinted.

"Guile. And cunning."

Crystal's mouth hung open. "Those aren't weapons!"

"And yet," said Kenzie, "you lay there, defeated. And utterly at my mercy."

After a moment of silence, Crystal started to laugh. The laughter started low and rueful, from the pit of her stomach, and it evolved into a mad howl that filled the room. Creeped out, Kenzie turned and left, the door whooshing shut behind her.

In the cockpit, Kenzie saw Jo waiting for her in the copilot's chair. Her lavender skin was faded and ashen, and she kept her hand over her midsection where Katak had slashed and poisoned her.

"It worked?" she said, grimacing in pain.

"Yeah," said Kenzie. "She's in the cell."

"Is she your 'loyal soldier' now?"

Kenzie sat in the pilot's seat. "Maybe?"

"Good enough," said Jo, panting. She sounded exhausted. "Now what?"

"Now," Kenzie said, picking up the communicator Crystal had left on the console, "we find Dash."

Beep

25

Vor's face beeped for the third time in fifteen minutes, and Dash tried not to get annoyed. But that was getting harder with each new beep. The Crag's techno-mouth was already hard to look at. But the fact that it could also be so consistently annoying to hear didn't make it much easier.

Dash looked over his shoulder.

"What's with the beeping, man?"

Sitting behind him, Vor shrugged. "Gas?"

Dash narrowed his eyes, then turned back to the helm console.

The cockpit lights were turned low as Dash tried once more to refocus on the task in front of him. He pored through the latest feeds and news reports on his display. While in the middle of a particularly dense summary about transgalactic traffic patterns, Ravi burst into the cockpit, smiling that confident smile of his.

Vor—finishing repairs to the console Kenzie had fried—and Squix—sitting to Dash's right in the copilot's seat—turned along with him as the science officer entered.

"Captain, I have news," said Ravi as the door swished closed behind him. He sat in one of the faux-leather seats, and the fabric creaked a little under his sleight frame.

Dash's heart skipped a beat. Ravi had been trying for hours to track down any signs of Crystal's ship, a task that had turned out to be even harder than they'd imagined.

"You found them?" said Squix, his skin taking a hopeful, purple hue.

"No," said Ravi, his smile now revealed to be less confident and more of the awkward, uncomfortable variety. "In fact, I wanted to let you know that I am certain I have no idea where they are. Or how to locate them."

"Oh," said Squix. He turned and continued his calculations.

Aside from Vor, all three of them were trying to find their missing crewmates. Dash searched for any sign of a Forger ship appearing in the media. So far, he'd had no luck. Squix, meanwhile, was calculating different possible routes that Crystal's battlecruiser could've taken from where they'd last been in contact with her. No luck on that end, either.

He wondered how it'd all gone so wrong. Not just the last few days…but everything. For a lazy coward, you couldn't ask for a better setup than the one he got. Being called a war hero without actually doing anything heroic? Money and fame just for not dying when he was supposed to? And accidentally saving the galaxy in the process? How could he take a gift like that and turn it into…this?

He looked around the dank, dingy cockpit. Squix and Vor were working hard. Ravi spun in his chair, having apparently given up. How did he get here? Dash was once again faced with the task of trying to save civilization, and he was looking for a fourteen-year-old girl who was way, way smarter than him so she could tell him what to do. And he couldn't even manage that.

Dash let out a heavy sigh. He decided to redouble his efforts and see what he could find in the news feeds. He wouldn't stop until he'd found

Kenzie—or until the Forgers had taken over the galaxy. He was determined. He had resolve.

He lasted six minutes. Then Vor's face beeped again. Dash gritted his teeth and shook his head.

"Is anyone going to answer that?" said Ravi behind him.

Dash didn't turn around, but he shut his eyes. "Ignore it," he said.

"But what if it's something important?" said Ravi.

Dash opened his eyes and turned around. "What do you mean, 'something important'?"

"Wellllll," said Ravi, "in my experience, when you get a priority call like that, it means someone probably has something, y'know, important to tell you?" Ravi grinned nervously. "Because it's a priority?"

Dash pointed at Vor.

"It's Vor—Vor's face is beeping."

"He thinks it's gas," added Squix without turning.

Vor looked at Ravi, pointed to his mouth, and waved.

Ravi squinted at him, then looked at Dash. "That's a long-range communicator."

"That's Vor," said Squix, who finally turned from his calculations to point two shaky tentacles at the Crag. "He's a teenager."

"No, I mean on Vor's face—that's a long-range communicator."

Dash looked at Squix, then at Vor, who looked as confused as he felt. "It is?"

"Yes," said Ravi, walking over to Vor and grabbing his head. He pointed at various components Vor had strung together to make his mouth. Vor didn't seem to mind. "There are bits and pieces that were clearly part of a communicator." Vor's face beeped as if in response to Ravi's diagnosis. "And that particular beep is universally recognized as a high-priority signal."

"Really?" said Squix.

"Of course," said Ravi, rolling his eyes with a smile, as if to say Dash and Squix were just about the silliest Billies he'd ever met. "Haven't you ever gotten a high-priority call?"

Dash and Squix looked at each other, then back at Ravi.

"No."

"Oh," said Ravi, releasing Vor's head.

Dash stood and looked closer. There *was* something weirdly familiar about some of the pieces on Vor's face, now that Ravi had pointed them out.

"Vor," he said, "where'd you get some of this stuff?"

"Oh, you know, Technica Outpost, some scraps from here and there, couple bits from the trash compactor…"

The trash compactor.

This was the communicator Crystal had given him. It was in pieces, rescued from the garbage, and grafted onto Vor's face.

"This is the thing! The thing she—this is it! This is how we find Kenzie! I mean—Kenzie's found us! I think!"

Squix flashed a few different unsure colors. "Huh?"

Dash grabbed both sides of Vor's face and yelled into it. "Kenzie! Do you read me?"

Aside from the terror in Vor's eyes, Dash didn't get anything in response. "Somebody help me with this thing!"

Ravi leaned in close. "Hmmm…right now it's only receiving the priority call signal, but it can't quite carry anyone's voice. Maybe we could boost the reception, though."

"I've got some more cables in my bunk," said Vor, freeing his face from Dash's grasp. "I bet I could hook into the ship's communications array."

"That's a start," said Ravi.

Vor raced from the cockpit.

Squix curled and uncurled a tentacle. "What if we repositioned the ship further from this star system's sun? The interfering radiation is probably muddying the signal."

Ravi snapped his fingers and pointed at Squix. "That's an excellent idea, Mister Squix."

"Do it!" said Dash excitedly. He sat at the helm and looked at his first mate. "When'd you learn that? I never heard you talk about 'interfering radiation.'"

Squix curled a tentacle under his chin, thinking. "Well, I have two PhDs. I think they might've covered that during Intro to Astrophysics. Sorry, Cap. I'm really not sure I remember when I learned it. But I guess I never really, y'know, needed to know that on any of our other jobs."

He turned from Dash to plot a new course.

"Oh," said Dash.

Twenty minutes later, the *Gremlin* was at a new position, further from solar radiation interference. Dash winced as Vor plugged his face into the console, and Ravi fine-tuned the communications array to try and get a message to Kenzie. After a minute, Vor's face beeped.

"Try it now," said Ravi.

Dash spoke into the comm in his right hand; he clutched its spiral cord in his left.

"Kenzie? Kenzie, this is Dash. Come in…do you read?"

Static.

"Kenzie, do you copy? This is Dash and we…we're really trying here, Kenzie."

The radio hissed in response.

"What's going on?" said Squix.

"I'm not sure what's wrong," said Ravi, chewing on his index finger.

"Normally this is when I'd smack the radio," said Dash.

"Let me try something," said Vor. Suddenly, he balled a fist and conked himself on the back of the head, making a sound not unlike someone sinking a shot on a billiards table. And then he did it again, Vor ball, corner pocket.

A voice broke through the static.

"Dash? Dazkrzzzkkkzz…opy? Do you copykrrzzzzkkkzz"

"Hit him again!" yelled Squix.

Ravi looked at Vor and half-smiled.

"Sorry," he said. And then he smacked Vor right across the face. They each said "ow." Ravi massaged his bruised hand while Vor rubbed his cheek.

"—zie to Dash, do you copy? Kenzie to Dash, do you read me?"

"Kenzie!" said Dash. "Yes, we hear you! Where are you?"

"Transmitting coordinates now," said Kenzie. "We'll be waiting there. It's Jo…she's hurt." Dash felt his smile disappear. He turned back to see the glitter fade on Vor's face.

"We need help," she said.

* * *

Dash had never seen Squix plot a new course so quickly despite the tremor in his tentacles. And yet, the next few hours through jump-space felt like they took a week. No one spoke.

Finally, the *Gremlin* emerged in a part of space Dash had never seen, surrounded by small, lazily spinning asteroids. Kenzie had picked a spot within the asteroid field to meet that looked free of any errant bits of space rock. Through the viewport Dash saw Crystal's angry, red ship—along with a hulking, partially broken megacruiser that looked suspiciously similar to the *Valor*.

Dash docked with the Forger ship, then he and the crew waited in the dimly lit corridor. The airlock hissed open, and Kenzie and Twilliam pushed a hovering cargo pallet through the docking tube. Jo, eyes closed and clutching her side, lay on top of it. Crystal, dressed in full armor, but with her helmet retracted and her face exposed, followed, her head bowed low, her gaze on the floor as she walked.

Twilliam muttered under his breath, avoiding Dash's eyes as they pushed Jo aboard. "I didn't have the correct...the equipment aboard that ship is dreadful." Vor, Squix, and Ravi followed Twilliam, who pushed Jo into the medbay. Crystal looked up at Kenzie, and Kenzie nodded approvingly. Crystal turned and followed the others. Dash arched an eyebrow at that but didn't say anything. He heard the medbay door whoosh open, and Doctor Bill said, "What, you again?" and Twilliam said, "You're still here, I can't believe—" and then the door shut.

Kenzie walked to Dash and without speaking put her arms around his middle. Dash surprised himself by hugging her back.

"Thanks," she said.

Dash let go after a moment and put his hands on her shoulders. He looked down at her face—it was still Kenzie, but she looked...thin? Sunken? He couldn't figure out what had changed.

"Listen," he said, "the Forgers...they're—somehow they got into the jump-chains project. We have to warn the council. Get to IA Prime or...something."

Kenzie stepped back and shook her head.

"It's more than that, Dash. The Forgers didn't just get into the project."

"What do—what're you talking about?"

"There never was a jump-chains project," she said, looking at her feet. "The council, IA Prime...they're all Forgers. They've been Forgers all along."

Dash didn't understand. "What?"

Kenzie looked up at Dash. Her brown eyes were wet.

"You were right," she said. "You were right this whole time. You were right and I was...I was just so, so wrong. There's no point even trying. It's too late. We've already lost."

She turned and ran to her bunk, leaving Dash alone in dark of the corridor.

The Truth

Kenzie sat on her bunk eating a candy bar she liberated from the captain's stash, absently tracing the small hologram of her mother's face with her finger. There was a knock at the door.

"Come in," she sniffed.

Dash shuffled in quietly.

"Hey," he said. Then, pointing at the candy, "That one of mine?"

"Yeah," said Kenzie. She took another bite.

Dash sat at the foot of her bunk.

"Who's that?" he said.

"My mom. She was in the Forger War, but…" Kenzie trailed off.

"Oh. She looks—uh, she looks a lot like you."

"Yeah," said Kenzie. She looked at her half-eaten candy bar and tossed it limply onto the bed. Dash scooped it up.

"Do you want to…" he said, taking a bite. With a mouthful of chocolate and peanuts, he said, "Do you want to, um, call your dad or something? He must be pretty worried."

"No," said Kenzie. "He's fine."

"Did you—did you call him already? How do you know he's fine?"

"He doesn't know I'm here," she said with another sniff. "He thinks I'm at jiu jitsu camp. He hates all this Fleet stuff. Ever since mom...y'know..."

She trailed off. They were quiet a moment.

"Is Squix okay?" she asked, feeling her chest go tight as she spoke the words.

"He's okay," said Dash, chewing. "I mean...he's not great. He's still a little, uh, shaken up from...well...everything. But he'll be alright." Dash swallowed and took another bite. "I think. I hope."

Dash crumpled up the empty candy wrapper. "So...what...uh...what were you just—" Dash cleared his throat. "I guess I'm kinda..." He let out a frustrated breath. "What's going on, Kenzie?"

"It's the Frawgs."

Kenzie looked up from the hologram of her mother and saw the confusion on Dash's face.

"What's that now?"

"The Frawgs," she said again. "We...have you ever wondered about the Frawgs, Dash?"

"Not really," he said. "They're dangerous. They eat people."

"You've been traveling through the Alliance for years since the War, right?

"Yes," said Dash. "Where are you going with this..."

"Before this trip, though, did you ever actually see a Frawg? I mean with your eyes, in person—not just hear about them on TV or the news or something."

"Sure, I—uh..." Kenzie saw Dash look away, doing some mental math. He looked back. "Actually, I'm not really...I could've sworn..."

He frowned. "No, I never did."

"They've lived on the outskirts of space, in small pockets, just scraping by and surviving on whatever they can find. Because the Alliance forced them there. Because the Alliance has been run by the Forgers ever since the War ended."

Dash's eyes went wide. Kenzie retrieved her handset and pulled up a photo of the governing council: three Crags, three Aphids, three Humans. She pointed at them.

"The Human members of the governing council—I'm pretty sure they're all Forgers."

"John-Dean Clifford," said Dash with a hint of venom.

"I think so," said Kenzie. "Look."

She accessed his public record and pointed out his council appointment date, which was four years after the end of the Forger War. Then she pulled up Lucy Reese's record and highlighted the date she'd gotten the security chief job at Technica Outpost. It was the same day.

"Probably not a coincidence," said Kenzie.

"That *creep*," said Dash. "I always knew there was something about that guy…"

"We met them, the Frawgs, back on Sheaffer Colony's moon. We found out that, after the end of the War, the Alliance started experimenting with their—well, with their jump-chains. The planet-stealing thing we saw at Technica. They kicked the Frawgs off some planets no one cared about, tested their technology on them. And then they made the Frawgs enemies of the Alliance to sell us on increased security. On jump-chains. And no one knew the Forgers were Human anyway. They've been here, for years, just planning…all this."

"Holy moly," said Dash, staring at the floor. He ran his hand through his hair. Kenzie thought it looked thinner than the last time she'd seen him—which, she reminded herself, was only a few days earlier.

He turned back to her. "So, what do we do?"

Kenzie shook her head.

"We don't do anything," she said. "It's like I said. We already..." Kenzie pressed her palms into her eyes and saw splotches of red and purple. She sniffed and opened her eyes, blinking away water.

"We already lost, Dash. The Forgers are in the Alliance. We can't do...anything."

She looked back at Dash and saw him frown. She wasn't sure what he was thinking, but she was surprised by what he said next.

"Bullshit."

Her eyes went wide. "What?"

"You heard me," said Dash, folding his arms. "You're...c'mon, you're Kenzie Washington. I've only known you for a few days, and I've never seen you stop. Never seen you give up. Even when you really, really should. You're not giving up now—not when you're so close."

"So...close? Close to what?"

Dash stood and spread his arms wide, like he was offering her the most threatening hug she'd ever seen. "So close to saving the whole stupid galaxy, you idiot! Just—come on! Ever since this whole thing started, it's all been—it's been all about this!"

"I don't...I don't think..."

"Don't make me say it."

Kenzie watched Dash, waiting to hear what he'd say next.

After grunting at the ceiling in frustration, Dash counted on his fingers as he spoke.

"You hacked your way through Technica Outpost and found Vor. You hacked us out of there so we could escape. You salvaged a new jump-shield. You stopped a tribe of Frawgs from eating us—" He held up an extra finger. "—twice. You broke us out of the galley and stopped an evil cyborg from killing us, and then you made him *stop* being evil! I don't know what the hell you did to Crystal, but you did a whammy on her too—"

"Stop it," said Kenzie, quietly. Her face was hot, and a pit had formed in her stomach. Everything Dash said...all of it was true, but...

"What?" said Dash. "What is this?"

Kenzie drew her knees up to her chin and wrapped her arms around them. "Everyone keeps getting hurt. Everything you just...everybody's been...everything I do hurts someone. Squix, you...Jo. I've never had...I've never had any real friends. Ever. And now I know why. I'm dangerous. Everyone I know, everyone I care about just gets hurt. Because of me."

Kenzie looked at the hologram of her mother, floating a few centimeters above the bed, the face staring ahead blankly like a bored ghost.

"I'm cursed," she said. "I'm a monster."

Kenzie buried her face in her knees. Her voice was muffled and her face was wet. "You were right this whole time. About everything. You fired me, and—and that was...you were right all along."

After a few seconds of silence, Kenzie peeked above her knees to see Dash looking down at the floor, hands on his hips.

Finally, he said, "Look. You're a monumental—a phenomenal pain in my ass. That's always been true. You're awful."

Dash looked up at her.

"But you're also the smartest, most talented, most creative cadet I've ever met. No," he shook his head, "that's wrong. You're the smartest *person* I've ever met—period. In a few days you've pushed me and Squix and the other cadets to do things that...well, I never thought I'd do much more than move boxes from one dirtball to another. And now—now it looks like *you* were the one who was right this whole time, Kenzie. I've got a chance..."

He sat on the bed and put his hand on her knee.

"...*we've* got a chance to save the galaxy. And on purpose this time. But we're running out of..."

Dash put his hands in his lap and looked at the floor.

"There's a ceremony on IA Prime to activate all the jump-chains tomorrow...they're gonna—I can't believe I'm saying this—they're going to steal all the planets in the Alliance. We're the only ones who know—and we have to stop them. Somehow. I can't do it without you. I don't even know where to begin. Tell me."

He looked straight at her, his eyes wide.

"Help me save the galaxy, Kenzie. Please. Tell me what to do."

Kenzie bit her lip. A week ago, hearing Dash Drake say this to her would've been a dream come true. But now, all Kenzie could feel was cold, damp shame in the pit of her stomach. She was no hero. She wasn't even in high school yet.

There was nothing she could do.

"I...I can't. I just can't."

Kenzie saw Dash deflate before her eyes. He let out a quiet sigh, and his mouth hung open, almost as though his jaw had simply gotten tired and given up. In the cadet quarters' dim light, Dash looked pale, and Kenzie wondered if he might actually throw up.

And that's when the *Gremlin* shook. Kenzie and Dash both crashed onto the floor.

"Oh God, what now?" said Dash.

The speaker in the wall crackled to life.

"Cap! They found us!" Squix cried. "The Forgers—they're here!"

Dash looked at Kenzie.

"We're doomed."

* * *

Kenzie steadied herself in the cockpit doorway as the *Gremlin* took another hit. A swarm of angry Forger ships floated nearly everywhere she looked through the viewport, filling the spaces between the asteroids. At least all those space rocks would make it harder for the Forgers to maneuver and shoot them all to death. That was something.

"What's going on?"

Squix, sitting in the pilot's seat, spared a nervous glance backward as she and Dash stumbled toward him.

"Bad guys!" he yelled. "They just jumped in and started shooting!" Squix turned back to the helm, then glanced behind him again and added, "Shooting at *us*!"

Ravi, sitting next to him, a nervous grin plastered on his face, tried his best to use the nav-computer to help plan an escape route. The flop sweat on his forehead told Kenzie he wasn't having much luck.

"It's not my fault!" said Ravi, sensing Kenzie's thoughts. "We're still docked with Crystal's ship!"

Dash ran ahead of Kenzie and yanked Ravi to his feet. Then he scooped up Squix and lobbed him over to fill the copilot's chair, sitting to take the helm himself.

"How'd they find us?" he said, jamming the stick forward and sending the *Gremlin* into a sluggish dive. The extra weight of the *Orzo* made it harder to maneuver. "I thought—I thought we made a clean getaway!"

Kenzie sat at the nearest console. She recognized it as the computer console she'd accidentally broken during the chase on Sheaffer Colony, now apparently fixed. That was helpful.

Back to Dash.

"What's this about a 'clean getaway'?" she said.

"From Motomondo, said Ravi from his new seat behind the copilot's chair, away from anything important. "That woman, the one from Technica Outpost that Dash doesn't like…"

"Lucy Reese," said Kenzie.

Ravi snapped his fingers with recognition. "Yes! Her. She arrested us and put us in jail." There was a brief pause. "And then we escaped!"

Dash, Ravi, Squix, and Vor all escaped from jail? By themselves?

"How did you—"

The ship shook again, combat shields absorbing another blow.

The cockpit door slid open. In the doorway stood Crystal, her face exposed, her glare looking particularly menacing.

"Commander Washington," she growled. "I await your order—"

Kenzie held up a finger to her. Crystal's face darkened, but she said nothing. Kenzie returned to Ravi.

"How'd you get back to the *Gremlin* when you, uh, got out of jail?"

"That's the best part," said Ravi, excited despite the Forger battalion raining hot plasma death all around them. "They had impounded the ship, so it was right there waiting for us!"

"It was right there?" Kenzie repeated. That didn't make any sense.

"Permission to speak, Commander Washington."

Kenzie gave Crystal a nod.

"Tracking module," said the Forger, rolling her eyes.

Kenzie's eyes went wide—of course they'd installed a tracking module in the ship. Of course their clean getaway was too good to be true. Of course. She turned and saw Dash slap himself in the forehead.

"I can't believe it," he said. "Lucy was looking for Crystal—and I...I led them right to her. I'm such an idiot."

Kenzie realized that the cold, damp feeling in her stomach was gone, and instead felt something warm suddenly spring up inside her chest—a strange sort of pain that itched a little and filled her completely. It was sympathy. All those years she'd worshiped at Dash's altar, she'd never known he was just a regular guy, thrust into a role he'd never earned and never wanted. When he finally revealed himself as the fraud he'd always been, she was furious. Then numb. And now? She finally understood him.

Dash really, truly was an idiot.

And she finally understood something else too: she needed to save him. Who else would?

The viewport spun as Dash threw the ship into a corkscrew, though, again, it moved like molasses because it was still docked with the *Orzo*. Kenzie turned to Crystal.

"Where?"

"Usually attached to the nav-computer, sir," said Crystal obediently. "That makes it easier to track a ship's position and destination."

Kenzie jumped from her seat and dove under Squix's console.

"Hey!" he said, tentacles whipping with panic, his skin flashing between yellow and red with each moment.

Lying on her back, Kenzie looked up and saw it: a small orb with a single blinking blue light plugged into the bottom of the console.

"How do I deactivate it?"

"You unplug it," said Crystal.

"Really?" said Dash. "No explosives or—I don't know, nerve gas or anything?"

"When Forgers find our quarry, they do not survive long."

"Oh," said Dash.

Kenzie unplugged it and hauled herself out from under the console.

"Well, I guess we're in luck," continued Dash. "The High Smith wants to cut my head off with a laser sword, so maybe that's why we haven't all blown up yet."

"Indeed," said Crystal. "Such a spectacle would delight many Forger children. But I believe it is my ship's combat shields that has kept us from destruction so far—"

"Quiet," said Kenzie.

Crystal's mouth went tight with rage, but she didn't say another word.

Kenzie looked at Dash and Squix, frantically trying to keep the ship from becoming critically damaged. Then she looked at Ravi—a lieutenant in the IA Fleet. She looked at Crystal—a Forger under her command, in full battlesuit. At the tracking module in her palm.

Lucy had fooled Dash and the others into thinking they'd escaped. Twince had fooled her into thinking she could trust him. The Forgers fooled the entire galaxy into thinking that they were gone. The owner of the Milky Wow and whatever shady dealings they did there. Even Dash Drake, hero of Gantoid IV. Nobody was ever what they seemed.

Even Kenzie had fooled *herself* so many times.

A light went on in her mind. She had a plan.

"Crystal," she said, pulling out her handset and tapping away. "Get to the *Orzo* and prepare to jump to the coordinates I'm sending you now."

"Retreat from battle? You want me to run and hide like some kind of—"

Kenzie looked up at her and glared. "You dare question your commanding officer?"

Crystal narrowed her eyes at Kenzie. The ship shook with another impact.

"Aye, Commander Washington," she said.

"Dash, Squix, you go with her."

"What?!" cried Squix.

"We're kind of—we're kind of in the middle of something here, Kenz—"

The ship took another hit, this one rattling Kenzie's teeth hard.

She stood and put her hand on Dash's shoulder.

"Go," she said. "Now."

Dash looked at her, saw she was serious, then stopped arguing. He hopped up, grabbed Squix by the tentacle and dragged him from his seat. She sat in his place, adjusting the seat so she wasn't so low to the ground.

"Ravi, get over here and spin up the jump-drive," she said. The lieutenant reluctantly took his place beside her. She punched some numbers into the computer console next to the helm. "We're going here." Then she turned and tossed Dash the Forger communicator she'd brought from Crystal's ship.

"I'll contact you in twelve hours," she said. Then she smirked, "Don't die before then, okay?"

Crystal turned on her heel and left the cockpit, Squix and Dash following behind her. Dash looked back as the ship shimmied.

"You're sure about this?"

"Hey," she said, smiling for the first time since coming back aboard. "Trust me."

Dash chewed his lip nervously and left the cockpit. Once he was out of sight, he called out.

"I'm trusting you!"

A minute later, the *Orzo* detached from the *Gremlin*, and suddenly Kenzie's efforts to evade the blaster fire got much easier. A flash of red told her that Crystal's ship had jumped away.

"Jump ready, Kenzie," said Ravi.

She punched the jump-drive button. Another flash of red in the viewport and they were gone.

The Next Day

27

The Forgers' battlesuits were marvels of technological advancement. Still, Dash was surprised at how incredibly hot and sweaty they got. His face, neck, torso, arms, legs—everything felt moist and prickly.

This was how he coped with stress: focusing on physical discomfort to ignore his existential dread and abject terror. It rarely worked, but he did it anyway.

"Friends, we gather today to make history," said the voice coming out of the speakers in Dash's helmet.

Minutes earlier he'd awkwardly clambered into a torpedo tube on Crystal's ship. A small countdown timer in the battlesuit's visor told him he'd soon be fired at unfathomable speeds toward IA Prime. He'd become a Human-shaped missile.

"It's fitting, then," continued the voice, "that we do so in the historic capital building of IA Prime, surrounded by the lawmakers and engineers who worked for a decade to make today possible."

There was probably a button he could've pressed to cool off, but Crystal kept its location to herself. She'd climbed into a torpedo tube of her own, but when Dash asked her about the suit's functions over their shared comm channel, she claimed she couldn't hear him over some conveniently timed audio interference.

"I am sorry, Captain Drake," Crystal said with a smirk in her voice through their perfectly clear comms. "I simply cannot hear what you are saying through all of this static."

"I thought," said Dash, "you were supposed to follow Kenzie's orders and help me figure out how this suit works."

"And I would, if only I could understand your request through all of this disruptive audio interference," snickered Crystal. For a warrior from another dimension, she sure did act a lot like a petty teenager. Ever since she'd begun recognizing Kenzie as her superior, she seemed to take satisfaction in finding ways to be annoying.

Dash sighed, resigned to sweating and watching the broadcast from the surface of IA Prime play across his visor's display. Councilman John-Dean Clifford—that pasty, round, secret Forger creep—led the jump-chains ceremony. The room was somewhere between dull gray and beige, filled with rounded tables and chairs. The Alliance's governing council chambers were designed to appear as neutral as possible so as to avoid offending the sensibilities of any member world. Its utter lack of design was a marvel of modern politics.

"Never before has such a wide-ranging, life-changing initiative ever been attempted on such a grand and impressive scale," continued Clifford.

"Do you recognize him?" Dash asked Crystal over their shared comm.

"Who," said Crystal, "the corpulent blob speaking at the podium?"

"Um, yeah…is he—have you, y'know, seen him at any of the meetings? The Forger meetings and…stuff?"

There was a pause as Crystal considered Dash's question.

"You think we have meetings?"

Dash thought about how he should answer.

Crystal continued. "I defected before I could meet with anyone involved in this 'jump-chains' plan of theirs. However, I do not know how a man of that…stature could fit inside a battlesuit."

Dash glanced nervously at the countdown timer in the corner, slowly ticking to zero.

"My friends," said Clifford in that skin-crawling voice of his, "it is my absolute and utmost pleasure to represent Earth in the Interstellar Alliance's governing council and to lead this ceremony with the blessing of Grand Chancellor Gork."

"And you're doing great!" interrupted Gork. He was a gangly, brownish-green Aphid sitting in a slightly elevated gray-beige chair on the impressively unremarkable dais behind Clifford's podium. Gork was surrounded by other politicians and members of the Fleet brass, like Ravi's boss, Commander Sharp, who cracked a small smile despite his no-nonsense haircut.

Gork's interjection was rewarded with mild chuckles and applause. Clifford winked at the camera. Dash fought the urge to barf.

"Thank you, Grand Chancellor," said Clifford into the microphone, "for giving me the opportunity to do the honors and push this button at today's ceremony—" He held up an ornate and very official looking tablet, festooned with ceremonial writing, official-looking seals, and a single red button. "—and usher us into a new age of security and prosperity."

Dash zeroed in on that tablet. He needed to get that tablet. If he didn't get that tablet, the whole galaxy was doomed. It was all on him.

Dash thought again about how much he did not like this plan.

It had been a surreal twenty-four hours, all leading to this moment. After the Forger ambush, Crystal wordlessly led Dash and Squix from the

Gremlin into her ship, which she was now calling *The Spaghetti Liberator*. Or maybe it was *Linguine*. Or *Lasagna*? Dash couldn't quite remember which noodles had inspired her.

Anyway, soon after boarding, they strapped in, and Crystal set them on a series of jumps sent from Kenzie's handset with the express purpose of throwing Lucy and her cronies off their scent. And it worked. By the time they'd arrived at their final set of coordinates, there was no hint of the ships that had pursued them from Motomondo.

When Kenzie raised them on the communicator some hours later, she told Dash what he'd already guessed—she'd taken the *Gremlin* on a similar series of jumps and esacped too. That's when she filled him in on the plan—well, his half at least. He didn't like it.

And now that he was encased inside a lethal suit of alien battle armor, housed in a rocket-propelled pod, waiting to be fired out of a torpedo tube toward the capital planet over a half million kilometers away in order to stop the ceremony…

Well, Dash liked it even less now.

"Before we push that button and usher in a new age of safety and prosperity," said Clifford, repeating that safety-prosperity bit again as if no one would notice, "I'd like to take a few moments to describe some of the struggles we've endured, as a society, in our quest for peaceful coexistence with the rest of the galaxy…"

Dash rolled his eyes and wished he could wipe the sweat from his nose. Just then, the countdown hit zero.

"Uh-oh," said Dash.

A split-second later, he was a Human missile, traveling at speeds best left to inanimate objects.

He felt his spine compress, his skull pushing against the hard helmet. He rocketed through space like a bullet. His suit's jets rumbled in his ears, drowning out Clifford's voice. The ceremony's video feed reduced to a corner of his visor's display. Dash gazed at the blurry streaks of stars that were suddenly everywhere. He was surrounded by other red dots—the rest of Crystal's collection of Forger battlesuits fired from the *Orzo* in a barrage. He wondered which ones were empty.

Now, Dash looked up towards his target. Dead ahead, he saw the big blue and green world known as IA Prime. It was surrounded by what looked like a gigantic belt—jump-chains. The remote Hub, which powered the jump-chains network, spun lazily above IA Prime like a spiky metal moon. It was dotted with small gray specks—the security detail of vessels on-hand to play guard duty.

"Would've expected more ships," said Dash through gritted teeth.

"They are unprepared for what is coming," said Crystal over the comm. She wasn't bothered by the inhuman speeds. Dash figured she was used to this sort of thing. "Commander Washington is a…surprisingly cunning adversary."

Usually IA Prime was where the business of governing took place. Today, it was the scene of a Forger invasion—well, two Forger invasions. Only the folks watching at home didn't know the first one had been underway for years— or that the second one was about to begin.

About halfway to their destination, the planetary defense canons began firing.

Bright beams of energy arced from the planet's surface, slicing through space, threatening to obliterate anything in its path. Dash felt his suit adjust its angle slightly, its sensors knowing how to avoid the particle canons. The other suits' computers likely did the same, keeping the small battalion of Forger armor heading straight for IA Prime.

"They're shooting at us!"

"Indeed," said Crystal, satisfied. "All is going according to the commander's plan."

"But that doesn't mean I have to enjoy it!"

Crystal barked out a genuine laugh.

This *was* all part of the plan, Dash told himself. This was supposed to happen. The suits were too small for the canons to accurately shoot at. So small, in fact, that the planet's defenses couldn't detect them until they were already mostly there. Kenzie had explained it all to him, with Ravi chiming in to sell him on it, using math and equations and other things Dash couldn't hope to understand to convince him it was statistically impossible he'd be killed via particle canon.

Besides, Ravi said, he was much more likely to die on impact with the planet's surface itself.

As Dash replayed that conversation in his head, the planet grew larger, and soon it took up the entirety of his view. For a moment, Dash forgot his fear and watched as his perspective shifted with each passing second. First, he saw continents then mountains. What first looked like a computer circuit board sharpened into an actual place, alive with smears of cities, composed of buildings and bridges—then traffic, people. Before he knew it, he spotted the capital building's domed roof.

Dash glanced at the broadcast in the corner of his display and saw an aide walking toward a visibly annoyed Clifford to whisper in his ear.

"What do you mean, 'an incursion'?" he muttered, not realizing his voice still carried into the live microphone. "Order the orbital security ships back!"

Behind Clifford, Chancellor Gork was approached by a different aide, presumably to tell him that IA Prime was currently under a multi-pronged attack. Dash felt kinda bad. Gork had always been nice to him the few times they'd met.

Suddenly he and the rest of the battlesuits crashed into the titanium-reinforced faux-stone of the building's domed roof and reduced it to scientifically enhanced and expensive rubble that rained down onto the ceremony floor.

As Dash tensed up, his suit angled itself for a proper landing. Hitting the ground was jarring, but his spine and skull were happy at the journey's end. Something resembling normal gravity reasserted its hold over his body. He looked and saw another suit make a similar landing—Crystal.

The other thirteen suits, meanwhile, just crashed into crumpled heaps on the floor. They lay in smoking craters, arms and legs splayed in all the wrong directions. Shiny red bodies of Forger battlesuits littered the floor of the governing council hall, the tables and chairs previously surrounding the great podium where Clifford stood having been reduced to gray-beige chunks and smoking planks.

Everywhere Dash looked, he saw scared people, either gaping at his arrival or simply running toward the exits. Glowing red targets appeared on his display, the battlesuit's tactical AI attempting to identify the retreating, defenseless people as imminent threats. Guards and soldiers had yet to pull their weapons, so stunned were they at the sudden arrival.

Dash turned and saw Clifford—holding the tablet—and he lunged right at him.

"Gimme that!"

The councilman jumped at the boom of Dash's modified voice. He grabbed the tablet out of Clifford's hands, taking care to not even graze the red button that spelled the galaxy's doom.

Clifford may have been a secret Forger agent, but he was no match for the battlesuit's powerful grip. And in the blink of an eye, he had it. The galaxy was saved. The tablet was his.

It was all over. Right?

He let out a heavy, happy sigh.

"Freeze!"

"Hands up!"

"Drop the tablet, now!"

It took a second for Dash to realize that the capital guards were yelling at him and not someone else.

"Oh, I, uh," he stammered. "Just—hang on a second…"

A Short While Earlier...

28

"There," said Ravi. "See that pointy, spinny bit?"

Kenzie squinted through the viewport. The orbiting Hub reactor powering the jump-chains network floated in the distance, surrounded by a blockade of slate gray security ships—though, as she expected, no red Forger vessels were among them. Keeping up the ruse until the end—and clearly not expecting a counterattack.

"I see several pointy, spinny bits," said Kenzie.

"Yes, but I'm trying to draw your attention to that one," said Ravi, pointing emphatically. "On the left side."

"My left? Or the Hub's left?"

"Yours."

"Okay...yes."

"I've cross-checked the plans I downloaded from the Alliance database with Crystal's Forger technical manuals." Ravi nodded at the list of sources he'd just cited out loud. "I'm certain: *that's* the main reactor."

"Great," said Kenzie. "Nice work."

Kenzie punched some commands into her console, and her display came to life with a shot from inside the *Gremlin*'s weapons control room. A layer of soot still blanketed the controls, a result of the fires that cut short their laser battle against the Frawgs and Crystal's ship above Sheafer colony a few days before.

Vor, holding his plasma-torch, turned and greeted Kenzie with a smile, his new, mechanical mouth a combination of genuinely sweet and extraordinarily creepy.

"Hi!" said Vor, very happy at the chance to talk. "Repairs to the weapons holding steady, Kenzie."

"So we're operational?"

"Well," Vor demurred, "I don't know if I'd go so far as to say 'operational.'"

Ravi leaned over to make eye contact with Vor.

"What's lower than 'operational'?" he asked.

Vor thought for a second. "Functional?" He nodded. "Marginally functional."

"So if we need to shoot—" Kenzie started.

"There's definitely a plausible chance we might be able to see about doing it," said Vor.

Kenzie sighed. "Good enough for now, I guess," she said. "See if you can get us from plausible to probable."

Vor shrugged. "Sure!" He turned and got back to work.

Next, Kenzie dialed up the engine room. Jo sat at the controls with Twilliam by her side preparing another dermal patch to help heal her injuries from the fight with Katak. Behind them, the *Gremlin*'s reactor glowed with power against the dark nanocarbon patch that they'd used to seal up the breach in the engine room. The reactor was brighter than Kenzie remembered, and shimmered with heat haze. That didn't seem like a good sign.

"How're things down there?"

Jo tapped a few buttons and flicked her gaze up at Kenzie through her display.

"Fine? I guess?" Jo shrugged. "I told you, I don't totally know what I'm doing down here—ow!"

"Hold still," said Twilliam, who attempted to draw blood from Jo's arm. "I need to check for toxicity levels, and I can't do that if you keep moving."

"Ugh," said Jo, who stuck out her arm for the cyborg. "Anyway…I think the reactor's stable." She pointed at her console. "The little picture on here is orange, but it's not red. And it's not flashing. So I think that's…okay."

"Okay," said Kenzie, aware that things were actually not really that okay but that there wasn't much she could do about it. "Keep me posted. We're getting close to zero."

Jo made a mock-salute. Aye-aye, Captain Kenzie," she said and signed off.

Kenzie smiled and switched her display to the broadcast coming from the ceremony. Councilman John-Dean Clifford lumbered up to the podium, and all around him other members of the council stood and applauded. Grand Chancellor Gork. Minority leader Lengg. Commander Gerald Sharp. She wondered how many knew Clifford was secretly a Forger, plotting the downfall of the Interstellar Alliance from within.

Kenzie tightened her grip on the helm.

"Thank you," said Clifford. "Thank you all. Friends, we gather today to make history…"

The ceremony was starting. Kenzie took a breath. Time to cause some trouble.

Kenzie activated the tracking module, just as she had every few hours since hatching her plan a day ago. Every time the *Gremlin* jumped to a new set of coordinates, Kenzie switched the tracker on. But Kenzie had hacked the device. Instead of Lucy and the Forgers learning their position, now it sent tracking signals to someone else. And it was only a matter of time before they showed up.

She punched the throttle, and the *Gremlin* shot towards the Hub at full speed, the blue-green world of IA Prime lazily turning below them. She couldn't help but notice that, with its engines at full burn, the ship shook a little more than usual. No…a *lot* more. Between that and the too-hot reactor, it seemed the *Gremlin* had taken more of a beating in that Forger ambush in the asteroid field the other day than she'd realized.

"It's fitting, then," said Clifford, "that we do so in the historic capital building of IA Prime, surrounded by the lawmakers and engineers who worked for a decade to make today possible."

Kenzie checked the timer in the corner of her display. It wasn't long until Crystal's ship would launch its small fleet of Forger battlesuits. Fifteen tiny missiles would soon rocket their way to IA Prime's surface to break up the party. Time to provide some cover.

"Enemy ships moving to engage, Kenzie!" Ravi gave his report with gusto. Kenzie had discovered in the last day that Ravi had never actually been in combat before.

"Once you get past the urge to pee your pants, it can be quite exhilarating!" he'd told her during one of their stops, recalling the last few times the *Gremlin* was attacked. "I'm starting to see why you like this so much."

In the here and now, the broadcast continued. "Never before has such a wide-ranging, life-changing initiative ever been attempted on such a grand and impressive—"

Ravi talked over Clifford's words: "They're closing in fast…"

Kenzie checked the scope. Twenty ships—a small patrol of five broke off, and she zoomed in to assess the situation. Four short-range fighters, one light battlecruiser in the back of the formation. That one was probably in charge.

The comms crackled to life.

"Unidentified vessel, reverse course and leave this area immediately. This is a restricted zone, and we have been authorized to use deadly—"

Another voice broke through, interrupting.

"Drake? Is that you?"

Kenzie got goosebumps.

"Did you really grow a spine since the last time I saw you?" It was Lucy Reese. And she was being *really mean*.

"It's over, Drake. Prepare to be boarded."

The battlecruiser broke from the approaching attack wing and sped towards the *Gremlin*—that one *had* to be under Lucy's command. Meanwhile, Councilman Clifford kept blabbing.

"My friends, it is my absolute and utmost pleasure to represent Earth in the Interstellar Alliance's governing council and to lead this ceremony with the blessing of Grand Chancellor Gork."

Kenzie saw Lucy's ship through the main viewport as it approached. Apparently, they expected the *Gremlin* to slow down and allow her to dock and take a boarding party to round them all up. Not today.

Kenzie jammed the helm down hard, pushing the ship into a nosedive away from Lucy and her flunkies. The ship's shuddering intensified as the injured *Gremlin* struggled to keep up with Kenzie's flying. Or maybe she just wasn't that good at flying the ship—that was a distinct possibility, Kenzie thought.

"Oh good," said Lucy, a smile in her voice. "You're giving me an excuse."

The first hit from Lucy's blaster bolts would've thrown Kenzie out of her seat if she hadn't been strapped in. Soon, the other four ships of Lucy's attack wing—the fighters—flanked them, easily outmatching the *Gremlin*'s speed. She looked up at her display and saw them approaching from all sides, weapons hot.

The ship took a pounding and started shaking worse than ever before. Kenzie's vision blurred as she jostled in her seat.

"Combat shields are being torn to shreds!" yelled Ravi over the din. She didn't look, but she figured he wasn't smiling now.

"We can't take this!" came Jo's voice over the speakers in the cockpit. "All the pictures are flashing red! I repeat, all the pictures are red, Kenzie! Red is bad!"

"Just hold tight!" said Kenzie through gritted teeth. Where were they? They'd be dead in a minute if they didn't show up soon...

The blasts started letting up when another voice broke through the comms. One of Lucy's thugs: "Chief, we're picking up an unexpected signal at the edge of sensor range—it's one of ours." There was a moment's pause. "I mean, a *red* one of ours."

That was Dash. She didn't count on Lucy's forces being able to detect Crystal's ship so far away. Time was running out...

Lucy didn't hesitate. "Jensen, Poole, Mong—blast that traitor out of the sky." Kenzie looked on her display and saw three of the fighters turn from the *Gremlin*. "Fredericks and I will handle things over here..."

A loud beeping suddenly filled the cockpit. The helm console's old jump-warning system was going bananas. They were about to have company...and from the sound of things, a lot of it.

Kenzie smiled.

The blackness of space outside the viewport was suddenly overrun with flashes of red—and green. Dozens of bulbous, swamp-colored Frawg ships jumped in with no end. The new arrivals immediately started firing on everyone and everything in sight.

Kenzie's tracking module hacks had beamed their location data to the Frawgs holed up in the Sheaffer system, rather than back to Lucy and her undercover Forger gang. She knew she'd left an impression on Katak and the rest of her tribe during their last encounter, so she figured they'd probably jump at the chance for payback. She'd realized recently she had a particular effect on some people. It was about time it actually paid off.

"Yes!" yelled Kenzie. "They're here—"

The *Gremlin* shook again, struck by…well…something. Kenzie looked at her scope and could barely tell one ship from the other, there were so many firing in all directions.

A new voice piped in on the comms. "Diiiiie!"

Katak, Frawg chieftan, was here. Apparently, she'd decided to lead the hunting party personally. Kenzie wasn't totally sure if Katak directed that scream at her specifically or really just anyone tuned to the general frequency. She decided she didn't want to stick around and find out. She deactivated the tracker again and listened to the chaotic comm chatter.

"They're everywhere!"

"Got one on your six—"

"We need fire support!"

"Call in reinforcements from Prime! We can't handle all these—I don't care what Clifford says!"

"Where'd all these stinkin' flippers come from?"

The radio was filled with similar cries as bedlam erupted around her.

She checked her scope—the blockade of ships stationed around the Hub was moving to intercept the new arrivals and provide backup…leaving the Hub unprotected.

"What have you got for me?" Kenzie said to Ravi as she turned the ship sharply to narrowly avoid a blaster bolt.

"Calculating…hold on—there."

A new escape vector appeared on Kenzie's display, and she followed the flight path to the letter. He wasn't as quick as Squix, but Ravi was catching on.

Kenzie found a hole in the battlefield and directed the *Gremlin* through it, getting some distance from the melee. She glanced at the countdown timer and saw it was pretty close to zero, so she lowered the comm volume to a dull roar. Down on IA Prime, Clifford was still talking.

"—like to take a few moments to describe some of the struggles we've endured, as a society, in our quest for peaceful coexistence with the rest of the galaxy..."

The timer clicked to zero. Kenzie knew Crystal's ship was launching its full complement of Forger battlesuits like rockets. All they had to worry about were the planetary defense canons once the suits were in range. And even then, trying to hit any one of those suits would be like using a water hose to soak a specific flea on a dog two blocks away: basically impossible.

Minutes later, the *Gremlin*, shimmying and shaking as it flew, was within weapons range of the Hub. Launching the battlesuit assault was just one part of Kenzie's plan—ensuring the Hub was destroyed was the other. This would be their best—and probably only—chance to stop the Forgers.

Kenzie glanced at the broadcast and saw an aide interrupting Clifford during his speech.

"What do you mean, 'an incursion'? Order the orbital security ships back!"

Moments later, Kenzie saw the ceiling of the capital building collapse and over a dozen Forger battlesuits crash onto the ground. Clifford scurried away and hid. Dash was doing his part—now it was time for them to do theirs.

Kenzie retrieved her trusty handset and entered some quick commands. In moments, she'd hacked her way through the Hub's security systems and lowered the combat shields surrounding it. She shoved the device back into her pocket, thanking her past self for getting so good at breaking through Forger computer networks. She was almost sorry this was probably the last chance she'd get to virtually wedgie the Forgers' entire digital security forces.

She tapped a few commands onto her console—made somewhat more difficult by how violently the ship shook—and the broadcast of the now-ruined ceremony switched off. The weapons room replaced it on her display, with Vor at the controls.

"Are we charged and ready?"

Vor looked up from his console: "Well, Captain," he said, giving Kenzie a momentary thrill—until he continued. "We're charged, but there might be a problem…"

Kenzie's heart sank.

"What kind of problem?"

"The *Gremlin*'s been pretty banged up in the last few hours. And also yesterday. And the days before that. Let's just say the ship's not in, uh, ship shape."

Jo broke into the comms from the engine room, her display now split between Vor and his sister.

"He's right, Kenzie. This thing says structural integrity is at forty-five percent."

"It's a miracle it's hung together this long," added Twilliam from behind her.

"But can we fire? At all?"

Vor cocked his head to the side. "Yes. But I'm not really sure what'll happen to the reactor if we do."

Kenzie twisted her mouth. They'd come too far not to try.

"Fire weapons, Vor."

The Crag nodded, tapped in a few commands, and hit the switch.

The laser canon on the roof sprang to life. A green beam of energy filled the *Gremlin*'s viewport, racing through space to hit the spinning, silver reactor on the Hub. But had it caused any damage?

"…energy levels on the Hub unchanged," said Ravi. "We didn't even make a dent."

An alarm started blaring.

"Weapons offline," said Vor.

"The reactor's completely overheating," said Jo. "Red on my screen everywhere."

"Can we stabilize it?"

"I...I don't think so, Kenzie...it says we're out of spare coolant." Kenzie remembered she'd dumped all the coolant back in the quadronium mine on Sheaffer Colony. This was all her fault...again.

"I think we have to shut it down," continued Jo, "or it'll just melt into slag..."

The alarms continued to scream, filling the cockpit with the steady sound of the *Gremlin* finally giving up.

Kenzie slumped in her seat. They were so close.

She sighed. Kenzie didn't want to have to do this, but she always figured it might be a possibility. Now she knew for sure.

She grabbed the ignition dial and turned it counterclockwise. The reactor powered down and the lights went dark. She flipped a row of switches on the console to activate the auxiliary power reserve. The weak emergency lights flickered on, bathing everything in a sickly orange glow. She spoke into the comms.

"Abandon ship."

Meanwhile, on IA Prime

29

"I said put your hands up and surrender now!" yelled Commander Sharp. The Fleet commander with the efficient haircut had taken up a position towards the center of the room and had his pistol trained at Dash. About a half dozen guards flanked Sharp, their weapons drawn and pointing at Dash's head.

"Just—just hold on, guys," said Dash, suddenly aware that several guns were targeting him. Clifford, he noticed, had retreated to a safe distance behind what was left of an overturned table. That...was an odd move for a secret Forger mastermind...

Dash pushed a button on his wrist and his helmet retracted, revealing his damp, sweaty face for everyone to see. He brushed his matted hair from his forehead.

A voice came from a few meters away. "Captain Drake?" It was the buzzing, clicking voice of Grand Chancellor Gork. Dash looked to his left and saw the old Aphid crouching behind what was left of his chair, chunks of rubble from the now-demolished dome littering the floor around him.

"Yes!" said Dash. "It's me! I'm, uh, I'm here to save the galaxy!" He paused for a second before adding, "Again!"

"But you're dead," said Gork matter-of-factly.

"No, no I'm not—not dead, me, I'm not—" Dash stuttered.

"Just what…" started Gork, straightening and fixing his ceremonial robes. "What is the meaning of this?" He blinked his inner eyelids nervously.

"Listen," said Dash, stalling for time. He pointed at Clifford. "That guy? That guy's a Forger."

Gork, Sharp and his retinue of guards—everyone still in the room who hadn't fled when the roof collapsed—turned and looked at the crouching councilman hiding behind some rubble in the corner.

"I'm not…I'm not a Forger," sputtered Clifford. "You're the one wearing Forger armor!"

"Well, okay, right—" said Dash. "Yes, that's true, but I'm here to stop—just trust me, okay? He's definitely a Forger." He paused for a second. "Aren't you?"

Dash straightened, trying to remember where he'd left his dignity.

"Look, I'm Dash Drake, right?" He furrowed his brow to its most authoritative position. "I'm the hero of Gantoid IV. And I say that guy's a Forger, part of a years-long plot to undermine and infiltrate the Interstellar Alliance's governing council. And steal our planets."

He glanced at Crystal for support. She just shrugged. Great.

There was a pause as everyone considered Dash's words. The thirteen other Forger battlesuits, still crumpled in smoking craters all around them, quietly sizzled and popped.

"Okay," said Gork, finally. "Arrest him."

No one moved. A capital guard to Sharp's left looked back to Gork on the dais. "Uh…which one, sir?"

"Both of them."

"Wait, what?" said Clifford and Dash in unison.

"The ceremony is ruined, something insane is going on, and we'll sort this all out somewhere safe. Arrest both of these men."

Dash saw the guards advancing on him—until another voice interrupted and stopped them in their tracks.

"That won't be necessary," said Commander Sharp with a sigh, holstering his pistol. "Guards, belay that order."

Sharp pushed a button on his wrist, and suddenly the guards' pistols all melted into slag. The men and women cried out in pain as their weapons burned their hands and fused with their skin. It was extremely gross.

Gork sputtered incredulously at the scene unfolding in front of him, the capital guards writhing in pain on the floor. "Are you…what are you…"

Dash was unsure whether to be relieved or terrified at Sharp's decision to ignore the Grand Chancellor's orders. He settled for highly suspicious—and still pretty terrified—and clutched the tablet tighter.

Commander Sharp walked toward Dash, stepping over Forger battlesuits and flaming wreckage.

"Years," he said. "Years spent, plotting, planning." He spoke slowly and deliberately. He pointed at Clifford. "Convincing Councilman Dummy over there that jump-chains were the only path to peace."

"Hey," said Clifford from his hiding spot. Clifford wasn't the Forger—Commander Sharp was.

"Convincing him to appoint and promote my soldiers throughout the Alliance and its Fleet. All the games, the lies, the waiting…"

Sharp stopped walking, sniffed the air, sized Dash up.

"Uhh," said Dash. "Hang on a second…"

"I could've waited just a few more minutes, until after the ceremony was over," he said, "but I suppose you have ended it prematurely." He reached toward his belt and grabbed a small metal rectangle, with a sort of hand grip on it.

Sharp thumbed a button and a beam of light appeared from the device. Suddenly Sharp was holding a laser sword. Not only was Sharp apparently a secret Forger but also the High Smith. Kenzie had been right about the Forger infiltration of the Alliance. She'd just been wrong about which ones had done the infiltrating. That kid.

"No more waiting," said Sharp.

"Crap," said Dash.

"Yes," said Crystal. "That man definitely makes more sense as a Forger than the round one."

"Now," said the High Smith. "I'm going to cut your head off."

Screaming, Sharp lunged at Dash and his exposed, very vulnerable head. Even if he'd remembered which button could make his helmet reappear over his face, Dash was sure he wouldn't have had enough time to push it. And it might not even matter, right? Could a laser sword cut through a battlesuit?

While these thoughts collided in Dash's mind, he put up his hands, cowering as Sharp charged at him, laser sword raised high.

Before he could discover what having your head cut off by a beam of pulsating energy felt like, he heard a clanging buzz. He lowered his hands and saw a battlesuit standing before him, blocking Sharp's path to his neck—Crystal. An energy shield had sprouted from her arm, and she used it to stop Sharp's blow. Then, with her other arm, she clocked him right in the face, knocking him to the ground.

"Crush it, Captain Drake," said Crystal, her booming voice making his ears ring. "Crush the tablet and end this!"

Dash realized he was still holding the ceremonial tablet, had *been* holding it this whole time, and without another moment's hesitation, he crushed the device in his heavily armored hands, reducing it to a warped, metal ball. Sparks whizzed out of it, popping and buzzing as the tablet was reduced to an inert hunk of garbage.

"I did it," said Dash. "I—I really did it...I stopped the Forgers!" Dash thought for a second, then said, "Again!"

"Well done, Captain Drake," said Crystal, standing over Sharp, who'd curled into the fetal position, clutching his bruised face. She kicked him and he flew across the ruined room.

He landed a meter away and rolled over, coughing. Then...laughing. Uh-oh. Laughing was never good.

"You absolute—" Sharp coughed again. "You idiots. Morons, all of you! You thought that device controlled the jump-chains network? You thought we spent years putting our plans into action to finally take what is rightfully ours...and had it rely on a single, red button?"

Dash frowned. "Kinda?"

"You've done nothing, Drake," said Sharp, crawling onto his knees, then to his feet. He spat a blob of blood onto the floor. "It's a prop. The button is useless. This one, however..."

He entered some commands into the device on his wrist. Suddenly Dash felt his battlesuit seize up. He tried to move his arm, but it wouldn't budge. Nothing would. In an instant, it went from a suit of armor to a metal prison.

"No!" yelled Crystal. "Please, no..."

Sharp entered more commands, and he and Crystal fell to their knees. The rest of the suits that had formerly been nothing more than crumpled forms on the ground clambered to their feet and surrounded him, forming a protective wall of automated Forger bodyguards. He had total control over the suits.

"You came here thinking you could make a difference, save the Alliance, stop the Forgers. But you never had a chance. And now you're too late."

He punched a few more keys on his wrist and spoke into it.

"Activate the jump-chains—now."

The Gremlin's Last Stand

"Hurry up, Twilliam," said Kenzie.

"I'm trying," said the cyborg, shouldering a bag of medical supplies while hugging Doctor Bill's flat body to himself. He awkwardly jogged to the escape pod door on the *Gremlin*'s port side. "Doctor Fatty's heavy."

"Hey!" said Bill, whose power supply was plugged into the back of Twilliam's skull.

Twilliam shuffled his way into the tight quarters of the six-person pod, taking his seat and strapping himself in next to Jo so he could monitor her vitals.

The pod was cramped, designed to support the minimal crew that would normally work on such a small cargo ship. But mathematically speaking, there'd be enough room for all of them to fit.

Vor shuffled in after Twilliam, consulting his handset as he went.

"I don't like the look of this projected escape vector," he said, taking his seat on the other side of his sister. "I estimate a seventy-five percent chance of capture by the enemy on this course…"

"Oh, stop it," smiled Ravi as he followed Vor in and strapped himself into his own seat next to Twilliam. "Those numbers don't factor in the pod's automated defense measures or even the distraction being provided by the battle currently being waged in the area. My estimates are much closer to forty-eight percent chance of capture."

Vor shook his head. "That's too low. And you shouldn't factor in the automated defense measures at all, since it's probable they've been rendered inoperable because of the damage the ship's sustained so far."

"Don't be such a pessimist! Have a little faith."

"Well," interrupted Twilliam, "once the jump-chains activate, there won't be any Alliance holdings still present in this reality anyway. So, really, chance of capture is closer to ninety-nine percent."

"What about Dash down on IA Prime?" asked Vor, looking up from his handset.

"Make my estimate one-hundred percent," said Twilliam.

"Ha!" laughed Doctor Bill from his position in Twilliam's lap.

Standing in the corridor outside the pod's entrance, Kenzie couldn't help but smile to herself. She'd miss this.

"Come on, Kenzie," said Jo, still weak. She motioned to her from her seat between Twilliam and Vor. "Let's get outta—"

"I forgot something…be right back!" said Kenzie, slapping a button on the corridor wall.

"No, wait!" yelled Jo.

The door slid shut with a thump and Kenzie sprinted back to the cockpit.

A minute later she was at her seat at the helm, the faux leather in the chair creaking under her weight.

A glance at the dimly lit display told her the fight between the Forgers and the Frawgs was still raging. Then she punched up the broadcast from the ceremony—the cameras were still rolling. The chaos of what unfolded in the capital building would be on every channel in the galaxy by now.

"—arrest him," was the first thing Kenzie heard. It was Grand Chancellor Gork, and he looked pissed. Things didn't seem great for Dash either. She had to hurry.

Kenzie looked out the viewport and saw the Hub's reactor spinning, innocently awaiting the Forgers' order to send power to jump-chains across the galaxy and suck the Interstellar Alliance's planets into another dimension. No matter what happened with Dash and Crystal down on IA Prime now, Kenzie couldn't let that happen. Not when they were so close.

She typed some commands into her console and launched the escape pod.

Kenzie heard a loud "thoom," the pod's engines roaring to life and pushing away from the doomed cargo ship. The *Gremlin* shuddered once as the pod with her friends flew into the inky blackness.

She sighed and put her hand on the ignition dial, turning it clockwise and powering the *Gremlin*'s reactor back up. The cockpit's main lights brightened, the ship began shaking, and the alarms filled her ears once more. The *Gremlin* was dying again.

Kenzie grabbed the helm, gently pushing up the throttle. She didn't want the ship's power core to melt too soon—not yet. Not before she could bring the *Gremlin* to its final landing spot, right on the Hub's reactor.

Within minutes, Kenzie had managed to close the distance to the Hub. She lazily set the ship down onto the reactor with a thud, then jumped from her seat. There wasn't much time left.

As she ran out of the cockpit, she grabbed her helmet and jammed it onto her head.

She skipped the lift, opting instead to slide down the maintenance ladder. She made it down to the cargo bay in record time, her feet stinging as they collided with the floor. She wished she could move even faster.

Kenzie ran to the chalzz pen—the little, yellow critters had been herded back into their enclosure since she'd left the *Gremlin* for Crystal's ship. She hit a few commands on her handset, and the nearby anti grav pallets—the ones she, Vor, and Jo had reprogrammed when they first came aboard the ship—rose with a hum. They hovered themselves into position and slipped underneath the pen, raising it up off the floor, and gently carried the box full of the chattering, stinking hexapods towards the engine room.

Kenzie punched the button on the wall to open the door separating the engine room from the cargo bay, and looked inside.

It was easy to feel the heat haze rising from the reactor cores. They were already destabilizing, throwing off a sizzle of sparks and a steady plume of smoke billowing up toward the ceiling, the off-white paneling already blackening with soot.

Once the pallets were in position, they deactivated, lowering the pen to the engine room floor. Kenzie pulled the pen's airlock release lever. The door opened, and soon the jabbering, toxic monsters would trundle out, filling the room. And that's not all that would soon fill the room, Kenzie thought with grim humor.

The engine room would be choked with dihydrogen-sulfide—the toxic sewer gas that the chalzz produced naturally. That was the stuff that had knocked Twince unconscious a few days earlier. But in addition to being poisonous for any creature who breathed oxygen, the gas was also extremely explosive.

As the first few chalzz marched from the pen, Kenzie ran to the cargo bay and shut the door, sealing the critters—and the explosive gas—inside as the reactor began melting down.

It wouldn't take long now. She had turned the engine room into a bomb. The *Gremlin* was going to explode—and take the Hub, and the Forgers' scheme, right along with it.

Kenzie smiled to herself and sighed again, taking one last look around the cargo bay. She wondered if Dash would be mad when he found out.

Probably.

Only One

Dash, frozen in place in his immobilized battlesuit, waited for the world to end. But then…it didn't. It was confusing.

From within his protective circle of Forger suits, Sharp looked visibly annoyed. He spoke into his wrist again.

"Do you copy? I said activate the jump-chains——"

Sharp was interrupted by a burst of static from his comm and then screaming.

"Sir!" A panicked voice cut through the din. "The jump-chains won't come online, they—there's no power—" More explosions and screaming. "Everything on this end is getting fried! Nothing's—nothing's working at all, sir!"

Dash smiled. He recognized the sound in that soldier's voice. Kenzie—only Kenzie could have that effect on someone.

"Slow down, soldier, just—wait, just take a second and—"

"The Hub! It's—it's gone, sir!"

The color drained from Sharp's face. He'd lost. Kenzie had done it.

Dash tried to think of something amazing to say, some clever way to rub it in.

"Way to go, idiot," he said. "You lost."

So maybe not Dash's best effort, but to be fair, he'd had a tough few days, and he was kind of tired.

Sharp didn't dwell on the ruination of his plans for long. He looked Dash square in the eye as he punched in some more commands.

"Well, I suppose I did lose—today."

One of the empty Forger battlesuits in front of him opened like a flower. He was going to get away, and Dash still couldn't move a muscle.

"But if you think you've stopped the Forgers—if you think you've won here, Drake…" Sharp stepped toward the waiting armor. "…then I suggest that you—"

The sudden sound of rushing water interrupted Sharp's final taunts. Surprised, he swiveled around to see another of the battlesuits opening, with several gallons of water pouring out like a waterfall.

A squishy, maroon blob jumped out of the suit and glommed onto Sharp's face.

"What the—blorgph!"

Sharp stumbled, unable to see and make his escape. Squix started slapping Sharp's head with his damp tentacles and offered Dash a small salute as the High Smith tried to keep his footing.

Squix extended a couple tentacles and tapped commands into Sharp's wrist device. Three of the suits flew off into the sky at odd angles, with one merely colliding into a wall and crumpling back into a heap. Squix kept tapping despite clearly having no idea what he was doing. A moment later, Dash could move again, and the rest of the Forger suits fell back down, landing on the ground with simultaneous crashes.

Soon, Sharp fell too, and Crystal wasted no time in crossing the distance to where he landed.

Squix saw her coming and hopped off the High Smith, a blob of ink staining his face—just in time for her to step on his shoulder with a sickening crunch. Sharp cried out in pain.

Crystal retracted her helmet, revealing her wild green eyes and a look of immense glee plastered on her face.

"I'm sorry, I couldn't hear you with that helmet on," she said, grinning. "What were you saying?"

* * *

The capital guards soon regained control and took Sharp into custody. Likewise, once the arrest of the High Smith was broadcast throughout the galaxy, reports began pouring in that a surprising number of Alliance security ships had jumped away without a word. Secret Forgers making a getaway. Dash learned that Lucy Reese had vanished along with them.

After news came back about the mass exodus of Alliance and Fleet personnel, the Grand Chancellor shook Dash's hand and thanked him once again for his service. Dash turned and half-apologized to Councilman Clifford for accidentally accusing him of being a murderous traitor. Clifford just sort of whimpered at him and left quietly.

Next, Dash set to the task of extricating himself from the Forger armor. Before leaving to debrief with the capital guards, Crystal provided some assistance. Dash had never seen her look happier.

After removing the left boot from his damp, sweaty foot, Dash sat amid the rubble and took a breath. He looked to his right. Someone had fetched a bucket of salt water for Squix, the hero Octopus, who'd blasted down to IA Prime without his trusty exosuit.

Squix stuck two tentacles out of the water, and jammed them together into a ball. Then he poked the tip of one up through it. Dash returned the thumbs up.

His handset beeped—it was Jo.

"Hey," he said, grinning. "You guys did it! Tell Kenzie she did an amazing—"

"Dash," said Jo, her voice choked. It sounded like...like she'd been crying.

"What's going on?"

"She's gone," sobbed Jo. The joy he'd felt a minute ago evaporated in an instant.

"What do you mean 'she's gone'? I don't understand," he said, lying.

Dash heard the muffled sound of the handset being passed to someone else.

"The ship" said Ravi, clearing his throat. "The ship's weapons weren't working. The *Gremlin* had taken too much...it wasn't going to be able to...she put us all in the escape pod and, and she..."

There was a pause. Dash waited for him to say the words.

Ravi cleared his throat, the smile obviously nowhere to be found in his voice. "The captain went down with the ship."

Dash stared at his handset. His hand felt numb.

She—she couldn't really have...could she? Why would she—this...

This couldn't be happening.

"I—"

A wet tentacle tapped Dash on the knee. He turned and saw another of Squix's tentacles sticking out of the bucket and pointing into the sky.

Dash turned and looked where he was pointing. He saw a small, dark line...slowly getting bigger with each passing second.

Ravi's voice came over the handset.

"Dash, are you there? The line just went dead. Do you read?"

The line grew bigger, forming a familiar shape. Blue and silver. An older model fighter—a classic Mark 6 Dart.

Dash stood so quickly he instantly felt dizzy.

"Kenzie?"

The Dart sped down toward the capital building, and what had looked like only a line in the distance just a moment ago was the fighter he'd kept under a tarp for so long—kept out of a sense of obligation that he'd never quite understood or appreciated.

The fighter landed a few meters from Dash, kicking up dust and debris. The few capital guards who'd filled the room after Sharp's arrest drew their weapons and aimed at the ship. Dash put up his arms and shouted.

"Stop, no!" yelled Dash, waving his hands. "Stand down!"

Apparently saving the galaxy twice in one lifetime got people to take you at your word. The guards lowered their weapons and watched as the cockpit swung open—and there she was.

Kenzie Washington, the fourteen-year-old girl who'd dispensed justice…and saved the galaxy. She turned and took off her helmet. Underneath she was all smiles.

"Captain Drake," she said, climbing out of the fighter. "Mackenzie Washington, reporting for duty…"

She hopped down and walked toward him. He didn't wait for her to reach him and ran to hug her. He realized after he'd gotten his arms around her that his face was damp.

"I can't believe you," he said, sniffling. "I cannot believe you."

He let go of her and grabbed her by the shoulders. He looked into her eyes.

"I cannot believe you blew up my ship," he said. He felt weirdly okay with this.

"Yeah, well," Kenzie said sheepishly. Then she gestured to the Dart with her head. "But only one of them."

Dash shook his head and barked out a short laugh.

"So," he said, "where'd you learn that maneuver?"

"Sometimes you just have to blow stuff up," she said. "Washington, page one."

Epilogue

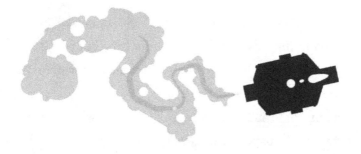

Kenzie reached under her seat and pulled the little bar. Then, she scooted the chair closer to the helm console with her feet, walking like a turtle who was getting ready to fly a spaceship.

Her spaceship. Well, okay not really *hers*, but, like, kind of.

"Hey Kenzie," said Jo to her right in the copilot's seat. "We've got a problem."

Kenzie turned to her friend, whose skin had returned to the right shade of glittery lavender slate in recent weeks. Katak's poison seemed to finally be out of her system.

"What's that?"

"Well," she said, swiveling her chair toward Kenzie and pointing at her handset with disgust, "I can't get on the network. Still."

Kenzie narrowed her eyes at Jo.

"Right—because this is basically the same ship it was before, and it's still a military vessel, and it still blocks comm signals."

"I thought we weren't doing that anymore," said Jo blankly.

Kenzie just shrugged. "Sorry, Jo. And, y'know, we're not gonna have access to the network for much longer anyway, so…" She turned back to her station and began prepping for takeoff. She swiveled back when an idea struck her. "Oh, I could loan you a book!"

Jo just sneered and rolled her eyes. "Ugh, pass," she said. "I know all about your taste in books."

Before Kenzie could think of something snarky to say back—she was trying to get better at that—her display flashed on. On the screen stood Crystal, a pained expression on her face and an Interstellar Alliance Fleet uniform on her body.

Kenzie would've thought that she'd look small out of her usual battle armor, but something about that scar and her fierce green eyes kept her presence as big as it ever was. That, and all the yelling she typically did.

"This is an outrage," she said, her hands balled into fists at her sides. She was standing in the mess hall, having apparently just changed. "I cannot—I cannot be expected to wear this…this…" She pawed at the clothes on her body, looking at them with bewilderment. "…*this*."

Kenzie sighed and slumped a little. She was getting kind of tired of constantly ordering Crystal to do normal things.

"Look," she said, trying to sound patient. She heard Jo laughing quietly to her right. "We're working with the Alliance on this. They're already freaked out enough with this whole situation, but they really don't like the idea of having someone totally decked out in Forger gear wandering around the ship—"

"A *Forger ship!*" hissed Crystal, getting way too close to the display. "The *Orzo* is a Forger battlecruiser, tested in the fires of battle, baptized in the blood of all who have stood against the Empire—"

"That sounds very exciting, Crystal!"

Kenzie saw Ravi enter, wearing his usual blue and white Fleet uniform and a smile. He was carrying an armload of scientific equipment and had stacked a box of cookies on top of his heap, apparently grabbing those on his way through to his new lab on the ship.

Crystal immediately puckered her mouth like she'd just sucked a lemon. Her cheeks flushed red, matching her short hair, and she crossed her arms in front of her body.

"Oh, uh, Lieutenant Sidana, hello, I did not, erm…"

"You know, I would be very interested to hear all about some of these violent 'baptisms' sometime soon, perhaps after I've finished setting up my station in the laboratory. You've kept this ship very clean!"

Crystal's face went a brighter shade of red, and she looked at the ground, bringing her hand to her ear awkwardly. It looked to Kenzie like she didn't really know what to do with that hand—and sure enough, seconds later it was back to being crossed with the other one around her middle.

"Thank, um, thank you Lieutenant, and—I…yes."

Ravi looked at the display and met Kenzie's eyes.

"Hi Kenzie!" he said.

"Hi Ravi." She waved at him through the display. "Say, Crystal, do you think you can help Lieutenant Sidana carry his things down to the lab on deck three?"

Crystal started shaking her head at Kenzie, but Ravi—who didn't see that—only smiled even wider.

"That would be extremely helpful!" he said as he started piling things into her arms. Kenzie switched the display off before Crystal could protest.

"So," said Jo. "That's weird."

"Uh-huh," agreed Kenzie. She arched an eyebrow. "Speaking of weird…"

She punched a few commands into her console. The *Orzo*'s severe-looking medbay appeared on her display as well as its four occupants. Twilliam was crouched in front of Vor, who sat on an examination table with an annoyed look in his eyes. Next to him sat Squix in his exosuit. Doctor Bill hung from the ceiling above him and probed the Octopus's mottled maroon skin.

"Stop fidgeting," said the doctors in unison. They did that a lot, and Kenzie wasn't sure if it was on purpose or not.

"I swear, the job you've done on this," muttered Twilliam as he jabbed a cybernetic welder into Vor's mouth. "It's a miracle your whole *face* hasn't fallen off of your head…"

"Thowwy," lisped Vor through his mechanical lips, the words mangled by Twilliam's instruments.

"You think that's bad?" said Doctor Bill. "You should see some of these readings! Squix has ingested so much more salt than his body needs, his actual cells might melt. I think he's halfway to becoming a jellyfish at this rate."

"That's not something that can happen," said Squix, then, worriedly added, "is it?"

"Keep eating those Cheese-flavored Sodium Blocks, and you might find out. Here, I'm going to begin the desalination process." Doctor Bill produced a new probe and started squirting water onto the top of Squix's head.

"Does that actually do anything?" asked Kenzie.

Vor, Squix, and Doctor Bill looked at her through the medbay's own display screen, apparently noticing her for the first time. Twilliam, whose back was to the display, kept working.

"Maybe," said Doctor Bill. "It probably wouldn't hurt the smell, though."

Squix flashed green. "Do I really smell? You—you know I've always wanted a nose, Doc…"

"How's the conversion process going?" asked Kenzie.

Twilliam stopped mid-operation and turned to face her. "The medbay's still in dreadful shape," he said, "but it's far more functional than it was the last time I was aboard. Now that we've stocked it with the proper tools—" He cocked his head toward Doctor Bill. "—as well as the outdated equipment you insisted on installing—"

"I'm not listening," interrupted Doctor Bill as he started dabbing at Squix's head with a small towel.

"—the medbay should be ready for all our needs."

"Hi Kenthie!" said Vor with his not-quite-installed new cybernetic mouth. "Hey thith!" He waved at Kenzie and Jo through the display.

"No talking!" said Twilliam, turning back around and resuming his work. Twilliam had insisted that Vor have a proper modification, saying that the one he'd grafted onto his own face by himself—his special project—was giving cyborgs a bad name.

"Thanks guys," she said. "We're almost ready to go."

"Almost?" said Squix, slightly damp. "You mean he's not here yet?"

"Of course he's late," said Doctor Bill and Twilliam.

"He's just finishing up with the last-minute briefing," said Kenzie. "That's all. I'm sure he'll be here any minute. I'll let you guys know before we're heading out."

"Bye Kenthie, bye thith!" waved Vor. Kenzie switched off her display before she could hear Twilliam berate his patient again.

She gave a little sigh, then looked around at all that had changed within the cockpit of the *Orzo*—no, it was the *Sojourn* now, wasn't it? That's what the Fleet admirals had decided when they approved this mission. Just one of many changes Kenzie was getting used to.

Where before the cockpit of Crystal's battlecruiser was spare and uncomfortable, the Fleet's retrofit had managed to fill the small space with a brand-new suite of sensors and tracking equipment, not to mention a couple of small, extra seats for people to operate it all. But beyond that, the Alliance's designers did what they could to smooth out some of the edges, adding more comfortable flourishes wherever they could: console layouts more familiar to Kenzie and the rest of the civilization that had lived on their side of the dimensional divide; fewer decorative spikes on every wall and surface; seats that didn't feel like sitting on granite slabs. It wasn't quite the *Gremlin*, but it was a start. She felt a pang of guilt at the thought of the old ship she'd blown up.

Kenzie was shaken out of her thoughts by the sound of shouts and clanks from behind the cockpit door.

"I said—let me through! What even are you?"

"Halt!" Clank.

"Ow! Don't do—"

"Desist, vile fleshling!" Clank.

"Ow, stop it!"

Kenzie swiveled in her chair and ran to the door, which opened at her approach automatically. Before her stood Dash, already looking rumpled in his new Fleet Captain's uniform, trying to juke past the spiky, floating traffic cone that ran the ship's automated security force. Attempts to remove the drone from the ship's systems proved impossible—every time they tried, the drone threatened to flood the rooms with poison gas—so Kenzie settled on slightly tweaking the system's programming instead. Judging by the way it was bludgeoning Dash with its robotic arms as he tried to enter the cockpit, she surmised that it wasn't working all that well. Or maybe this was what working really well looked like.

"Drone, stand down," she said.

The cone spun around to face her and gave a clanking salute with its arm. "The commander speaks, I obey!" The drone hovered up into a hatch in the ceiling and disappeared.

Dash rubbed his forehead, which sported a bright pink welt.

"You gotta do something about that thing," he said, walking past Kenzie and into the cockpit."

"I did," said Kenzie. "He used to carry a gun."

Dash leaned against the wall and thought.

"Oh. Yeah, this is better, then."

Dash turned and nodded his head at Jo, who just gawked back at him. "What?"

Dash kind of made a motion with his head at her. Then jerked it backward to one of the smaller seats behind the co-pilot's chair. "You're in my, uh…"

Jo curled her lip like she'd walked past an open garbage chute and scoffed.

"Fine," she said, shaking her head. She stood and slipped out past the two of them and took the smaller seat Dash had indicated. She plopped down and immediately put her feet up on the console. "Let's go already. We've been here for*ever*."

Dash sat in the vacated copilot's chair and turned to Kenzie, ignoring Jo.

"So we're good to go?" asked Kenzie as she took her own seat at the helm. "The admirals? The grand chancellor?"

"They all signed off on the mission, yeah," he said, running a hand through his hair, a vague look of terror lurking in his eyes. "I'm to captain the *Orzo*—I mean the *Sojourn*, um…into Forger space. In another dimension. And I have command of this crew to try and gather information and intelligence on the location of Technica Outpost and all the rest of the people the Forgers have abducted. That's…that's what we're doing…"

"Don't get *too* excited, Dash," said Jo, who was now absently tapping at her handset despite not being able to connect it to the network.

Dash exhaled loudly. He looked like he might throw up.

"I am very nervous, Kenzie," said Dash.

"Yeah, I know," she said. "But don't worry—this is just a recon mission, right? Just look, learn, and leave…"

Dash squinted at Kenzie.

"Let's not kid ourselves," he said.

"What do you—what're you talking about?" Kenzie replied in her best *I'm not being crazy; you're being crazy* voice. "You're the captain, right? Captain?"

"Uh-huh," said Dash, a small smile peeking out at the corners of his mouth. "I'm the captain. I'm in charge and everyone always listens to me—especially you—and that's definitely what's going to happen when we fly this undercover Forger battlecruiser into enemy territory and go snooping around—with you at the helm. Right?"

Kenzie felt her face spread into an all-out grin.

"Right," she said.

Dash leaned back in his chair and sighed. "Well, no more use delaying the inevitable. I'm the hero of IA Prime now. Gotta go rescue everyone and bring peace to the multiverse. Is everyone aboard and ready to go?"

"Yup," said Kenzie, reaching into her pocket. "We're all set. Just give the word, Captain Drake." She pulled the round, black disk with the single button on its side and placed it on the helm console in front of her. She pushed the button and the hologram of her mother appeared. She looked into her mom's eyes and, as ever, couldn't quite meet the ghost's gaze.

"The word is given, Captain Kenzie," said Dash, putting his hands behind his head and closing his eyes. "Let's head out."

As Kenzie punched some commands into her console, she switched on the ship's comm system.

"All hands," she said, "prepare for dimensional jump. We're going to find them."

Kenzie could just barely hear the crew's cheer and applause go up through the metal door to the cockpit.

She looked at her mom one more time as she entered the final commands.

"I'm coming to get you."

Kenzie flipped the last switch. The viewport flashed red, then green, and they were gone.

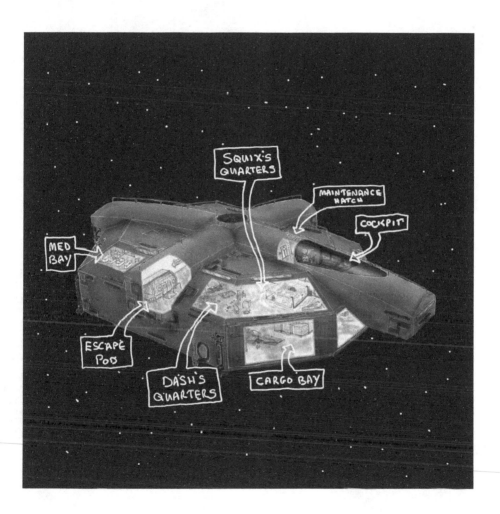

Acknowledgments

This novel was too long by at least two, maybe three pages. Even still, I'm going to try and spend a few more pages to thank all the kind folks who helped make it happen in one way or another. But before I do all that, I'd like to thank YOU, the reader, for taking the time to read my silly little book. If you liked it, please leave me an Amazon review. And if you didn't like it, please don't leave me an Amazon review. How'd you even get here? Do you always finish books you don't like? I'm honestly impressed…I should leave you a positive review for being such a dedicated reader.

Big thanks to my early readers: my friends Will Lakey, Collin David, Jeff Giles, and Greg Williams. They kept me on the right track and helped me get this book to where it is now.

Will is a fellow sci-fi fan, and an extremely talented artist. In addition to providing me valuable feedback, Will whipped up the design for the Gremlin early on in my writing, and it stuck in my head from there. You can find a full illustration of it on the title page of the book, and I love it.

Collin, likewise, is also a fan of all things spacey and alieny, and he's also a very gifted artist. He and his partner, Beckie Hermans, are responsible for the cover of this book. Once I saw it, I knew it was perfect, because it makes the novel seem much classier than it really is. If you decided to try this book based on the cover, you have them to thank.

Jeff is a great writer and critic, and he's never shy about sharing his opinions no matter what they are. So knowing he actually liked it helped keep me positive in the face of rejections, and his encouragement motivated me to finally self-publish the thing. Now that we're here at the finish line, I kind of wish I'd taken his advice even sooner.

And Greg read all the very earliest material here, literally the first person besides me to read the first pages of this novel. Chatting with Greg about writing, about movies, about all the things we love (and hate) is what motivated me to write this in the first place. He was the guy who helped me work out the Dash-Kenzie dynamic in the first place. Simply put, without Greg, there would be no book. I honestly can't thank him enough.

An absolutely huge thanks to Supergroup, the writing group that so kindly welcomed me into their circle despite not knowing me. Double huge thanks to them for allowing me to stay in the group once they did know me. Kate Schultz, Kaethe Schwehn, Sarah Hanley, Coralee Grebe, Jana Hiller, Sean Beggs, Christine Brunkhorst, and Kristi Belcamino: You're all wonderful writers, readers, and people. Your insightful critiques, enthusiastic support, excellent questions, and most importantly regular deadlines kept the engines of the book humming. The snacks were good too. Okay, the snacks were the most important. Without this writing group, the book would've sputtered to a halt, another half-finished project to join the rest of the abandoned ideas buried in the depths of my computer. If you're a writer struggling to finish something, anything, do yourself a favor and find yourself a writing group. Just don't join my writing group—they're mine.

D.J. Schuette of Critical Eye Publishing is the guy who helped me get this novel from gathering digital dust on my hard drive to gathering actual dust on your bookshelf (or more digital dust on your E-reader). From the jump, D.J. has been extremely supportive of this book and my writing. Once I made the decision to self-publish, he's been a sharp editor and partner in getting Dim Stars out into the world. Thanks so much for helping me make this book happen. If you want to self-publish and want an absolute pro to help you get it done, D.J. is the person for the job.

Thanks to my mom Marilyn, my dad Roger, and my older brother David for fostering a love of reading, writing, thinking, and bickering. The people in my family are passionate about what we believe and how we feel, and we won't hesitate to let you know. And honesty in moments of crisis is usually a pretty good recipe for comedy, I've found.

My mom's love of language set me on the path to become who I am today. As a result, I've written this book, and managed to forge a career as a professional writer and editor. She always encouraged me to read as a kid, especially when I was punished by having TV privileges taken away for not doing my homework. There's rarely a better time to pick up a book than when you literally have no other choice. Meanwhile, my dad's sense of humor and his decision to introduce me to Bugs Bunny and Mel Brooks at a young age pretty much molded my brain into whatever strange shape it's in now. Extra special thanks to David for inadvertently getting me into Star Trek back when I was just a small sponge. Extra special no-thanks to David for watching that scene from Star Trek II that one time when I was still in grade school. You know the scene, where Chekov got those creepy worms jammed in his ears. That definitely left a few scars.

And of course, thank you to my wife, the lovely Teréz Iacovino. She has always been a dedicated supporter of my writing, even (and especially) when I haven't been. A talented artist, curator, baker, and one of the funniest and sweetest people I've ever known, Teréz has always encouraged me to take whatever time I needed to write, no matter how lousy the outcome turned out to be on any given day.

Late last year, Teréz gave birth to our son, Henry, and life's been pretty wild since then. Suddenly this partnership between two people has grown into a family. I was not prepared. The process of figuring out how to make life work with a new person with new needs and a whole different set of priorities has been messy at best. Henry makes me laugh and smile just moments after he does something that makes me want to put him on the floor, pat him on the head, and flee into the street, never to return.

About six months after Henry was born, the Coronavirus pandemic spread to the United States, and we've been more or less hermetically sealed inside our house ever since. As I write this in mid-June, we've barely left the house for about three months. Feels kind of like being stuck in a spaceship with a cute, weird, totally frustrating small person suddenly invading my space and messing up all my stuff.

But I figure it'll probably work out okay in the end.

About the Author

Brian P. Rubin is a writer and editor living in Minneapolis, Minnesota with his wife, Teréz Iacovino, and their son, Henry. Dim Stars is his first novel. His favorite food is soup.

www.brianprubin.com

CPSIA information can be obtained
at www.ICGtesting.com
Printed in the USA
LVHW091546271020
669964LV00001B/131